Frigg's GIANT

J. P. HALDENWANG

Barnegat, New Jersey, USA

Cover design by Ravenborn Covers.
Interior formatting by John Ryers.
Edited by Rebecca Odelius.

ISBN-13: 978-0578439754

For Rielly

Dedicated to Richard and John

Acknowledgements

Thank you to all the members of the Phoenix Quill. Special thank you to Rebecca for all the hours we spent talking about this story until we made it as perfect as we could. To John Ryers for formatting this for me and helping me with each step of this process.

To my brothers, Ray, James, Al and Andrew. To my nieces and nephews who are too many to name, especially Lori, Chrissy and Michael. To my mother and my father.

Thank you to Anika Willmanns from Ravenborn Covers for the cover design.

Table of Contents

CHAPTER ONE

"Giants!" Saga exclaimed while her hands rushed out to her sides. Frigg jumped in shock at her tutor's outburst, but it was the way she always told her stories. Saga didn't just say the words; she brought them to life.

In truth, Frigg preferred when her father told her stories, but the Lord of Southrend was busy with obligations. Many nights she went to bed without hearing her father's voice tell her the tales of the ancient creatures who once walked the North World.

Saga grinned and even cackled lightly at Frigg's reaction. Saga had an evil sounding laugh, making her stories increasingly terrifying. "The giants once ruled all of the north. Back then, human men and women ran from them and hid in caves. Those who weren't fast enough were picked up with one hand and swallowed whole. Some of those who got away were eventually caught and eaten slowly, ground up between the giant's teeth or made to suffer for making the giants chase them."

Frigg felt the chills down her spine, and her body began to shake. She fought herself from blinking and kept her eyes wide open while hanging on Saga's every word. "What else happened?" Her words were nothing more than a whisper, too excited to say them aloud.

"The giants became greedy," Saga continued. "They made slaves of mortal men, forcing them to do labors in order to stay alive. The giants were merely playing with them though. When they eventually grew tired of the men as slaves, they found other pleasures in watching them die. The giants tossed them to the black wolves in fighting pits and watched them struggle for their lives. Even if a man was lucky enough to survive the wolves, the giants simply stepped on the man afterward and laughed. They made mortal women dance for them for hours without stopping. If they did stop…" Saga paused. "Well, by the punishments I've already told you, I'm sure I don't have to go into detail."

"Tell me," Frigg whispered.

Saga smiled, exposing her yellow and rotted teeth. "Well, you know how your father squashes bugs when he finds them in your room just by placing his thumb over them?" Saga chuckled as Frigg's eyes widened. "That's enough stories for the night. If I tell you more, you won't be able to sleep."

Frigg arose from the stone ground of her father's meeting hall. The only window inside was boarded up, but the sounds of the thundering wind collapsed against it, especially at night. The room was warmed by two braziers on both sides of the room, placed in back by the main seats around Lord Damari's table.

The hall sat empty for hours after Damari met with his closest advisors. Frigg always watched for him at night, knowing when he returned he would immediately go to the meeting hall where his ale waited for him. He occasionally caught her in there and warned her to never come in this late again, yet she would return the next night. After a small lecture, he would pick her up and tuck her into bed just before talking to her for a few moments.

Like most nights, it seemed the Lord of Southrend would miss his chance to tuck in his daughter. Frigg stood in place and looked to the open door in the corner, hoping to see her father's presence. Saga looked herself, knowing what Frigg anticipated.

"If your father sees that you're not in bed, he'll be disappointed," Saga assured her.

"I want to know where the giants went," Frigg said. She stood straight and pounded her right foot into the ground. "I'll go to bed if you tell me what happened to the giants."

"You've heard this story a hundred times," Saga reminded. "You are well aware of what happened to them."

"Tell me again." Frigg raised her chin and exhaled loudly.

"Giants were killed by brave men," a familiar voice interrupted. In the doorway off the meeting hall stood her father. His arms were crossed and he leaned against the open doorway. "Little girls shouldn't be told stories about giants this late at night."

He took a few steps into the room. Even with his arms still crossed, a grin emerged when he glanced at his daughter. His emerald eyes shone differently whenever he looked in Frigg's direction. A wide smile always followed, even as he tried to fight it away.

Frigg kept her strong stance, even though she wanted to leap into her father's arms. She stretched her neck up as if trying to look over his six-foot frame.

Damari returned his daughter's stubborn stare. "Why aren't you in bed?"

"I wanted to hear a story, and *she* wouldn't tell me one," Frigg replied, pointing at Saga.

"I'm sure Saga told you many stories, and you just wanted more," Damari said.

"I did not!" Frigg said loudly.

Damari raised his eyebrows at her outburst. "Calm your tone to your Lord Father. You know better than that."

His voice was still soft, trying to act like the noble lord who commanded all the servants and warriors, but he could never take a harsh tone with Frigg. It was always loving and affectionate, but it irritated her. She knew she was still a child in his eyes based on the way he talked to her. Even when she would get angry with him, his voice never changed.

"I demand another story before I go to sleep," Frigg said as loudly as her tiny voice would go.

Damari looked at Saga. "I'm getting demands from an eight year old."

His voice was normal pitch when he spoke to Saga. Frigg squinted her eyes in frustration. "Another story," she repeated.

Damari chuckled softly as he walked over to her. As if she were weightless, he picked her up and pressed her against his body. The cold iron of his armor made her shiver, but just to be in the arms of her father warmed her heart.

He carried her from the meeting hall to her room. With a light kick of his foot, the slightly ajar door swung open, and he walked toward her bed. A small brazier burned on the other side of the room, so she could sleep comfortably through the night. Her father placed her on her feathered bed and grabbed the bearskin to cover her. Frigg shook from the chill, pinching the blanket closer to her. She sat up excitedly and put her back into the pillow.

Damari adjusted the blanket around her. "It is far too late, Frigg. It is time for sleep."

"Just one more?" she begged.

He exhaled. "Fine, but it won't be a story. It'll be history."

"History?" she asked.

"History is important, little love." He gently ran his hand through her golden curls and swept them from her eyes. "We learn it, so we don't repeat it."

"Like what?"

He reached back, pulled out her pillow, moved her further down the bed, and forced her to lie down. "Like the fact that our kind, humans, were once slaves to the giants." He took the bear skin and adjusted it so it covered her from the neck down and stuffed her pillow back behind her head. "We had to be in order to survive. You see, there was something out there more dangerous than giants." His face went to stone for a moment, a small smirk emerging from his lips as he whispered, "Dragons."

Frigg's eyes bulged. "Drrr...Dragons?"

Damari bowed his head and tucked the bearskin under her body. "Dragons were unpredictable creatures. They would lie dormant for years, mortal men and women thinking they were long gone, and then they would emerge and wreak havoc on the land, burning everything made by men and killing anyone that got in their way."

Frigg felt a dark chill, not the kind of exciting one she felt when she heard about giants, but a frightening one. The blanket warmed her, yet she couldn't stop trembling at the thought of dragons. "How did they stop them?"

"With the help of giants," he said softly. "Of course, this meant compromising with a race of beings that would rather pound us into the ground than talk to us. There weren't many of them at the time—maybe twenty or more. They lived in Direwood, just before the Great Mountains of the north. They had a king as well. His name was Alatrex. We mortal men had to pay homage to him by groveling at his feet and begging him to help us with the dragons. He spat in our direction, mocked us because, you see, there was only one dragon left. His name was Valstrath the Vile. Described by those who survived his wrath as a black scaled dragon with a red underbelly, wings that blocked out the sun, and a breath of fire that incinerated everything it touched and left nothing but ash."

Frigg continued to shake, but she tried not to look scared in front of her father. If she showed it, she worried he would stop telling her stories all together.

"The humans asked Alatrex if he knew how to stop this dragon from returning and destroying everything after they rebuilt it," he continued. "Alatrex just scorned them with his mighty voice and told them they should ask the dragon. The men were cowards in the face of a dragon, so they begged him to ask. Alatrex said he would only do it if they did whatever he commanded from that day forward, and they agreed because the dragon was far more dangerous than the giants."

"Did...did he find out?" Frigg asked.

Damari nodded. "Valstrath told him they needed to provide a young girl who was pure, four times a season, to be sacrificed in order to ease his rage against humans. You see, dragons once ruled this world by themselves. No one knows how it was that only he remained. Scholars will tell you men killed them, the giants killed them, or they just died out. Valstrath saw humans as beneath him. The fact that the gods created humans in the first place was an insult because the dragons were mystical creatures with great knowledge and power. Humans compared to them was trivial. To Valstrath, it was insulting the world replaced his great race with such beings. Our ancestors finally gave in."

Frigg gulped. "They agreed?"

"They had to. What other choice did they have?"

"They could have fought the dragon."

"Fought the dragon?!" he asked. "Did you not hear me describe him, little love? He was larger than the giants the stories say, and he could fly and breathe fire. How would mortal men fight that?"

"Then how did he die?" she asked curiously.

"Well, first I have to tell you what happened." Damari once again pushed the strands of hair away from her eyes. "The humans did as Valstrath requested and took a young girl up to his lair, four a season, as was told to them. They chained her to a post outside the cave and ran off."

Frigg pulled the covers to her chin. "How did they know he killed them?"

"They heard the screams when they traveled away from the cave," he said sadly. "The girls were often chosen at random, but Valstrath told them if she wasn't beautiful, the agreement would be broken, and he would punish them if they didn't comply. Parents begged the gods for ugly children, so they didn't have to be sacrificed for Valstrath's pleasure. After a while, humans stopped breeding so they didn't have to send their daughters to their deaths. This was not pleasing to Valstrath because soon nothing but ugly girls were sent to him."

"Am I ugly?"

"Of course not, little love," Damari said. Then his face changed to concern. "You need not worry, Frigg; he's no longer around."

"Then what?"

Damari kneeled on the side of the bed. "Well, Valstrath then requested that mortal men only send him girls of noble blood, future ladies and princesses."

"So…girls like me?"

He nodded. "But the lords and nobles of the world said no, and this enraged the dragon. The commoners turned against those of power because they wanted to know why their daughters had to be killed, but, when it came to title, they decided to fight. So all of the North World seemed to be in chaos."

"Did they ever stop fighting?"

"Eventually. When Valstrath didn't get a new gift, he attacked, forcing all the people to unite to fight against him. He scorched most of the north, killing as many men, women, and children as he could, and headed south for what would be our home. As he destroyed the castles and villages in the north, our ancestor, Balder the Bold, went to the giants and begged them for help. He asked them to kill Valstrath."

"And they did?"

"They agreed, but Alatrex and his giants wanted more than just human slaves," Damari said. "They wanted all of the north to themselves. No humans to live here ever again. Balder agreed because it was better to risk our lives in the south against the Wild Men and the Southern King than to stay where a dragon lived."

"Did they kill the dragon?" Frigg asked in quiet excitement.

Her father paused with a smirk when he heard her eagerness. "They did, but at great cost." His eyes lowered and the smirk left his face. "They all died trying to kill him—all except Alatrex. He was so enraged by the death of his giants that he decided to rid the world of our kind."

"Did he?"

"If he did, I wouldn't be telling you this story," he said with a small laugh. "Go to sleep, my little love. I will show you what happened to him in the morning."

"But I want to know now," she whined.

"Patience, Frigg. I promise that when I show you, you will be very pleased."

Damari kissed her ever so gently on the cheek and then again on her forehead. He ran his hand over her hair and rose to his feet. With a quick smile, he turned and headed for the door.

"Father," Frigg called. Damari faced his daughter. "If they asked you to sacrifice me to a dragon, would you?"

"Never," he said in a whisper. "I would kill every creature in this world who asked me to do so."

After her father left the room, Frigg turned to her side and closed her eyes. The story about the dragon scared her, but the thought of her father being so protective of her took away all her anxiety. He would slay a dragon or kill a giant who tried to harm her. Her father was more powerful than any of those creatures. The thought of his protection cleared her thoughts of horrible dragons and revenge-seeking giants. Her eyes closed, and she drifted into a dreamless sleep.

CHAPTER TWO

Frigg awoke suddenly. Her room was deathly quiet and dark. The brazier died down, but she could still see the embers glowing in the corner of the room. There was an eerie twist in her stomach. Then it came—the vibration of voices. They rumbled through the walls in an incoherent echo.

She sat up, practically feeling the aggressive waves of the deep voices on the other side of the wall. She wanted to investigate, but she knew her father would be quite upset if he found her roaming the halls this late at night. Frigg wondered if the voices meant danger. She decided it was better to find out what was going on than to stay in bed and wonder.

Her feet dropped to the stone ground, and she instantly felt its chill as it rose up her legs. She thought about taking her bearskin with her, but it was far too big for her to carry and the blanket would weigh her down.

She opened her door slowly, so it didn't creak. She stepped through the doorway, tiptoeing quickly and without a sound. At the end of the hall, in her father's private quarters, the voices took on words of what sounded like an argument between two people. Damari's voice was distinct; she heard him yell at many of his warriors a time or two when he felt they didn't live up to his expectations.

Soon, the second voice rang out, loud and sharp. "I am to be king one day. A king's reign does not begin when he takes the crown. It begins the moment he is born and far before he is given the title. If you expect me to do nothing like a weakling, then you have mistaken me for someone else."

The voice belonged to Tadeas, Frigg's older brother. She hadn't seen him in nearly a year, since he was mostly near Westerland and Ravengale acting as a representative of Southrend for their Lord Father.

"I don't expect you to do nothing!" Damari yelled back. "I expect you to act like a king in the ways of patience until the true enemies reveal themselves."

"When?" Tadeas asked. "When they place their swords in my back?"

"Lord Gustav is not to be trifled with," Damari shouted. "He is a methodical man who picks at his enemy until he finds a weak spot, and then he exploits it. Your anger has always been your weakness. Continue to show it, and he will pick at it further like a festering wound."

"He mocks us to the rest of the kingdom, and you do nothing!"

"Do not think my lack of action means I'm doing nothing!"

Frigg heard a chair being dragged across the ground, so she knew Damari stood and the chair pushed back from his momentum.

"You are my son, my only son left," Damari said in a softer voice. "If you go after men with power, they will come right back at you with everything they have."

"Let them," Tadeas said defiantly. "One day the crown will be mine. I will not sit and do nothing while Gustav takes everything from us under the nose of the king."

"Whatever you have, take it to the king before you do anything," Damari pleaded.

"Why? So he can sit on his throne and hear witnesses for Gustav lie for him?" Tadeas asked. "I need ten good men."

A dead silence came from the room. It went on for so long Frigg questioned whether she was in some kind of dream, mere moments from waking up in her bed to the realization that her brother wasn't actually there. "For what purpose?" The question came quietly, yet it held an undertone of rage.

Tadeas didn't back down. "I will take the problem to Gustav and handle it like a warrior."

Damari gave an uneasy exhale. "You will take ten men to Westerland? Gustav has an army of five thousand men."

"If he is a man of honor, he will face me with ten of his own," Tadeas said.

Frigg heard Damari's fist strike the table. "You are not dealing with a man of honor!" Damari exhaled again. "Gustav wants one thing—the throne. He's already the richest lord in the kingdom and has the most men. One word from him and he can cause an all-out war that would wipe us from the North World. I am prepared for this battle because one day it will happen. Once Graylyn falls, which I pray to the gods happens when he is old and frail, the crown will pass to our house. When that day arrives, Gustav will march his way here with everything he has and go to war with us."

"So why are we standing here and doing nothing while allowing him to get away with petty insults?" Tadeas asked in outrage.

Damari voice softened. "You go before the king and tell him of what you've seen, along with any evidence or witnesses you have to confirm your suspicion."

"Gustav will only deny the claim."

"But the claim will be there and when Gustav slips up and exposes himself to the rest of the kingdom, Graylyn will make an example out of him."

There was another loud thud. "I'm not waiting for that crooked-nosed knave to stand by until Gustav makes a mistake."

"You do not speak of your king that way."

"Well, if I ever see him again, I'll be sure to apologize."

"This is getting us nowhere," Damari complained. "I forbid you to speak with Gustav until you've seen Graylyn about it."

"Forbid me?" Tadeas' tone grew louder. "I will march with my men right to his gates if you're too cowardly to do so yourself."

Now there was a great amount of rumbling in the room. Frigg's heart sank as she thought about the two of them engaged in some physical confrontation. When the door opened, she froze in fear. Damari stormed from the room, and, with two quick leaps of silence, Frigg made it to her room and hid in the darkness. She looked out slightly, watching her father march down the hall with his fists clenched and his face beet red. He didn't even look toward her room. He just brushed by and left the hall toward a different portion of the castle.

Frigg released a sigh of relief and stepped out once again. Standing in the hall, outside Damari's private quarters, was Tadeas. He had his head down, and his fingers rubbed his brow. He was dressed in his armor, head to toe, draped in a blue cloak with his longsword at his waist. When he raised his head, much like his father, his emerald eyes stood out. His own face was flush, certainly from all the arguing with their father. In just a split moment, his eyes met hers, and the furious look turned soft.

He raised an eyebrow as he slowly walked toward her. "What are you doing up?"

She drifted back toward the door to her room and leaned against it in reserve. Tadeas matured since she last saw him. He must have grown a few more inches while his once smooth and perfect face gained a few wrinkles and scars. "The yelling woke me."

Frigg's words made his face drop. "I'm sorry." When he reached her, he kneeled down so he could look her in the eye. He took his fingers and removed the hair from her face, just like their father. "I didn't mean to wake you."

"Why were you and Father fighting?" she asked.

He rubbed his chin gently and looked up. "It's hard to explain right now. Perhaps when you're older you will understand."

"I can understand!" she exclaimed in anger.

He rubbed her shoulder and grinned. "I'm sure you think you can, but things are far more complicated than you know. You need not worry about these little things. Your only thing to do is to be a little girl, get dressed up, get dolls and trinkets, and be spoiled with gifts."

She stood up straight, stomped her foot into the floor and said, "I want to know!"

"You sure have Mother's spirit." Tadeas chuckled, but she caught the saddened look in his eyes. "Things are complicated, my sweet sister." He looked her up and down. "By the gods, if I didn't know any better I'd swear you've grown. What have you been eating?"

Frigg blushed. "I didn't grow."

"Sure you did," he said confidently. "At least a few inches if I had to guess."

There was the sound of walking behind her. For a moment, Frigg panicked, thinking it was their father. Two forms came into the hall dressed identical to Tadeas with the same type of longsword.

The fat one gave Frigg an odd look. "What is she doing here? It is far too late for little girls to be up."

"Loke, do you not recognize the lady of the house?" Tadeas asked. "You will address her with respect from this point forward."

Loke's shoulder's dropped, and his intense face turned pale in embarrassment. "I…I didn't realize, milord." He looked quickly toward Frigg. "My apologies."

"Milady!" Tadeas stressed.

"Milady," Loke said quickly. "My apologies, milady."

"My sister looks cold, Loke. I suggest you find her a fur," Tadeas commanded.

"A fur?" he asked, wide eyed.

"She is going to see me off," Tadeas clarified. "She can't sit outside the gates in just a simple robe this time of year."

"But what about Father?" Frigg asked him.

Tadeas grabbed her with one arm, lifted her, and held her against his body. The feel of his armor against her was chilling. "Father is calming his anger somewhere. It won't be a problem that you see me off, sister." Loke remained in the same place and looked to the two of them. Tadeas' eyes lowered. "Did you not hear me? Find my sister a fur!"

The warrior turned as quickly as his stumpy legs would allow him and ran off. The remaining soldier snickered and then asked, "Is there anything I can do for you, milord?"

"Gather my horse, Brynjar, and make sure we have plenty of supplies," Tadeas commanded. "I want to take at least ten good men with me."

"Milord, milady," Brynjar said as he bent at the waist and walked off. Tadeas stared Brynjar down until he was out of sight then looked back to his sister. "Tell me what you've been doing since I've been gone."

Frigg thought about it as he carried her through the castle. "Father has been teaching me how to ride."

"How to ride?" he asked in excitement. There was that belittling voice again. If Tadeas and her father talked like this all the time, she wouldn't be able to tell them apart. "Do you sit upright?"

"Of course," she said with a soft laugh.

"Just remember, put your heels into the horse when you want him to go, and snap the reins when you want him to go as fast as he can," Tadeas explained.

"I'm not there yet. It is still kind of scary to ride," she admitted. "Father is afraid if I go too fast, too soon, the horse will throw me off."

Tadeas walked down the spiral steps, still holding Frigg firmly against his body. "You have to know the beast before you try to go fast. Father is right. You should listen to him. He taught me how to ride, too."'

"Yes, I know, you and Erland," she reminded him.

His pace down the steps slowed slightly, and he looked to his sister with pain hidden behind a grin "Yes, he did."

Frigg could sense his sadness and almost regretted the comment. "I'm sorry."

"For what?" he asked.

"For mentioning Erland," she said. "I didn't know it would hurt you."

Tadeas reached the bottom of the stairs and gently placed her down. "Sometimes I wish the gods would have brought you to us sooner, so that you could have known him."

"I wish that, too," Frigg replied. "What did he look like?"

"Much like Father," Tadeas told her with a reminiscent expression. He seemed to drift off for a moment, lost in his own thoughts as he looked beyond into nothing. "The gods blessed him with being born first. That always meant he was taller, stronger, faster and, of course, more handsome, but I had yet to grow. I always told him when the time came, when I reached my peak in youth, I would be better than he was. He never had the chance to prove me wrong."

"Was he brave?"

Tadeas bent down to her. "Very. Do you remember how he died?"

"In the war with the Wild Men in the South World," Frigg recalled. "He got killed in the final battle holding the Dread Gate."

Tadeas combed the side of her hair with his fingers. "That's right. He and two hundred men had to hold back three thousand Wild Men while waiting for Father and King Graylyn to arrive with reinforcements. He was their commander, and he could have waited until all his men were wiped out and rode away to safety. Instead, he did something no one expected. He fought them head on. They held the Wild Men just long enough for Father and King Graylyn to arrive, destroying the Wild Men forces and claiming victory." Tadeas swallowed and looked down, his face turning red for a split moment until he gained control of himself. "Victory came with a price. Erland was far too wounded to survive and died in Father's arms only moments after we claimed victory."

Frigg had heard the tale but never from Tadeas. Not even her father uttered the story. She was forced to hear it from Saga, who numbed any emotion when she told it. It felt nice to see someone with feeling tell her about it. It made Erland feel real to her.

"Do you think he would have liked me?" Frigg couldn't help but ask.

"He would have loved you," Tadeas replied.

Loke returned with a black wolf fur and held it out toward Frigg. Tadeas' eyes nearly came from his head and his face turned crimson. Loke jolted when he saw his reaction and quickly took the wolf fur and wrapped it around Frigg.

Frigg brought it closer around her shoulders. "Thank you, Loke."

"Of course, Frigg," he answered. Another quick look from Tadeas made him add, "Milady."

Frigg looked back at Tadeas. "I think he's learned his lesson."

Tadeas snickered as he touched Frigg on her shoulder and directed her toward the door. Loke jumped at the chance to open it for them. A brush of chilling wind struck Frigg as he opened it. She nearly lost her fur from its power, so she grabbed it and wrapped it tighter. The chill covered her face, and she felt it surge in her bones.

From the castle entrance, she could see the one hundred foot stone wall that surrounded Southrend, guarded by archers and warriors standing post by bolt throwers. In the back corner of the wall sat a bolt thrower that had a dragon spear in its flight groove. The machine was more of a relic from the past, only used a few times when Valstrath came from the Red Mountain to rain carnage on the humans.

The courtyard outside of the castle was lined with warriors. Occasionally, one of them held up a torch to guide the way for the future lord of the garrison. When Tadeas and Frigg passed, every head bowed to them out of respect. She heard them mutter, "My lord," and "My lady," every so often.

She walked at her brother's side, holding his arm tightly and hoping it would help her warm up. Her eyes kept looking to the bolt thrower with the dragon spear. Ever since she could remember, it had always made her feel uneasy.

"Dragon spear," Tadeas said, reading her gaze. "Father said Southrend was once filled with them in the age of dragons, along with all the cities in the North World. It is made of an ancient steel that no longer exists that is said to be able to pierce a dragon's hide with ease."

"Father told me," Frigg said. "But why do we still have one of them?"

"It is to remind us of what we once had to fight off in order to survive in this world. Giants came after us only when we journeyed too far into their lands. But dragons? Dragons always thought of us as an abomination to this world. When Valstrath the Vile fell, they were no longer needed. The king removed most of them and tried to melt down the dragon spears to make swords, but he was unable to do so. Our bloodline preserved that one remaining bolt thrower as a reminder of the evils that once threatened this kingdom."

Frigg's eyes locked on her brother as she walked beside him. He held his head up proudly when the warriors addressed him. He would be a great lord one day. She always saw how much the others respected him. He never demanded any kind of loyalty from his men or those of Southrend; he simply had a presence about him Frigg sensed whenever she was with him. She always felt slightly intimidated around him, even though he had never given her a reason to feel nervous. The attention given to him by his men made her feel like she was around royalty. He would be king one day, and she couldn't wait to see it.

The rank Tadeas requested stood ready—strong men mounted on horseback, heavily armored, and wearing horned spectacle guarded helms. The remaining warriors were part of the city guard, commanded to keep a watchful eye on the castle to assure no one tried to harm the lord or his family.

"Where are you going?" Frigg asked.

Tadeas' face brightened as he looked down at her. "Trivial things, little sister. I ride north to handle things for Father."

"Will you be gone long?" she asked.

"I wish I could say I will return soon, but things are complicated." Tadeas stopped at his horse and adjusted the strap on his saddle.

"I just haven't seen you in a long time," she reminded him.

He frowned. "I know, and I truly hate that every time I see you, you get bigger! I hardly recognize the little girl I saw the last time."

"Will you try to hurry?"

Tadeas walked away from his mount and went to one knee so he could look at her. He turned his head and pointed up at the sky. "Do you know what star that is?"

Frigg took a long look, and near the moon was a bright star outlined in red. "Yes, I've seen it."

"We call it the Gods' Hammer," he said. "It points to the north. I know that all I need to do to come home is face away from it and keep going. Whenever you see it at night, I want you to look at it for a while—not too long, just for a few moments. I will do the same, and perhaps on one of those nights, you and I will be looking at it at the same time, and, just for a moment, we'll be together. We'll do that from now until I come home, and we can be together again. When things in the north are settled, I'll come back and stay for a few days. I promise."

Frigg's face sank at the thought of him being gone again. Tadeas reached down and hugged her tightly. He kissed her forehead, something he had done ever since she could remember. It always made her feel protected.

"Now you take care of Father while I'm gone," Tadeas requested. "Make sure he doesn't get too angry."

Frigg managed a small laugh.

"And don't fear riding," he added "You have to be brave."

"It is hard to be brave when you're small," she replied.

"Nonsense," he said as he looked at her. "Do you know how Erland held back all those Wild Men with only two hundred men?"

Frigg shook her head.

"He lured them in by standing in the valley of the Dread Gate all by himself," Tadeas said in a whisper. "He dared them to come after him, knowing their thirst for war and battle would make them clumsy. When they charged at him, archers within the cliffs let loose arrows upon them. They poured black tar all over them and arrows with tips coated in fire set them ablaze. He took that small force and then confined that large army in a small valley so he and his men could fight them on even ground. You see, his army was small. Being small doesn't mean you can't be brave, it just means you must use your wits to defeat something much larger."

"I'm too young to have wits," she said.

"They'll come to you when you need them the most."

"How does a story about battle help me get over the fear of riding?" she asked.

"Think of it as a challenge that you must use your bravery to overcome," Tadeas replied.

"Frigg!" the call came from behind her, and she turned suddenly to see their father walking toward them, eyes enraged and face flush with anger. "What are you doing up?"

Before she could try to come up with an excuse, Tadeas came to her rescue. "She came to see her brother off."

Tadeas' stern voice made Damari stop. His fatherly eyes went soft as he looked at her. "Go inside Frigg. It's cold out here."

"She has a fur," Tadeas said as he mounted his horse.

Damari approached Frigg and stood behind her, hands resting on her shoulders while he looked at Tadeas. "How many men are you taking?"

"I just need ten good warriors," Tadeas told him.

"You could take more," Damari offered.

Tadeas shook his head. "I'm only going to Astongale."

"What about Westerland?" Damari asked.

Tadeas looked to Frigg and replied, "I'll bring this to the king, this time."

"It is the right choice," Damari said.

Tadeas gave a nod before he put his heels into his horse and rode off. The cavalry followed, causing the ground to rumble and the quiet night sky echo with the sounds of clanking armor. One warrior didn't ride yet.

It was Brynjar, torch in hand as he looked to the Lord of Southrend.

"I'll keep a good eye on him, my lord," Brynjar said with a slight bow of his head.

"Thank you, Brynjar," Damari replied.

"Milady," Brynjar said with a deeper bow of his head just as he snapped the reins and rode off.

Frigg slowly looked up toward her father, who seemed to be seething with anger. His eyes still followed his son, riding through the garrison and toward the main gates. He peered down at her with his piercing gaze. She smiled at him, reminding him he could never be angry with her for too long.

"Don't give me that smile," he commanded, but that belittling voice seeped through. He rolled his eyes and reached out his hand. Frigg grabbed him by his pinky finger. "Come along now."

CHAPTER THREE

"Back to bed?" Frigg asked in disappointment.

"Not yet," Damari said as they walked forward. "I want to show you something. I was going to save it for the morning, but, since you're up now, we might as well visit it." Her father's voice sounded angry, but he smiled down at her. "Perhaps the fact that you are awake is a good thing after all."

Frigg looked up at him. "What do you mean?"

"Men often react with anger when it comes to those they have disagreements with." Damari kept his eyes forward as they left the castle's courtyard. "We lash out and try to use brute force to win confrontations, never realizing the consequence of what can happen when those actions unfold. Our people have a saying; 'a warrior will throw an ax at an enemy, while a smart warrior will make sure it is sharp and accurate before he throws it.'"

Frigg crinkled her eyes as she looked at him. "I don't understand."

"A smart warrior will think before he throws," he explained. "He will make sure that when he does throw an ax, it will, in fact, hit his enemy. In times of war and battle, this will not due; a man needs to react instead of think. Against an enemy you're not yet in war with, it is best to be patient. Find his weakness, and then, when you have exploited it, make sure the weapon you use is deadly enough to be effective. I think you helped your brother learn this very important lesson."

"What does this have to do with Tadeas?"

"Your brother wanted to act off his emotions," Damari said. "I believe he took one look at you and realized what could happen if he acted in anger. He knew that an act of war would be met with another act of war, and the reaction to that may have caused the ones he holds dear to him their lives."

"Like me?"

"I don't like to think something could ever happen to you, little love, but I believe he may have," Damari admitted.

When he looked down at her, he lifted the right side of his lip in a small smile. Frigg couldn't help but blush. "So does that mean you're not mad at me?"

He shook his head. "I'm still mad at you. When a father tells his child to sleep and stay there until morning, he expects her to obey."

She looked down in shame. "I just haven't seen Tadeas in so long."

As she held his pinky finger, he stroked the back of her hand. "I know. I truly wish you could see him more, but he has duties as my heir and must uphold them. You, on the other hand, are still my child. You're supposed to do as I say."

"Tadeas doesn't do as you say?"

Damari grunted. "The proudest day in a father's life is when his children stand up to him. The little boy I held in my arms when he was brought out of your mother is long gone. Now, a great man is there—one I am proud of."

"This is the first time he stood up to you?" Frigg asked.

"By the gods no! He's been doing it since he was fifteen," Damari said. "This time though it was the ravings of a man and not a spoiled boy. True, he wanted to do things the wrong way, but he finally realized the right thing to do."

Frigg blushed. "Because of me?"

"Yes, because of you," Damari said as he leaned in to her and nudged her lightly.

"Is he going to be in trouble?" Frigg wondered, scared of the answer.

"Trouble? No, he's going to the king," Damari assured her.

"It's because of Lord Gustav?" Frigg asked softly.

Damari could only nod with his face going cold. "I'm afraid so."

"Who is he?"

Damari looked down at her and asked in surprise, "You don't know who Lord Gustav is? Saga needs to start teaching you the other kingdoms in the North World. I'll make sure she starts on them soon."

"Well, who is he?" Frigg asked again.

"Lord Gustav is the Lord of Westerland, just northwest of here. If you walk the North Road, there is a fork that will take you there. It's the biggest city in the North World, even larger than Astongale."

"How big is Southrend?"

"Southrend is the smallest of the cities."

Frigg never saw any other place outside of Southrend, and to her it was massive. Trying to imagine the size of all the others was incomprehensible. "Why is Gustav a lord?"

"By birthright, just like you and me, but Gustav is the richest man in all the kingdoms," Damari said. "He also has twice as many men as all the other kingdoms combined, and that includes the king."

Frigg's eyes widened in surprise. "If he has all that, why is he causing trouble?"

"Because Gustav is just like every other man that has everything; he wants more."

"What is more?"

"The crown."

"But King Graylyn is king."

"Exactly, and King Graylyn doesn't even have as much as Gustav. Imagine what that must be like for the richest and most powerful man to have to bow to another being who he feels is inferior to him. It must disgust him."

"He wouldn't be a good king?"

"No," Damari said without hesitation. "Gustav would rule with fear and intimidation. A king must have many qualities to rule. Those can be some of them but not the only ones. A king must be just, kind, honorable and respect even the lowest of people in the kingdom."

"No one can teach him those things?"

Damari chuckled. "You have a good heart, little love. Once a man reaches a certain age, he is permanent in his ways. He can never change. A man with Gustav's temperament cannot become a king and rule. How can a people love a king who treats them horribly?"

"Would you be a good king?"

"I would like to think so," he said humbly.

They walked through the common square as Frigg's thoughts swirled about what her father had told her. Guards and commoners bowed their heads in respect to the lord and his daughter. Frigg always felt awkward when people who were much older than her bowed before her. She never understood what made her more special than the rest of the world.

It was still early in the morning. The sun was not up, yet she saw shopkeepers and vendors preparing for the day ahead. Many merchants sold furs, fruits, and bread—even an armorer walked by them.

The commoners were easy to spot because most of them had disheveled faces filled with dirt and grime. Their clothes were ragged and torn. Their eyes held a kind of wildness that made her fear being around them. Southrend was filled with many poor folk. Her father did what he could for them, but even in the south of the North World it was hard to come by a decent living. She felt comforted knowing she was with her father and a few guards. She grasped her father's finger tightly in this portion of the garrison, and he looked to her in concern when she did.

"Are you scared, little love?" he gently asked.

Her eyes went to his, but, even as she tried to hide it, the trepidation still came out. "No."

Frigg could tell her father knew it was a lie. "There is no need to fear. These people know who you are without having to introduce yourself. You are Frigg, Daughter of Damari, who is Lord of Southrend. Anyone of them would give you all you asked for if you were so bold as to request it—a free piece of bread, a fruit, even a piece of jewelry from a merchant. If one was good enough for you, of course."

When they began to leave the common quarter, Damari reached back to his escort of guards and held out his hand to stop them from following. It was rather odd that he didn't want guards, but, then again, he was still dressed in armor, sword by his waist and walking with purpose.

For as long as Frigg could remember, her father had no enemies—at least, none in Southrend. For as small and young as she was, she listened quite intently whenever she heard whispers of her father. There was never a threat on his life, never an insult, not even the slightest mocking about his abilities as a lord. He was always greeted with great respect, whether by the commander of his forces or the baker. Damari returned the esteem, no matter the man, whether he was of title or not.

They came to a large, barred gate on the edge of the garrison. It stood about twenty feet in the air, spiked at the top to prevent any brave soul that attempted to climb it. This post only had two guards, but they were large men, giants in Frigg's eyes and both holding double-sided axes. Whatever was beyond the gate must have been of great importance.

Frigg could recall passing by here once or twice but never questioned the nature of guards being posted. Guards stood all around Southrend, and she never knew the purpose. Frigg could never remember a time when they were needed for violence. Some of the taverns got rowdy every once and a while, and they were forced to calm the confrontations, but in all her life, she had never seen them remove their swords or have to be violent with anyone they encountered.

Frigg believed Southrend to be the most peaceful of the cities. Saga often told Frigg of the thieving and murdering that happened elsewhere, the dishonorable commoners and warriors who caused harm to the people of their own city. She felt blessed being part of a garrison that was tranquil. They resided in a place where her Lord Father could walk down the streets without worry of his safety or hers.

The guards moved from the gate as one of them opened it for Damari and her. Her father took his finger from her grasp and walked forward. Frigg hesitated. She began to take a step but stopped herself. On the ground, several feet away, loomed a barred floor. It stood a hundred feet wide and across. A chain attached to the front of it and stretched in the air and connected to the back wall of the courtyard. The chain went into a pulley system with a crank, so someone could raise the cage when need be.

Damari held out his hand to her, but Frigg still felt cautious. *Why would there be a cage on the ground?* She wondered. *Is there something inside?*

"Come, little love," Damari called. "If I remember, you wanted me to finish the story."

"The story?" she asked. Then it struck her—the bedtime story her father stopped only a few short hours ago. She hurried to him but came to a halt when she noticed she was getting closer to the bars on the ground.

"Geir!" Damari called. One of the large guards who took a post outside the gate entered and walked around the caged ground. He went to the pulley and began to turn it with all his strength. He groaned and winced with every turn as Frigg watched the cage rise from the ground.

Frigg closed in on her father and nearly leaned into him when she saw the chasm below. It was on a slope toward the shallow end where she and Damari stood. She crept her way up to the edge where the stone began to sink.

Damari snatched her hand quickly. "Be careful, little love. You could trip."

Frigg glanced back into the hole. She couldn't see a thing beyond the shadow that crept over the steep stone. Geir locked the chain when the cage rose all the way. Without having to ask, he took a torch from one of the walls and walked it over to his lord.

Damari nodded to Geir, and the guard returned to his post. Damari held out his hand, and Frigg instinctively grabbed his pinky. Damari chuckled as he took her whole hand. "I won't risk you falling in."

"Can you fall in?" Frigg asked.

"More like roll," Damari joked.

Damari walked down first, taking each step carefully as he held her hand tightly. Frigg saw unlit torches on the walls. Damari stopped to ignite each one on the left side of the pit.

"Why not the ones on the right?" Frigg asked him.

"If I light them all, it would take forever to get to the ground floor," he told her.

"What's there?"

He smiled at her. "You'll see."

With each torch lit, she began to see a little better down the pit. It sloped for a while until Damari put the flames to the third torch, and she could see where the ground leveled out. When they both reached even ground, she felt relieved.

Her father walked forward again and lit up the rest of the torches on the left side of the pit. When the light from the flames gave her more sight, Frigg noticed a massive rock near the end of the wall with the largest chains she had ever seen attached to it. Even her father, who frequently lifted heavy swords and armor, would not be able to lift the chains from where they hung.

Damari slowly walked over to her. "Where did we leave off in the story?"

"All the giants died except for Alatrex," Frigg reminded him.

"That's right," Damari remembered. "This enraged the King of Giants. He wanted to destroy all of us for it, blaming the humans for begging him to kill the dragon and, when he tried to help, his people were wiped out. He went after those he felt were responsible...our people."

"So he came for us?" Frigg asked in a trembling voice.

Damari nodded. "And he would have succeeded if our ancestor didn't prepare for him."

"Balder?"

Damari gave a second nod. "You see, ever since he had become the Lord of Southrend, he knew the giants would one day come for our people. He knew their treaties with our kind would end because of some horrible incident, so he had this pit made—one so deep that it would fit a giant of sixty feet tall if need be."

"How big was Alatrex?" Frigg asked in quiet excitement.

Damari walked over to the right side of the pit where it was still dark. His torch lit up a brazier, and the fire spread in a circular pattern around an altar with a portion of indented wall. Beyond the flames, sat the biggest skull Frigg had ever seen.

She could recall the skulls of men in the pits of the catacombs that belonged to her ancestors. Damari's father was nothing more than a skeleton, stuffed in a tomb that Damari would open once a year to honor his father by cleaning his sword. Frigg was told that her family believed whatever was buried with you went with you to the afterlife. To assure her grandfather could defend himself in the afterlife, Damari sharpened his sword in preparation for the evils in that realm.

This skull was unlike one she had ever seen before. Despite its size, it wasn't one that matched that of a human. The skull was missing the lower jaw, and the top row had several knocked out teeth. The top of the head was cone shaped with the cheek bones enlarged and the eyeholes taking up much of the top half of the skull. Giants had been described to her before by Saga many times as hideous and evil, and now she tried to imagine what it would look like with flesh covering over it. She agreed with her tutor about the description.

Frigg stepped slowly toward the skull, fearful that it would somehow come to life and attack her. It was grey with a few cracks near the top of the head, and it slanted to the right because of the lack of a lower jaw.

"They estimate from this skull that he was forty feet tall," Damari said, his voice echoing inside the empty pit. "He came for Southrend, his footsteps said to echo throughout the land making villagers and even the bravest men run from his presence. Three thousands men stood outside the gates of Southrend, ready to defend their home from a creature that planned to destroy every member of our kingdom. What Valstrath didn't destroy in his anger, Alatrex did. The North World was covered in the bodies of brave men who fought a dragon they couldn't defeat. Those who remained tried to fight a giant whose only goal was to destroy everything in his path to make up for the death of his own people."

Frigg was enthralled by the skull, slowly taking her steps toward it, still afraid that it could come to life. For a moment, she reached out her hand to touch it but stopped herself. She looked to her father for permission. He lifted the right side of his lips and nodded. Her tiny arms could only reach the side of the skull. She could feel the joyfulness come across her face, but then she thought of the fate of the creature that captured her imagination.

"How did he die?" she couldn't help but ask.

"Balder used the dragon spears," Damari told her as he walked toward the skull. "There were four around our city. They were made in preparation for Valstrath, but, when he was killed, Balder found a new use for them. While Alatrex stomped his way through the lines of three thousand warriors, who knew far before the giant came that they were destined to die, the dragon spears were loaded in the bolt throwers, moved to one of the walls, and fired upon him."

She looked to her father in horror. She knew the kind of weapon a dragon spear was. Cast in black iron, the head curved into a deadly point, so when it made contact it would tear the flesh large enough to be a devastating blow, even to a giant.

"He was struck twice," Damari said as he strolled closer to her until he was standing next to her, admiring the skull as well. "He didn't die, but he was wounded badly. It took the remaining warriors to drag him inside here and chain him to the posts." He turned his head and motioned to the two squared rocks with the chains connected to the top. "For days, he sat in here and screamed an unnatural cry that could be heard for miles. He pulled at his restraints to no avail. For days, he continued with his threats until his screams of anger and rage turned to silence. He sat slumped against the wall, eyes looking into the sky at the stars and beyond the cage that covered over him. The only reason they knew he was there was because of his soft breaths."

"He didn't beg?"

"Never," Damari said with admiration in his voice. "Balder told him if the giant gave his word he wouldn't harm Southrend or the rest of the North World, he would let him go, but the giant wouldn't give in to terms. He wouldn't lie. He would never go against his word. Besides, even if he agreed, it was no longer Balder's choice."

"Why not?"

"Because King Torvald came from the safety of Astongale and gave Balder a command." Damari's eyes were locked on the holes were the giant's eyes once were. "'Starve him. Starve him to death,' he commanded."

The thought made Frigg swallow in sadness. "And he did?"

"The king gave a command, and Balder had to obey," Damari replied. "While Torvald stayed in his protected castle high in the mountains of the north, our ancestor watched his people get killed and slaughtered with no remorse. When it was all over, when our people did all the work, the king decided the fate of Alatrex. We live to serve, and we must do what we are told, when we are told, by those who are in power."

"Did Balder want to starve him?" Frigg asked softly.

Damari dropped his head and looked at her with weary eyes. "I'm not sure. All I know is he did what the king commanded. King Torvald said he couldn't risk Alatrex being alive. The rest of the giants were killed by Valstrath, and he had the last one in a cell. The safe choice was to make sure he died, so he couldn't cause the world anymore harm."

She had to step away from the skull as she felt a knot in her throat. "That was wrong."

"Was it?" Damari asked. "Alatrex was going to have our people removed from the North World if he succeeded. Then he swore he was going to kill us all. I feel sorry for the giant, but the end meant we went on. Their race is now gone from the world to never harm us again."

She understood what her father told her, but she still couldn't help but feel saddened that she would never get to see one for herself. It would just have to remain in her imagination, a place where giants were always living, every time the stories were told to her.

"Why today?" Frigg asked him.

He looked at her with confusion until he realized what she meant. "About telling you what happened?" He took a deep breath, torch in hand, and walked away from the skull. "I know you always asked, and today I could no longer hold the truth from you. You'll be starting your studies soon, and I suspected that, when given the books about the giants, you would read it for yourself. Since I was the one who mostly told you the stories, I wanted you to hear it from me."

"Saga told me there were no more," Frigg admitted. "She just never told me how."

"Dragons and giants are of the past, little love—stories to remind us of the evil that once dwelled in our world. Men took over the right to do harm to others and strike fear into those who are weaker than them." Damari looked around the large prison. "Giants are still very much alive; they're just the same size as us now and call themselves lords and kings."

Frigg glanced one last time at where Alatrex once sat. She imagined his enormous body leaning against the back of the wall, hands shackled and looking up through the cell at the stars, just as her father described.

"I believe it is time for bed once again," Damari said as he stood before her. "You got to see your brother, and I showed you the final place of the last giant to ever live. I think that is fair enough, wouldn't you agree?"

She submitted with a nod. Damari held out his hand for her to join him, and they walked back up the slope.

CHAPTER FOUR

The rain sang a song of gentle comfort while the wind whispered a northern breeze. Frigg stared out the open window and looked to the grey skies that covered the horizon. She could hear the thunder every so often, rumbling inside those dark clouds like a soothing growl. She never feared rainstorms or the sounds that followed them; they always helped her sleep at night.

It was midmorning, however, and sleep was the furthest thing from her mind. Tadeas left a few days earlier, and she missed him dearly. She recalled how he promised to come back and spend time with her. The anxiousness she felt to see him again started to become unbearable. To get her mind off of her brother, she decided to walk through the town—anything to get out of the castle for just one day.

She stepped off the chair in front of the window. It was the only way she could look outside. It wasn't as frigid as it had been the nights before, but a slight coolness still brushed against her skin. She picked up the fur from her bed and wrapped it around herself. The tiny chill subsided, and a mild warmth overtook her.

She heard a quick knock at her bedroom door, and a guard entered her room. At first sight of the man, Frigg felt frightened. He was dressed like most of the guards, heavily armored throughout his body, sword at his waist, and helm tucked under his arm, but it was the warrior's face that scared her. He had a gash over his right eye and a large scar running down the length of his face. Both his cheeks were slashed, and the way the wounds healed made it look like a permanent smile. His real lips didn't mirror the scars. They curved downward in an angry frown. His head was bald, once again having a few scars visible around the sides of his head.

He quickly cleared his throat and got the snarl off his face. With his blue eye down in shame, he moved the helm in front of his waist and held it with both hands.

"Milady," he greeted with a rough voice, despite clearing it before he spoke. "Your father has requested that I escort you outside. He wishes to speak with you."

Frigg could only nod, still in shock at the disfigured man.

"Do I frighten you, child?" he asked softly.

"No," she said quickly, trying not to stare at his mutilated face. When she looked back at him, she tried her best to forge a smile. "I'm sorry."

"It's all right, milady," he assured her.

She knew she offended him and couldn't help but feel embarrassed. "What is your name?"

"I am Olaf." The warrior introduced himself with a bow at the waist.

"You do not need to bow to me," Frigg said with a slight giggle.

He looked relieved. "I was told to serve you as I would your father. I would have done the same to him. You are a lady of title, after all."

She approached him with caution, still out of sorts with the way he looked. She bravely looked him in the face, staring into the only good eye he had left. "Do you know what my father wants?"

"He only asked that I escort you," Olaf said. His mouth rose, but Frigg was unsure if it was a smile or because of the scars. "Now if you don't mind, milady, it would be helpful if we go."

Frigg lowered her head and motioned toward the door.

"After you," he insisted.

Frigg walked out of her room with Olaf closely behind. When she left the castle, her father was waiting for her on his stallion with a white mare next to him. He held out the reins to her and smiled.

"Are we going riding?" Frigg asked.

"Yes," Damari said. "But we're going somewhere. I have something I want to show you."

Frigg slowly approached the horse. Her fear of riding came to her, but she remembered what Tadeas said. She summoned her bravery and felt at ease, but she still wondered how she would manage to mount the horse. She felt hands grab her and lift her up. She thanked Olaf with a quick smile, and then grabbed the reins from her father.

"One day you'll have to get on that horse on your own," Damari said to her. "I assume that will be the day you've grown up completely."

"Where are we going?" Frigg asked.

"South," Damari said in his belittling voice.

"How far south?"

"As south as south will allow us." This time he smiled.

Frigg gripped the reins. She tried to remember what she was taught by her father. She gently turned the reins so her white mare would turn around slowly. Damari did the same, but at a much quicker rate.

When Frigg's mare and her father's stallion turned around, Damari looked to his daughter and motioned with his head for her to go first.

She rolled her eyes, knowing he only wished to see her start off right. Gently, she put her heels into the mare and made it go forward. Her father picked his horse up just slightly so they were next to one another.

With the sound of other horses behind them, Frigg turned to see their escort of twelve guards. They were all armored, and with Olaf among them. The disfigured warrior positioned himself up front, the scowl back on his face and looking ahead in a trance.

"Do you like your new bodyguard?" Damari asked.

Frigg couldn't keep her eyes off the scarred warrior, amazed and astonished that a being could go through so much and still live. "Why do I need a bodyguard?"

"You're of age now," Damari told her. "Your brothers had bodyguards when they were your age. So shall you."

"I've never needed one before."

"That's because you were too little."

"Why now?"

He glanced at her as his horse trotted along. "You are my daughter.

Men who want to hurt me would use you as a way to do that."

Her eyes narrowed. "By killing me?"

"No!" he snapped. His eyes flared in anger and then it faded. "Don't say such things."

"I'm sorry," she said.

He reached over and tapped her chin. "Head up now. You don't want to ride without seeing where you're going."

"I'm sorry," she repeated.

"It's all right," he assured her. "You're far more mature than your brothers were at your age. It's going to take some getting used to."

She smiled shyly. "Is that a good thing?"

"In some ways," Damari said. "Others…not so much. It means you know things I wish you didn't."

She kept her grips on the reins as she felt like her mare was going to rock her off. "This is because of Gustav, isn't it?"

Damari didn't look at her directly. "You are the daughter of the Lord of Southrend. If someone wished for me to give up that title, they could hold you ransom or try to harm you in some way to get to me. I won't let that happen."

"But why Olaf?" Frigg asked. "He's very…"

"Ugly," Damari finished.

She looked at her father then looked back at Olaf to make sure he didn't hear. When she didn't see him react in any way, she looked back at her father. "I was going to say scarred."

Her father chuckled. "Olaf is one of the greatest warriors in Southrend, little love. The scars only prove that men have nearly killed him but couldn't. The only thing you need to assume about a warrior with scars is that he's a survivor. I asked Olaf to leave his post as a foot soldier in the forces and become your protector. He may look ugly now, little love, but I assure, one day, you won't see the scars."

She always trusted her father's word, so she didn't object anymore. True, Olaf was scary, disfigured in ways she could never imagine, but what other kind of warrior would she ask to take this duty? His intimidation could be useful when it came to her protection.

When they left Southrend, they traveled south just as her father told her. The rain let up, the grey clouds parted, and, by midday, the sun showed its presence along with its warmth. Fall had always felt like this—warm in the afternoon and deathly cold at night. She felt herself sweating in her fur, but she refused to take it off because she knew in only a few hours she would have to put it back on.

They stopped in a forest just near the southern end of the North World after a few hours of travel. Damari made camp near the river, built a small fire, and requested some of the bodyguards hunt down some food for the party.

Frigg sat on a small log in front of the fire. Before he went off on the hunt with four other guards, Olaf gave her some of his bread, no doubt a way to warm up to her because of the horrible first impression he made with his appearance. The remaining guards stood around the small camp and looked out for any disturbances in the forest.

Damari set up a small table near the fire with a casket of wine and a small chalice for himself. Frigg ate her bread and looked around at the surrounding trees. Nothing but red oaks surrounded them. Dead leaves covered the ground, and the wind started to pick up.

"Where are we going?" Frigg asked between bites of her bread.

Her father sipped his wine and looked around him at the sights of the forest. He seemed to take in the atmosphere, inhaling with both his nose and mouth after a long sip from his vintage. For a moment, she didn't think he heard the question as his eyes looked all around them.

"Do you know where we are?" Damari finally asked her.

Frigg looked around again. She knew it was south, the last forest in the North World if she recalled, but she wasn't sure if it had a name. To save herself from assuming or saying something stupid, she shook her head.

"Because of the red oaks, they call this the Red Forest," Damari told her. "If you head east and stand on the mountains, you will see red all the way into the horizon. Our ancestors called it the Blood Forest. This is where the Wild Men once lived."

"Once lived?" she asked cautiously.

He laughed at her discomfort. "Yes, once. You need not worry about them. They are far south now because of our people."

"We're going south though," she reminded him.

Damari took one large swallow to finish his wine. "I'm showing you the Dread Gate."

Her eyes lowered as she thought. "The…the Dread Gate?"

He nodded and rose from his seat. "Our family has been protecting it for generations, and we will be protecting it far after you and I are gone. Tadeas will take over Southrend one day and be protector of it, and then his children after him and so on."

"Why show it to me if Tadeas will protect it?" she asked.

"Because it is part of you." Damari walked around the table and stood in front of her. "I am the Lord of Southrend, Defender of the Dread Gate, and you are my daughter. Lords of other cities let their children live in ignorance to what the world is really like. This world is filled with evil and wicked men, but they would have their children blinded to it. Most daughters of those lords never see the outside of the city they live in, but not you. You will see what our family has lived and died for since that gate was put up nearly five hundred years ago."

Frigg noticed how things had changed significantly since Tadeas returned and news of Gustav came to her father's attention; the guards around the castle increased, a bodyguard, and a trip to the Dread Gate. Frigg felt a twist in her stomach she didn't like. At times, it was so intense she felt like she couldn't breathe. She kept her composure in front of her father and never allowed her nerves to show in her face or body. When she felt her hands shake slightly, she clenched them together and hid them in her fur.

"What will happen to me once Tadeas becomes lord?" she asked.

Damari looked up in thought. "I assume he will take care of you."

"I won't be a child forever," Frigg reminded him.

"Like I said on the road, Frigg, you're far too mature for your age. I feel like I'm talking to a girl of sixteen and not one who's eight."

"Will you or he make me marry someone?" she asked.

Before Damari could answer, there was a small sound in the forests ahead. The guards removed their swords and surrounded both Frigg and her father. She tightened her fur to hide her trembling shoulders. She looked to the brush as it shook and rattled. When the guards who went on the hunt emerged from them, she exhaled loudly.

Damari gave her a quick glance, and she turned away to hide her fear. The four hunters came back with a boar and a few rabbits. They cooked the animals by the fire, and all of the party enjoyed the fresh meal. Frigg sat with her small plate, only taking the rabbit. She never had a taste for boar.

As she softly chewed her food, she looked at the twelve guards, ripping at their meat like savages. They chewed with their mouths open, which made it difficult for Frigg to enjoy her own food.

Damari stared at them, and a cold silence settled over the camp. They all looked at him, eyes filled with shame because of their immoral behavior. *They must not be used to eating in front of others*, she assumed.

"You're in the presence of a lady," Damari reminded them.

"Sorry, milord," rang out from each of them, followed by, "Sorry, milady."

The sounds softened after that. Damari looked over at Frigg and winked. It didn't quite get her to laugh, but she looked down and blushed.

Olaf finished his meal and placed his plate on the ground. Frigg still had some food left over, so she held the plate out to him. At first, he looked at the plate with no emotion, and then his eyes met hers. He shook his head and tried his best to smile at her with his scarred face.

In less than an hour, they were back on the road, leaving the Red Forest and entering the Southern Plains. The wind was brutal. Frigg felt like she would be blown from her horse at any moment. Even her mare stopped or slowed down when a strong enough gust hit it. Her father stayed close, reaching over when the wind increased as if to stop her from being harmed.

They couldn't even talk because of the force of the wind. The gusts made a powerful and vibrating sound that required a scream for anyone to hear a word. The horses traveled through a rocky hillside, climbing higher and higher from the flat ground. When Frigg looked to the side, she saw the steep drop if the wind did knock her from the horse. She would roll down a rocky hill for hundreds of feet. The very thought began to take over her imagination.

She looked to the horizon ahead. The thought of striking rock and her limbs hitting against the hard surface still lingered…until the sight of the Southern Mountains. They proved to be a feeling of relief for her because now her sight could concentrate on something else. The hill finally began to widen, the rock surface turned to grass, and they traveled back down to the plains. The only emotion she felt was awe.

The Southern Mountains were the last monument in the North World—said to be unclimbable by mortal men. They stretched for two miles reaching both the Western and Eastern Sea. The only way to travel through them was the Valley of Bones, named for all the wars fought between the Wild Men of the south and the Northern Kingdom ruled by King Graylyn. The valley was blocked off by the infamous Dread Gate, a one hundred foot wall made of stone with a small gate at the base of the structure. It blocked anyone or anything from coming in from the South World—as their kingdom wanted.

From what Frigg was told of the South World, it was nothing more than swamps, wetlands, and deserts that were undesired by King Graylyn. It was constantly cloudy and foggy according to the books, but there were tales of the Southern Kingdoms, just no proof that they still existed.

She didn't realize how large the Dread Gate was until she got closer. A flicker of birds was perched on top of it; a few glided around the peaks of the wall and gave her a sense of its height. It was all her eyes could see, giving her a case of vertigo until she spotted the small garrison and guards standing on the northern side. It seemed the guards below were preparing for a confrontation, but one guard with Damari stopped riding and waved the flag at the top of his spear. The golden hammer of Southrend shone on its blue background as it ripped into the wind. There were a few shouts from the garrison, and then the guards stood up straight, heads raised and arms at their sides, with one of them gripping the hilt of his sword.

Frigg counted at least thirty of them, but one warrior stood in front of the others. When the cavalry got closer, the warrior bowed in the direction of Damari.

"My Lord Damari, you honor us with your presence," the warrior greeted. "What do we owe this visit?"

Damari dismounted from his stallion and approached the warrior. "I wanted to show my daughter the Dread Gate."

"It's been nearly a year since your last visit," the warrior said. "It's been far too long."

"Indeed," Damari agreed as he turned toward his bodyguards. "Olaf, help Frigg down from her horse."

The scarred Olaf quickly left his own horse and grabbed Frigg at her waist. She pressed her hands on his shoulders as he guided her to the ground.

"Thank you, Olaf," she said.

"Milady," he replied with a nod.

The wind had calmed, but a big gust suddenly ripped through the plains when she went to her father's side.

"With all due respect, milord, the Dread Gate is no place for a little lady," the warrior said to Damari.

Damari's death stare pierced toward him. "Captain Vidar. Frigg is my youngest child, but she is still my child. That means she can go wherever her father does."

"As you wish," Vidar said with an apologetic bow of his head.

Damari walked toward the gate, only a hundred feet in the distance. Vidar walked beside him while Frigg lagged behind with Olaf. The clanking of armor made Frigg turn to see the guards who awaited the Lord of Southrend marching back toward the Dread Gate.

"What news?" Damari asked.

"There hasn't been a Wild Man sighting since the summer," Vidar said.

"Is that when one hundred of them tried to break through?" Damari asked.

Vidar nodded. "We killed most of them, but the others retreated. Hasn't been an attack since. We did have two riders go beyond the gate. The horses returned, but the men were beheaded."

Damari cleared his throat and glanced toward Frigg. "Careful with your words, Captain."

"My apologies, milord," Vidar replied. "Other than what I've mentioned, there has been no real attack from the Wild Men."

Damari lowered his chin as they got closer to the small garrison. Vidar walked off toward the stone wall while Damari walked around the wooden fort toward the base of the cliffs. He motioned for Frigg to accompany him, and then immediately put his hand out to stop the bodyguards from following them.

Frigg walked around the wooden wall of the garrison with her father and came to a small shrine hidden behind the fort. The statue of a warrior stood proudly with an authentic sword stabbed into the base of the monument. It didn't look like much to Frigg, just a warrior who resembled those who fought under Damari and defended Southrend. He wore a sculpted helm that covered the upper half of the head, only exposing the lower jaw with a closed, expressionless mouth. He stood with a sword in his right hand pointed to the ground and a shield strapped to his back.

Damari stepped gingerly and paused when he was within a few feet of the statue. He looked at it, almost frozen by its presence like he stood before a mighty god. Frigg wanted to say something, but she didn't know how he would react if she did. She continued to look to the statue herself and wondered what made her father look at it with such awe. When her eyes went to where the real sword was, halfway in the stone, she recognized the name, *Erland.*

It was a monument to her older brother—the one she never met but heard stories about, including his early death. He was buried in the catacombs back in Southrend. She didn't understand what this memorial was for.

Damari finally kneeled in front of the statue, something Frigg had never seen him do; men always kneeled before him. His head lowered in prayer, and she heard him whisper something under his breath. After a short pause, he turned his head slightly in back of him.

"Come, Frigg," he said in a saddened tone.

In all the years with her father, never once had he used such a voice. It sounded for a moment like he had something caught in his throat. He quickly cleared it and looked at the statue again.

Frigg sat cautiously with her eyes to her father. He had to squint because of the gust of wind and tears came down the sides of his face. She wasn't sure if it was because of emotion or the wind. Because his face was stone, she figured he was fine.

"Say hello to your brother, Frigg," he said with a motion of his head to the statue.

She looked to the rock structure but was not as taken by it as her father. "But he's back in Southrend, with Mother."

"His body is," Damari whispered. "But his spirit was left here."

His words still confused her. She gazed, as he did, and tried to find the same emotion he showed while he admired the statue. It was nothing more than rock and stone, sculpted to resemble a warrior who had the title of her brother. To her, Erland wasn't a rock replica with a blank expression. Admittedly, it was better than him being a story, but she always imagined sharp features on him, and handsome, much like Tadeas but more matured. In her imagination, Erland was a giant among men who towered over even her father by the way everyone spoke of him.

How can a statue represent a man? she wondered. It didn't tell of his dreams, his thoughts, his actions, nor did it resemble the type of man he was. How could she get to know him from a piece of stone?

"My apologies, Lord Damari," Vidar interrupted with a shaky voice. Her father rose and joined Vidar. "But the patrol from the south just returned. I assume you want to speak with them and find out what they've seen."

"Frigg," Damari called in a rough voice.

She got to her feet immediately and walked as quickly as she could to her father's side.

Damari glared at Vidar before he walked off. Frigg followed, moving quickly around the garrison and heading toward the stone gate. A loud creak came from the Dread Gate. Frigg noticed the stone doors open and her heart jumped. It was only when she saw three riders, all wearing blue cloaks with heavy furs on the shoulders and golden hammers on their chest that she relaxed and knew they were her father's men. They were towering warriors, much like the two who looked over the giant pit back at Southrend.

One removed his helm and revealed a thick grey beard that touched his chest and long salt and pepper hair. His upper lip was without facial hair, cheeks filled with scars and black diminutive eyes. He wore the grimace of a madman, with pure intensity surging from his eyes as he gazed upon the other warriors. His attention shifted to Damari, who quickly approached as Frigg trailed several feet behind.

The other two removed their helms, as well, but their presence seemed diminished compared to the first. The first warrior had a long stride as he walked to the Lord of Southrend and dropped to his knee. Even when he knelt, he looked massive. Just as he rose, the other two kneeled with bowed heads.

Damari paused and looked up at him. Frigg felt intimidated by the man and took small steps so she stood behind her father.

The warrior suddenly took one giant step forward and wrapped Damari in his arms. Both men laughed and patted each other on the back as they embraced.

The large warrior grabbed Damari by the shoulders as he pushed him away and looked at him. "What are you doing here?"

"I came by to see how things were," Damari said with a final pat on the warrior's shoulder. "How are you, Rangvald?"

"Just got back from the South World. We were gone for two weeks," Rangvald said. "Should we go to the tavern and talk further? It would be nice to eat something rather than rabbit and drink something a little stronger than water."

"Of course," Damari replied.

Frigg felt invisible. Her father didn't speak to her or even look in her direction. She felt Olaf's shadow on her. The bodyguard kept his glance forward and walked with his hands by his waist only an inch or so from his sword. He had a presence about him that she found comforting. While her father and Rangvald continued to laugh over the old times, Olaf still did his duty. His scarred face kept glancing from one warrior to another, all the while sizing them up as if to make sure they wouldn't cause any harm.

When their group made it to the entrance of the garrison, the wooden doors already stood open. A few of the warriors sat on horseback and snapped their reins as they rode by and headed toward the wall. It looked like a new party of men was about to go out, which, Frigg assumed, gave Rangvald and his two men a chance to stay at the fort and rest.

Frigg thought the garrison looked rather plain. It had a barracks to her left where a few warriors lingered and a hut to the right with smoke exhaling from a chimney. Laughter came from the hut, along with dancing shadows from inside. When the doors opened, the voices silenced at the sight of Damari. Four men sat at a table at the end of the room, all with cups in their hands. Four more tables stood empty, and the bar at the far end of the tavern didn't have anyone sitting in front of it nor behind it.

"My lord, Damari," one of the men called as he stood up and hurried over to them.

Damari held up his hand to assure he didn't need any praises. "I just want a cup of ale for myself, Olaf, and Rangvald."

"A meal for me, as well," Rangvald added. "Anything but rabbit."

"Of course," the warrior said.

Frigg felt the atmosphere shift. When she glanced at the other warriors, they spoke quietly. It was nothing like the sounds she heard before they entered.

It wasn't until the men took a few more swigs of their ale that the sound returned. The warrior who initially greeted Damari looked to be the current bartender. After giving three requested cups of ale to Damari, he filled the cups up for the other warriors. They raised their glasses to their lord, then to Rangvald, and even to Frigg. She suspected they only did so just as an excuse for another swallow.

Damari and Rangvald sat at the nearest table to the door while Frigg and Olaf sat on the other side. Olaf held his cup with one hand as his eyes looked to the other three off duty warriors. He took small sips but made no sound.

"Did you lose any men on this trip?" Damari asked after a swig of his ale.

"No," Rangvald answered quickly.

"I saw you come back with only two men. I thought patrols went out with five?" Damari asked.

Rangvald sat back in his chair. "We decreased the patrols."

Damari's eyebrows lowered. "Why?"

"Three men is all we need now."

Damari tilted his head. "Only three?"

"Two years back, two hundred of those Wild Men came charging at that door," Rangvald began as he placed his elbow on the table and leaned forward. "The archers took out most. They pounded on the stone wall with battering rams. I feared the gate would eventually break, so we opened it and charged."

"I remember this," Damari said as he looked off in thought. "We lost forty men from that battle."

"Fifty," Rangvald corrected. "After we killed off the first few pushes, they retreated through the valley. I sent out the first patrol to kill off the others. Seven riders, heavily armed, all of them my best killers. When they returned, only five came back. I went out with my own to finish off the remaining forces. I expected hundreds of them, or at least to be outnumbered, but there were only small groups of them."

"What do you think would cause this?"

With his cup raised to his mouth, Rangvald said, "Ask me how far I rode this last time."

"How far did you ride?" Damari asked.

"One hundred miles," Rangvald revealed.

There was a silence between them just before Damari asked in awe, "One hundred miles? How many Wild Men did you encounter?"

"The same as the last two times I've gone out." Rangvald gulped down his remaining ale and slammed the cup on the table. "Not a one."

"Not one?"

"After they attacked in the summer, the last Wild Man we encountered was fifteen miles south of the Dread Gate," Rangvald said. "There were only ten of them. They're still a savage bunch of bastards..." Rangvald's gaze instantly went to Frigg, "Sorry, little lady."

"It's fine," Damari absently assured him, his attention still taken by the news. "Nearly a year?"

Rangvald nodded. "They haven't changed much, wearing nothing but bear furs and using the steel weapons of the men they've killed." The guard acting as bartender walked over with a large pale of ale and refilled Rangvald's cup. When it was filled, the brute waved him off with a hand. "I'm lucky I wear armor. They took the heads of two of my men..."

"Rangvald," Damari said with purpose, motioning his head toward Frigg.

"I thought you said it was fine?" Rangvald asked.

"The language, but not the description," Damari clarified.

Rangvald nodded. He slurped his ale and wiped his mouth with the back of his hand. Some of the ale beaded on his long beard, but he made no attempt to remove it. "Two men died. Good men. I made the Wild Men pay for it."

Just by his tone, Frigg knew it was vicious. His eyes relived what happened and projected it toward Damari. His stare was haunting. Frigg could only imagine the one he expressed in the heat of battle.

"I didn't understand it when I was hunting them after the attack, but when they pounded on the Dread Gate, they weren't trying to get in to kill us. They were trying to get away from the south." Rangvald sipped again. "Based on what I found, they've been gone for months. I tried to find some kind of sign of them and tracked them as far south as the horses would allow. I got to the Deserts of Krane and headed back. If those bastards went beyond the deserts, they're not coming back."

"So there are no more Wild Men?" Damari asked.

"Not from what I can tell." Rangvald looked ahead and took two quick gulps. His ale was gone again. "They could be hiding in some forest or taking refuge in the mountains somewhere that I couldn't get through with my horse, but this is a race of men that has never run from a fight. They thrive to kill our kind. They live for it. They wouldn't just run away."

"So what do you think?" Damari asked.

The guard came back again with the large pale, poured it for Rangvald, and dropped a plate of food in front of the brute. It included two chickens, a side of potatoes, and a bowl of stew.

Rangvald ripped off a leg from his first chicken and nearly ate all the meat with one bite. With a quick swallow of ale, it was down, but the grease glimmered on the sides of his mouth. "I think they were running from something."

After Damari absorbed what he said, he glanced at Frigg. "Perhaps we can speak about this when the time is more appropriate."

"But..." Frigg began.

"I will hear no more, little love," Damari interrupted. "It's bad enough stories of giants and dragons keep you awake at night."

"Perhaps we can talk about it more in Southrend," Rangvald suggested.

Damari's glance went back to the large man. "You're the leader of the patrols here. Why would you go to Southrend?"

Rangvald sank his teeth into the second leg of chicken. With his mouth full, he managed to say, "There are no more Wild Men here." He chewed like a savage while the contents of the chicken rolled in his mouth as he spoke. "My place will be best suited next to you in Southrend, protecting the city."

Damari spun the chalice in his hand while it was still on the table. "What does Vidar have to say about this?"

Rangvald chewed some more. "He knows my only real talent is killing. I'm not doing much of it here."

"You won't do much of it in Southrend, either," Damari told him.

"At least there's a chance." Rangvald shrugged. "No more Wild Men, no more beasts in the south to keep me up late at night. There are nothing but bears, deer, and wolves, and I've killed plenty of them. I need to kill something that makes me fear once again."

"The North World has been peaceful for years," Damari reminded him.

"Exactly," Rangvald said with a point of his finger at Damari. "Too peaceful if you ask me. You and I are well aware that years of peace are followed by years of war. It has been too silent in these recent times." Rangvald put down his cup, leaned in toward Damari, and uttered, "I feel a time of war is upon us. You will need my sword and my counsel."

Damari nodded as Rangvald leaned back. The Lord of Southrend took a small sip of his ale and exhaled. "Trusted men are hard to come by, my old friend. My father always said I could trust you. I have never questioned your loyalty."

"And you never shall." Rangvald motioned toward Frigg and added, "My duty is to you and your little lady, as well as your son, Tadeas. I can't be much help at this forsaken wall. Let me show you the true meaning of my service to you and your family."

His words were passionate and direct. His tone was filled with purpose. Frigg was taken by him and could see the determination in his eyes. He begged, yet he didn't. He simply wanted his wishes to be heard by the Lord of Southrend, and they spoke volumes.

Damari gave in with a nod and rose to his feet. "I will speak with Vidar."

Rangvald stood up and bent at the waist. "You will not regret that decision, milord."

Frigg rose when Olaf did, and they followed Damari out of the tavern. Once more, the Lord of Southrend was greeted with praise by other off duty guards. They all looked to be on their best behavior when he was around. Frigg had no idea where her father would go next.

"Milord," a guard on the wall called. He pointed his finger to the north. "A rider approaches. He wears the golden hammer of your house."

Damari rushed toward the front gate. Frigg jogged a little to stay behind him. When she looked to the horizon, a lone rider rushed toward the garrison. When Damari headed out on foot, Olaf held out his arm and stopped Frigg from following.

"Stay back," he commanded.

"He wears the mark of my house," Frigg reminded him.

"The best way to look like an ally would be to wear the mark of your house," Olaf said.

With the mention of a possible trap, Frigg worried for her father's safety. "What about my father then?"

"He can handle himself, milady," Olaf assured her.

Damari and the rider finally met. Frigg was too far to hear anything. After a quick exchange, Damari motioned with his head for the rider to head toward the garrison. When the rider rode toward the entrance, Damari made no attempts to follow him. Instead, he just looked to the north with his back turned.

A pit formed in Frigg's stomach. Something was wrong, though she didn't know what it was. She looked to Olaf for reassurance, but even he gave her a quick glance of concern.

The rider brushed by them, but Frigg followed him with her eyes. He rode to the stable and quickly dismounted. His expression was somber until he looked in her direction. He almost looked angry, and it made Frigg turn away.

Her father walked back to them, but his steps were slow. Frigg took a step forward and was about to call to him, but, when she saw his expression, she froze. His face mirrored the rider.

"Olaf," Damari said, gritting his teeth. "Get my daughter ready to ride."

Even the wind that he caused as he walked between them held

tension. She never saw her father this angry before. The pit in her stomach increased, and she felt herself shaking from anxiety.

"Come, milady," Olaf called softly. "Let's do as your father asked."

CHAPTER FIVE

Her father's horse rode ahead. When the party saw Southrend in the distance, Damari gave his orders to Olaf and Rangvald to look after Frigg. She wanted so badly to ride beside him, but her mare was far too slow to ever catch his stallion.

The knot in her stomach twisted. She knew there was something wrong. Something happened that forced her father to immediately ride back to their city. Damari whispered to himself, but the muttered words made no sound. Only the vain in his forehead pulsated, ready to burst open. The thing that bothered Frigg, the one that hurt the most, was that he didn't say a single word to her. He didn't look at her once as they traveled through the gusty trails.

Even the bodyguards kept silent. Their eyes remained focused in front of them with an occasional turn of their heads when they came through the trails in the forest. For as loud as Rangvald was in the tavern, his sudden silence unsettled Frigg.

Damari rode ahead with the closest bodyguard several feet behind him. Even the Lord of Southrend's horse seemed to walk aggressively. Damari's shoulders slouched forward, his head nearly hanging down. Frigg could only see him from behind, but it looked nothing like her father from her perspective. He always had a strong posture, no matter the situation or company.

By the time he rode off, all she could see was the dust from his horse rising through the landscape before he vanished. Frigg took a deep gulp and looked at Olaf. Her bodyguard glanced back and gave an uncertain smile.

"Can we ride faster?" Frigg finally asked him.

He shook his head. Even when she fished for words from him, he refused to give them.

"Is there something wrong?" Frigg asked.

"Just ride forward, little lady," Rangvald answered as he rode up on the other side of her. The towering warrior glanced down from his stallion. Even his horse was a giant, nearly twice the size of her mare. "It's best we stay quiet."

The gates of Southrend were already opened. There was usually the sounds of pounding steel from the blacksmiths, chatter amongst the people, or distant sounds of the city moving, but right now there was nothing…until she heard the yelling. She felt so anxious to get off her horse that she nearly fell. Luckily, Olaf dismounted quickly and was on the side of her mare to catch her.

"Easy," he said with worry.

Frigg didn't stop to thank him. She rushed toward the main courtyard where warriors of Southrend gathered just outside the stables. There was shouting and screaming while armor-clad men bottled up at the entrance. She easily walked around them because of her size. She heard Olaf calling in the distance, but she needed to find her father.

The warriors stood unaware of her presence, and with each one she walked by, more of them were in her way. Soon her small stature couldn't maneuver around them. She began to collide with some, and they didn't bother to apologize or even check for her safety. Among the warriors inside the stables, were Loke and Brynjar. Loke was the only one not standing. Instead, he leaned against a table, head fallen in his hands. He looked up at Frigg with the residue of tears on his cheeks and dried blood on his armor. He looked away, rose from the table, and walked forward.

Frigg spotted her father through the guards in the stables. He stood with his back turned much like he did at the Dread Gate. His head hung, too, but she couldn't understand why.

The chaos of the warriors made Frigg's head hurt. She couldn't even make out what any of them said. To her, they were just aggressive shouts that rattled her mind. Brynjar's armor matched Loke's, and dirt covered his face. He screamed at the others inside until there was a pushing match between him and another warrior. They both grabbed each other by their armor and screamed obscenities.

Frigg jumped back when she saw the confrontation; Brynjar pushed one guard so hard, the guard drifted back and collided with her. When she hit the ground, everything went silent except for a soft ringing in her ears. Everything was blurred. She felt a rough vibration as she sat up and thought she saw Olaf push his way to the warrior who collided with her. The scarred bodyguard turned the warrior around and struck him with a vicious punch. The warrior's whole upper-body twisted and collapsed to the ground. Olaf's next target was Brynjar, but someone grabbed him before a fight could break out.

"SILENCE!" screamed Damari.

Damari's voice covered all the other shouting. The room went still, and all eyes looked to the Lord of Southrend as he stood with an icy stare.

Frigg rose from the ground and looked beyond the warriors. Damari stood in front of a wooden table, but she couldn't see what lay on it.

"Everyone leave at once," Damari said quietly.

After a long pause all the warriors quickly dispersed. Olaf took his place next to Frigg, so no warrior came close to her. This time, they were careful around Frigg as she finally got a better look at what was on the table in front of her father.

When the last warrior walked behind her, she saw it—a body. It wasn't just any body; the pit in her stomach told her that. The lifeless form lay high on the table, but she saw the hand hanging off the side of it. Her lower jaw quivered, and she could feel the tears in her eyes.

"Tadeas!" she tried to call in a strong voice, but it came out as a whimper. "Tadeas!"

Her cry got her father's attention, and he turned his head toward her. "Olaf, take her away."

When Frigg started forward, her bodyguard reached down and grabbed her. "TADEAS!"

"Olaf!" Damari said louder. "Take her away now!"

She squirmed in Olaf's grasp and tried using every ounce of strength to get by him, but he was too strong. He held her back with just one arm wrapped around her body. Her arms reached out for her brother, but she knew in her heart he was dead.

"TADEAS!" she cried again as the tears fell from her eyes.

As Frigg screamed, Olaf pulled her from the stables. She kept her eyes on her brother's body with his head turned toward the wall so she couldn't even see his face. She wanted to see him, even if it was just one more time.

After she realized she couldn't break Olaf's grasp, she turned into him and struck him in every way she could. His armor absorbed most of the hits because her arms weren't long enough to reach his face. Even through her cries, she heard him hush her as he got her outside the stables and into the courtyard.

Olaf carried Frigg back to the castle. She fought the whole way. Her eyes were filled with too many tears to notice, but Olaf eventually dropped her on the comfort of her bed. Olaf didn't say a word as he walked away from her and closed the door.

Frigg immediately rose from her bearskin and rushed to the door. It was locked from the outside, and she pounded on the door with her fists as if she were strong enough to break it down. With each strike, her hands bruised from the force, but it was nothing compared to the pain in her heart.

Images of Tadeas' smile came to her from the last time she spoke with him before he rode north. His words started to pierce her as well as the image of him embracing her. "Now you take care of Father while I'm gone. Make sure he doesn't get too angry." She struck the doors so hard the skin broke on the sides of her hands. They swelled, bled, and pulsed as her skin ripped open.

She struck the door, cried tears of anguish, and yelled to be let out, but no one answered her call. When the adrenaline finally left her, she felt the throbbing pain in her hands as they shook from the agony. She curled in her bed, hugged her knees, and moaned into her pillow. It muffled the sound, but it didn't stop her heartache.

She didn't know exactly when she fell asleep, but she dreamed of Tadeas. He stood on a hill with his back to her as the sun set in front of him. She tried to climb the terrain to reach him, but her legs burned from the effort. The more Frigg ran toward her brother the further away he became. She pushed herself to reach him, but the harsh wind picked up and kept her back.

Her legs could no longer move. She collapsed to the ground and slowly slid down the hill. Suddenly, the hill got too steep, and she dug her hands into the cold grass to stop herself from falling. The world tilted, and she almost lost her grip. In a last effort, she called out to Tadeas.

He turned from the top of the hill in slow motion. Despite the distance between them, she could see his gentle smile. The sun set in a timeless moment and gave way to the stars in the cloudless sky. Tadeas pointed upward. Frigg's eyes looked to the Gods' Hammer, the bright star outlined in red. Without warning, she lost her grip on the ground and fell. The wind brushed her face as her stomach sank. She opened her eyes, but there was nothing.

Frigg felt herself rise from the bed, shaking in a cold sweat. It was only a dream. When her hands spread over the bed, the blankets were soaked. The wet bearskin reminded her why she cried, and she felt the tears start again. She sat on the edge of her bed, head in hands, and sobbed as the tears soaked through her fingers and trailed down her arms.

It had to be a lie. Tadeas couldn't die. Everyone loved him because he was a leader and a good man. Why would the gods take someone like that from the world? The image of his motionless body haunted her. Each time she saw him in her mind, more tears poured from her eyes.

Her door slowly opened, but she didn't bother to hide her sadness. It didn't matter who it was as she wept for her brother.

"What is that?" Saga asked in outrage.

She said it with the same anger she used when Frigg spilled something on the floor or misbehaved. Frigg turned toward her with wet eyes and a runny nose. Saga slammed the door and rushed over to her. She kneeled in front of Frigg and grabbed her by the shoulders.

"There is no time for this."

Frigg's mouth opened in surprise at Saga's callousness.

"You don't think I'm sad?" Saga asked while she cleaned Frigg's face. Her fingers were rather rough at first, but the fire in her eyes was gone. "I'm heartbroken. I watched that boy come from your mother, be brought into this world, and helped raise him up to be a great man. You don't think I want to hide away and shed tears until the next full moon?"

If Frigg wasn't searching for it, she might have missed the sadness in her tutor's eyes; she hid it well.

Saga lightened her grasp on Frigg's shoulders, and her voice softened. "You have to be strong for your father. If he sees you sad, it will tear him up worse than how he feels right now. Trust me—he feels it, as well. He is the Lord of Southrend, the Defender of the Dread Gate, and heir to the throne of the North World. He will suffer in silence, much like what you need to do. Whether you want to accept it or not, the people of this city look up to you. You determine how they feel. If you show sadness, they will see it, and it will resonant off of you and grab a hold of them. Sadness makes you weak."

"I'm only eight years old," Frigg reminded her with a frown.

"I know, little one." Saga hugged her tightly. While Frigg was still cradled in her arms, Saga added, "But even little girls know to be strong when the time calls for it." Saga grabbed her by the shoulders again and pulled back from their embrace. She stressed the words, "Be strong! Be strong!"

Frigg nodded, taking a deep breath until her face settled. She wiped away every tear until she felt her face swell from the pressure.

Saga rose and walked toward the door. "Wash your face, put on a new dress, and meet me in the hall when you are ready. Your father wishes to speak to you."

Frigg nodded while two fresh tears hit her cheeks. She wiped them away as quickly as they came and rose from her bed. As her tutor requested, she washed her face with the bowl of water in her room. Because of the cold weather, the water felt chilly, and she could feel her skin turning red. When she thought her face was clean enough, she got a new dress from her clothing chest and put it on. She chose a white chemise with long, baggy sleeves and finished with her fur.

Frigg wiped her eyes even though she was out of tears, but she wanted any evidence of them vanished from her face. She placed the hood of her fur over her head and opened the door. As promised, Saga waited for her in the hall.

She reached her hand out to Frigg, and the saddened girl took it. The halls of the castle were quiet and chilling. The guards who took post, and never said a word unless spoken to, stood with slouched shoulders and lowered heads. The echoes of her and Saga's steps were the only sound, and even they seemed melancholy.

"Keep your head up," Saga whispered.

Frigg lifted her head higher and looked beyond everything in front of her. She concentrated on spots in the walls of the castle. She felt the eyes of some of the warriors on her but ignored them. She bit the inside of her cheeks to keep a stone expression. For the first time in her life, when she walked outside of the castle, a silence shrouded the city. There wasn't even the call of birds or the sound of the wind.

When they left the courtyard of the castle and entered the streets of Southrend, the commoners stood outside taverns and housing areas. Mothers silently cradled babes in their arms, and no one who watched Frigg walk with Saga uttered a sound. Frigg felt very stiff as she walked and stared at the horizon above the city. Even a small glance to the people of her city may have given away her grief.

The great cathedral sat at the edge of Southrend. Constructed from old, coarse stone, it looked ancient. Frigg always hated going inside because she feared the structure would collapse and trap her with the dead. Only a few years back, she dreamt about that exact thing: The ceiling fell in on her as she ran to the catacombs below so she wasn't crushed. She heard the sounds of the tombs opening, and all her ancestors rose, most of them skeletons but a few with rotted flesh just hanging from the bone, groaning and reaching their arms out to her as if wanting to catch her. She froze and couldn't move. She would awake moments from them grabbing her, clutching her pillow with both hands and shaking.

At least that nightmare wasn't real. The real life tragedy that came before her was far worse than the dead giving chase.

Each guard bowed his head to her and gave her the quiet call of,

"Milady." Her eyes swelled, but she gently cleared her throat and stood before the entrance. The guards parted quickly, and Saga let go of her hand.

Saga motioned for Frigg to go inside. Frigg raised her head as she marched amongst the men. She walked through the dark entrance and found herself in the gloomy cathedral. Immediately to her right was the door to the crypt. For a moment, she paused. She let her head drop as a few tears found their way down her face but quickly removed them before they could stain. She stood up straight, sniffled to get rid of the sadness, and opened the door.

Frigg walked down the winding narrow steps to the crypt and steadied herself by placing her hand on the wall. About halfway down, she felt the chill of the underground world. The catacombs were always a dark and dreary place surrounded with the cold silence that only came in the presence of the dead. It was always dimly lit—only a few torches on the wall separated the resting places of Frigg's ancestors.

Her father stood in the middle of the hall, as if he expected her, torch in hand and face shrouded in the darkness. The shadows danced all around and took forms Frigg knew weren't real, yet each one was a reanimated corpse roaming in the shadows about to jump out and grab her.

"There you are," Damari said in a quiet and kind voice. She caught the glimpse of a smile. "I know you always feared this place."

He looked at the pillars that stood two at a time across from one another and then lined all the way down the passageway. Between the pillars, a small room with a closed tomb inside housed the dead members of her bloodline.

Frigg felt ashamed to think she didn't know most of them, even though she visited the catacombs many times with her father to pay respects to the dead. He always called them out while passing them, giving her a brief history of the ancestor inside, where they stood in the family tree, how they died, and even the children they left behind. There were at least twenty tombs in the beginning of the passage before she got to the two she knew: the final resting place of her mother, Asta, and eldest brother, Erland.

"I admit that when I was a child I feared it, as well," Damari said.

"But one day you'll realize that the catacombs of our bloodline are the safest places in the city. The dead can never harm you." She saw him smile again and wondered if he used it to mask how he really felt. "How are you?"

She readjusted herself again, stood straight with her head up, and cleared her throat. "Fine."

She feared anything more than a word would make her sob.

Damari reached his hand out to her. "Come now."

Frigg paused and glanced toward the first tomb on her right. She put one foot in front of the other and hurried after her father. The catacombs were haunting. She would prefer a hundred stories about dragons that might give her nightmares over a few moments alone in this place.

They were her fallen family—their souls long gone into the afterlife. Stories of the dead who rose from the grave as empty vessels feeding off the flesh of the living used to dominate her thoughts in this place. Her father swore to her the stories were mere fables, but as she walked, the fear of the dead rising was the furthest thing from her mind.

The two of them passed her mother's tomb, but Frigg could never look at it. The next tomb held her eldest brother, Erland. It was still new, not as dusty or cracked as the older ones.

Lastly, she saw Tadeas, lying on top of the tomb for anyone who wished to visit and pay their respects before he was locked away for eternity. His flesh was pale, eyes closed, and sword grasped in his hands as it lay in the center of his body. His golden hair looked near perfect. It had most likely been combed for hours by the servants, so he looked suitable even in death. His face sagged, yet he still looked handsome. Frigg heard that one of the benefits of dying young was that you never grew up to be old and ugly, but the thought of her handsome brother lying in the tomb made her wonder if there were any benefits to dying young.

Damari kneeled in front of his son's tomb with his head down and his eyes closed. Without having to be asked, Frigg joined her father. She looked to Damari's blank face and then looked to Tadeas' tomb. While she knelt, she could only see the bottom of his boots. It made it easier, so she didn't have to see his face again. His pale face would be the final memory of her brother, and the less she saw it, the quicker she thought it would fade from her mind. She wanted her last memory of him to be how he smiled and winked toward her before he rode off.

Her father was too quiet next to her. Damari gave her a few smiles, but it was as if he wasn't really there. She thought of ways to comfort him, like grabbing his pinky finger like she always had when they walked together or just telling him something to make him feel better. But she was just a little girl. What words could she possibly conjure to comfort him?

She saw him mouthing something, but she couldn't make out his words. His lips stopped moving. He squeezed his eyes shut, and finally opened them. Frigg quickly looked forward, so he didn't catch her staring.

Frigg still didn't know what to say. The sound of dripping water bounced off the stone walls. Her mind played tricks on her, and she thought she heard the sounds of the tombs opening. It was the nightmare all over again, so she thought of something soothing. She imagined Tadeas rising before her with a loud laugh. Damari and she would jump back from shock, and Tadeas would point at them and mock them for believing he was dead.

When she looked up, his motionless boots were still there, and the fantasy faded to the reality that he would never rise. She almost reached out to him, wanting to touch him again, but then his last hug wouldn't be the last time she was close to him.

"Do you know what I wanted for you?" Damari asked in the silence. The low pitch he used to talk to her for her whole life vanished. Her father spoke to her as an equal. She found it unsettling and hated that it came in a time of death.

She shook her head and felt the tears behind her eyes begging to get out. She feared a single word would release them and show her sadness to her Lord Father. She remembered what Saga told her. *Be strong!* Even in her thoughts, her tutor's words screeched.

"I wanted you to be spoiled," he continued with a quick smile. His lower lip trembled for a moment but it quickly stopped after a deep swallow. "You were supposed to be the one who didn't have to deal with this. You were going to grow up feeling nothing but love and affection from your mother and me. We were going to watch you grow and give you everything you ever desired."

She couldn't help but smile, hoping it would bring him some comfort. He managed to look at her with eyes she didn't recognize. She didn't know if it was because of Tadeas, or if he no longer saw her as a child.

"Do you know what happens now?" he asked in a whisper.

Once again, she could only shake her head.

"King Graylyn has no heir to the throne of the North World. The first three attempts by his wife, the queen, were all stillborn. On their fourth attempt for a child, she and the babe died." Damari's face hardened. "When we went to war with the Wild Men, your eldest brother, Erland, died. The king felt so guilt stricken when I lost my eldest son that he made me his heir. If the king should one day die, I will be king—not just of Southrend but of all the North World. If something happened to me, Tadeas would have been king." Damari looked again to his fallen son, followed by another swallow of sadness. "You are now my heir, my only child who will inherit all that I have and will gain in the future."

The screaming match between Tadeas and Damari came back to her. Her father's words about how Tadeas would be king one day started to make sense. Her mouth dropped. If her father were king, then she would be…

"You will be a princess," Damari said. "A title very fitting to you, but that would mean you will be queen when I am gone."

She stared at her father, but then tried to look beyond him. It made her want to breakdown. The thought of him gone was far too much to bear. The pain she felt at the loss of Tadeas was still too fresh, and Damari's death would certainly be the twist of the dagger that dug at her heart.

"Don't say that," she managed to say.

She could see his warm smile through her blurry eyes. He reached out a finger and caught a tear before it could trail down her cheek. He hugged her tightly. He quietly hushed her, and the strength she managed to conjure because of Saga's words broke with his simple gesture. *Be strong! Be strong!* The words lost all meaning. She sobbed into his armor loudly. She gripped his cloak, closed her eyes in shame, and let go. He tightened his arms around her and gently rocked her. She felt ashamed to break in front of him but relieved because the burden of the pain wrenched her.

He finally pulled her away and looked at her. "Listen here and listen well. I will not leave you any time soon, not now that this has happened. I promise I will gain revenge on anyone who had something to do with the death of your brother."

"That won't bring him back," Frigg managed to say.

Damari grinned. "Did my little girl just teach me a lesson?"

Despite the unbearable sadness that took over her, she managed a small smile.

His face went somber again. "I didn't want this for you Frigg, I swear. You were supposed to be a little girl, at least for a few more years. But now, you inherit something you do not understand. You will have to seem much older than eight. You will rule one day, which means we must prepare you."

She took the cuff of her sleeve and dug into her eyes to remove the tears. "How will we do that?"

"You must know everything I know. You will be taught about the other cities, the history of the kings that ruled before Graylyn, how it was he became king, and his bloodline before him. You will learn the mistakes they made so you do not repeat them, their good qualities so you may absorb them, and all the ways on how to rule a kingdom." He looked at her. After a short while, he released a light laugh and combed his hair with his hand. "You know, I remember the day I did this for Tadeas."

"Did what?"

"Had this same conversation and explained to him what his duties would be when he became a man and what was expected of him." His emerald eyes gazed up at his fallen son just a few feet in front of them, motionless on the tomb. "He was a clumsy boy, your brother. You know he used to fall off his horse?"

"Really?" Frigg asked.

Damari nodded. "I used to yell at him for it. Erland would tease him endlessly. There was a time or two when I had to get between them. Erland was far too big and knew he could easily hurt Tadeas, but Tadeas was relentless when it came to trying to stop Erland's mockery. Erland would just laugh at him, making Tadeas even angrier. At that age, I saw what Tadeas had inside of him, the fire that took over when he couldn't conquer someone who was taller and stronger."

Damari's eyes danced all around, and Frigg wondered if he was reliving those moments in his mind. "Your mother always thought I was too hard on your brothers and told me to be more gentle. My father was harsh with me, as was his father before him. How was I supposed to be gentle? It was never taught to me. Your mother lectured me on the importance of love and caring for your children, but those are the ways of gentle hearts." He paused with a sigh. "Sadly, gentle hearts don't make it in this world. The world is forged by men who are created in the likeness of those who raise them. I was told to bring warriors into the world, so I did."

His hand cupped the side of her face as he looked at her. "And then the horrible day came when she died while birthing you. My heart shattered in a thousand pieces when they told me the news. I felt a pain no sword could replicate, and I thought I was a broken man forever. Then they put you in my arms and that heart, the one I thought was gone, managed to awaken with just one glance from your beautiful, innocent eyes. They were your mother's eyes. It was the gods' way of telling me everything was going to be all right. I thought I was lost because of your mother's death, but I found something I never knew existed. Unconditional love."

"What was she like?" Frigg knew the answer to that question by heart, but the familiar sting still came to her throat from even mentioning her.

"Your mother?" he asked distractedly. He slowly shook his head. "The most beautiful thing I've ever seen in my life. I let her provide all the kindness for your brothers because she knew how to do it. She was loved by her father. She always said that to me, but I never understood it. I mean, I loved your mother, the way a man in this world does, but I didn't love her as much as I could have." He took a deep breath. "It took losing her to realize that. That's why I coddled you. I tried to make up for it, I think. You were her final gift to me, and I wanted her to see in the afterlife how I loved you." His eyes glassed over. It was the first time in Frigg's life she saw her father cry. The back of his hand wiped the tears away. "She would have loved you. By the gods, she would have held you in her arms for as long as she could, rocked you gently, and sang you to sleep. When you got older, she would have taught you how to be a proper lady, just like her."

Frigg looked up at the bottom of Tadeas' shoes. Three immediate members of her family were now in the crypt. Two of them she didn't know, and the most recent was one of her heroes. "I wish I could have known them all better."

"So do I, little love," her father whispered. Damari cleared his throat, and his eyes turned sharp and determined. "You will be queen one day. Do you know what that means?"

Though she didn't understand the magnitude of that duty, she nodded.

"No, you don't." He rose and held out his hand to her. He knew. "But you will. Come now, little love. I will make sure you are prepared."

She grabbed him by the pinky finger and stood up. Damari's eyes locked on the body of his son once more. With just a nod of his head, he slowly turned. Frigg lingered at the tomb where her mother lay.

"Is there something you wish to say?" Damari asked.

Frigg looked up at him. "Is Tadeas with them now?"

Damari nodded to her and glanced at Asta's tomb. "Good night, my love. Kiss my sons for me, and show them the love I was never able to express." Damari tussled Frigg's curly hair and said, "Say goodnight to your mother."

Frigg's eyes finally looked to the stone box. She let go of her father's finger and walked to it. With a sweep of her hand over its top, the dust cleared, and she saw her mother's name carved into the stone. She stood on the tips of her toes, leaned forward until her lips touched the cold rock, and kissed it. She had no face to the woman who gave her life, nor did she think her mother had a face for her wherever the fallen went, but she still felt she was with her for just a single moment—together like they never had been before.

She quickly grabbed her father's finger again and headed down the dark hall. The fear of the catacombs faded as she walked with him. The pain of losing Tadeas still lingered in the pit of her stomach and dominated her thoughts, but having her father next to her eased them, even if it was for just a little while. He stayed by her side up the winding stone steps, despite the fact they were narrow. Damari kept her near the wall, so she didn't slip on the edge of the staircase. She held his pinky finger the whole time to keep her balance.

Loke waited for them outside the cathedral when they walked out. He dropped to one knee and hung his head. The other guards stood in a circle, giving the broken warrior his space in front of the lord and lady of the city.

"You may rise, Loke," Damari assured him. The gentle voice he used in the crypt faded, and he returned to being the Lord of Southrend.

The fat warrior did as he was commanded and lifted his head, yet it still looked like it sagged. "My apologies, my lord, but there is news from the north."

"What news?" Damari asked.

"It's King Graylyn, my lord. He comes to pay respect to your son," Loke replied.

Damari nodded his head slowly several times. "Inform the guards. We'll need to prepare the town for his visit."

Damari tried to walk by, but Loke held out his hand and stopped him. "There's more."

Damari raised an eyebrow.

Loke leaned in and whispered, but Frigg still heard it. "Lord Gustav is coming, as well. The rider says he commanded five hundred men to escort him."

"Five hundred men?" Damari asked. "Why would he be bringing five hundred men?"

Loke could only shrug for an answer. "It's pretty suspicious, my lord."

Damari paused. With a nod of his head, he dismissed Loke. The thick warrior bowed at the waist and walked off with quick feet. Damari realized the other guards around him heard the conversation. "You all heard what's going on. Double the guards at the wall and in the streets. We will have the king arriving soon, and I want the city to have the presence of our warriors for his safety. He will no doubt have bodyguards, but I don't want to take any chances. Our city doesn't harbor murderers or men with ill-will toward him, but we need to be safe. You all have your orders."

The men walked away in different paths except for Damari's four bodyguards. Olaf was among the crowd and approached Damari with a quick bend at the waist.

"Take Frigg back to the castle and inform Saga she is to start teaching her the history of the North World," Damari commanded. "Tell her we also need Frigg to have a new dress for when the king arrives, and teach Rangvald his new duties."

"What duties are they, milord?" Olaf asked.

"He will take a post at the castle," Damari replied. "He needs to be told how to protect it and how to evacuate myself and Frigg in the event of an invasion."

"Of course, milord," Olaf said with a bow of the head. The guard's scarred face turned to Frigg. She could feel his eyes on her. "Milady."

Damari looked down at her. "I have things I need to do, little love. I'll be back at the castle when I can."

She nodded, still unable to speak without having to fight tears. She returned the hood of her fur to her head as she walked, standing straight, head up, and biting the inside of her mouth.

As the sound of Olaf's armor clanked while he walked, Frigg turned her head back to her father. He watched her walk off, bodyguards surrounding him and a distant expression on his face. They both held back their emotions. He had his way and she had hers.

CHAPTER SIX

She read for hours. She read books as thin as her finger and books as thick as her hand. One looked endless. When she turned the page, the binding groaned from the weight and threatened to close making her lose her place. For two days, she didn't leave her room, immediately opening a new book whenever she finished one. Just when she thought she was nearly done with the history, Saga came in and dropped more books on the table.

Frigg wanted to scream from boredom, but her father stressed to her how important it was to study. She read for so long yellow dots flickered in front of her eyes.

One morning felt particularly cold. The wind pushed its way through the window. The wood covering the window wasn't very flush and let in a chilling breeze that was accompanied by the sound of an annoying clank. The brazier in her room was nothing more than embers, but she feared the amount of smoke a large fire would cause in the room.

Servants brought her food every few hours while her eyes looked through the pages. If she didn't eat quickly, it was like eating ice. Saga noticed the temperature in the room, so she kept bringing in fresh stew from the cauldron for Frigg.

Her tutor tested her every so often with questions. She asked Frigg about what she read and whether or not she understood the meaning of certain events. Frigg realized her teacher had read these books, as well. Whenever Saga asked a question, it was always right after Frigg read a certain passage. Saga lingered behind her, looking at the pages herself.

Near the afternoon, her freshly crafted gown was brought to her and put on her bed. It was made from blue velvet with patterned sections running down the front, including the sleeves. Frigg stared at it in admiration for a while and wondered what the fabric would feel like once she put it on. She snapped out of her trance when Saga realized Frigg's fascination with the dress.

"Pay attention to the book," Saga said. She seemed angry, but Frigg wondered if she was thinking of Tadeas. After she talked to Frigg about her true feelings, Saga did what Frigg and her father did to keep them inside; her way was just a little rougher. Saga's words had venom in them, while Frigg's words held little emotion.

"Sorry," Frigg said gently. She tried to only use one or two words when she spoke. The tears may have left her eyes, but she feared what would happen if she said more than the minimum.

"Who was Graylyn's father?" Saga asked as she tried to get the creases out of Frigg's dress.

"Audun the Admired."

A light sigh came from Saga as she pressed her hand down the gown. "And how did he come to reign?"

"By killing the king of the North World," Frigg said.

"How is that possible?" Saga asked in false surprise. "How was Audun the king if we already had one?"

"Audun came from the South World with all his people." Frigg recited what she read only a few moments earlier. "His people were at war with the Wild Men for many years. In the south, all of the kings fought the Wild Men, but this war was different. The Wild Men were stronger than they ever were before. They burnt down cities, villages, and all safe havens for Audun and his people. It pained him to do so, but Audun needed to accept that the war was a failure. With nowhere else to go, he decided to come north and make peace with the North

World King, Sven."

Saga picked up the dress and inspected her work as she raised it in the air. "And did he agree?"

"At first," Frigg said. "He had to give up all titles and swear loyalty to King Sven the moment he crossed the Dread Gate. His crown was handed over to Sven and melted down. Sven had a necklace crafted from it and wore it as a victory against Audun's people. Audun thought it was an insult but wouldn't go against his word."

Saga folded the dress in her arm and gently placed it back on the bed. "So Audun gave up his crown to Sven, but how did Audun become King of the North World?"

For a moment, Frigg forgot, but when she flipped back a few pages and saw the explanation, it came back to her. "The Wild Men headed to the Dread Gate with thousands. Warriors of Southrend, Westerland, Astongale, Ravengale and Morendorn raised their banners and marched through the Dread Gate to meet them in the South World. Because Audun had experience fighting the Wild Men when he lived in the South World, he knew what ways could be used to defeat them."

"Did he now?" Saga asked. "What were they?"

Frigg flipped to the next page. "Wild Men fought well in the open. Because of their numbers and size, they could intimidate warriors, even ones who were well trained. Audun warned Sven of this, but he didn't listen. King Sven is written as a stubborn man who always tried to use strength to defeat the Wild Men instead of strategy. He thought fighting them any other way would be considered weak. For the first few weeks of battle, many of the men from the North World were slaughtered. Audun took his own men and baited the Wild Men into a valley in the South World—one he knew well. When the Wild Men were bottled in, they couldn't run freely and didn't know how to fight in ranks. Audun crippled the Wild Men and pushed them to the Deserts of Krane."

Saga walked toward Frigg and stood behind her, looking over her shoulder at the book. "So they won?"

Frigg nodded. "For the time being."

"What does that mean?"

Frigg hated being belittled this way. By her tone, Saga knew everything already and just tested her memory. Frigg felt far too exhausted to start an argument. "King Sven took exception to Audun's victory. As the entire army celebrated the foreign ruler as the true victor, it drove Sven insane. He eventually declared war on Audun and all who followed him. Allegiances were formed, lords took sides, and the North World was at war with itself."

"And who won?" Saga asked as she walked around the table.

"Audun won by killing Sven in the battlefield of Westerland," Frigg replied. Saga chuckled, so Frigg questioned her own knowledge of the events. With a raised eyebrow, Frigg asked, "What's so funny?"

Saga finally took a seat across from Frigg and placed her worn hands on the table. "The book you are reading is written by the scribes of Astongale, which means it was written by someone loyal to King Graylyn. The book at the edge of the table is of the same event," Saga pointed out, "but it is written by a scribe in King Sven's city."

"What's the difference?" Frigg asked in frustration.

"Well if you read it, you will see why," Saga said with a grin. She seemed to take pleasure in watching Frigg get angry. Frigg stared at her for several moments, but Saga just gave that familiar giggle with her rotting teeth coming through in a pleasurable smile. "All the cities of the North World wrote about the events that took place in the history of our world. Various nobles, lords, and kings all have their opinion on how things unfolded. Even when things didn't happen the way they remember, they write it their own way, so they don't look weak in the eyes of their own people. Half of the pages you read are manipulations and deceits, so those in the future are confused by the past. Men in this world lie, sweetling. The trick is trying to figure out which is the lie and which is the truth."

"Well, how will I do that?" Frigg asked.

Saga shrugged. "Sometimes you never do. That's how difficult things are for a ruler. You must decide what the truth is and what the lie is. When you come to rule, you will hear lies from the mouths of men who claim loyalty to you but actually wish to deceive you about their true intentions."

"And I will be expected to know the truth?"

Saga shook her head. "You're simply supposed do what you feel is best."

"And how will I do that?" Frigg repeated with her voice raised in annoyance.

Saga slowly blinked in surprise at Frigg's outburst. "Settle down now, young lady. Children throw fits, not young ladies of Southrend."

"I'm not a young lady from Southrend! I'm a little girl!" Frigg said as she rose from the chair. "I didn't ask for this."

"Neither did your father when your brother died!" Saga snapped. "Tadeas knew all the things we are trying to teach you. He was ready for whatever position was given to him. If the king died tomorrow and something happened to your father, he would have been able to take the throne with no worry coming to the empire." Saga stood with authority and pressed her hands into the table. "Now the gods saw it fit to take him before his time and before he could fulfill the destiny your father envisioned for him. They pointed the finger at you. You are the only remaining child of Damari, Lord of Southrend and Defender of the Dread Gate. You may be a child and may not understand what that means, but you will."

Saga gritted her teeth with a slight snarl in her tone. Frigg bit the inside of her mouth and hid the urge to cry. She stared angrily right back at the old woman. In times like these, Saga wasn't her teacher; she was an angry crone who didn't understand anything.

Saga pointed to the table while looking at Frigg. "Now, sit down."

Frigg took her time. She slowly pulled out her chair and sat back down, inching it forward so she could sit directly in front of the books.

"Tell me the rest," Saga said.

"The rest of what?" Frigg asked.

Saga exhaled loudly. "Tell me how Audun became king."

Frigg ran her finger through the page but kept her glance on Saga. "Why should I tell you if it isn't the right story?"

"Tell me the version you were reading," Saga snapped. After a few moments of silence, the tutor adjusted herself in the chair, sat back, and rested her hands in her lap. "Go ahead."

"Audun became king," Frigg repeated.

"And what did Sven's family do about it?"

"Sven's only brother, Kensley, tried to raise forces after the fall of his brother, but he was easily defeated," Frigg replied. "Kensley was executed, but his son was spared."

"And who was his son?" Saga asked.

Frigg hadn't gotten to that portion of the story yet. She leaned forward and looked into the book as quickly as she could, so she could satisfy Saga. After a few lines, she caught the name and looked up in shock. "Gustav?"

Saga nodded. "King Sven had no children. His bride, Eira, was said to be barren. He was only twenty two years old when he died, and Kensley, just a year younger, had a wife who was with child."

"Gustav," Frigg repeated in a whisper.

Saga nodded again, but this one was more somber. "Eira was given to Audun to make peace with the North World since the people already loved her. A year or so later they disproved she was barren with the birth of his son." Saga held her hand out toward the paper, commanding Frigg to see for herself.

Frigg's fingers went through the pages again, faster than the last time. She stopped when she found another name. "Graylyn." Her eyes widened. "So Gustav hates Graylyn?"

"Perhaps, though he pretends to be a loyal subject to the king." With the tension gone and their argument long in the past, Saga rose and walked around the table again. She didn't stare over Frigg's shoulder this time. She just slowly walked, her arms tucked into her sleeves and her steps hardly making a sound on the stone ground. "Gustav's hatred is mostly directed toward the man who executed his father. Did you happen to come across the name of the man who removed Kensley's head from his shoulders?"

Each new discovery seemed to make things worse for her, and she sensed this would be another answer she didn't like. Sure enough, she came to the name and looked up at Saga. Frigg hardly said the words, "Inghard, Lord of Southrend and Defender of the Dread Gate."

"That's right," Saga confirmed. "Your grandfather. Lord Inghard took Audun's side in the war—a betrayal that the bloodline of Sven will never forget. Each child born of Sven's blood is reminded of how his family was removed from the throne of the North World and whose sword did the deed. They may blame Graylyn's father for being the new king, but they will never forget the bloodline of the one that took him from this world."

"That's why Gustav hates us?" Frigg asked.

"Lord Gustav of Westerland, better known as the Dragon Lord of the West, hates everyone," Saga admitted. "There was a time where we feared more than the Wild Men beyond the Dread Gate. We feared a people who were no different than we were, but we fought them simply because they were on the other side. Men are fools like that."

The night Tadeas and Damari fought flashed in Frigg's mind again. She remembered that Tadeas was going to talk to the king about some kind of conflict with Gustav. "Did Gustav kill Tadeas?"

Saga stopped walking and quickly turned to Frigg. "Who told you that?"

"The night Tadeas left, he was fighting with father about a problem with Lord Gustav," Frigg informed her.

Saga's eyes flickered from side to side in her head. "Did you tell your father this?"

"He would have already known," Frigg reminded her.

Saga looked to the ground for a few moments. "I'll bring that up to him later. The truth is we still don't know what happened to Tadeas. Your father sent couriers out to every lord in the North World asking for help in the matter."

Frigg had yet to ask the question, fearful of the descriptive story about how her brother was taken from the world, but she wanted to know. "How did it happen?"

Saga looked at her. "That's not my place, sweetling. When things have settled, you should ask your father."

Frigg only nodded and glanced back at her book. "I'm scared to bring it up with him."

"Why?"

"I'm fearful I will start to cry."

Saga's face changed. "What have I told you about tears in a time like this?"

"But they are necessary for those we love!" Frigg said with great passion.

Saga nodded. "You are right; they are, but one day you will

understand why you must keep them in."

Saga circled the table again. The tutor's eyes lingered, and Frigg wanted to scream for her to leave. She had studied enough and been forced to read stories that may or may not be true and learn of all the dead men who ruled before she was born. She didn't understand why she needed to know the past, nor did she care.

"Was Graylyn an only child?" Saga asked, breaking the silence.

Frigg was done; she no longer cared about the questions. Saga made it around the table and stared at her. Frigg knew Saga wouldn't stop looking at her until she answered the question. She reluctantly looked at the page, but the words blended together like incoherent sentences.

A name suddenly struck her in the family tree of King Audun and his bride, Queen Eira. They had two offspring; the first, of course, was their son, Graylyn, but the second was a daughter named Asta.

Frigg looked up, and her eyes blurred with tears. "My mother?"

Saga nodded. "She was the Princess of Astongale, the prize of King Audun, and the glimmer in the eyes of Eira. Lord Inghard and King Audun became very close friends after they defeated Sven. Audun visited Southrend whenever he could, bringing Graylyn and Asta with him. Naturally, your father and Graylyn became very close friends, and when they came of age, Asta and your father grew fond of one another in a different way."

"They fell in love?" Frigg asked.

Saga took her seat across from Frigg again and nodded. "But the Princess of Astongale was not to just be given away. Even if she truly loved your father, she was to be fought for."

"Saga!" a voice called from the doorway.

Frigg jumped a little when she saw her father standing there. He didn't look too pleased with what Saga told Frigg. He slowly walked in the room, but his glare looked like he was about to yell.

Saga shrank in his presence, head down and shoulders dropped. She cleared her throat for a few moments and finally met his eyes. "Milord."

"Frigg," Damari demanded. "Come with me."

Frigg eagerly stood up and joined him. Wherever they were headed had to be better than reading books.

"Milord," Saga repeated before Frigg could run out. "She needs to put on her dress."

Frigg rolled her eyes. Even a few more moments in that room was torture.

"Put on your dress and meet me outside," her father commanded her.

Frigg had never changed so fast in her life. After she finished dressing, Saga looked her over to make sure her face was clean and her hair was presentable. Saga's fingers repeatedly plucked and picked at her curly hair. Frigg stood there counting the moments until it was over. With a loud sigh, Saga finally dismissed her.

Damari stood in the hall when Frigg walked out. Olaf and Rangvald stood behind him. The brute, as Frigg had come to call her father's new guard, stood with his hand on the hilt of his sword as if he expected a fight.

Damari looked her over. "It's a lovely dress suited for a lovely girl."

She blushed and grasped his pinky finger. Olaf and Rangvald turned to escort them out of the hall. Frigg couldn't get over the height difference between the two of them. Rangvald was a beast of a man who wore armor twice the size of a normal warrior.

"The courier has returned," Damari said, disrupting her thoughts. "The king is only a few miles out."

"You mean my uncle?" Frigg asked.

"I see you have been reading," Damari replied.

"Why did you never tell me?"

When she glanced up at him, he looked back at her with a sunken face. "Your brother didn't learn all the things about the North World until he was twelve—the same age I planned on having you learn. With recent events being what they are, you have been rushed into learning."

"I've been reading for days," Frigg complained.

He clicked his tongue. "I know. I'm sorry, little love, but it is needed. You will have to rule one day."

Frigg stopped walking and took hold of her father's hand with both of hers. He stopped and faced her with puzzled eyes. "What if I don't want to rule?"

Damari motioned for Olaf and Rangvald to go ahead. He kneeled in front of Frigg and took her hands in his. "You need not worry, little love. If something should happen to the king, then I will rule until you come of age. That will be when you are mature enough to understand what is happening. You're only eight. I know this is all so much for you to take, but I will be right here to help you along the way."

Frigg looked down and gave in with a nod. She still didn't want to do it, but she also didn't want to let him down. That would only break her heart further.

CHAPTER SEVEN

When Frigg and her father walked out of the castle, the entire courtyard was filled with ranks of warriors who stood waiting for them. Olaf and Rangvald were the only two not standing in formation. The wind picked up just as Damari and Frigg reached them. Olaf seemed to struggle with it, his cloak ripping into the gusts, but Rangvald stood like a mountain against a storm.

"Olaf," Damari called to Frigg's bodyguard. "Take my daughter to the jeweler. There is a gift there for her."

Frigg looked at him excitingly. "A gift?"

"If you are to meet the king, we need you to look exceptional," Damari said. "Not saying that you don't already, little love. We just need you to look proper for a man who is worthy of his title as king."

Olaf approached and gave a simple nod to Damari. Then he stood and waited for Frigg to join him. Frigg let go of her father's finger and practically sprinted away with excitement.

Her mutilated bodyguard captured the attention of the commoners as they walked through the alleyways. Everyone whispered, and a few gasped at the sight of him. She was getting so used to him and didn't mind what he looked like anymore, so she glanced at him to see his expression. He seemed used to the reactions he received.

Other than the bizarre responses to Olaf, most of the commoners looked pretty happy. The merchants laughed as they gathered in the main square of the Common Quarter. Frigg saw nothing but smiles from most of them. She thought it would be a relief after the many days of sadness all alone in her room, but she couldn't help feeling angry. She wanted to see them mourning the loss of Tadeas, yet their exultant nature made her brother seem long forgotten. She traded sadness for anger.

Her eyes searched the walls surrounding the Common Quarter and something gained her attention. With the comments made by the people toward her bodyguard and the anger she felt from them smiling, she figured she'd pass the time with her bodyguard. "Olaf."

"Yes, my lady," he said.

"Why are there no stairways to the wall in the Common Quarter?"

"Balder made that in case of a revolt by the people," he replied. "If they decided to go after their lord or his men, the archers could just loose their arrows and no commoner could reach them."

That makes sense. "Interesting. The people love my father, though. They would never do that to him."

"I surely hope you're right, milady," he said.

When they left the main square, Frigg exhaled loudly to release her rage. The small talk did little to help. It would be some time before they reached the jeweler. Loke approached her near the stables, the same place her brother's body laid when she got back from the Dread Gate. Brynjar lingered behind him and leaned against a tavern with goblet in hand and a scowl covering his face. He looked to Frigg and gave a slight nod of respect.

Loke's eyes were still glassy when he approached her, and she could see on his face where the dirt was washed away with tears. Her anger melted away because she wanted to do the same thing, but she kept hearing Saga's words in her head. *Be strong. Be strong.* Those two little words jabbed at her mind. She said them over and over again to stop herself from crying. She didn't want to let Saga down or show her father she was sad.

Olaf reached for his sword by his waist when Loke got near, but Loke raised his hands to assure Olaf he meant no harm.

"I just want a word," Loke told him.

"Be quick about it," Olaf muttered. "She is expected to be with her father soon."

Loke managed a nod to the bodyguard then looked at Frigg. "Frigg... milady, I mean. I would like you to know that I now serve you if you wish. Tadeas was my commander and my friend. I owe him everything I have. If you command it of me, and your father approves, I will protect you with my life and make sure nothing ever happens to you."

Frigg swallowed slowly. "Dry your tears, Loke. There is no more time for them."

Loke looked offended by the statement. Brynjar lifted himself from the tavern wall and headed toward them. This time, Olaf removed his sword halfway from its sheath.

"Olaf!" Frigg said in alarm.

Brynjar grabbed Loke by the shoulder and motioned for him to walk away. Olaf's eyes stayed on Brynjar, sword still ready to be removed completely. Brynjar scoffed.

"You disrespected the Lady of Southrend," Olaf reminded him. "She was knocked over because of your anger. You owe her an apology."

Commoners stopped in the streets to watch the confrontation. Olaf took another step forward and stood inches from the warrior. Brynjar still looked irritated, but a calmness seemed to wash over him. He looked at Frigg and slowly approached her with the occasional glance toward Olaf.

Brynjar dropped before her. "I apologize to you, milady, for being the reason you fell in the stables. Ask anything of me, and it shall be done."

With a drop of his head, Frigg recognized his sincerity. It seemed the scowl and the drinking were his way of dealing with the death of her brother. She was too emotional to give a response.

"Come, Olaf," she called to her bodyguard.

She walked by Brynjar and Loke with Olaf at her side. She felt horrible for ignoring both their statements of loyalty, but she needed to be strong.

This was the new Frigg—a hardened version of her former self who was no longer allowed to be a child. If Tadeas were still alive, she wouldn't have to worry about all these things.

When they reached the jeweler's, the street was crowded with commoners. Frigg heard expressions of pleasure and excitement at the possibility of seeing the King of the North World, but many of them stopped chattering at the sight of Olaf.

There was a long pause while their eyes focused on the bodyguard. Frigg loudly cleared her throat. At the aggravated sound, the townspeople looked at her.

"Would you excuse us?" Frigg asked a little too politely.

"And who might you be, little one?" one asked.

"I am Frigg, Daughter of Lord Damari," Frigg answered with power in her tiny voice.

Gasps of surprise and pale faces filled the crowd. Olaf gently tapped Frigg on the shoulder and whispered, "It's Lady Frigg."

She wanted to be angry with him for correcting her, as was her right, but a smile slowly came across her face while she looked at him. He returned the gesture but only for a quick moment.

She looked back at the commoners in front of the door and cleared her throat once again. They scattered like rats and made a clear path for Frigg and her bodyguard.

With a glance toward Olaf, she said, "Don't correct me again."

He raised his eyebrows, but she smiled to show she was joking. He gave a sigh of relief.

When she opened the door, a bell jingled above her. The deserted shop had an exotic smell. Several plants were aligned against the far wall. With a small step toward them, she discovered them to be the source of the nice aroma. It was a rather small shop with a wooden counter, too tall for her to see over, but she had a clear view of the top shelves behind it with sparkling gems, necklaces, and what looked to be earrings.

"You must be Frigg," the shopkeeper greeted as his head peered over the counter. He smiled, walked around the counter in the small shop, and greeted her with a bow. "So very nice to finally meet you, milady. I am Jerrick."

"The honor is mine, Jerrick" Frigg insisted.

Olaf stepped between them, and Jerrick looked shocked. "Is there something wrong?"

"It's Lady Frigg," Olaf corrected him.

"Apologies, Lady Frigg," Jerrick said, but his eyes remained on the disfigured bodyguard.

"Do you know my bodyguard?" Frigg asked. She was tired of everyone staring at Olaf.

Jerrick snapped from his trance and gave her his full attention. "No… no, I don't."

"Then why would you stare at him?" Frigg asked.

He hesitated. "Well, milady…there is…well…"

"Say it," Frigg demanded.

He was taken aback by her statement and stopped stuttering. "His face is quite displeasing."

Frigg could only nod. "Do you know how he received those scars?"

"I'm not quite sure."

"He got them by defending our people against the enemies of the North World," Frigg said. "We could only hope that all of our warriors would sacrifice themselves the way Olaf has for the safety of the people. Wouldn't you agree?"

Jerrick's eyes looked to Olaf, and his head lowered in shame. "My apologies."

Frigg didn't bother to look at Olaf to see his expression. "I was told you had something for me."

Jerrick pointed his finger in the air with excitement as he walked around the counter and picked up a small chest. He grinned as he made his way to her, but quickly halted when Olaf reached for his sword.

Frigg looked back at her bodyguard and just nodded to him. When Frigg turned back to Jerrick, she caught a glimpse of his terror. "He is very protective."

"I can see that." Jerrick kept his eyes on Olaf. He opened the chest and tilted it toward Olaf to show there was nothing inside that could harm Frigg. He removed a circlet lined with pearls and sapphires. Jerrick looked at Olaf and asked, "May I?"

"Yes," Frigg answered him and took a step closer, so he didn't have to reach.

"I hope it fits," Jerrick said. "I had to guess the size based solely on your age."

He placed the circlet on her head and slowly adjusted it. He took a step back and examined her. He finally gave a big smile and squeezed one hand in the other in pleasure. He tucked his hands under his chin and stared at her. She could have sworn she saw tears in his eyes.

"I'm sorry," he said. "I'm just proud of my work. You are certainly ready to meet the king."

Frigg turned toward Olaf. "What do you think?"

"I'm not fit to give you a proper opinion, milady," he said.

She looked back at Jerrick. "I thank you for making this for me. I am forever grateful."

"Thank you for wearing it, Lady Frigg. I will brag to all who request my services about the circlet I made for you." He bowed at the waist and even looked to Olaf and nodded his head.

Frigg moved to leave, but something caught her eye. There were several pieces of beautiful jewelry in the shop, but one piece gave off a radiance that made her head turn.

Among the necklaces, made from golden threads and silver lace, was a simple linen rope that held a small ruby the size of a single tear. It certainly wasn't glamorous compared to the others, but it was small like her.

Her feet made their way to it, and she couldn't help but pick it up and hold the gem in her hand while it hung on a small hook.

"The friendship ruby of protection," Jerrick said.

"Excuse me?" Frigg asked with a turn of her head.

"It's a simple piece." Jerrick went to her and took it off the hook. "You give this to a friend for protection. It's a gift more than anything else."

"How much?" Frigg asked.

"For you, my lady, nothing," he replied.

"I couldn't," she said.

"I insist." Jerrick unhooked the simple clasp and wrapped it around her neck.

"You said it was a gift for someone?" Frigg asked.

"Ah, but that's the trick," he said with a smile. "It represents your protection over a friend. All your love and care go into the ruby as you wear it until you find someone who is worthy of it."

She looked at it against her chest. "All my love and care goes into the ruby?" Frigg rolled her eyes. "I may be eight, sir, but I'm not stupid."

"I never said you were." He went to one knee and looked her in the eye. "It is important that we still believe in the power of love and friendship. Jewels such as this hold that power. The more you care and love for a person, the more powerful it becomes."

"Lady Frigg," Olaf said. "I am sorry to rush you, but your father will be waiting."

She looked at Jerrick. "Thank you. I will pay you for it one day."

"Pay me back by giving it to someone worthy." Jerrick rose and smiled at her.

Frigg gave a slight bow to Jerrick and walked outside to the sounds of the cheerful commoners again. A few groups stood around once more, and their jovial talk irritated her all over again.

She felt Olaf touch her on the arm. He guided her to the side of the street. He grasped her by the shoulders and looked at her. She looked at him curiously.

"I wanted to thank you."

"Thank me?" she asked.

"For what you said to the shopkeeper," he replied with his eyes resting on hers. "Most people, when they see me, see a freak."

She looked down. "I admit that I did the same."

"I know," he said. "Why is it that you no longer look at me that way?"

"Because now I don't see the scars," she said. Olaf exhaled softly. She grinned and added, "I read about you."

He raised his eyebrow. "Read about me?"

"In the history books I was given," she said. "You were at the Dread Gate with Erland."

His hand went to his face. "That's where I got many of these."

"They said you stood with him when he was surrounded," Frigg said.

Olaf nodded and cleared his throat. "Enough with sad times, milady. It was already rude to pull you aside without being commanded. Your father will be waiting."

"Don't ever let it happen again," Frigg joked.

Olaf grinned and bowed. He motioned with his arm for her to go forward. They headed toward the front of Southrend. The one hundred foot wall had a larger presence of guards than normal. They paced the walkway with their gaze to the open field in the north—no doubt waiting to give word that the king's escort was within view.

Through the crowds of warriors that had gathered, Frigg could see her father, mounted on horseback and looking behind him. When he spotted her, he motioned for her to hurry to him.

"Make way for Lady Frigg," Rangvald's deep voice shouted.

The warriors parted, and Frigg walked quickly through the pathway to where her father waited with the reins of her mare. Just before Frigg reached her father, Rangvald stopped her.

"Pardon, milady," Rangvald said. He looked at Olaf. "You won't be needed for this, Olaf."

"Why not?" Frigg asked for him.

The large warrior looked down at her with irritation in his eyes. "The command came from your father, milady. I am only giving the order."

"He is my bodyguard," Frigg reminded him.

"Milady," Olaf said as he stepped forward. "It's quite all right. Commander Rangvald will be by your father's side, and he will look after you. I won't be far behind."

Olaf bowed at the waist, turned, and vanished into the crowd of warriors. Frigg's eyes narrowed as she asked, "It's because of his scars, isn't it?"

"Your father awaits," Rangvald said through gritted teeth.

The commander turned around and walked away without honoring her with a bow or any other salute. She got the feeling that the commander didn't take too kindly to speaking to a little girl so properly.

Frigg made her way to her father where one of the warriors helped her mount her mare. A smile emerged on her father's face when he noticed the circlet. "It looks very nice. Very fitting for a girl of your title."

Frigg said nothing.

Damari pointed at the ruby around her neck. "And what is that?"

Just as she was about to answer her father, the gates opened. Damari adjusted himself in his armor and checked the clasps on his cloak to make sure it didn't fall off. Her father never acted so nervous when it came to any of the other lords. Of course, this was the king. When he adjusted the helm on his head, Frigg cleared her throat. Damari looked at her and smirked softly as he realized what he was doing.

"It's been years," he said to her.

"You act like he's some woman you're going to marry," Rangvald said on the other side of him.

The gates opened completely and exposed the empty field with the grey horizon in the distance. Clouds rolled in; it was possibly a storm. Frigg saw it as a bad omen. If it rained, they would have to stay out there, hours if need be, just to make sure they greeted the king outside the gates. *It was expected.* The thought rang out in her mind as she saw flashes of lightning in the distance. It would be a shame for her velvet dress to get soaked, but it didn't matter.

The guards were the first to walk forward. After twelve ranks, they began to march. Damari snapped the reins and his stallion trotted onward. Frigg was a little hesitant; she still wasn't used to riding a horse by herself. Luckily, her mare was small and stunted, much like her. Her father said the mare would grow with Frigg; they would eventually be one when they got older.

The bannermen held the flag of Southrend high as it ripped into the southern wind with each step. The warriors marched in unison to the sound of light drums. Even their armor seemed to clank in unison. Frigg had an uneasy feeling. This wasn't the first time they met with a man of title. It was usually just a small rank of men, Damari, and herself. This time the size of the ranks made it look like they were going to war.

A few of the warriors in front of her held boxes that ranged in size from small containers to large chests. The merchants wanted to give their greatest works to the man who ruled over the entire North World. The last time the king visited, Frigg was only two years old and too small to remember him. Everyone, including Frigg, wanted to make sure they made an impression.

The revelation that he was actually her uncle made her even more nervous. If it weren't for the chill of the day, she may have shook out of anxiety alone. She reminded herself on what to do: *head up, sit tall, and speak properly.*

Damari, Rangvald, and Frigg rode ahead of the ranks but stopped just a few feet in front of the massive welcoming party. Frigg saw some movement on the horizon. At first, it was nothing more than shadows moving inside the fog, but then the mass of horses and carriages broke through and headed directly toward them.

She saw warhorses covered in strange armor. They wore white with red spots, brown with white patches, and grey with black stripes. The warriors were covered in armor that shone gold and silver that was polished and clean. The bannermen held up flags for two houses. One was the red dragon head of Westerland, and the other was the side profile of a standing bear of Astongale, colored green on a white background.

The horses sounded like the thunder in the clouds behind them as they rumbled across the terrain with such vast numbers that Frigg felt overwhelmed by the sight. There must have been a thousand or more! On the right side, were the king's men and on the left were Lord Gustav's.

The massive army that came with King Graylyn stopped about a hundred feet away and spread out. A pathway was created for two horsemen, one of them in black armor with a red cloak and the other in silver armor and a green cape. By the banners, Frigg knew the one in the red cloak was Lord Gustav, and the other was King Graylyn.

"Dismount," Damari whispered. Rangvald went to the ground with a quick whip of his leg. When Damari touched down, he held out his arms and lifted Frigg off her mare. "Do not speak unless spoken to."

"I know," she whispered.

Damari stood up straight. Frigg did the same and watched Gustav dismount from his horse and slowly approach them. He was a tall and lean man with long hair as black as his armor and skin as pale as milk. He had an expressionless, clean-shaven face as if he was etched from stone. His features didn't move except for his shifty, blue eyes. There was a large red ruby hanging around his neck. Frigg thought it must have weighed him down.

Gustav kept his hand on the hilt of his curved sword and slowly approached Damari with his chin up and a swagger to his walk. He stopped a few feet in front of the Lord of Southrend and bowed his head without lowering his eyes.

"Lord Damari," he said in a low voice.

"Lord Gustav," Damari greeted with a bow of his own. Her father's eyes darted toward her. Frigg bowed, as well. "This is my daughter, Lady Frigg."

"Lady Frigg," Gustav greeted as he shifted himself and stood in front of her. "I knew your mother. If the lady would permit me, you are just as beautiful as she was."

"Thank you," Frigg said.

Gustav looked behind him as a warrior wearing the same black armor and red cloak approached with a box in his hands. The warrior wore a helm with a steel mask over his face. Gustav took the box and held it out toward Frigg. "This is for you, my lady."

Frigg didn't know what to do. She looked to her father for approval then held out both hands and took the tiny box. She opened the lid and saw a necklace decorated in rubies. They were breathtaking, and it was difficult not to look like she was in awe. She was to be proper, and she kept reminding herself of that. She closed the box and looked up at him. "Thank you, Lord Gustav. I feel unworthy of such a gift."

"Nonsense," the Lord of Westerland replied. He gently took her hand, reached down, and kissed the back of it. He gave her a final grin before stepping away from her. Gustav looked at Rangvald, who was on the other side of Damari, and didn't even acknowledge him except for a sharp glare.

Gustav stepped back and looked behind him at King Graylyn still mounted on his horse. The golden crown he wore was decorated with large sapphires, rubies, and citrines. There were several other tiny gems of which Frigg didn't know the names. The arches on his crown looked like flames from a fire. It stood proudly over his brown curled hair that fell down over his shoulders onto his silver armor. He grabbed the side of his green cape as he dismounted, so he didn't get caught on it. When he was on the ground, he needed to balance himself. He was a heavyset man with armor crafted round so it could fit his large frame. He combed his hand through his long, bushy beard and chuckled as he made his way toward Damari, Rangvald, and Frigg.

Like Gustav, he grabbed the hilt of his sword as he walked. His face straightened when he saw Rangvald. It made Frigg wonder if the king had a problem with the commander.

Damari dropped to one knee, followed by Frigg and Rangvald. Behind her, she could hear the wave of clanking armor from the welcoming army of Southrend doing the same.

"Get up," the king roared. "I tire of the groveling."

Rangvald was the first to rise, and the king continued his stare. "Back from the Dread Gate, I see."

Rangvald nodded. "Last time I saw you, you were standing over Wild Men with a bloody sword."

"Last time I saw you, you didn't have so many scars," Graylyn replied. "Still ugly, though."

Rangvald managed a small smile, but Graylyn gave a hardy laugh and hugged the large commander. He broke from Rangvald and stepped toward Damari. Graylyn looked at Damari for some time.

"As a man who lost many children far too soon, you have my sympathies, my old friend," Graylyn said. "It is custom for the Lord of the City to be at the king's command, but now I am at yours. I came to pay my respects to your brave son, Tadeas. I saw him a year or so back. He was a brave boy, and I am honored that he shared my blood."

Damari bowed his head and looked down. "I thank you, my king."

Graylyn hugged Damari, but he towered over the Lord of Southrend when they embraced. Graylyn broke from him and couldn't help but smile. "Lord Hackett and Lord Egil send their regards."

"I received their blessings from couriers they sent."

"There are small quarrels in their portion of the North World. I hope you can forgive them for their absence," Graylyn said.

"Lord Egil's wife died many years back. I had Wild Men to fight off at the Dread Gate," Damari remembered. "He forgave my absence. I certainly understand when a city is in need of their lord."

"Lord Hackett spoke highly of your son," Graylyn said. He even smiled when he recalled the event. "Nearly every time we spoke, he said he was a good lad, worthy of being your son, and one day, future lord of Southrend."

"It warms the heart to hear that," Damari said.

Graylyn inspected his friend. "By the gods, it's good to see you."

"You, too," Damari said as he patted the king on his armored chest. "Just wish it was under different circumstances."

"As do I," Graylyn said sincerely. He finally stepped in front of Frigg and looked down at her. She kept her head straight and made sure to keep her eyes on his. "You must be Frigg."

"Yes, my king," she said.

He held out his arm. "Last time I saw you, I held you with just this arm, and now you've grown to be quite the little lady. You look a lot like your mother."

"That's what everyone tells me, my king," she said. She felt her father's glare, like she made some kind of mistake with the statement. "Hearing it from you is the highest honor."

She caught the grin behind the king's mustache. "I look forward to getting to know the Lady of Southrend."

"The honor shall be mine," she replied, as she kneeled slightly and rose.

Graylyn looked to Damari. "You raised yourself a proper lady here, Damari. You should be proud."

"I am, my king," Damari said.

"Now if you don't mind, I would very much like to feast and drink into the long hours of the night," Graylyn said with a turn toward his escorts. "We feast!"

A roar exploded from the king's men, and a wave of cheering echoed all the way back to the ranks in the distance. The whole mass of warriors pumped their weapons in the air with excitement. Frigg watched in awe of the impact a few single words created from the mouth of a king.

CHAPTER EIGHT

"I don't understand why!" Frigg hollered as a servant picked at her new dress. "I had a perfectly fine dress on when the king arrived. Why can't I wear that one?"

"Because that was the dress in which you greeted King Graylyn! You will need another for the feast. That's the way it goes," Saga impatiently explained.

"That makes no sense," Frigg replied.

"It's not supposed to, Frigg," Saga said. "The cooks and servants have worked tirelessly to prepare meals and ale. They also decorate the Lords' Hall for everyone who's expected. The king brought thousands of men with him. Things could be worse; you could be a cook or a servant, and you wouldn't survive one day doing their duties."

As Saga inspected the new dress, Frigg took the opportunity to stick her tongue out at her. The old woman seemed to feel it and looked up. Frigg quickly put her tongue back in her mouth just in time. Frigg closed her eyes as a servant combed her hair. She sighed, knowing Saga was right. All she needed to do was show up and look proper. She currently had three servants with her—one for her hair and two to work on her new dress. This dress was green velvet, the color of Astongale, to honor the king.

She had been standing for far too long, to pass the time she started to twiddle her thumbs because she was getting restless.

"Don't do that!" Saga snapped when she noticed. "A lady doesn't twiddle her thumbs."

She almost stuck her tongue out again, this time right to her face, but she knew it would only come with more reprimanding. Besides, her anger came from elsewhere and Saga was only doing her duty.

From her room, Frigg could smell roasted meat and fresh bread. She could hear the laughter in the lower halls from all the new guests. The whole city was in celebration because of Graylyn's arrival.

Outside, beyond the sounds of the rain, Frigg heard cheering and adulation.

"They forgot about him," Frigg said. The words slipped from her mouth, but she didn't care. She could no longer keep it inside.

Saga stopped pacing around her. She snapped her fingers and motioned for the servants to leave. Saga gave Frigg her infamous glare. "What are you talking about?"

"Tadeas," Frigg said. She hated the tone she used to say her brother's name. "Do you hear them?"

"The people?" Saga asked. Saga grinned, which made Frigg furious, but this was her way. "Kings have a way of making people forget. The king is far more important. You have to understand that as much as your brother meant to them, he was no king. He would have been…" Saga looked away as her voice trailed off. "When your father finds out who killed your brother, he will have his vengeance. You have a loving father in your memories, but you've never seen the warrior he can be, and none of us have seen the father who goes to avenge his son."

Saga stroked Frigg's face, gave it a gentle slap, and smiled. "You look fine for tonight. You do your best to smile and be proper. I'm sure there will be a discussion about your brother tomorrow."

"Why are they waiting until tomorrow?" Frigg asked.

"This is the way of the world, little one," Saga stressed. "The death of someone to a king is nothing, even if he is the boy's uncle. Their greatest concern will be you now because you have the blood of Graylyn in you. They concentrate on what they can do—not what they can't. Whether you want to hear this or not, Tadeas is gone. His fate has been sealed."

The harsh reality hit Frigg as she stood there fighting off every emotion that came to her. She hopped off the platform on which she stood. She went for the door but stopped and looked back at Saga. "If Father doesn't find out who did it, I will."

Saga grinned. "I know, but you just worry about that if the time comes."

Frigg walked out and headed downstairs toward the Lords' Hall with Olaf right next to her. They only used the hall for a feast or a meeting between large groups.

When they reached the entrance to the hall, Frigg saw nobles in silk robes, warriors decorated in polished armor, and women in dresses who, Frigg thought, showed off far too much flesh. She may have been eight, many years away from understanding why their attire looked that way, but by the way these women flaunted themselves, she didn't look forward to that age. Many of them weren't in the Lords' Hall yet, but she could tell by their glazed eyes they were drinking already. The servants stood silently next to their lords and ladies.

"Lady Frigg," a voice called.

Frigg turned to see Gustav behind her. He wore a red doublet with a dragon pendant on his chest and a black cloak. His raven hair was tied back into a tail, and the large ruby hung from his neck.

"Lord Gustav," Frigg greeted him with a bow of her head.

"You aren't wearing the necklace I bought you," he said while looking at her neck. Then he pointed to the small gem she was given at the jewelers shop. "That one you're wearing now is not fit for a lady of your title. Why such a tiny gem?"

"I'm wearing green," she said quickly. "I was told to wear a dress that honored King Graylyn. If I was asked to wear something to honor your house, I would have. This necklace was a gift from someone else."

He nodded. "I was told that I had the honor of escorting you inside the feast. May I?"

"Of course," she replied.

In truth, she hated the idea, but she knew enough not to turn down a lord's request. Gustav held out his elbow to her, and she reluctantly looked up and took it. She looked around for her father but didn't see him. Gustav took one step forward and, without saying a word, the crowds of nobles and warriors parted for him.

He certainly had a presence—the kind a king would have. She remembered the history books and how Gustav was supposed to be king if it wasn't for Audun. Sven was the last king of his bloodline and the last to be called the Dragon King. Every lord after Sven who came to power in Westerland was now called the Dragon Lord.

"Perhaps I should have waited for my father," Frigg said as she looked around.

"He's already inside, my lady," Gustav replied.

Frigg reluctantly walked with him down the long hallway toward the Lords' Hall. Her skin crawled from the touch of the man who may have been responsible for killing her brother. She kept her posture straight and her head up. They waited behind several other couples. She could see by the pace it would be some time before they entered the hall. Eventually, curiosity took over. "Why do they call you the Dragon Lord?"

He glared at her. "You don't know why? I would have thought you knew."

Frigg felt his eyes. "I do, but I wish to hear it from you. I've come to find the things I read in books are often the thoughts of lords who commanded scribes to write them."

Gustav laughed. "You're very smart for your age, little one."

"And you're very judgmental for yours," she replied. She hadn't meant to insult him so roughly, but it irked her to hear this man use a nickname instead of her proper title.

Gustav stared at her. She paused and turned to him. His eyes were on fire, and his flesh turned crimson as he broke from her. "You dare speak to a lord that way?"

"You are a lord, and I am a lady. I asked you a question. Instead of answering it, you chose to assume I knew the answer," Frigg reminded him. "I wish to hear it from the man who holds the title—not by ink written on parchment."

Gustav paused for a moment. "You're right. You did. I apologize for belittling you."

"And I apologize if my words were offensive," Frigg said.

Gustav held out his arm and invited her to walk with him once more. "May I ask the lady another question before answering hers?"

"You may," she permitted.

"Why so curious?" he asked.

"If I am to rule one day, I would like to know about all who live in this kingdom. Since you are here, I wanted to hear from you. Who would know it better than the Lord of Westerland himself?"

"That is the truth. I thank the lady for showing such interest. I shall do as she requests." They took a few steps before Gustav answered. "Dragon Lord is a title given to the Lord of Westerland, much like Defender of the Dread Gate is given to whomever rules Southrend."

"Its origin has to do with dragons," Frigg added.

"Do you like dragons?" Gustav asked.

"Not particularly," she admitted. "I favor the tales of giants."

"Giants!" he exclaimed. With a glance toward him, she realized he was belittling her again. "Sorry, my lady. You must understand that I'm not used to being in the presence of a princess."

"I'm no princess," she insisted. "Now, if you don't mind, please finish the origin of your title."

"I thought I told you," he said.

"You told me it's given to the Lord of Westerland. You didn't tell me where it came from," she reminded him.

"You're right," Gustav said in a mocking tone. "My ancestors gained control of the dragon we all know in legend as Valstrath the Vile by taking a very precious ruby that was said to control him."

She glanced at the obnoxiously large ruby around his neck. "Like the one you're wearing now?"

He took the ruby in his free hand and admired it. "Yes, just like this one. It is given to the Lord of Westerland on the day he takes power. I was so young when I took over that it weighed me down."

She gulped. "I heard the tale of your father and uncle. You have my sympathies."

She felt his glance. "I appreciate that, but like you with your eldest brother and mother, I did not know them. I didn't understand death until much later."

"As did I," she whispered.

"Tadeas. He was a good man." For the first time during his visit, Gustav looked uncomfortable. He looked in every direction except into her eyes. He finally looked at her. "Your brother and I had our differences. Despite them, you have my sympathy."

It was hard to read his tone. Her only option was to nod to him as though she believed him, even though deep down she felt he was responsible for Tadeas' death.

He seemed to mask his discomfort with a smile and a bow of his head. "If the lady would permit me, I will escort you the rest of the way in silence. Not that I don't enjoy our talk, but voices are known to travel. We don't want others to hear what should be a private conversation."

"Of course," she said.

A booming voice echoed throughout the halls. One of her father's servants stood at the entrance of the main hall and introduced the guests as they entered. Names and titles were shouted out. She thought she should try to memorize them because of her own title, but she had read for far too many days and only wished to rest. Her turn finally came. The crier needed no reminder about the future lady of Southrend or the most powerful lord in the North World. While he shouted their names, Frigg looked at the overwhelming amount of guests in the Lords' Hall. Beyond all the faces of the guests, she looked to the dais where her father sat with Graylyn. There were two empty seats left—one to Graylyn's left one to Damari's right. She already knew the seats were reserved for Gustav and her. An exhale of relief escaped her knowing they weren't next to one another.

After the final introduction, Frigg curtsied to Gustav and quickly walked away as Olaf lingered behind her. She turned to Olaf and noticed Gustav still looked at her.

Frigg moved through the crowds. Before she reached her father, Rangvald stepped in front of her. The brute stood in clean armor with hair still wet from a bath.

"Olaf," Rangvald barked. "Do we need to go through this again?"

"He is staying," Frigg said with quiet conviction.

Rangvald's eyes lowered to her level. "Pardon me?"

"He is my personal bodyguard, and I say he stays," Frigg said. Her voice sounded steady and her posture tall, yet her heart raced as she fought herself from shaking because of the intimidating warrior. "Olaf wears scars he gained by defending our city. You wear them yourself." Frigg pointed her small finger up at Rangvald's face. "I figured you would understand that."

Rangvald took a step forward with clenched fists. "If you weren't the lord's daughter…"

"But I am," Frigg snapped. "Which means you have to do as I say. The only command I have for you is to move away from me so that I may take my place next to my father."

Rangvald's face twitched. He finally stood up straight and marched away.

Frigg looked around to make sure she didn't cause a scene. The heated exchange was done with quiet tones, and no part of their conversation gained the attention of the guests. The others around her continued to drink and talk amongst themselves.

When Frigg reached the dais, her father's eyes followed her. Frigg curtsied to Graylyn, but he barely seemed to notice. Olaf pulled out the chair for her, and she could still feel her father's eyes watching her every move.

Damari leaned over to her and whispered, "What did Rangvald say to you?"

"It was nothing," she lied. With the king in Southrend and her brother's death on her father's mind, it seemed like a small matter.

She knew there was no fooling her father. He kept his gaze on her until the dais vibrated with thundering steps. Frigg glanced at Lord Gustav as he made his presence at the table known. His stiff lips made a small smile toward her before he bowed his head to Damari and then bent at the waist to Graylyn. A few moments later, the king slammed his cup on the table and commanded everyone to be silent. Graylyn praised Damari for the preparation of the Lords' Hall, the beautiful sculptures of Southrend, and the reception the people gave him. There were several more toasts, but Frigg stopped listening from boredom.

A small cup, with just a mouthful of wine, was given to her for the occasion. With each toast, she took a small sip. At her age, the vintage tasted vile, and she was happy when it was all gone. When the toasts continued, she pretended to sip when there was nothing in her cup.

When the tributes concluded, the food was finally brought out. Frigg counted so many pigs, she thought they killed off the entire winter supply of food. They ate fresh bread, stew, and clams brought in by Lord Gustav from Westerland. There were fruits—fresh, dried, and some even preserved in honey. Lemon cakes and cream custard tarts were some of Frigg's favorite foods, but she was too overwhelmed with the atmosphere to enjoy them. Many times her father asked her why she didn't eat, but she simply answered, "I'm not hungry."

Graylyn laughed and drank for hours. His annoying chuckle dug at Frigg's ears each time she heard it, and after many cups of ale and wine, she heard it often. He shouted like a drunken fool to those he saw below the dais. He raised his glass to each new man he recognized. A few he toasted many times. Frigg wasn't sure if the king forgot them, or if it was customary for Graylyn to toast them whenever they came into his view.

When the maidens came up to fill his cup or give him more food, he groped them right in front of Frigg and told them all the filthy things he wanted to do. He even kissed a few then commanded them to disappear. The maidens smiled and laughed, but Frigg caught a glimpse of disgust on a few of their faces when the king turned from them.

Lord Gustav showed no one any praise. He sat with his elbows on the table, cup in one hand, and he took small sips every so often. He studied the room. His cold eyes searched like a hawk stalking a mouse. Frigg tried not to look at him, but his glare continuously drifted in her direction. Frigg found it difficult not to stare back.

Damari was far too quiet for her liking. He barely smiled to those who called to him. Occasionally, he raised his glass but never took a sip. Frigg watched him as he looked down and ignored the feast. His eyes looked somber and small, as if he could hardly keep them open.

The feast continued for many hours. Several of the nobles and warriors within the ranks of Southrend and Astongale had to be carried out by servants from their heavy drinking. Frigg found it odd those in red robes or black armor didn't partake in drinking like the others. Gustav's men were scattered all around the hall. Their eyes mirrored those of their leader as they searched the room. The knot in her stomach grew. Frigg wasn't sure which concerned her more: the drunkenness of the king or the sobriety of Gustav and his men.

"My king," Damari said softly.

The king laughed at some joke he told himself while ale dripped off his beard and food stained his chest. He tried to focus on Damari with drunken eyes. "Did you say something?"

Damari stood up. He looked at the king and with a much louder voice said, "I think it is time for those of title to have some privacy."

His voice traveled through the hall and caused a quick silence among the rowdy feast. For the first time, Frigg heard nothing but the ringing in her ears.

"There is time for politics in the morning, Damari," Graylyn assured his brother-in-law. His eyes were glassy and bloodshot. "I've been riding for days. I need sleep before we speak."

"I'm afraid this can't wait," Damari said as he walked to the side of the table and stopped just in front of Olaf.

The king seemed to notice his urgency. Graylyn gave an uneasy smile and looked out to the crowd inside the Lords' Hall. He raised his cup for what Frigg thought was the thousandth time. "Good men and beautiful women, the king will be left alone with those of title."

The crowd of people stood stunned by the command before they slowly made their way to the doors. A few stumbled, and a few more leaned on others as they left while Gustav's men walked without hindrance. Damari's men exited last. All that remained in the hall was a mess of food and drink spilled on the floor.

Frigg felt Olaf press her shoulder with his hand before he made his way off the platform. One of Gustav's men remained; it was the warrior in the mask. She wondered why he kept his face concealed.

Isn't that disrespectful? she thought. The king may not have noticed because of his state of mind, but the fact her father said nothing was odd. He constantly reminded her of things not to do in the presence of King Graylyn, and she knew wearing anything that concealed one's identity was forbidden.

Frigg watched Gustav nod his head to the warrior, and he disappeared with the rest. Rangvald pushed his chair as he reluctantly stood and headed away, leaving only Graylyn, Damari, Gustav, and Frigg in the room.

The king looked in Frigg's direction and then glanced at Damari.

"Perhaps this is a conversation where children shouldn't be present."

Frigg didn't wait for another word. The king made his command, and she quickly stood up.

"Frigg," Damari demanded with his eyes still on Graylyn. "Stay where you are."

"We are to discuss the state of the kingdom, Damari," Graylyn stressed. "What can a little girl gain by hearing talk of politics?"

"She is my heir," Damari reminded him. "With the death of Tadeas, all I have will pass to her once the gods call me to the afterlife. She is also your blood and will rule once the both of us are gone. How is she to rule if she knows nothing about the land she will inherit?"

"A little girl as your heir?" Gustav mocked as he walked off the dais and sat in one of the empty chairs below.

"She is my eldest child and last remaining," Damari said. "I'm about to put my son to rest, or have you forgotten already?"

Gustav sipped his ale. He masked any emotion he was feeling with a plastered smile.

"That is what we are going to discuss," Graylyn replied.

"What do you mean?" Damari asked.

Graylyn smiled at Frigg. "I'm sure you will make a great ruler of Southrend one day, little lady, but a queen…I'm not sure."

"What do you *mean?*" Damari repeated.

"We agreed that the title of king would pass to your son," Graylyn explained. "Your son is dead. Tadeas was a man, Damari, your daughter…"

"She is of your blood. Your sister was her mother. The line of lineage goes to her by birthright," Damari said.

Graylyn put his cup back on the table, and his expression sent a chill up Frigg's spine. She was so used to seeing him laugh and act like the court jester rather than the king. For the first time, she saw the depth of his authority.

Damari pressed his fist into the table. "My son died in your war against the Wild Men, giving up his life to keep control of the Dread Gate, and my second son was murdered by a man who, I believe, is in this room."

Gustav almost rose from his chair, but Graylyn held out his hand

and stopped him before saying, "*My* war? It was *our* war."

"I only went to war because my king asked me to." Damari leaned off the table and walked toward Graylyn. "If you recall, I told you how to handle the Wild Men without having to go to war, but you insisted that we needed to show them our strength. My son died because of that strength. You promised me, the day we sent him to the catacombs, that his death would not be in vain. You took out your sword and swore, when you were called to the eternal world, that my family would be the rulers of the North World because your blood ran in their veins." Damari was now a foot away from Graylyn. "Don't tell me now that my sons died for a lie."

Graylyn exhaled and placed his right hand on Damari's shoulder. "I know what it's like to bury a child. I buried four of them myself. I didn't get to watch them grow up and become great leaders, warriors, or men who changed the world. I watched them get placed in tombs, locked away, never to have the life brought back into their eyes." Graylyn's eyes watered as he looked down and closed them before the tears could escape. "If the gods gave me a choice to bring back all of my children, as well as my beloved wife, or just your son, I would choose your son because I would want to honor the promise I made. Damari, I don't have that choice. The gods placed this fate before us, and what we have is an heir who does not have a son to rule after him. If I die tomorrow, you would rule in her stead until she was of age, but what happens after that?"

Damari clenched his fists. "So what are you trying to say?"

Graylyn glanced in the direction of Gustav. "Lord Gustav presented me with a proposal to unite your family with his."

"Absolutely not!" Damari snapped. "None of his sons will marry my daughter."

"I didn't expect Tadeas to lose his life," Graylyn cut in. "Your son was a good man, a true leader, and worthy of a kingship if I was to pass, but he was called to the gods."

"It wasn't their decision," Damari said with malice in his voice. "It was the choice of an assassin."

"It was the choice of a Wild Man," Gustav said from his chair.

"That has yet to be proven," Damari said.

Gustav chuckled with his mug in hand. "So what do you propose, Lord Damari? Graylyn dies, you die, and we bow at the feet of an eight year old girl?"

"That's what was promised by the word of King Graylyn!" Damari yelled toward him.

"It was promised when your son was alive!" Graylyn boomed.

His voice resonated in the hall and nearly made Frigg jump.

Damari stood in Graylyn's face, an absolute offence from what Frigg had read; it could have cost her father his life. While Damari pointed at Gustav, he said, "My son was murdered by this traitor."

"What proof do you have?" Graylyn asked.

"My son rode off to tell you about a quarrel with Gustav, and he died before he reached you." Damari's eyes locked on the Lord of Westerland.

"Do you think me a great fool?" Gustav asked as he crossed one leg over the other. "How foolish would I be to kill the Lord of Southrend's son? What would I have to gain?"

"The throne of the North World," Damari reminded him. "I find it odd now that my son has died, all of a sudden the king proposes I have my daughter marry one of your sons." Damari looked back at Graylyn. "How could you be so blind and not see what he is doing?"

Damari would not back down—not even to the king. Frigg felt uneasy. All the lectures her father gave her about respect and being a lady, yet when it came to the death of Tadeas, respect seemed irrelevant. Frigg realized, even though she was only eight, there were times to kneel and times to rise.

Gustav's laughter purred from his lips as he rose from his chair. He placed his cup down softly on the table to the side of him and looked up at the heated Damari. "I will recount what has already been proven based on what I heard only days after your son was kill. An arrow from a Wild Man's bow was found in the side of the boy's neck, and he was covered with wounds caused by a spear, which we all know is the main weapon of the Wild Men."

Damari's face turned crimson with rage. Her father seemed to ignore Gustav's explanation. Frigg realized her father was doing the exact same thing she did; the anger boiled over in him. The dancing, the praising, the raising of cups and the drunken fools who surrounded him must have felt like his son's loss meant nothing. Even after all that, he had to greet the man he thought took Tadeas from this world in the field outside Southrend and then feast with him in the night, all the while wondering if, in fact, the Dragon Lord of Westerland killed his son.

Graylyn placed his hand on Damari's chest to calm him. The king tried to get into Damari's line of sight, so he was no longer staring at Gustav. "Damari, my old friend," he muttered. "I think you have your anger in the wrong place."

Damari's rage soothed, but only a little, as he looked at the man he called his best friend. "My son came to me before he left and told me what Gustav was doing in Westerland. He wanted an act of war for it, but I suggested he bring the problem before the king."

"And what was the problem?" Gustav asked from below. He stood arrogantly, picked up an apple from one of the tables, and cleaned it against his doublet. Gustav took a bite from the apple, but he made a disgusted face and spit it to the ground. With a flip of his hand, he tossed the apple away and walked up to the dais. Graylyn positioned himself in front of Damari. Gustav stopped a few feet short of the king and placed both hands behind his back "Every lord of this kingdom believes I'm trying to get rid of you all. Lord Hackett, Lord Egil and you, Damari, have your minds made up that I'm some kind of monster who plans to rid the kingdom of all of your families. Lord Hackett and Lord Egil may have sent word that they couldn't come because of some pathetic excuse, but we all know they didn't arrive because they do not wish to be in the same room as me. At least I showed up to honor your son."

"You came here to mock him and stand before me with a smile because you knew Graylyn wouldn't allow a fight between us," Damari said. "You planned this. Graylyn might be fooled by you, but I am not."

"Watch your tongue," Graylyn warned.

Damari looked deeply into the king's eyes. "How could you allow this snake to trick you? How could you think I would ever allow one of his sons to marry my daughter?"

Gustav smiled. "She won't be marrying one of my sons."

Damari's face dropped. Frigg watched as it went pale. His eyes turned wild, and his chin shook. He looked like he wanted to scream, but the only word he said came out in a murmur. "Never."

"Damari," Graylyn started.

"I will have his head on a spike before I let him go near my daughter." Damari seethed.

Damari lunged toward Gustav, but Gustav simply backed away and chuckled under his breath at Damari's attempt. Graylyn was struck unexpectedly, but his large frame absorbed most of the shock. When the king regained his balance, he stood up and wrapped his arms around Damari.

"Have you lost your mind?" Graylyn screamed as he pushed Damari back.

The king's strength nearly made Damari fall to the ground. Frigg had never seen her father so incensed in all her life. He looked ready to try to get by Graylyn again, but he took a breath and pressed a hand over his silks. He was still angered, but he gained control of himself and didn't attack.

"I invoke a duel," Damari said.

The king's eyes widened, and Frigg's heart jumped in her chest.

"Father…" Frigg began.

"Stay out of this, Frigg!" Damari commanded.

"Watch yourself, Damari. That's my betrothed you're speaking to," Gustav said with a pompous grin.

Damari rushed toward Gustav again, but Graylyn caught him in his grasp. Despite their size difference, the king struggled to keep Damari from reaching Gustav. The Lord of Westerland continued his taunting by chuckling as he backed away.

"Guards!" Graylyn shouted while trying to contain Damari. "Guards!"

The doors to the Lords' Hall opened with force and slammed against the wall. Olaf pushed his way through the rushing crowd with his sword in hand as he headed toward Frigg.

The king tried to keep Damari away from Gustav, but Frigg could see her father pushing his way closer with each moment. By the time the guards reached Graylyn, Damari was being pulled back by his own men, and warriors from Westerland surrounded their lord. Rangvald stood in front of all the men from Southrend, sword half unsheathed—a warning to the guards from Westerland.

Olaf directed Frigg out of the hall, but she kept her eyes on her father. Even with so many surrounding him, Damari still tried to get to Gustav. Her heart sank when she saw an overwhelming number of warriors wearing red and black. She could no longer see her father. Olaf kept his hand on her shoulder and guided her out the door and into the main hallway.

There were screams of panic behind her, and she looked in the direction of the entrance to the Lords' Hall. With so many warriors trying to get by them, Olaf picked up Frigg with his free arm and ran through the oncoming masses. The knot in Frigg's stomach turned, and she kept her eyes on the Lords' Hall even as it faded from her vision.

Down a different hallway, among some other warriors, Frigg spotted Loke. When he saw Olaf carrying Frigg, his eyes went wide and he started toward them. Among the yells and calls, Frigg could hear Loke call to her bodyguard. When Olaf reached the stairs, he turned in alarm with his blade ready.

Loke came to a sudden halt and put up his hands. "It's only me, Olaf. What is going on?"

"Damari was going after Gustav," Olaf explained. "I need to get Lady Frigg to safety. I don't know what's going to happen."

"I'll get to Damari," Loke said.

The heavyset guard set off running. Frigg shook in Olaf's arm as the halls echoed with the sounds of running feet and clanking armor. She didn't know if the confrontation turned violent, but she knew with how angry her father was the tension could boil over.

"It's all right," Olaf whispered in Frigg's ear.

Olaf got Frigg to her room where Saga lingered in the hall. Her face turned near pale when she looked at Frigg.

"What is going on?" she asked in a low breath.

"Damari went after Gustav," Olaf said as he placed Frigg down just outside her door. "A fight broke out, and the king had to get between them."

"About what?" Saga asked.

"I'm not sure," Olaf admitted. "I think it would be best for you to stay with Frigg in her room."

Saga looked like she wanted to say something, but Olaf opened the door and gently pushed them both inside. With his hand about to close the door, he added, "Lock this."

Saga barred the door just as Olaf commanded. She turned and looked at Frigg. "What has happened?"

"King Graylyn told father that I was to marry Lord Gustav," Frigg said.

"That's preposterous," Saga scoffed. Her chin trembled. "He's far too old. How could they propose such a thing?"

"It's no different than what I read in a few of those books," Frigg said. "There were lords who married girls nearly three times younger."

"This is different," Saga claimed.

"How?"

Saga took a moment to gain control of her anger. "None of those girls were you."

Saga said no more, and Frigg had no reply. They both stayed quiet. Frigg could hear sounds of running and faint shouting from below. Her heart jumped when Saga grasped her shoulder. With each sound outside, Saga's grip increased. Frigg was so scared, she hardly noticed.

After a while, they heard a rumble of footsteps. The thundering vibration got closer as Frigg's heart rate increased. The steps halted just outside her door. The knob turned, but the bar stopped the door from opening.

Someone pounded on the door. Four bellowing strikes followed by, "Frigg, open the door!"

She knew her father's voice. A breath escaped her. A tear fell from her eye, and her shaking increased. Saga removed the bar, and Damari opened the door. Four warriors followed Damari with their swords out. They quickly looked all around the room. When they saw there was no one inside but Saga and Frigg, they put their weapons away.

"Father," Frigg went to him, ready to leap into his arms.

Damari caught her by the shoulders and stopped her. She was shocked to see his face still enraged; he didn't look too concerned for her. "Wipe your tears."

The statement didn't sound like him at all. Her father always showed her some kind of concern when she was upset. He pushed her away from him and looked at Saga. "Why was the door locked?"

"Olaf told us to come in the room and lock the door," Saga said.

His eyes flashed, and he subconsciously pushed his tongue against a fresh split in his lip.

Rangvald walked in from the hall and pushed his way by the four warriors. His shadow took over the entire room. "How many do you want posted outside the door?"

"At least four," Damari said. "We can't be too careful. I want Gustav watched."

"Of course, milord," Rangvald said with a nod of his head.

Damari paced the room. He walked to the window and opened it to look outside. Frigg still felt uncomfortable with how her father was acting. Damari looked outside and leaned his hands on the stone. "In the morning, you will go to Ravengale."

"You can't mean…" Saga began.

"I do," Damari said with a turn as he looked at Frigg. "It is not safe here. Not while Gustav is lingering around the city."

"But I don't want…" Frigg started.

"It's not about what you want!" Damari yelled. The whole room shook, and Frigg's body jolted in fear. "You'll leave tomorrow with Rangvald and an escort of one hundred men."

"Milord," Saga jumped in.

"I don't need lessons from you, crone!" He snapped.

Saga's face sank with Damari's comment, but she continued. "Tadeas was in Ravengale when he died, milord. It wasn't safe for him. What makes you think it'll be safe for an eight year old girl?"

"Tadeas didn't have one hundred men protecting him or Commander Rangvald," Damari said in a low, but vicious tone. "Now you will go to your own quarters at once and remain there until I need you."

"I will not accompany Lady Frigg?" Saga asked in shock.

Damari tightened his fists. "She is going to be taught by someone else from now on. Now leave."

Saga covered her mouth with her hand and stormed out. Damari didn't even look in Frigg's direction as he headed for the door. "I'll have your things packed for the morning. Now go to sleep."

With his guards following him, Damari walked out without saying good night or tucking her in. He had never done that. When the door shut, Frigg stood in the center of her room and watched for him to come back inside. She felt the tears flow down her face and didn't bother to remove them. When they began to drip from her chin, she looked down to see a small puddle on the floor.

She stood there for a while. The only sounds she heard were the shuffling of the guards' feet outside her door and their muffled voices talking to one another. With a slow walk to the door she locked it from the inside.

She didn't bother to change out of her dress. With a walk toward her bed, she stopped, and headed first toward the window. It was a clear night, with all the stars in the sky shining brightly down on the world. Out of all of them, one seemed to mesmerize her more than the other. *The Gods' Hammer*, she remembered her brother telling her. The red hue around it made it stand out among the thousands of lights in the heavens. She remembered Tadeas' words and hoped, wherever he was, that he could see it, as well.

"Everything's changing, and I don't like it," she whispered as if Tadeas could hear her. "Father's changed. They're trying to make me change. I don't know what's real anymore, and I could really use you." Her eyes welled, and the tears came once more. "Please, Tadeas, if you can hear me, please help me, or at least guide me to someone who can."

Her words seemed to drift outside the window and linger in the air with no hope of anyone hearing them. After a few moments, she wiped her eyes and turned from the window. She sank into her bed, covered herself with her bearskin, and put her head into the pillow. She could feel the tears until her whole world went dark, and the silence of the night came over her.

CHAPTER NINE

Frigg awoke suddenly in the night. She sat up in a panic as her heart raced in her chest. She couldn't find the source of the sudden rise from her sleep. It was silent. It took her a moment to realize it was, in fact, the eerie silence that woke her. The familiar knot in her stomach returned, and her lip quivered.

She could still only see darkness in her room because her eyes hadn't adjusted. There wasn't a single sound around her—not even the wind. It usually ripped through her room from her closed window, but tonight it was gone. Not even a gentle breeze.

She wanted to call out to Olaf but remembered her father had four other guards outside. Olaf may not have been one of them, but it would be unlikely. He was near her night and day, and she often wondered when he slept. Before she fell asleep hours earlier, she vaguely heard the four guards outside, talking amongst themselves, but there was nothing now—not a word, a grunt, or a footstep.

She dangled her feet over the ground as she sat on the edge of the bed. When she dropped to the floor, the smack of her feet sounded like thunder in the stillness. She tiptoed her way over to the door. About a foot or so from the door, she stepped in something wet. It was deathly cold and sent a chill up her leg. When she moved away from the puddle, her heel stuck to the ground.

She ran her fingers across the bottom of her foot and raised them to her eyes. Her eyes adjusted to the darkness, and she saw the crimson hue of blood. She nearly screamed, but a quick placement of her other hand over her mouth muffled the instinctive reaction. She breathed quick, panicked breaths, over and over again, until she felt lightheaded.

Blood meant death, and death meant bodies. She stood in shock for a few moments, knowing that somewhere outside her room was a corpse so close its blood leaked under her door. She wanted to hear anything that would give her a sign of life, but the silence still shrouded over her. The longer she stayed inside the room, the longer she felt in danger. If there was death around her, she needed to find some kind of way to protect herself or find someone who could. With a quick lift and a slight ringing sound, she quickly unlatched the bar that locked her door. Afterward, she didn't move, waiting to hear footsteps or voices, but once again, there was nothing.

A slight creak, like a cry of pain, sounded when she pulled the door open. The dim lights of the torches enabled her to see the corpses of four guards. Like the moon over a pond at midnight, the reflection of the flames danced in the puddles of blood.

Her eyes brushed across each guard with their throats cut open and blood spilling onto the ground. The one closest to the door, the one whose blood leaked under her door, stared blankly up at her. She knew he was dead, but she couldn't help but think he was looking right at her with his eyes wide and tongue hanging from the side of his mouth. She wanted to look away, yet she couldn't. This was the first time she saw a fresh corpse not prepared for the catacombs. The look of death made her freeze with fear.

A yell from down the hall broke the silence. Frigg looked up, and her whole body shook. She stood against the wall of the hall while her feet soaked in the puddle of blood from the guard next to her door. She quickly retreated into her room and made her way back to the window.

The voices were a mix of hostility and laughter, and she assumed there were more than two of them. Her door was wide open as she heard their voices getting closer. She knew it was far too late to close the door and put the bar back.

She heard one of them clearly say, "The door's open."

Her heart dropped. There was only one place for her to go, and she rushed to get under the bed. The moment her body touched the stone it chilled her to the bone. She took a deep breath, taking in all she could just as she heard the footsteps come into her room. The moment the first footsteps echoed through her room, she held her breath. She knew in the silence that even the slightest sound would give her away. When the footsteps got closer, she closed her eyes tightly and put her hands over her mouth, so she didn't gasp in fear.

"Where is she?" one voice asked.

"She could have left the room," another said.

"She would have walked by us in the hall," the first voice reminded. "Check everywhere inside here. Then we'll check the other rooms if we need to."

She heard them toss her clothing chest over. Frigg turned her head and saw three pairs of dirty legs covered in scabs and scraps. These weren't warriors from any city that she could tell, but, then again, she only saw their legs.

A scream came from the hallway. Frigg nearly crawled from under the bed in panic. She looked over to see the intruders pause as another figure entered her room. Just by the hanging robe she saw when the form came in, she knew it was Saga. Her teacher walked right into the hands of three invaders, and there was nothing Frigg could do to help her. Even if she wanted to scream a warning, Saga was far too close now to get away, and it would let the intruders know where she was. By the dead guards in the hall, these three men only had one thing on their minds.

"What is the meaning of this?" Saga asked defiantly.

"Where is the little lady, crone?" one of them asked.

"Even if I knew, do you truly believe I would tell you after what I've seen? You obviously plan to kill her," Saga stated.

"Her fate is already sealed, and, now, so is yours," the first voice told her. "Save us the trouble."

"Never," Saga whispered.

The first warrior lunged forward, and Frigg heard the sound of flesh ripping followed by a grunt. Frigg tightened her hands around her mouth just as a flow of tears poured from her eyes. She watched Saga's knees hit the ground as the tutor fell forward. One of the other intruders kicked Saga's body, and she rolled until her face looked directly at Frigg. The shocked look was still on her face, along with blood flowing out of her mouth. Saga's eyes widened when she saw Frigg in her hiding place. Saga's jaw shook as she lipped the words, "Stay here."

Her mouth no longer shook, and her eyes faded along with the life inside her. Saga's eyes looked beyond Frigg as the blood still dripped out of her open mouth.

"I think the crone came to delay us," one suggested. "She probably hid the girl in her own room."

"Check it," another said.

"Wait," one of them called. Frigg's heart stopped. "Those look like bloody footprints of a child leading under the bed."

Fear froze her once again as she closed her eyes and embraced her fate. A raging scream didn't even make her jump. It must have been one of them, lifting his weapon, ready to strike her down. Flesh began to tear, sickening gurgling sounds came, and she heard bodies fall. She wondered if somehow she was numb to the feel of a blade, and her soul was drifting to the afterlife.

"Frigg!"

For a moment, she didn't recognize the voice, but then a familiar lisp found its way to her ears. "Olaf!"

"Frigg!" he called again. Frigg crawled from under the bed, and her bodyguard grasped her with his free arm and picked her up. He inspected her to see if there was anything wrong. "Are you hurt?"

"No," she said through tears. She looked down at the body of Saga and relived what happened in her mind. "They killed her..."

"I know," Olaf said. "We need to get you out of here."

"Where's Father?" Frigg asked.

"He met with Gustav and the king outside of the castle courtyard," Olaf explained. Frigg looked at the bodies of her intruders. They were unarmored and covered in what looked to be blue paint.

"Wild Men?" Frigg asked, but she knew.

"There are at least thirty of them," Olaf said as he carried her. "They came in through the back of the castle and then locked the courtyard gate so no one could get inside," Olaf paused as if unsure to continue, but added, "including your father."

Olaf walked through the halls and in each one, warriors of Southrend scattered the ground. Only a few of the bodies were the Wild Man invaders. Frigg finally got a better look at them. Blue paint covered their faces, mostly around the eyes and lower jaw. Every one of them had pitch-black hair, long and knotted. They wore loincloths on their waists and rags on their feet. Her first time encountering them she could only see their scabbed and dirty legs, but their bodies were filled with dirt and grime along with more blue paint in creative designs on their chests and stomachs.

"Rangvald said there were no more Wild Men," Frigg said.

"Well, little lady, as you can see, there are," Olaf replied.

They reached the staircase and went down the spiral steps. Olaf stopped halfway when he saw four Wild Men about to rush up the stairs. They backed up when they saw Olaf with Frigg in his arms. Each one of them held two weapons, an ax and a short-sword, already covered in blood. Directly behind them were three freshly killed guards.

The Wild Men took their stances, weapons in hand and ready to attack. Olaf gently placed Frigg down on the stairs, so she was out of harm's way. "Frigg, if the worst happens…run."

She wanted to beg him to run with her, but the bodyguard jumped forward, his longsword swinging down and breaking the defense of the first Wild Man. Olaf plunged his sword deep into the attacker's stomach. The next Wild Man tried to take advantage of Olaf while his sword was occupied. Olaf ducked the swipe and used his armored hand to backhand the Wild Man. He removed his sword from the other with a push of his leg to the Wild Man's stomach, freeing him to attack with his sword once more. With his weapon back in front of him, Olaf awaited the third who swung violently at his head. Olaf blocked and countered, slicing the Wild Man across his chest. The fourth leapt at Olaf, and Frigg gasped when she saw a spray of blood. Olaf backed away and felt the fresh wound on the side of his neck, but it didn't look mortal. Olaf yelled in rage as he stepped forward.

Frigg watched the second Wild Man rise to his feet, but, instead of trying to overwhelm Olaf, he went after her. The Wild Man lost his footing while he scaled up the steps. He reached his hand out as he fell forward and grabbed Frigg's ankle. She was so frightened that she couldn't even scream. He pulled her down and raised his ax. Frigg turned her head away, so she didn't have to see what he was about to do. Instead, she heard a thud and someone choking.

Frigg opened her eyes and nearly jumped back in horror. The Wild Man who grabbed her was still there, but he had a sword jabbed into the back of his head with a blood-dripping blade protruding from his mouth. Olaf stood behind the Wild Man. With a quick pull, Olaf removed his blade, and the Wild Man's head hit the stairs. Behind Olaf, the third Wild Man lay beheaded. Frigg looked at Olaf's neck and saw it dripping with blood.

"Are you okay?" Olaf asked her.

Frigg nodded and reached for him. Olaf picked her back up and headed for the entrance of the castle. The doors slowly opened, and Olaf stopped and held out his blade. He nearly dropped Frigg to the ground in preparation. A hurling sound headed toward them. Frigg felt herself get tossed to the side, and a crashing sound erupted in the room followed by a loud grunt.

The stone ground was unforgiving as Frigg's elbows and knees scraped against it as she fell. Olaf threw her with such force that she rolled until she hit the wall. She ignored her own wounds and looked around for her bodyguard. She was nearly crippled with shock when she saw a massive spear sticking out of his stomach. He lay on his side, gasping as his free hand tried to pull the weapon from his body. He screamed again just as Frigg realized the spear pierced all the way out his back.

With a twist of his hand, the spear broke, but a piece of the weapon still protruded from Olaf's stomach. He slowly got to his feet, grabbed the spearhead behind him, and pulled it out through his abdomen and out his back. He howled with each movement until the spearhead and the stub of the weapon were completely removed.

An unarmed Wild Man screamed from the open entrance. Frigg assumed it was the one who threw the spear. He tried to charge the bodyguard, but Olaf backhanded the Wild Man with his gauntlet and jabbed his broadsword deep into the unarmored flesh of the savage. Olaf used his foot to push the Wild Man off the blade and chopped his sword into the Wild Man for good measure.

Olaf took a step toward Frigg but collapsed. He managed to catch himself before hitting the ground face first. Blood pooled around him as he sat up. He shifted himself until his back rested against one of the pillars.

Frigg ran and dropped next to him. His hands pressed against his abdomen, trying to stop the blood leaking from his pierced armor.

"We need to leave," Frigg managed to say. She knew it was too late, but she hoped her mighty bodyguard could somehow miraculously ignore the mortal wound.

Olaf managed to muster a small laugh. "It's too late for me, little lady."

"Don't say that," Frigg begged.

He looked into her eyes. "You know it's true."

"But I'll be by myself." She could hardly see as her eyes filled with tears. "There are still more of them. I need you, Olaf."

He tried to rise but winced and fell back down. He looked down at his hands covered in his own blood. His face turned red. "You're right, little lady. I'm still breathing, which means I still have fight left in me."

Olaf slid his back against the pillar and used his broadsword as a crutch to help him to his feet. He kept his other hand on his abdomen to try and stop the bleeding. When he rose, he exhaled loudly.

Olaf had a brief moment to rest before the entrance of the castle opened once more, and six Wild Men entered. They paused when they saw Olaf and readied themselves for a fight with the bodyguard. A few of them snickered when they realized he was wounded. With the struggle to rise, Frigg wondered how her protector would fight off six more of them.

Olaf pushed Frigg back again and put his sword in both hands. Drops of blood from his abdomen hit the ground. When he walked forward, Frigg saw the exit wound in his back and noticed it was trickling blood as badly as his stomach. He nearly collapsed when he walked forward but caught his balance.

A Wild Man wearing a black mask stood in front of the others. He was much taller and larger in muscle compared to the other five. The blue paint of their people covered his entire chest in the form of thorns. In his hands was a single sword, covered in blood that still dripped from a recent victim.

Another Wild Man jumped forward, ax and short-sword in hand. With a quick deflection of the Wild Man's attack, Olaf countered with a cut to the scoundrel's throat. A spew of blood shot from the wound, and the Wild Man dropped to his knees. Olaf threw his foot out and kicked him away.

The leader took a few steps back and motioned for the others to attack. Two more closed in on Olaf. The first engaged Olaf in a sword fight while the other snuck behind Olaf and swung at the bodyguard's leg. Olaf yelped in pain, forcing him to drop to one knee. Frigg had to look away after seeing Olaf's wound. When she looked back, Olaf jabbed the hilt of his sword into the Wild Man's face who wounded him. With his attention to the rear, the Wild Man in front of him stabbed Olaf in the chest. The Wild Man snickered in victory, but Olaf grabbed the blade and shoved it further into his own torso. This got Olaf within range of the Wild Man, and he chopped his sword down, piercing through the Wild Man's shoulder and going all the way to his chest.

Olaf spit blood from his mouth as he stood up and kicked the disoriented Wild Man away. The Wild Man who cut Olaf's leg recovered and came at him with a swing. Olaf ducked his head backward just in time and beheaded the savage.

Olaf grabbed the hilt of the blade that was inside of him and pulled it out with a grunt of agony. The next Wild Man tried to take him by surprise, but Olaf used the sword he pulled from himself to chop into the side of his attacker. His victim wailed loudly as Olaf let go of the sword, gripped his own broadsword with both hands, and stabbed the Wild Man in the chest. Despite the wince of pain on his face, he took out the blade with a swift pull and stared down the leader.

With a weakened lean forward, Olaf picked up one of his victims swords from the ground. With a windup, he tossed the sword at the masked warrior who ducked, but it floated passed him and hit the other Wild Man in the chest. Only Olaf and the leader remained.

Olaf stumbled and swayed back and forth. The leader pounced with a quick attack. If Frigg blinked, she would have missed it. Olaf somehow saw it and managed to block, turn to the side, and push the masked warrior in back of him. The masked warrior couldn't stop his own momentum and stumbled. Olaf regained his own feet that were still a little shaky.

Thundering steps came from the entrance, and Rangvald emerged. The Commander's armor was soaked in blood, and his blade shared the same crimson tint. There were even a few splatters across his face, but he didn't appear to be injured.

Olaf barely glanced at him before turning toward the masked warrior in case the Wild Man made a move, but Frigg had time to notice something different in Rangvald's eyes. He took a step as Frigg screamed, "Olaf!"

Olaf heeded her warning and turned back around. Rangvald stuck his blade deep into Olaf's chest before her bodyguard could even raise his guard. Olaf sank to his knees with his eyes wide open in shock. His own sword dropped from his grip as he gasped.

"You piece of..." Olaf didn't get a chance to get out the rest of his statement. Rangvald removed his sword from Olaf's chest and swung for his head.

Frigg turned away, and a chilling silence surrounded her. She pressed her eyes closed, but the stench of death took over her nostrils—the same kind of awful smell she remembered while kneeling before her brother's tomb. This was all too real, and the sound of Olaf's body crashing to the ground made her realize she was all alone.

Her eyes opened, and she stared at the stone wall in front of her. She refused to face the Wild Man who now stood before her. She could hear his breathing.

"Lady Frigg," the masked warrior said in a muffled voice. "There is no use in running."

Her legs shook so much she wasn't sure if she could run.

"Handle this," was all Rangvald said as he turned and headed for the door. She could hear fighting and yelling coming from outside, but they went mute as Rangvald slammed the door shut and turned toward the masked warrior. "They broke through. Grab her already."

Frigg turned and ran. She headed for the stairs and quickly turned her head to see if anyone followed her, but they all just stood there. Just as she went to look forward again she slammed into something hard. She hit the ground as the back of her head struck the stone floor. With blurred eyes, she looked up to see a Wild Man standing over her with the forms of others behind him.

There was a voice behind her, but it was muffled and distant. Just before her eyes closed, she saw the Wild Man with the black mask reach his hand down to grab her. She wanted to scream, but darkness overcame her just before she went unconscious.

CHAPTER TEN

A sudden jolt launched Frigg's entire body in the air. Her eyes opened wide in horror just before she landed on a hard, wooden surface, and her elbow dug into the floor. A sharp pain went through her arm as she rolled to her back and groaned. The back of her head also ached. The last thing she remembered was falling on her back and striking it against the stone ground with the Wild Men surrounding her.

She was alone now, or so she assumed. She tried to look at her surroundings, but darkness shrouded her. A few glints of light peaked in around her, but she was still unsure where she was. The ground rumbled below her, and she could feel herself moving.

When she sat up, her hand grazed the wooden floor. A suffocating feeling hung in the air. Nearby, horses neighed, and their hooves stomped the ground. *A carriage,* Frigg thought. She felt the bars and realized the carriage was covered with a thick cloth.

She heard a few voices from outside, but the words were more like vibrations because of the obstruction from the cloth and the noise from the rattling carriage. The horses pulling her weren't the only ones she heard. The rhythmic trot of a horse echoed on the side of her cage every few moments. She heard the rider on her carriage crack the reins and command the horses forward. Their pace felt rather slow. Her last memory was of a battle just outside the castle, yet she heard no sounds of a confrontation or any kind of hostility.

If she was in a cage, it was because she was captured, and it meant the Wild Men had successfully gotten her out of the castle without her father's men stopping them. A deep sense of panic took over her as her breaths increased with every moment. Her father would have fought with everything he had to make sure they didn't take her, and, if she was captured, that meant he was...*no.* She wouldn't even think it. She covered her mouth to keep herself quiet. The Wild Men captured her, but she didn't want them to know she was awake. *If they know I'm awake, they may kill me. Or do they need me alive?* Maybe if they needed her alive, that meant her father was alive, too.

Small glints of light came from small slits in the fabric of the cloth. One seemed low enough that she could look out if she wanted. She crawled slowly to where the tear was, inch by inch, pressing her palms into the floor to stop herself from sliding.

She grasped the bars and lifted herself up to her knees. With one eye, she looked out and saw the carriage rider. He blocked most of her view, so she couldn't see anything beyond him. She looked to the other side of the cage and saw another small hole. She would have to stand up in order to see out of it. She moved from one bar to the other until she reached the opposite side. Her knees shook as she unsteadily got to her feet.

Just as she was about to look out, the carriage struck a dip in the road. She held onto the bars with all her strength as the jolt pulled her body back. She barely managed to stop herself from falling. When the path became smooth again, she lifted herself up and looked out. She counted six Wild Men on horseback next to her carriage and, in the background, loomed a forest.

In Southrend, forests looked very inviting with the warm green and umber trees all spaced out so one could see inside of them without fear of the unknown. The forest she spotted now looked dark; the trees bunched together and grew around one another in a thick line of bark and twisted trunks.

She knew she was far from home.

As she studied the landscape, one of the Wild Men on horseback seemed to glare right at her as he rode by. In a panic, she lost her balance and landed on the floor of the cage. Her cage came to a stop, and she could hear faint voices again. Shadows appeared at the back of the cage. When they pulled the cloth free, the sun blinded her vision, and she was forced to look away.

"Well, look who's awake," said a familiar, chilling voice.

Frigg tried to look, but her eyes still hadn't adjusted to the sudden burst of light. She heard a key go into the lock. The door creaked open. A massive form only needed to take one step before he snatched her by the shoulder and yanked her from the cage.

This is it, Frigg thought. *This is where they kill me.* She decided she wouldn't go without a fight. Despite her hindered sight, she threw her tiny fist. She connected to something, or someone, and then threw her fists again and again. Sometimes she hit her target, but she mostly grazed or missed completely. Her first punch got a surprised grunt, but the ones afterward got nothing but evil laughter.

Her kicking legs felt the ground once more, and the large form pushed her by the head toward the outline of another cage, but this one didn't have a cloth over it. Frigg suddenly wished her eyes hadn't adjusted to the light of day when she saw the two black shapes inside. One of them crouched close to the floor while the other paced in the background.

"Black wolves," Frigg whispered.

At the sound of her voice, the one lying down rose with a vicious snarl while the second wolf lunged toward the cage but was stopped by the bars. "That's right," her captor confirmed. "Vicious beasts that feed off the flesh of humans and hunt in packs. If they stood up, they would be nearly ten feet tall."

Frigg stared at the blood red eyes of the wolves looking at her while they scowled their teeth. She was close enough to the cage to feel the hot breath of the beasts.

She turned and looked at the captor that held her by the back of the head. *Rangvald.* His armor was still covered in dry blood and those eyes of his were bloodshot and cold. The armor gauntlet he wore as he grabbed the back of her head chilled her to the bone, and she could feel some of the blood smearing into her hair.

"Don't get too close to the cage," a second voice said.

"I'll handle this, Halvar," Rangvald replied.

The second voice belonged to the masked Wild Man who Olaf nearly killed until being betrayed. He peered through the eyeholes of his mask—the only part of his face Frigg could see. There were three small slits near his mouth and two near his nose, so he could breathe.

"Do you know what the good thing about black wolves is?" Rangvald asked. The hungry wolves lashed at her from the cage. Their eyes appeared as red as the blood they lusted for. As the beasts scratched and clawed, the bars shook, and Frigg feared a powerful enough hit would unleash them. "Once they get a smell for something, it drives them insane," Rangvald said, answering his own question. "They become fiends. They go into a state of madness until they finally capture what they're looking for and get to sink their teeth into it. It is rumored that one of the wolves will grab you by the neck and hold you with just enough force to keep you down. They won't kill you, you see. They want to hear their prey scream and groan. It makes up for the scent driving them crazy. The other wolves will surround you and rip open your flesh, and only when the other wolves eat your legs will the first let go and join in. Since there are only two of them, the process will be much longer and far more painful."

The rabid hounds barked with such intensity that their spit hit Frigg in the face. She tried to back away, breaking Rangvald's grip, but Halvar stood right behind her. Rangvald violently grabbed her by her hair again and forced her face only a few inches from the cage. The wolf's hot breath scorched her. The sound of its horrid growl vibrated in her ears.

One of them reached its paw through the bars, claws exposed, and thrust it toward her face. Rangvald managed to pull her back just in time and tossed her to the ground. Frigg landed on her back and watched the black wolves try and free themselves.

Rangvald unsheathed his broadsword. The instrument of death measured nearly twice her size and still looked drenched in the blood of all the men he betrayed. He stood over her, blocking the wolves. "They have one other good quality," he continued. "When they find their prey and feel they are outmatched, they find a wild pack that they're not even a part of and join them. This way they can stalk you with greater numbers to assure a kill." He dropped to his knees, so he could look right at her. "Now they have your scent. They only need to get within a few feet of you to know what your blood smells like. The only thing stopping them from getting at you is this cage. So if you scream, yell, fight or make any attempt to try to get away, I will make sure these men throw you in with the wolves with no regard for the screams you will make when they sink their teeth into you."

Frigg's face quivered as she looked up at the gigantic man. With a slight motion of his head, Frigg felt herself grabbed by two Wild Men who roughly placed her back in her cage. They locked her up and haphazardly replaced the cloth, but Frigg still had plenty of light and could also hear their conversations more clearly. "She's awake," she heard Rangvald say. "I have done my part in this and assured she was alive."

"I told you she was," a muffled voice said. Frigg assumed it was Halvar.

"I had to be sure," Rangvald said. "I'm heading back to Southrend."

"Without suspicion?" Halvar asked.

"This was part of the plan, you fool," Rangvald spat. "I will go back and tell them I followed for as long as I could until I confronted a few of you. I will tell them I fought and killed several Wild Men, but the pack that took Damari's daughter eluded me. If they decide to send a party to find her, I will be able to throw them off your trail. This will give you time to reach Gustav."

Gustav! Of course! Frigg thought. *But why would Rangvald help Gustav? And how did Gustav get the Wild Men to help him?*

She heard the sounds of a horse riding off until it became nothing more than a fading trot in the distance. Someone readjusted her cloth, and she was once again shrouded in darkness. In another moment, the reins snapped and her cage resumed movement. A panic took her. Rangvald had said nothing of her father, and his fate was still unknown to her. He would never suspect Rangvald to be a traitor, especially with how highly her father had spoken of him. *Did he kill Father, as well?* She wondered. *Is his fate sealed?*

Chatter came from outside the cage, but she still couldn't hear anything clearly. She gave up when the voices continued to be nothing more than suppressed sounds. She crawled into the corner of the cage and felt like her cell was closing in on her. The road was still bumpy, and she often had to grab the bars to stay in place.

Frigg did not know where her kidnappers were taking her or what their intentions were. She kept having visions of being thrown in the other cage, something that a Wild Man would surely do for pleasure if it suited him. After a while, the bars rattled, and she couldn't understand why until she looked at her hands and saw them shaking.

She felt as though they had been traveling for hours. Her body ached from lying on the uncomfortable wood surface. The carriage finally stopped rattling when the rocky road turned smooth. By the feel and the sound of the terrain, Frigg assumed they now traveled on grass.

Suddenly, a loud cheer erupted from outside, and she jumped slightly. There was an echo of cheering voices that came from further away. The reaction in the distance puzzled Frigg.

The voices increased outside the carriage as the cloth slipped slightly from her cage. Frigg heard greetings and laughter as everything came to a halt. She began to fear for her life again. The party who captured her must have met up with another group. As she listened closely, she heard hammering, crackling fires, the neighing of horses, and distant voices. *This must be their camp*, Frigg thought.

She saw shadows heading toward the back of her cage. The cloth fell, and the blinding sun impacted her eyes once again, but her eyes were able to adjust more quickly this time. When the cell opened, Halvar stood there with a few others behind him. He reached in and grabbed her.

When Halvar pulled Frigg from her prison, the crowd erupted in cheers so powerful it pierced her ears. Frigg looked around and realized these were not Wild Men but Gustav's warriors.

Halvar pushed her forward, and she walked slowly toward the crowd. The warriors stood in her way but only parted when she got within a few feet of them. Many of the warriors held their weapons, pumping them in the air in celebration. They jeered at her as she walked by while each man yelled a swear word or threatened her life. Her eyes welled up, and her face felt flushed. Saga may have been gone from the world, but her words were still very much alive inside of Frigg's mind. *Be strong. Be strong,* she said to herself as she continued down her emotional gamut. She knew now, more than ever, she needed strength.

Something wet suddenly struck the side of her face and dropped from her cheek. Her hand wiped away the spit, but she was soon littered with more. She tried to pick up her pace but tripped on the ground. When she fell, the crowd erupted in laughter.

Next she was pelted with scraps of food and small pebbles. She held her arms in front of her face to protect her eyes. Frigg hoped the faster she walked, the quicker she could get through the crowd. Without warning, she felt as if she struck a tree, and she found herself back on the ground. Another round of mocking came from the warriors.

She looked up and saw that one of the warriors had held out his leg and tripped her. She tried to ignore it and get to her feet. There was a push to her spine, and she slammed back into the ground. She rolled to her back to see the same warrior that tripped her chuckling with glee.

A part of her wanted to stay on the ground and crawl into a ball. The tears threatened to fall from her eyes, but those two little words kept coming to her. *Be strong.* They were her rallying cry and the only thing in the world that helped her get through this moment.

When she finally got to her feet, she continued her path. More spit and scraps were tossed her way, but, this time, she made no attempt to stop them. She kept her head up, kept her steps steady, and drowned out the sounds of the mocking warriors. They may have had her as a prisoner, but she wouldn't allow them to break her mind. She would walk with pride and show them their words and trash couldn't break her.

The crowd of warriors looked to be endless, but the last of them finally parted, and she saw a tent draped in red. The cloth at the entrance was slightly open, and Frigg saw the flickering candle light inside gleaming off Gustav's face as he sat behind a small table with a glass of wine and a wicked grin.

Frigg stopped and glared at him. Halvar's shadow came over her from behind, but she refused to walk inside. Even after a nudge to her back, she stayed in place. Her eyes locked on the man responsible for her kidnapping.

He chewed loudly as he turned to look at her, a steaming plate of meat in front of him and a large, clear chalice of wine in the center of the table. He motioned to the empty seat at the other side of the table. "Hello, Lady Frigg. Are you hungry?"

No words came to her—not because she didn't want to answer, but because she wanted to scream at him. She didn't know if a sudden outburst would make him violent. As angry as she was, she was just a little girl. Any outbursts of rage could put her already questionable safety at further risk. She could feel her face growing warm, and she tried to contain the anger. She knew the first few words would be filled with malice, but the ones afterward would come as tears.

"I am not," she finally muttered. Her stomached ached with hunger, but she would never accept food from a traitor.

He shrugged and motioned his head toward Halvar. "Were you followed, Halvar?" Halvar hesitated and looked at Frigg. "It doesn't matter if she knows. They won't get her back unless they do as I ask. She'll either die, or it'll be over by the time she even tells them what we know."

A dark chill crept up her spine, and Frigg tried to stop herself from shivering. She knew Gustav's current gentle tone was just a farce.

"Not sure," Halvar replied. "Rangvald plans to throw them off our path. That should give us more time to hide her."

Gustav nodded before taking a small sip of his wine. He put the glass down and looked at Frigg. "Then Damari no doubt gathered his army all morning and is preparing to follow. I want a rider sent with a message telling him if he pursues us, he will be given his daughter in pieces."

The relief of knowing her father was still alive was tarnished instantly by the threat that followed. Frigg felt Gustav's eyes on her after she looked away from him. "You should be thankful. The marriage between us is off."

That was the furthest thing from her mind at the moment.

"Why did Rangvald betray my father?" Her thoughts started to find their way to her tongue. He didn't answer. When the silence became uncomfortable, she added, "He loved my father."

Gustav rolled his neck as he adjusted himself in his chair. A smug look covered his face as he let the tension linger. "Rangvald loved your grandfather," he finally said. "He never liked Damari. You might understand that betrayal if you were the one sent to live at the Dread Gate. Rangvald is a warrior, not a tracker of Wild Men. He was rather easy to convince. All I had to do was promise him Southrend once I have the crown."

"And what will happen to my father?"

Out came his grumbling snicker. "That depends on your father."

Frigg's heart sank. "You're going to kill him anyway, aren't you?"

"You can't keep a man alive who you removed from power." The Lord of Westerland rose from the table and walked around it until he stood directly in front of her. "He'll give up once he knows his little lady is in trouble. I see the way he looks at you. You are the glimmer in his eye and his last remaining heir. With Tadeas' recent death, he will do anything to keep you safe—even give up all he has."

"And you'll still kill him?" the question came with gritted teeth.

"He'll have revenge on his mind," Gustav reasoned. "There will, perhaps, be those who would secretly follow him in hopes of rising up to take back what is his." He leaned down to her. "I cannot allow that."

Frigg summoned the rage that had built inside of her and went to strike him. He caught her hand with ease, as if swatting away a fly. "My father will kill you."

Gustav chuckled as he pulled her further into the tent and threw her to the ground. His strength was overpowering. The tears found their way out of her eyes and down her cheeks.

Gustav's smug smile turned into a snarl. "Your father can't kill me. He's miles away, conjuring an army to come here to only turn back when my rider meets with him. If he decides to go against that, he will be taken care of. Have you forgotten that Rangvald is still with him?"

"He'll know!" Even as she shouted it, she prayed for the statement to be true.

"You think I'd be foolish enough to make a pact with someone your father doesn't respect? Rangvald will keep an eye on your father." He crushed all hope that remained. "I am no fool, child. Rangvald will make sure that your father does exactly what I want him to, and, if he doesn't, the Lord of Southrend will meet his sons and wife sooner than he expected."

"I will kill you!" She rose from the ground and imagined hitting him over and over again. His face would be all bloodied and bruised, and it would take Halvar and most of his army to get her off of him. As she approached, however, Gustav released a sharp sting to the side of her face. She hit the ground with such force that it vibrated throughout her body.

The sting stayed on her cheek, and she managed to open her eyes and see him shaking his hand from the impact of hitting her. On one of his fingers, he wore a silver ring in the shape of a dragon—no doubt the reason her face stung far worse than normal.

Gustav picked up the chalice of wine and refilled his glass. "You're not in Southrend anymore, Frigg. No one here is going to bow down before you or honor you because of who your father is. Out here, among my men, savages will do unspeakable things even to a little girl. The wolves will feast on you if I see fit, and I can send parts of you back to your father as a warning. No one said anything about you returning to him in one piece."

He was no longer the lord pretending to be honorable; this was the true version of the Dragon Lord. His threats made her imagine horrible things. Even the stories of dragons didn't frighten her like this. She reverted back to the little girl she truly was, knowing her anger and attacks on him would do nothing. Frigg could only try to think of something she could say to make him change his mind.

"You were going to have your title," she reminded him. "King Graylyn said you were going to marry me."

"You and I both know your father would never agree to those terms." Gustav turned and leaned back into the table. "Even if he did, I'm not waiting for the king to die, and you to come of the right age, in order to take back what belongs to me. Your Southern blood is a disgrace to the legacy of my family. My ancestors were kings and queens while your ancestors were in the South World mating with Wild Men. My family has been sitting idle while King Graylyn disgraces the throne my descendants sat upon with honor and prestige. The name Dragon Lord comes because we ruled the dragons. They were our slaves hundreds of years ago, doing our bidding and ridding the world of bloodlines that were not fit to be among the kingdom. I will now purge the land of those I feel are unfit and bring back the legacy my family made far before yours came and tarnished it."

He didn't care that she was nothing more than a child. To him, her blood alone made her an enemy, even if she didn't have a choice in the matter. She was a walking reminder of what happened to his family, and he wanted to rid the world of everything that reminded him of his family's fall.

"You're going to kill me even if he does everything you ask," she realized.

Gustav managed to drop his expression of malice. For a moment, she thought she caught sympathy in his eyes. He took a short sip of his wine and put the glass on the table. "You'll join your brother in the afterlife. He'll be happy to see you."

"Did you kill Tadeas?" The question came forcefully. While he was being honest, she might as well know the truth about her brother. She was still on the ground, so she used her elbow to lift herself up. She didn't want to look completely helpless.

The Dragon Lord let a cold silence hang in the air before he finally confirmed her suspicions with a nod. "He died quickly. I can't promise the same for you if your father doesn't do what he's supposed to."

"So you aligned yourself with Wild Men to do your work for you?" she asked.

The side of his lip rose slightly. "Not exactly, but making it seem like the Wild Men did it worked to perfection." Gustav looked to the entrance of the tent. "Halvar!"

The masked warrior walked in and glanced at Frigg on the ground. He didn't seem too concerned as his eyes went back to Gustav. "The rider has been sent with your commands."

"Good." Gustav grabbed his glass of wine. "She will be taken to the north to Ashvale. Damari will suspect we are taking her to Westerland."

"But the king runs the north," Halvar reminded him.

"That's why the caravan will take the east road to stay out of sight, and then travel north near Direwood," Gustav told him.

Even with the mask on, Frigg could see Halvar's hesitation. He cleared his throat before he asked, "Direwood?"

Gustav rolled his eyes and exhaled loudly. "Don't tell me you believe those ridiculous tales, as well?"

"Tales often come from real stories," Halvar argued.

"That are as swelled up as a strike to flesh from a hammer," Gustav said loudly. "You need not worry, Halvar. You won't be going as far as Ashvale. I'll need you back here after your visit with our old friend. "

The masked warrior conceded. "Do you have the sacrifice?"

"Outside in the other cage." Gustav took a long sip of his wine this time. He finished it and placed the glass on the table before he leaned toward Halvar. "Keep this little lady away from harm, for now. If she misbehaves, do what you must, but do not kill her. We need her alive."

Frigg saw Halvar glance at her, and she couldn't help but look away. "I have a feeling she will be on her best behavior."

"Remove her from my presence," Gustav commanded with a final glare toward her.

Halvar reached down, grabbed her by the back of her dress, and pulled her to her feet. He cruelly tossed her in front of him, and she stumbled out of the tent. The jeers instantly came at her when the crowd of warriors saw her exit their lord's tent.

She paused to prepare herself for the ridicule once more, but, before she could take a breath, Halvar pushed her down. She stumbled and landed on her face. The roar of the men nearly made her breakdown and sob, but she stood up from the ground, not bothering to remove the dirt that covered her face. She lifted her head and walked forward.

The crowd parted again with the same greeting they gave her the first time. She kept her mind on her father and how he was alive instead of focusing on the other threats Gustav threw at her. She knew he planned to kill Damari, but that was yet to come. She thought her father would catch on to Rangvald. That's what she had to believe.

With her thoughts locked on her father, she walked through the crowd of men much faster than the first time. When she reached the carriage, the party of Wild Men still surrounded it. A new cage and carriage caught her attention just on the side of her own. Inside of it was a little girl, much like herself.

The other girl's cage wasn't covered in cloth like hers. It seemed the new prisoner was allowed to look out into the world as they traveled. Gustav's secondary torture for Frigg was to be in a prison of darkness as she went to her unknown fate. The little girl looked to be the same age as Frigg. She sat on her knees and grasped the bars in front of her. Dirt covered her matted hair and her face, but Frigg could see the trails on her cheeks where tears had fallen. She wore a ragged linen cloth that may have been a dress at one time. She looked filthy, but then Frigg remembered how she had been thrown to the dirty ground since she arrived at the camp. For all she knew, she looked worse.

The girl's eyes followed Frigg as Halvar pushed her toward her own cage. The little girl's expression was blank, like a statue of some kind that could only move its eyes. Halvar unlocked Frigg's cage and threw her in. After he shut the door and closed the cloth, she was left in the darkness once more.

The stare of the other little girl burned into her memory. Despite the lack of emotion, there was something in those eyes of hers that made Frigg think something terrible was about to happen. She had no choice but to wait for the carriage to move again and try to mentally prepare for what surely lay ahead.

CHAPTER ELEVEN

Frigg heard sobbing coming from behind her carriage. From her own experiences with crying, she knew it belonged to a little girl. She assumed it was the one she saw in the cage just as she left Gustav's camp. At no point did she hear the Wild Men reprimand the girl.

The entire party was silent. Not a single Wild Man had spoken for hours, and the quiet made Frigg uneasy. The carriage rolling against the rocks and the trotting horses were the only sounds that let her know she wasn't alone.

She passed the time by trying to remember the stories her father told her, but even filling the void didn't help. Her father was a much better storyteller, and even her imagination couldn't do the tales justice.

The story of the Old King and the Young Maiden played through her mind when, suddenly, gravity pulled her to the back of her carriage. The horses pulled her up some kind of steep incline, and the ground became rockier. She heard the voices of the Wild Men again, but no clear words came because of the restriction of the cloth. The horses cried out, and the worried knot in Frigg's stomach returned.

Shouting came from outside her carriage—warning cries from up ahead. She wondered if they were near a patrol of the king's men. *Could it be Father?* Frigg silently hoped.

She rose to her feet and went to the front of the cage to look through the tear. The man snapping the reins blocked her view once again, but she stayed in place. Perhaps he would shift himself, even slightly, and she could get a better glimpse. He seemed to be a rather large man, but she didn't get a good look at him when she was let out earlier.

They kept hitting rough patches, making it difficult to get a good look at what was ahead. She closed her eyes and concentrated. She kept telling herself to get a grip on those bars. If she was being rocked back and forth, then the carriage rider was as well, and even a slight movement to the side could give her sight to what was ahead.

She squeezed her eyes shut and promised herself she would focus her vision the next time the carriage rocked. The opportunity came when the carriage went up on its left side. Her eyes opened, and she saw the carter slightly shift his body to the right. He rocked back a moment later, but she saw the mountain. It was near dusk, and grey clouds covered the skies. She caught a glimpse of the Wild Men who rode in front of her carriage, but she didn't have enough time to count them all.

She recalled Gustav telling Halvar to visit their old friend. Perhaps it was another lord from the other cities, meeting up with Gustav's Wild Men to secretly make an allegiance against her father and the king. She planned to listen in once they stopped—hoping that she could catch a name. Her chances of getting out of the carriage were bleak, at best, but in the event she could get away and somehow get home, she could warn her father of the threat. She already had enough information to help her father; even more details of Gustav's revenge would be useful.

It became deathly warm and humid inside the cage—the kind of heat that not even summer could replicate. Usually, Frigg had at least a glint of light from the sun, but now it was pitch black. The carriage continued to bounce. She leaned back in the carriage and grabbed the bars to avoid getting tossed.

Something dripped ahead of them. Frigg assumed her cloth must have shifted again, and she frantically searched through the small hole in the cage for some kind of clue, but it was far too dark. Suddenly, a deep red glow emerged in the distance. A burning sensation momentarily filled the air. She moved her head back to avoid the sting, but it was impossible.

A few of the guards began to complain, as well. Frigg noticed the horses pulling her carriage were replaced with two Wild Men, straining as they dragged her along. When the red glow came within view, Frigg realized it was an opening into a cavern. An odd rumble sound echoed around them. She could also clearly see where they were. The party had traveled inside the mountain through a dark, slim path, and now they looked to be in the heart of it. A river of lava rumbled as it flowed below them. The mysterious sound she heard was bursts of heat coming from the surface of the lava.

The lake of lava looked to be endless with a few scattered, solitary rock platforms. Her carriage quickly turned. She could no longer see the river, but the bright red light lingered on the side of her cage.

The path turned on a downward slope. The Wild Men who dragged her cage took short steps to assure her cage didn't roll down too quickly and run them over.

The bright red glow soon faded, and the torches became the only source of light. Not one of her captors uttered a single word. She wondered if they feared this place as much as she did. They moved slowly and methodically around each bend.

She didn't understand why they were being so cautious. Especially since none of them carried weapons. Even if they did run into any adversaries, they had nothing with which to defend themselves.

"Stop." The word came in an echoed whisper from Halvar. The entire group froze. Frigg watched as Halvar took one of the torches and tossed it forward. The surface of a strange lake lit up in flame. Frigg thought Halvar threw the torch in order to light their way further down the path, but for many moments after the lake was on fire, no one moved.

"Does he know we're here?" one of the Wild Men asked.

"He knows now," Halvar answered as he snatched another torch from one of the men. "We woke him."

The entire party stood in a tense silence. Halvar looked to the right. If only the men pulling Frigg would just go down and join him, then she could be closer and get a better view. Unfortunately, a rock wall stood in the way, so she could only see the lake of fire before her. Halvar held the torch down the pathway to the right and waited.

A deep, rumbling sound traveled across the pathway and made the bars tremble on her cage. Frigg crawled backward until she hit the corner. As a dark presence captured the air, it felt like the source of the growl was inside the cage with her. As it got louder and deeper, Frigg curled up in a ball and hugged her own body.

"Put the cage down," Halvar called.

Frigg's carriage dragged forward and turned to the right, just as she had wished moments before, but now she wanted to go back. Her body slid downward to the front of the cage. She pushed her feet out in front of her and stopped herself from slamming into the bars. Because the Wild Men placed the carriage down, she sat at an awkward angle, but the cloth in the front opened slightly and allowed her a better glance at what was ahead.

She ducked down and saw a massive black shadow in the distance. She watched as Halvar and the others seemed to shrink as they walked closer to the strange figure.

A new red glow sparkled from the dark form, but it wasn't fire or lava. A deep rumble struck the ground and rolled its way to her cage where she felt its vibrations. Frigg held her breath when she realized the source of red light were eyes.

"We are here to make our arrangement," Halvar said unsteadily. "My lord is ready to uphold his part of the agreement."

A thundering reverberation touched the ground and shook Frigg's cage again.

"The agreement was to release me from these chains," a powerful voice said. It sounded unworldly. No normal being could conjure that much of a vibration.

"To release you once we had what we needed," Halvar replied with a little more boldness. "We are almost there."

"So you came here to tell me you're almost there?" The powerful voice rumbled.

"The plan is in order," Halvar assured the creature. "We only need you to do what you promised."

"Only when you uphold your lord's promise!" The statement rattled the cave and made the Wild Men back away. "What is that I smell? It cannot be." The creature sniffed the air. "Is that the essence of royalty?"

"The blood of Southern Royalty," Halvar confirmed. "The blood of King Audun."

"Bring her to me!" The voice rumbled as the vibrations bounced off the cave walls.

Frigg buried her head in her knees, and silently prayed to the gods to spare her.

"No," Halvar answered.

Never in all her life did that one word bring her so much relief.

"No?" The powerful voice asked in defiance.

"That will be your prize once you do what is commanded of you," Halvar said. "My lord promises."

"Promises from your pathetic kind?" Its laughter echoed throughout the cavern. "I don't believe in the word of humans."

"Believe in my lord's," Halvar said.

"So you come to me now with no sacrifice?" The voice asked.

"I didn't say that."

Frigg gasped loudly when a Wild Man ran by her cage.

A sobbing scream made Frigg jump. She suddenly remembered the other little girl—the one she only caught a glimpse of back at the camp. She gripped the bars as she watched the Wild Man drag the girl down the pathway to the black creature inside the cavity.

Frigg wanted to yell out. She wanted to scream at them to leave the poor girl alone, but her bravery left her long ago. The other little girl begged her kidnapper every step of the way as she tried to fight from his grasp, but he was too strong.

"No," Frigg whispered. Even that sounded too loud, and she placed her hand over her mouth. Tears soaked the back of her hand, but she managed to remain quiet.

The little girl still struggled with the Wild Man who dragged her toward the black mass. She was tossed forward with such power she hit the ground and went limp.

Halvar and the Wild Men backed away and scattered like rats. The black mass deeply inhaled and paused. Frigg saw the little girl slowly coming to from being tossed to the ground. The girl got to her feet and looked at the red glowing eyes of the creature.

A hellacious scream escaped her, but then a burst of fire exploded and covered over the girl until she became permanently silenced. The ignition of light gave a glimpse of the creature, but that was all Frigg needed to know for sure—*a dragon!*

Frigg buried her head in her knees once more and sobbed into her dress. She convulsed with fear and tried to muffle her cries. The silence only confirmed what Frigg already knew, and then it was shattered by the loud chomping and chewing of strong jaws. She covered her ears and leaned her body near the wall of the cage. In a panic, she moved away from the wall, but her trembling body rattled the bars.

A spewing sound followed a disgusted cough. "I want the blood of royalty! These peasants taste vile!"

"And you shall have it," Halvar promised. "All you need to do is one thing."

"What is her name?" the dragon asked.

"Lady Frigg of Southrend, the heir to the throne of the North World," Halvar said.

A cackling laugh came from the dragon. "A future queen? It's been so long since I've tasted such innocent, royal blood. Bring her before me."

The thought made Frigg sob, and she backed away in her cage as far as she could go.

"No," Halvar said. "How am I to trust you won't kill her when I put her in front of you? You think me a fool, dragon?"

"You're pretty smart…for a human." The dragon sniffed the air once more. "Her scent is beautiful, but I warn you, human—break your promise to me, and I will make sure you stand before me as my latest victim. I've never liked the taste of men, but I will make sure to make you an exception."

"Goodbye, great being of the mountain," Halvar said quickly.

Frigg could hear the Wild Men walking back toward her, but the dragon's voice bellowed once more. "You tell Lady Frigg of Southrend that she will not be able to run from me once these chains are removed. I know her essence now. She…shall…be…mine!"

Frigg's cage rocked once again; they were leaving. The suffocating feeling in the air lifted, and she heard birds chirping in the distance. The carriage rumbled back and forth, and the trotting ahead told her the horses now moved her instead of men. She assumed Halvar was on his way back to Gustav, but the thought brought her little comfort in the wake of what she just witnessed.

The rocking of her cage calmed after an hour or so, and she heard the familiar sound of the road once more. She stayed in the corner of her cage, arms grasping the bars, but she didn't need to. She was on level ground, and yet, she found herself frozen as the explosion of fire kept replaying in her head. She feared the memory of the dragon's face would haunt her forever. Her lower lip shook, and her entire body felt stiff.

The cloth surrounding her cage swayed freely until she heard the horses screech. She could tell the Wild Men were trying to calm them down, but the stallions only grew louder. Frigg's cage shook as she heard the horses walking over their own steps and slapping their hoofs into the ground.

The dragon, she feared. *It broke from its restraints and is coming after us.* She was sure of it. One of the Wild Men in the front of the party yelled back to the others, but she couldn't make out the words over the commotion from the horses.

Frigg heard howling, and she remembered the black wolves. They growled and snarled in their own prison, rattling the bars as if they wanted to break free. The horrible sounds they made turned into whimpering. *What would a black wolf fear?* Frigg wondered. *It must be the dragon.*

A rattle shook the ground, and Frigg felt the vibration of it travel up her body. Another tremor followed that trembled the very earth. Just as she was about to scream, a mighty roar sounded with such force she thought the source of it was right on top of her. It echoed, but even after it stopped, she could feel her heart pick up in her chest. This was no dragon; this was a new kind of terror.

She leapt to the tear on the side of the cage. She couldn't see any of the Wild Men, but she did hear one of them hush the others up ahead. A dead silence came over the party. Frigg ran to the front of the cage to the other tear, but, as usual, the carter blocked her view. She watched him shift his body and look to the distance, like he was searching for something. She could almost make out the trees from the forest in front of them. They stood mighty and proud until she watched them suddenly shake back and forth. Just before the carter blocked her view, one of the trees snapped with a sickening shatter, and she heard the thud when it hit the ground.

She backed away just as a thundering strike shook the earth, followed by a second, and then a third came so rapidly she had no time to recover from each shockwave of force. Screams from the Wild Men, ones of fear and panic, were drowned out by another deafening roar from this new terror.

There was definitely something out there. The horses screeched again, and her cage jolted forward so quickly she rolled backward until she struck the bars of the cage. This time, her prison rumbled out of control. Even when she grabbed the bars, she couldn't hold on to stop herself from crashing in all directions. The carriage hit a dent in the road, and it catapulted in the air and fell down on its side.

Frigg heard the horses running until their steps faded. Outside, the carter groaned. A bloodcurdling scream came afterward, followed by a cracking sound. The cloth around her cage shifted in many directions, and she could see outside better. She slowly crawled over to look. Frigg thought she spotted something, but it was too quick for her to get a good look. The carter twitched on the ground, but she couldn't understand why. She also wasn't so sure if she wanted to know.

She heard a loud crash next to her cage. She went to the tear in the side once more and saw the cage filled with the black wolves turned on its side, too. They whimpered again, and she saw one of them clawing into the ground trying to dig its way out.

All of a sudden, something struck the ground with such force that sand exploded up from the impact, and Frigg heard some of it graze the side of the cage. She closed her eyes and hoped it didn't hit her. When she felt brave enough to open them again and look through the cloth, the body of a Wild Man laid motionless on the ground.

A raging roar exploded. A nearby scream quickly faded. The panicked cries of the Wild Men were always followed by an aggressive snort, a packing sound, and then a snapping noise that made Frigg's stomach twist. The yells from the Wild Men decreased until there was nothing but silence—not even a whimper from the wolves or a screech from the horses. There was nothing. Then she thought she heard breathing. This was no normal exhale. At least, not one she had ever heard.

Frigg stopped thinking about the beast beyond her prison and realized she was breathing loudly, too. With the fear and anxiety that took her, it felt like it echoed. She took both her hands and covered her mouth, but even her muffled breathing seemed loud.

She grabbed onto the bars for her life, but, just as she tightened her grip, the cage lifted in the air with ease. Her cage shifted to the side. She tried to grab the floor to keep herself from rolling, but her fingers couldn't grip the wooden surface. The cage continued to turn over and over. The cloth fell, but Frigg couldn't see a thing while spinning in the air.

Each time her cage rolled, Frigg heard a frustrated grunt. Her panic faded and turned to complete horror. She tried to scream, but the cage jolted and crashed into the ground with such noise she couldn't even hear herself. She prayed for her father to charge in and save her from whatever attacked her cage. Soon the crashing faded, the noises muted, and everything faded to blackness.

CHAPTER TWELVE

As Frigg lay in the darkness, she recalled those rare times when she would awaken in the middle of the night in the comfort of her bed in Southrend—the blankets wrapped around her and everything so still and silent, yet she couldn't move. The best way she could describe it was her mind felt awake, but her body still slept. A state of paralysis overtook her as she laid there. Sometimes it was very frightening because her head was buried in her pillow, and she felt suffocated. To try to save herself, she would count to three in her head and, somehow, through pure will, she would move slightly. Just before her life looked to fade, she would move her head at the last moment and breathe. Yet, she still couldn't move.

Saga told her once that sometimes the spirits of those who were killed would come back and take revenge on the children of their enemies, trying to kill them while they slept, far away in the afterlife where no one would ever suspect them of the crime. The next morning she could hardly recall what happened. It wasn't until late in the day that she remembered the experience, and it always gave her a dark chill. To think that ghosts were trying to harm her was a hard thing to fathom.

She knew it was happening again. There she was with her head buried in the cold ground as the grains of grass tickled the side of her face. The temperature around her felt cold, and the ground was nothing like the comfortable bed back home. It irritated her flesh, and she wondered how her body had yet to fully awaken from the discomfort. Yet the silence around her felt peaceful—no horses, no muffled voices, not even the rocking of the cage. It was the first time she felt at peace since being in the hands of her captives, and it seemed her body yearned to hold on to that feeling.

Like before, she silently counted to three. Frigg lifted her head, and the grass no longer dug into her cheek. Still her body wouldn't move. *Just an arm*, she thought—one arm and perhaps she could awaken the rest of her body. She counted to three, but her arm didn't move. She begged her body to do what she wanted and counted once more.

One...two...three. Her fingers lifted slightly, but it was more like a spasm than a voluntary movement. She counted off in her head again, and, this time, her hand came up. Slowly, her body stirred, and she forced herself to sit up. Her eyes opened, but there was nothing but a blur in front of her. She could vaguely make out the cloth that once surrounded the cage. A blast of light came over her. She raised her hand to shade her eyes from the sunlight. The cloth had been torn off her cage in several places, so only a few layers of it remained.

She shook her head in an attempt to clear her vision. The cage lay on its side, and some of the bars twisted and pierced the ground. Frigg looked up and saw one of the broken bars only a few inches from her forehead. She scooched away from it for fear that she would accidentally scrape her head. When she shifted her body, she hit the bars again and turned around. A few of them were missing. The opening seemed slim, even for someone her size, but it was worth a try.

Her body ached from being tossed around, and she could hardly move her legs. She rolled to the gap in the bars and tried to push through. Her body wouldn't allow it. The bars weren't far enough apart for her to squeeze herself out. She grimaced with every push and tried to will her already tiny body to get smaller. A push of determination finally got her further, but the bars gripped her body so tightly she couldn't breathe. A deep inhale made her stomach sink in and she brushed by—but not before one of the mangled bars slashed her arm and tore open her flesh.

She ignored the pain as her body somehow got all the way out of the damaged cage, and she pulled her arm close to her body. She didn't want to see it and could only image the gash just by the feel of it. The blood soaked through her dress and quickly stuck to the skin on her stomach.

She glanced at the open ground ahead of her and saw nothing but bodies. Wild Men spread out on the green grass with their bodies twisted in all directions. She wouldn't give the horrible sight another glance. She turned her head and tried to run away from the aftermath.

A sudden gap in the earth made her stumble forward. With her arm curled into her stomach, she couldn't reach out to stop herself, so she fell face first into the ground. She rolled to her back and forced herself up. She could still see the destroyed carriages and bodies, but they were now at a distance. While her eyes panned what was in front of her, she noticed she was in a hole. It wasn't very deep, but it did make her realize why she fell.

She got herself back on level ground and heard howling in the distance. It had to be the black wolves. Whatever attacked the Wild Men had scared them off, but the creature was nowhere around now. She had a choice; she could stay in the open lands, and possibly get attacked by black wolves, or she could try her chances in the mysterious forests of Direwood. She knew of the dangers in the open fields, so she thought the forest was the only way to stay safe.

Frigg's little legs pushed toward the entrance of the forest. Her sight instantly set on how abnormal the branches on the trees looked. They twisted upward and downward and even wrapped around the limbs of other trees. The scene was quite chilling. The bark on the trees had several knots that swirled in every direction and reminded Frigg of morbid faces of ghosts or ghouls. She swore a few of them had deranged eyes that kept staring at her, and she couldn't shake the eerie feeling. She felt the hair on the back of her neck stand up when she walked by each tree. She almost expected one of the branches to snatch her up and squeeze her until the life left her. The thought made her shudder.

Her eyes looked up at one tree and a Wild Man sat at the top staring down at her. Frigg dropped to the ground and hid behind a log. She thought they had all died! That one must have spotted her, and she feared death or capture once again. Her body shook and her breaths picked up. With her eyes closed tightly, she started to sob. After several moments of silence, she wondered what was taking the Wild Man so long to come after her.

He's in the tree. Her eyes opened, and she reminded herself of his position once more. *He's in the tree? Why would he hide in a tree?* That's when she stood up from behind the log and looked at the Wild Man. His eyes seemed to stare into her soul, but he didn't moved. She took a few steps closer and saw one of the branches stabbed into his back and protruding from his chest. A combination of blood and spit hung from his lip. Blood flowed down the bark of the tree. She missed it the first time because of the blackness of the bark, but she saw it once the sunlight hit the tree.

How did he get up there? she wondered. She searched around but saw nothing. Frigg figured that whatever attacked the Wild Men was so powerful it could toss a man with little effort to the very top of a towering tree and impale him on a branch.

She found her feet again and walked further into the forest to get away from the sights of death. A thick mist came from the ground. Her feet vanished into the fog, and, like the trees, she thought something was going to grab her. She sighed in relief when she felt the solid ground below her and not the flesh of some monster hiding and waiting to pounce. She hugged herself because of the sudden chill she felt in her body. She didn't know if it was actually getting colder in the forest, or if it was just her fear that made her shiver.

The scent of stale water hung in the air and mixed with a musky aroma of rotting wood. The solid ground turned to damp soil, and she sank with each step. When she lifted her foot, the mud made a bizarre popping sound. The dirt covered the sides of her shoes, and she felt the grime cover over her heels and soak into her feet. She feared falling into some large puddle she couldn't see because of the mist on the ground, so she walked slowly and carefully. She heard squeaks, chirps, and high pitched screeching of which she couldn't find the source. Despite all the sounds around her, the forest itself had no movement or any creatures in sight. She hoped they were just insects that lived inside the fallen trees or hid in the fog at her feet.

Before her stood an opening without any of the twisted trees, but the fog seemed thicker. She walked through the opening and further into the forest without having to climb over logs or small rock walls. When she took her next three steps, the fog parted and waved beneath her. She stopped and watched the mist swirl around. Her tense shoulders relaxed, and the knot in her stomach lifted.

She finally began to see life in the dead forest just ahead. Trees blossomed with leaves, and their trunks no longer expressed hideous faces. The stale water stench gave way to the aroma of pine and flowers. Birds chirped. There were still remnants of the frightening terrain, such as the mud and the mist, but the sun peeked its way through the trees and kissed her face with its warmth. Though the trepidation inside of her faded, she was still in a strange place, so caution stayed on her mind.

She heard something running in the distance, and Frigg's fear quickly returned. Her eyes searched in front of her to see the blur of a fox rushing away. It was good to know animals inhabited this place. The haunted forest's reputation may have been swelled by stories of those who feared its presence. Here she stood, a girl of eight, and she began to see the beauty of it.

She scraped the dirt off her shoes against a log. The residue of grime still covered them, but they lost their weight. She kneeled down and pinned her wounded arm to her dress. With her free hand she began to rip the bottom of it until she held a large piece of fabric. Without looking at the cut, she began to wrap her wounded arm. It stung and she winced with each twisting until she finished.

She suddenly felt a tremble on the ground. She froze and looked around her for the source of the vibration, but there was nothing in view. It was so subtle she may not have felt it if she wasn't standing still. After many moments, she wondered if her mind was playing tricks on her, but then she felt it again. This time, it came with more force and felt closer to her. Once again, her eyes panned the forest, but there was still nothing.

There came a trembling so intense she nearly lost her footing. Just ahead of her in the trail, only a few yards away, came a parade of wildlife, including deer, squirrels, raccoons, rabbits, and a few species she didn't recognize. Predator and prey ran through the same trail and seemed to forget their place within the food chain of nature. Frigg wondered what could be within this forest that caused the animals to run in panic. A limping wolf slowly trailed behind the rest of the animals. It stopped, nose to the air, and shifted its head to look at her. It wasn't as large as the black wolves in the cage, but she was still prey, after all. It faced forward again and continued on the trail.

It took some time for Frigg's shaking legs to steady before she could walk again. With the drop in temperature, she knew the sun would set soon. The small chill of the forest started to intensify, and she hugged her body to try to keep warm. The chill descended to her legs, and each step came gingerly. When the sun completely set, it would be unbearable.

The sky had a fading blue tint. Crickets sang their song of the night. There came the uneasy feeling of someone watching her. The quake in her knees returned, and her eyes darted in all directions. She could feel the hair on the back of her neck rise.

The shadows shifted and curved in the darkness of the brush. Her mind invented things that weren't there. From the side of her vision, eyes came out and looked at her, but, when she returned the glance, she realized they were simply small glimmers of light peeking through the shadows. She looked for the eyes she knew were out there in the darkness, but they had yet to emerge.

The ground felt solid, but the surrounding trees looked wicked once more. Branches shifted in so many directions, and the trunks conjured their ghoulish faces. The sound of crickets was drowned out by howls deep in the distance, and each one made her snap her head in the direction from which it came.

Something wailed close by, and she leapt in the direction of the closest tree to hide. Where she expected the ground to be, it wasn't. She stumbled forward and nearly hit the ground face first. Luckily, she remembered to stick out her good arm, so she caught herself before she fell. This hole was much like the one out in the plains when she escaped her cage. She stepped back up on level ground, and, as she looked back at the hole, something caught her attention. She did a double take, and the hole wasn't a hole at all; it was a footprint!

She couldn't move or breathe. The pounding of her heart quickened. A grunting sound came from behind her, and she froze. Something exhaled, and a hot breath drifted toward her and brushed her legs. She slowly turned around.

Through the brush in front of her, there stood a large shadow. Two eyes glistened through the darkness as they darted back and forth. Frigg hoped they were just lights in the distance playing with her mind, but they moved again. This time, they fixed on her, and she watched them blink. A low, rumbling sound erupted, and she took a step back.

The darkness and shadows of Southrend had a way of dancing and conjuring horrid images that made her fear the dark, but this was no figment of her imagination; it was, in fact, something.

Her lower jaw quivered, her teeth chattered, and her body quaked. She wanted to run or scream, but she worried, if she did, the creature would give chase. Her only option was to stay still, hoping and praying it was questioning her authenticity, as well.

The shadow of the being rose and revealed its true size. The glimmer of its silver eyes rose to the brush on the top of the trees. It snorted and released a low, grumbling growl. She gasped at its presence and felt herself stumble backward. *It can't be,* she thought. *They're gone! The last of them died.* The back of her foot struck a log, and the sound echoed in the quiet night.

Frigg recalled Saga's stories about what stood before her, her own childlike obsession with their legend, and the tales of when they walked the earth. They were gone now, or so her father had once assured her. With a tiny whisper under her breath, she confirmed to herself what she already knew. "A giant."

CHAPTER THIRTEEN

Frigg turned and ran. The wind whipped against her face as she panted in horror, jumping over rocks and bushes, hoping her little legs would get her as far away from that thing as they could take her.

She heard a deep rumbling behind her, and she knew; it was coming after her. She ran with such force and speed that everything in front of her was a blur. Her torn up shoes struck the ground until she felt nothing but air as she suddenly fell forward. The ground sloped downward, but she had been too scared to notice. She flipped forward, and her small frame rolled down a steep hill, twisting her tiny body in all directions. Her shoulders struck rocks, and her feet snagged branches. She plummeted down the hill until she came to a violent halt. Her face smashed into the ground with such force that her legs nearly came up over her head.

The wind was knocked out of her lungs as she desperately tried to scream. Dead leaves and dirt fell from her mouth. When she regained her breathing, she vomited the contents that covered her tongue and stuck in her teeth. She blew her nose. A mixture of dirt and blood landed on a small rock in front of her. Her tongue touched a small laceration on the inside of her lip, and she tasted blood.

When her breath came back completely, she gasped with such force it echoed in the forest. She quickly placed both hands over her mouth to muffle the sound. After taking four quick breaths, she removed her hands from her mouth and looked at her palms. They were covered with the residue of tears and blood. Her face stung from the scrapes and cuts.

Her eyes tried to look around, but everything was dazed and doubled. She blinked a few times to try to recover. She felt the side of her head where it slammed into the ground. While fiddling through the strands of her blonde hair, she felt a damp residue. When she looked at her fingers, they glistened with fresh blood. She shook her head, and, finally, the world around her was right again.

She tried to lift herself up, but a sharp pain in her right ankle made her scream. She collapsed back to the ground. She didn't want to look. Based on the way it felt, she thought her foot might be dangling from her leg.

She forced herself to finally look at her ankle; it was definitely sprained or, worse, broken. She glanced at the top of the hill in panic, but she didn't see anything trailing her. If she were to get away, she would have to crawl. She dug her elbows into the dirt in front of her and dragged her body. She silently prayed the giant gave up its pursuit of her when she rolled down the hill. Even so, she wouldn't be caught in the middle of a trail if it happened to want to find her.

She groaned with each forward push of her body and winced when the slightest touch brushed her ankle. After only a few feet, she couldn't go any farther. Tears of pain rolled down her face, and her entire body ached from the fall. Her head sank into the ground. She wanted to stay there for hours and simply wait for her father to pick her up and take her home.

What if he never finds me? What if he thinks I'm dead and doesn't come looking for me? What if the Wild Men killed him? Each question broke her heart a little more.

She closed her eyes to fight off the tears and took a deep breath. When she opened her eyes and picked up her head, she realized she was no longer alone.

She recognized the beast standing before her by how many times she had seen the hunters in Southrend skinning them or felt the comfort of its fur at night. Frigg was unable to scream or move in the presence of a creature she had only seen when it was dead.

A grizzly bear stood before her on all fours. Its hot, nasty breath coated her face even from several feet away. She remained frozen, not knowing what she could do to escape. With pronounced shoulders, the grizzly bear suddenly stood on its hind legs. It snarled and growled toward her before it finally roared so loudly Frigg shook from its strength.

The bear gave off another loud roar, and she slowly backed away. The grizzly dropped to four legs again and took a step toward her. With her ankle twisted, she knew she only had a few moments to keep the inevitable from happening. When the bear got within a foot of her, she imagined what it would feel like when the bear's teeth tore her body apart.

A thunderous roar echoed behind Frigg, and she awkwardly turned her head to the hill above her. The black mass of the giant rumbled down the hill, slamming its feet into the earth with such force that Frigg felt her body rise from the ground. Even the trees rattled and lost their leaves as the giant came bounding forward. In the distance, birds retreated with panicked caws.

The shadowed form pushed through the trees as if they were twigs. As it descended further down the hill, it snorted and beat its chest. Frigg couldn't help but gaze at the bear, who slowly backed away from the enormous creature.

The giant grew nearer, and, for a moment, Frigg thought it would step right on her. She closed her eyes and curled into a ball. She tucked her knees into her chest and masked her face with her hands. The shockwave of a massive foot falling right next to her lifted her from the ground. She rolled to the side and opened her eyes, but everything in front of her was blocked by the giant's green and grey leg.

With her whole body trembling, she crawled around the giant's foot. The grizzly stood frozen—much like she did when she was alone in its presence. The giant lifted its leg and slammed it to the ground just a few feet in front of the bear. The quake lifted Frigg and pushed her several feet back. When she hit the ground, she rolled and noticed the grizzly bear did the same but with much more force.

The intimidating animal that roared at her only a few moments earlier whimpered like a frightened cub. It turned and quickly ran until it was nothing but a brown blur. She wished she felt more relieved, but there was still the monster in front of her.

A deep, low grunt came from the giant as it turned to look at Frigg. The setting sun still lingered behind its massive form, so its face remained shrouded in the shadows of the forest. All she saw was the flicker of its silver eyes and the jangle of bones from a choker it wore around its neck. She didn't know what it wanted from her; she only knew it followed her.

She slowly sat up. Frigg realized that, even if her ankle wasn't twisted, she wouldn't get very far if she ran. Her body shook uncontrollably, and it made her shoulders ache. The vertigo she felt when she looked at the Dread Gate came back to her as she looked up at the colossal being.

The giant took two thundering steps toward her and reached down. She wanted to scream, but the shock wouldn't allow her. All of a sudden, she was surrounded by darkness. For a moment, she thought the gods had taken her and spared her from the terrible demise the giant had for her. It wasn't until she felt the tremble of the steps below her that she realized she had been captured in its hand. Small glints of light peeked through the giant's colossal fingers. She pressed her hands up as if she could pry them apart. The texture of its flesh reminded her of the rough stone of the castle wall back home.

The giant's steps were rather clumsy. She kept swaying in its hands and even rolled a few times. It was difficult for her to try and stay in one place. She felt lightheaded and started to hyperventilate. Her panicked breathing wouldn't be able to hold up for much longer. She tried to calm herself, but it was hard to do in the hands of a monster.

The shock dissipated, and, with all the air that remained in her lungs, she let out a scream. The creature opened its hands and shifted her from its right hand to its left hand. Frigg reached her own hands out to the side to balance herself, and, with the moonlight breaching the trees, she saw the color of the monster clearly for the first time. Its flesh was near grey with tints of green. Its rough hands seemed covered in scabs and punctures.

She fit in one of its hands with little fear that she would fall unless it tilted its wrist. She relaxed a little until she realized it was looking right at her. She felt herself quaver, and she remained focused on its grey and green hand, not wanting to know what its face looked like.

The hand rose, and she gripped the flesh on its palm with her own once more to hold her balance as the fingers tilted upward. She looked down but then squeezed her eyes shut. She heard sniffing and opened her eyes. The nose of the giant was so close she could have reached out and poked it. *It's going to eat me,* she thought. Without thinking, she threw out her fist and punched it square in the nose. The creature grunted angrily, and Frigg wrapped her arms around her legs and prepared for the worst.

The giant cupped her with both hands once again as both the darkness and the muted sounds of the forest shrouded over her. It shifted her as it walked, and she fell to the bottom of its cupped hands right where both of them connected. There was a small crease where the hands came together, and she thought she might fall through. She tilted her head down and watched the forest ground go by.

The giant's thundering steps continued, and Frigg felt like she had traveled for miles. The many stories about giants told to her by Saga and her father used to intrigue her. Yet, here she was in the grips of one, and it was absolutely terrifying! The mystery of giants had always kept her attention, but that was when she was told they were gone from the world. The last of them supposedly had its skull at the bottom of a pit back in Southrend.

Frigg summoned another scream and let it out. When the hands opened again, she looked up and yelled, "Put me down! Put me down!"

The giant grunted, and she felt her body slowly descend to the ground. When the giant gently tilted its hand, she fell softly to the earth. She instantly winced because of her ankle and leaned to her left to avoid putting pressure on it.

The trees were so thick where they were, not even a small glow of moonlight came through. She looked up at the giant, but the darkness kept the detailed features of its face well hidden from her. Its silver eyes inspected her as it stood up and took two steps away from her.

While she sat on the cold brush, some of her fear finally dissipated. She looked up and inspected what she could see of the giant. The outline of its body looked like a brute, even for a giant. He had wide shoulders and muscular arms with skinny, lanky legs. His only clothing was a long loincloth that looked to be made of animal fur. It walked barefoot, and the top of its feet looked much like its hands—scraped and cut.

The sun had nearly set. It would be only a moment or so before it became pitch black, and the cold covered over the world. Even the slightest breeze gave Frigg chills.

The giant turned and walked away from her. It knelt down on the ground and looked into the forest as if expecting something. The top of its head was hairless and cone-shaped. It reminded her of the skull in Southrend, though the skull in the dungeon looked larger.

As her eyes adjusted to the darkness, she noticed the beast had a snaggletooth that rose above its lower-lip and rested just below its nostril. As it breathed, its throat rumbled. She couldn't tell if this was an act of aggression or just its normal breath.

She thought she could use this as her moment to get away. It seemed to be enthralled with the sights of the forest. By now, the crickets sang and the insects buzzed. The forest seemed filled with flashes from the lightning bugs. When she tried to stand, the painful reminder of her twisted ankle came back, so she decided to crawl.

She made her move to go, but thunder suddenly cracked above her. The sharp sound made her stop. Then the rain poured in through the thick trees and quickly soaked her as she sat in the middle of the forest.

The giant grunted as it rose, took just a few steps, and stood over her. The rain rapidly struck her as she tried to look up at the giant, but it was no use; the rain fell too hard and too fast for Frigg to see anything above her. The giant roared into the heavens as if its scream would frighten the storm. She felt perplexed by its behavior and watched as it paced back and forth while looking to the sky. After another deafening roar, it reached down to pick her up again.

"No!" She screamed as she crawled backward to get away from its grasp. Her hand landed over a rock. Out of desperation, she picked it up, reached her hand back, and threw it toward the giant, weakly striking it in its chest. Even she knew it must have felt like nothing more than an insect, but she had to try something.

The giant snorted and growled lightly as it bent down. She gripped the ground below her and curled up again, but her eyes couldn't stop looking at it. Its eyebrows were creased, and its lower lip rose with the snaggletooth nearly going into its right nostril. It didn't seem too intimidated by her rock throwing as its hands once again cupped her and picked her up from the ground.

This time she didn't act calm. She screamed and punched the inside of its palms, but she knew she couldn't break free from the prison of its grip. Eventually, she gave up any thought of freeing herself. She shivered from when the rain soaked her dress and hair. She could feel the fabric attaching itself to her flesh. The cold draft coming through the gaps of the giant's fingers made her teeth chatter. If she needed to think of a bright side, at least she wasn't getting wet from the pouring rain anymore. She hugged herself as her whole body shook from the cold. She felt it in her bones, and her water-soaked body made it practically unbearable. She crawled into a corner and imbedded herself between two fingers. That brought some warmth but not enough to stop her shaking. She feared the monster would feel the vibrations, loosen its grasp, and drop her to the ground.

The sounds of its thundering steps stopped, but the rhythm of the raindrops still pounded in her ears. Rain seeped in through the giant's hands and descended on her. She jumped as water ran its way down her neck and her already sodden flesh. She let out a loud gasp and tried to hug herself even tighter.

The rain faded, and the sound around her turned hollow. She felt herself descend and the giant's hands open. She felt stones under her and winced as she landed on her right ankle. She quickly shifted and looked up. Her new captor stood over her, shadowed by the darkness. She looked around, but she could only see the reflections of light coming off stone. About twenty feet away from her was the mouth of a cave.

The fissure was pretty small. The giant had to bend down, so its head didn't hit the top. The monster crouched now and sat itself against the wall with its knees up and its arms slumped over top of them. Even in the darkness, she could see the snagged tooth rising from its lower lip. She caught a glimpse of its eyes looking all around the cave. She knew this was a place it had been before based on the bedding of branches upon which it sat.

When her eyes started to adjust from the darkness, she saw remains all around the cave. There were bones of every size—some as small as her and others nearly twice the size. Some of the skulls on the ground were from animals she didn't recognize. A horrid stench permeated from the piles of bony debris.

Frigg felt desperate to flee, but there was no escaping the cave at that moment. She kept her eyes on the creature in the darkness, watching its head turn every so often and just gaze into the nothingness surrounding them. Its fat nose repeatedly sniffed the air. Despite taking her to this cavern, it didn't pay attention to her in the slightest.

Perhaps it's full, she thought. *Maybe it's going to eat me once it gets hungry again…or save me for breakfast.* Between her shivering and her soaked clothes, she would never get any rest. The stone ground itself was uncomfortable even as she sat on it. The feel of a feathered bed and a bearskin had spoiled her. She planned to wait and escape after it fell asleep.

She watched its large shadow sit up with its head bent down. It headed toward the mouth of the cave. When it left, Frigg looked around in worry. She tried to crawl away from where she sat, but the pain in her ankle felt unbearable. She sobbed on the ground as she attempted to crawl forward. Even when she tried to lay her right leg on top of the left, so it didn't drag across the floor of the cave, the pain still pierced her. It was only a few feet until she gave up, quivering from the cold with her ankle twisted beyond repair.

All the books Saga made her read didn't tell her how to survive in a situation such as this. Little girls had no place in the forest, especially Direwood. Even the bravest men didn't come back alive from the hunt, and now she started to understand why. For the first time in her life, Frigg was alone.

The creature that enthralled her for most of her life was just as terrifying as Saga and her father described. They had tried to warn her. They told her they were vile and evil, yet she always had a great feeling of wonder about them that she couldn't shake. Now when she stood before it, she lost all childhood fascination.

She could feel the steps of the giant before she heard them. She drifted back, making sure to keep off her right ankle as she did. Its form came through the mouth of the cave, and she saw something in its hands. The giant ducked its head down as it stepped toward her. She wanted to crawl as far back into the corner of the cave as she could, but she couldn't move because her ankle throbbed. She could only sit and await the fate the giant had in store for her. She closed her eyes and concentrated on trying to get her body to stop shaking.

Something struck the ground next to her, and she reluctantly opened her eyes. A black mass of something lay next to her, and, out of instinct, she reached her hand out and touched it. The rough surface of branches and sticks brushed against her palm.

At first, she didn't understand their purpose, but then she remembered the giant's resting place. It was trying to give her a place to sleep. *Does it expect me to find comfort from branches?* Then again, it was a beast from Direwood; what would a giant know of luxuries?

A horrible stench filled the cave. Then the giant dropped a dead deer with its antlers snapped from its head and its tongue hanging from its mouth. Frigg looked up at the giant, and it motioned with its head at her and then toward the deer. Frigg could swear it wanted her to eat it. *Why would it feed me?* She wondered.

"I'm not eating that," she said, still in shock at the corpse before her. He grunted and even nudged the deer closer with his foot. "I'm not eating that!"

Her raised tone echoed throughout the cave, and she saw the giant's eyes widen. For a moment, she thought she saw fear in them. *Does it fear me? No.* Frigg shook her head. She must have been mistaken.

The giant creased its forehead and squinted its eyes as it lowered its head until it was almost directly in front of her face. She could reach out and touch the enlarged tooth if she wanted, and, unfortunately, she got a hint of its breath. She had to turn her head away before she vomited. The taste of bile briefly rose to the back of her throat.

The giant snorted at her and sniffed in her direction. Frigg turned her head and closed her eyes, each hot breath coating the side of her face and neck. Then the horrible smells of both its breath and the deer were gone. She opened her eyes and watched the giant return to the corner of the cave. She saw its mouth rotating around while it chewed on the deer.

Even the sounds it made while eating turned her stomach—the sickening snap of bones and the chomping of flesh.

She curled into the branches. It wasn't much of a comfort, but it was better than stone. She stared at her captor, afraid to even blink.

She would never look away. She didn't care if she had to stay awake for days. Her plan would take hold once the giant closed its eyes and drifted to sleep. Even giants slept…or so she hoped.

A small explosion came from the direction of the giant—a series of pops and finally one, loud detonation. Then there came a smelly fog, one far more lethal than both the giant's breath and the dead deer. The vile creature had passed gas, and she had to hold her breath and turn her head. If it didn't plan on eating her, it was certainly trying to kill her with the unpleasant odor. Her hands clasped over her face, and she took in small breaths, trying to spare her nostrils from the unbearable stench.

Tears filled in her eyes. She didn't want to spend another moment in this cave, but what other choice did she have? The sounds of the rain from outside once brought her comfort when she slept in Southrend, but it reminded her that now she was stuck in this cavern with a monster. She could try to escape in the pouring rain, but there was no point in getting soaked and freezing to death. Frigg had no clear answer on what to do, so she waited and hoped one would come to her.

CHAPTER FOURTEEN

The giant's snoring awakened Frigg late in the night. She couldn't recall falling asleep. The broken branches of her bed poked at her and jabbed into her flesh. Her dress was still soaked from the rain, and her fingers and toes felt numb. She rolled in the sticks and winced from the gash on her forearm and the twist in her ankle.

Her captor snored away, and the sound echoed inside the small cave. The giant leaned into the stone with his head resting on a rock. The exhales of its snores pierced the air, and she covered her ears to stop her head from trembling.

She remembered her plan; the time was now or never. Beyond the sound of the giant, lay the quiet and still night of the forest. Sometime in the middle of the night, it had stopped raining. This was the best time to escape.

When she tried to stand, a sharp pain shot through her ankle. She would have to try and ignore the pain, but it was worth it if she could get away from this monster. Her first step softly echoed throughout the cave. Her head snapped toward the giant, but it didn't flinch. It laid there, unconscious, making enough noise to be heard back in Southrend. To be safe, she paced herself toward the mouth of the cave. The feel of the grass under her feet once she left the cave helped her relax a little. The moon peaked through the thick trees and reflected light on a creek not far away. Her throat felt parched, so she decided to quickly quench her thirst.

A little drink wouldn't take up much time and, besides, she needed it. She stumbled over the larger rocks as she reached the creek. She lied down and scooped her hand in the water, taking one handful after another. The water felt chilly and smooth as it went down her throat. She gasped from drinking so much and rose back to her feet.

The clouds in the sky opened, just for a moment, and she saw the Gods' Hammer. She thought of Tadeas and what he said to her. Then she remembered, *it points to the north.* She turned in the complete opposite direction and looked to the trees that stood before her. She couldn't see anything beyond them, just the shadows of the forest, but she knew this was her path home.

The pain in her ankle seemed to worsen with each step. She gasped when she took one wrong step and put too much pressure on it. It echoed in the quiet night, and she anxiously looked to the mouth of the cave. She heard movement from inside, and her stomach dropped. In a panic, she turned back toward the trees and tried to pick up her pace. A stomping behind her shook the ground. Suddenly, her legs kicked helplessly in the air. The giant caught her by the back of her dress with just two fingers, and all it did was take two steps from the mouth of the cave in order to recapture her. She screamed in panic as she felt her body get turned around, and there it was, staring directly at her with those silver eyes. It grunted angrily as it looked at her with its mouth turned into a furious frown, and its eyebrows lowered.

"Put me down!" Frigg yelled as she continued to kick her feet and swing her arms, but the giant was far from her range.

It gently placed her back on the ground. Frigg looked up and screamed at him. "I have to go home! Why don't you understand that? Why won't you let me go?"

Her voice carried to the surrounding forest, echoing and traveling into the night. Before she could say anything else to the giant, she heard wolves howling. Frigg's eyes went wide as she turned toward the dark forest. Glowing red eyes returned her stare.

"Black wolves," she whispered under her breath. Could these be the same ones the Wild Men captured? She remembered what she was told about them; once they have a scent, they crave it.

There had only been two of them in the cage, but now a half dozen growled at her from the forest. Frigg backed up until she nearly tripped over the giant's foot.

The giant brought its hand down and gently pushed Frigg to the side. She didn't understand what it was doing, but she didn't fight it. When she was at a safe distance, it breathed in, took a thunderous step forward, and roared into the forest.

A deep silence momentarily fell over the forest. Then branches and brush began to snap and break. Frigg could hear the wolves whimpering as they quickly ran in the opposite direction of the mighty beast. The giant gave one more roar as it pounded its chest with its fist. The giant took a few shallow breaths and looked at Frigg. For a split second, she thought she saw it smile, but it was too dark to tell.

"It's dangerous in the forest," Frigg said in a low voice. The giant looked down at her and nodded. He motioned with his head for her to return to the cave. "I can't," she complained. She looked down at her ankle. "It still hurts."

The giant reached down with one hand, picked her up, and walked back toward the cave. When they were back inside, it tilted its hand over her makeshift bed until she stepped off.

She grimaced again and sat down. "It really hurts."

It glanced at her foot and slowly reached out one of its massive fingers. Frigg moved her foot away, which made the giant stop and look at her.

"It hurts worse," she said in irritation.

The giant reached into the darkness of the cave before its hand came back toward her. A strange glow emanated from its finger, and she saw the hint of a gooey substance. The giant smeared the foreign medicine on her ankle. She looked up at the ceiling to try and forget the pain, but, as soon as the giant touched her ankle, she gave out a soft cry.

Its enormous finger pressed into her ankle. She wanted to leap back because of the chill. She winced as it covered her ankle with the wet, cold substance. The pain was nearly unbearable, and, out of instinct, she pulled her leg away from the giant's grasp.

After a breathy grunt, the giant grabbed Frigg's leg with its pointer finger and thumb and put pressure on the sprain.

"Will this really help?" Frigg asked.

The giant looked down at her but then returned to working on her ankle. The cave seemed darker, and Frigg assumed clouds in the sky blocked out the moon. She peered out of the mouth of the cave and thought the forest looked especially dark and haunting. The largest and scariest of what lived in the forest was right in front of her, yet she felt safe.

It did save her from the bear, roaring at the animal and scaring it off. The image would certainly stay with her for many years to come. She would also remember the way the wolves cowered in its presence. Though still unsure of the giant's intentions, Frigg felt fairy certain it did not plan on harming her.

She removed the cloth she used to wrap the laceration on her forearm. "Will it heal this?"

The giant carefully inspected the cut. Its fingers gently held her arm and rubbed the substance into the gash. She had to close her eyes and hold her breath, so she didn't scream out. The tear in her skin stung far worse than when the bars ripped it open.

"Mulga."

Frigg's head snapped toward the giant. "Did you say something?"

Its silver eyes locked on her.

"Mulga." This time she saw the giant's lips move.

"Mulga?" Frigg asked.

The giant tapped himself on the chest a few times with his finger. "Mulga."

She couldn't help but smile. "Your name is Mulga?"

He nodded slowly with his fingers still pressed on her forearm.

She pointed at herself and said, "Frigg."

He stared at her for a moment. "Frog?"

"No, not frog, Frigg...Friiiiiigg," she stressed.

"Friiiiiiigg," he repeated.

She rolled her eyes. "No, Frigg."

"Friiiiiiigg," he said again.

"Just Frigg."

"Frog."

She sighed. "Never mind."

He pointed at himself again. "Mulga."

"Yes," she said. "You are Mulga. I am Frigg."

"Friiiiiigg," he said.

"No, just Frigg."

"Just...Frog."

"Frigg!" she heard the echo of her own voice in the cave, and it made her jump.

His eyebrows lowered, and his elongated tooth nearly pressed into his nostril. There were a few howls in the distance because of her outburst, and they frightened her.

She wanted to forget the evils that dwelled in the shadows. She pointed at him. "You, Mulga." She then pointed at herself. "I'm Frigg."

He glanced down at her forearm as he lifted his fingers off the wound. It looked and felt like some kind of sludge or slime. She went to touch it, but a burst of air came from his mouth. She jolted and looked at him. He shook his head slowly.

"I have to stay still in order for it to work? I can't move?" she asked.

Mulga nodded. "Stay. No hurt if stay."

She finally nodded. With the way her ankle felt when she tried to walk, she had no choice but to believe him. If her ankle didn't feel better soon, she would try to find another way to get out.

She leaned against the wall while sitting on her bed of branches and rewrapped her wound. A strong gust of wind brushed through the cave, and her teeth chattered. She closed her eyes and hoped her exhaustion would take over so she could get some rest.

As she sat there and shook from the cold, she felt his finger push her shoulder.

"Why are you poking me?" she asked with chattering teeth.

"Shiny," he said as he looked at her and pointed at her chest.

Frigg looked down at her small ruby necklace. "Yes, that's a necklace. It shines."

His eyes darted back and forth as he looked at her. "You...shake?"

She nodded. "It's because I'm cold."

"Cold?"

"I'm soaked in water, and it's almost winter!" she said.

He didn't seem to understand her words. He dropped down in front of her and sat with one leg crossed on top of the other. "Frog, cold?"

She rolled her eyes when he attempted to say her name. It started to become clear to her that the giant wasn't very smart. Frigg wondered how he learned to speak at all.

"Are you not cold?" she asked.

He shook his head awkwardly. It looked rather funny to her, and she managed a slight laugh. Mulga's eyes got wide, and the edge of his lips raised as if he tried to smile but had forgotten how.

He reached his hand out to her, and she was caught in surprise when he picked her up. He raised her in the air and took his other hand and cupped her once again. This time though, her head stuck outside of his grasp, and the rest of her body was cocooned in his hands. Mulga pulled her closer to his face. He raised his hands to his mouth and took a deep breath. When he exhaled, a gust of warm air filled his cupped hands and even dried off some of her dress. She ignored his horrific breath that leaked its way out of the space between his fingers. He released two more big breaths, and her dress was no longer attached to her skin.

Saga once put one of her dresses near a fire, and the warmth when she put it on afterward felt like the summer sun. His breath nearly did the same, but it stained the fabric with its stench. He gave a final breath before he gently placed her back by the bed of branches.

Miraculously, her entire dress was dry. Her body felt warm, except for her toes and fingertips. They were still numb, so she balled up her fists and hugged herself.

"Warm?" she heard Mulga ask.

She looked up and could only nod. The breeze came through the cave, chilling her once more. He gave her a partial remedy, but she would need a permanent one if she wished to survive.

"It's going to get colder," she said to him as her teeth started to chatter again. "Can I make a fire?"

"Fire?"

It was clear he didn't know what she meant. She got to her feet, limping and looking around the ground of the cave. There were a few stones here and there, and she hoped she could make a spark. She grabbed a few branches from the bed the giant made for her and tried as best she could to make a pile.

She remembered learning to make a fire when she was five; Saga insisted on teaching her because she got sick of having to wake in the middle of the night to do it for her. Even with her hands numb, she struck the rocks together. Mulga grunted, but she didn't pay him much mind. She must have hit the rocks together a dozen or so times and began to lose all hope. Finally, she got a tiny spark, and this made Mulga's head jerk back. Again and again she struck them until the dry branches started to smoke. She blew on the branches and watched the tiny fire spread.

She could almost feel the warmth rush to her face, but then Mulga roared. She didn't understand why, but she quickly crawled backward as his fist came crashing down on the pile and extinguished the flames. She froze with her eyes wide and looked up at him. His silver eyes glimmered in the darkness as he slowly turned away.

"No fire!" he said as he went back to his corner of the cave.

A gust of wind struck her again, and Frigg shivered. She would be lucky not to freeze to death by the end of the night.

CHAPTER FIFTEEN

Frigg woke up warm somehow. She wasn't on the rocky ground or surrounded by branches. She looked around, but it was too dark for her eyes to adjust.

The ground below her shifted, and she jumped up. Light poured down on her, and she looked up into the silver eyes of Mulga. He held her in the palm of his hand with the other hand cradled under it.

"You kept me warm," she realized.

Mulga gently placed her on the ground and stood up. He stepped over her and headed for the entrance of the cave. Frigg watched him go until he reached the mouth and turned around. With a motion of his head, he beckoned for her to follow. Even after he disappeared, Frigg hesitated, unsure of what to do. She looked around at the bones of dead animals; then she decided to follow him.

She got to her feet and realized her ankle felt much better. She tested it by taking a step forward. It still hurt but not as bad as before. She touched the cloth on her forearm and untied it. The laceration had closed, and the skin looked to be healing rapidly.

She glanced back at the mouth of the cave and saw Mulga staring at her. With another motion of his head, he signaled for her to follow. She still needed to limp, but the movement felt less difficult. When she walked outside, the warmth of the sun embraced her.

Mulga knelt near the small lake and scooped water into his mouth with his hand. Frigg knelt beside him and just watched him drink. He stopped when he noticed her staring. He quietly grumbled. Frigg needed to reach in order to get to the water. She felt her leg slip and prepared herself for a fall, but Mulga caught the back of her dress. He motioned for her to get some water.

"Thank you," she said. She scooped the water with her hands and brought it to her mouth.

When she was satisfied, she looked at him and nodded. He pulled her back to level ground and continued to quench his own thirst. She watched as water slid from the sides of his mouth and soaked his chest. He was a bit of a sloppy drinker.

Frigg noticed a jar tied around Mulga's waist near his loincloth. He crossed his legs in front of him. He sat facing her and pointed to the ground.

"Frog, stay," he said.

She rolled her eyes. "It's Frigg."

"Friiiiiiig."

"Just say 'Frog,'" she said and threw her hands up in the air.

"Stay," he repeated.

Mulga reached for the jar around his waist and removed the cork. He reached into the jar with two fingers. When he pulled them out, a black substance covered them. He motioned for her to put out her leg. When she did, he covered her ankle once more using a gentle stroke.

"It feels better," she said to him.

He just looked at her and then back to her foot. Without gesturing, he covered her forearm, too. She figured he was shy with his inability to talk back when she said certain things. Either that, or he didn't know the words.

"How much can you say?" she asked him.

"Say?" he questioned.

Once again, she didn't know if he knew what the word *say* meant. "You can say certain things, but you can't say much. What words do you know?"

He placed the cork back in the jar and stood up without answering her. He walked toward the forest, yet now it didn't look so scary.

Willow trees, devoid of their leaves, lined the majority of the forest. During the day, their shadows didn't conjure false images, and she could walk through them without any fear. Mulga had to walk around them, which helped her keep pace with him, and he always stayed within a few feet of her.

She wished she could ask him questions he understood, but his mind capacity was probably less than hers. They strolled through the forest, though Mulga had to duck every so often so the branches high in the air didn't hit him.

In the brush, hidden bushes with flowers peaked up from the ground. When Frigg walked by them, she caressed them with her hand and inhaled their scent. The ground still shimmered from the rain the night before, and some of it crystalized from the cold. She watched the mist of water cover her hand as she touched each bush.

"In the light, the forest isn't so bad," she told Mulga.

Mulga looked over at her and grunted.

"When it's not dark, it isn't so scary," she clarified. She saw the greens on the trees once again. "Is this your home?"

"Home?"

"Where you live."

"No home," he said.

"How do you not have a home? Isn't the cave your home?"

"No home."

She didn't push the issue. "It's quite lovely in the light."

"Where...you...home?" he asked while brushing a branch away from his head.

"Southrend," she answered. His lips moved as he tried to repeat her words, but she could tell he struggled. "South-rend."

"South...rend," he finally said.

She smiled. "That's right. Now say it together. *Southrend*."

"South...rend...South-rend...Southrend."

Her smiled grew wider. "That's right."

"Where South...rend?"

He may have said it correctly before, but it seemed he still needed time to get it right. She grinned. "To the south."

"South?"

Frigg looked to the sky. The morning sun shone behind her, so she turned left and pointed. "That way."

He tilted his head. "You go home?"

Frigg looked to the thick trees and rocky terrain that stood before her. "It's very far away. Maybe when my ankle feels a little better I could try. That is," she paused, "if I'm allowed."

"Allowed?" he asked.

She stopped and looked up at him. "Why did you take me?"

He rubbed the top of his head with a finger. "Danger here. Frog in danger."

"So you were protecting me?" she asked.

He nodded. "Frog too small. Frog get hurt."

She chuckled lightly. "So you're not holding me prisoner?"

He shook his head. "Go home when feel better."

She laughed in relief. "And here I originally thought you wanted to eat me."

His eyebrows dropped. "Mulga no eat Frog. Frog taste bad."

"I taste bad?"

"Not Frog…men."

Her face crumpled in disgust. "You've actually eaten men before?"

"Try to hurt Mulga."

Her face stayed the same. "I guess I understand, but it's still disgusting."

Mulga nodded as he walked forward. Frigg joined him and thought, *I can leave when I'm better, but where will I go?*

"I'd be better going north to Astongale," she said aloud.

"North?"

Frigg turned right and pointed. "North is that way."

He pointed in the direction they were going. "What…this…way?"

"West," Frigg answered and then pointed behind them as she started to walk again. "East is that way. East is where the sun rises, and west is where it sets. That's how I'm able to remember it."

Mulga walked ahead, but then he struck one of the branches high in the trees and grunted. He placed his hand on his forehead and roared at the branch. With a full swing of his arm, the branch snapped from the tree and fell to the ground.

This outburst of anger concerned Frigg. She took a few steps back. His nostrils flared, and his eyebrows lowered. He looked down at her and slightly relaxed his frown.

She waved him toward her with her hand. He didn't seem to know what she meant, but she waved harder and faster. He finally knelt and lowered his head to her. Frigg touched the side of his face and examined his forehead. "It's not that bad. There was no reason to get so angry."

"Tree hit Mulga," he rumbled.

"No, it didn't. You walked into it."

He shook his head defiantly. "Tree hit Mulga. Mulga hit back."

"You walked into it," she repeated.

She tried to smile, feeling it might sooth him, but he rose up and stared at her. She searched her mind for something to say to break the odd tension but couldn't quite find the words.

Her stomach rumbled, and she rubbed it slowly. Mulga looked at her curiously and grunted.

"I'm hungry," she admitted. "I need food."

"Food!" he said in excitement.

"Don't kill anything," she said in alarm.

He lowered his eyebrows.

"How about fruit? You know, fruit? They're in trees." She pointed to the willows. "Not trees that look like that but different ones."

He scratched the top of his head, but then his eyes lit up. With a swipe of his hand, he picked her up and placed her on his shoulder. She reached out and grabbed the ropes around his neck that held his bone charms.

"Hold on," Mulga told her just as he began to run through the forest. His steps struck the ground in a thunderous rumble, and Frigg heard the birds withdraw from the bushes and trees.

She held onto his necklace with all her strength while the trees in front of them got pushed aside like twigs. Foxes, rabbits, and deer sprinted away from the giant as he rushed between the trees.

Frigg beamed as the trees blurred by. A cliff in the distance grew closer and closer. Frigg thought Mulga would run right into it, but, instead, she felt him lift into the air and grab onto the rock wall.

He grunted with each push, and the wind brushed through her hair as the giant scaled higher and higher. A cliff that would have taken even the best men hours to climb took him only moments. With a final push upward, he jumped and landed on the surface. Mulga gasped for air as he stood at the top. He reached for Frigg and placed her on the ground. She felt dizzy from the journey but also giggled because of how fun it was.

They stood on a large platform between the cliffs. A different kind of forest stretched out before Frigg. The green haven seemed to invite her into its heart. The oaks and maples shook from the wind, but they whispered a melody of comfort with their welcoming breeze. Most of the trees were green, but there were some others colored in deep reds, yellows, and oranges. Fallen leaves covered the ground because of the coming winter.

A small field of flowers blossomed in front of her with a mix of lilies, roses, tulips, and orchids. Most of Direwood was grey, and this array of colors and smells overwhelmed her senses. She slowly walked toward the field, looking back at Mulga like she needed permission.

He simply sat down and watched her. Frigg turned back around and ran as best she could with her ankle through the flowers. She couldn't help but fall to her back and inhale the scent. The intoxicating aromas made her laugh. She sat up and looked at Mulga whose face was still stone and expressionless.

"Well, come on," she called to him.

He snorted and slowly walked forward. "Frog, hungry?"

She was so enthralled by her surroundings she forgot about her hunger. With a jump to her feet, she raced through the field and looked at all the trees. She felt the rumble of Mulga's steps behind her. The cliffs above held several trees, and she managed to spot a few of them with apples. Her eyes lit up with excitement. *Finally, something edible!* Frigg thought. The tree closest to their level sat far above her head. When she stopped, she looked at the giant. Mulga stared up at the apple tree. Even for him, it was hard to reach. Its trunk sat on the edge of the cliff above them, but the rock wall was too smooth for Mulga to climb it. He reached his hand up, but he couldn't quite get to the apples, even when he stood on the tips of his toes. Frigg's stomach rumbled. There was food, something to satisfy her for just a little while, and not even a giant could get to it.

Mulga looked down at her and went to pick her up.

"What are you doing?" she asked while she took a step back.

"Frog, climb?" he said.

"Oh, no. Being on your shoulder or in your hand is one thing, but I'll have to climb the branches to get to the apples," she tried to explain.

He swooped her up into his hand and lifted her up. She held on to his palm while looking up and let out a scream. She felt herself come down a bit.

"Frog climb," he said again.

"I don't like to be in the air."

He scratched the top of his head with a finger. "Frog climb."

"IT'S FRIGG!" she shouted.

Her outburst echoed and made him jolt a little. She realized she upset him. "I'm sorry, but I don't like to be high in the air. It scares me. Like you with the fire."

He grunted and looked around.

"There's no fire. Don't worry."

He still looked around.

"I promise," she said in a soothing voice. "No fire. I'm trying to tell you that I feel the same way about being in the air as you do with fire."

His eyes darted from left to right several times, but then he raised his eyebrows. He scratched the top of his head again, and his bottom lip curled up. "Frog climb."

"I can't climb! I'll fall!" she shouted.

She expected him to get angry, but his eyes set on her with a gentle stare. "Frog fall...Mulga catch."

The very thought of having to climb up the branches horrified her, but there was something familiar in his voice; she felt the same amount of safety she would have if her father had said it. She nodded.

When he reached his hand up as high as he could, she was still a few feet from the closest branch. She breathed slowly to stay calm and stood on both feet. While her legs trembled and her heart beat wildly in her chest, she reached her hand up and touched the branch. She thought she heard it crack.

It's just your imagination, she told herself. Her second hand grabbed the branch, and she hung in the air. It got so quiet she thought Mulga was gone. She looked down to make sure, but his palm was still there.

"Mulga catch," she heard him say again.

She looked back up and saw the next branch not too far away. She pulled her body up and rested for a moment. The next branch was thicker, and the apples dangled in temptation just above it.

She stood up and reached out for it, but, once more, it was out of her grasp. Her upper-body swaying back and forth as she tried to keep balance. *Don't look down*, she thought as her eyes fixed on the fruit above her. She pressed her feet down on the branch again and again. When the momentum of her weight made the branch lift her as high as it would go, she summoned her bravery and jumped up. Her arms wrapped around the next branch. She closed her eyes and prayed to the gods that she wouldn't lose her grip.

Despite her mind telling her otherwise, she looked down and saw Mulga's palm still in position to catch her. She pulled herself up to the thicker branch and reached up for the fruit. With just a small tug, the apple came loose. She grabbed two more apples that hung near the first.

When she looked back down, her head started to spin. Mulga waved her in with his freehand, but, even knowing he would certainly catch her, she still couldn't jump off the branch.

"Mulga catch," she heard him say.

The knot in her stomach faded. She closed her eyes, held on to her apples with both hands, and hopped off the branch. It seemed to take forever, but then she dropped into his palm and opened her eyes.

She thought she saw Mulga smile as he lowered her to the ground. She took a moment to recover.

"Thank you," she finally said.

They walked along the platform looking at the trees. In the distance, she heard the gentle sound of falling water; she knew immediately what it was. She limped forward, anxious to see the waterfall, while Mulga strolled next to her.

She stopped just before a small, rocky surface and searched around to see if she could find an easier path. With her ankle, it was going to be difficult to climb. Luckily, Mulga picked her up, and, with one small step, landed on the rocky surface. He sat down, crossed his legs, and held Frigg in his palms.

She shifted herself and glanced at the waterfall, watching the water crash to the small lake in front of them. The cliffs rose about two hundred feet in the air with moss growing along the stone. She didn't see any caves or caverns.

The mist from the water sprayed all around her and Mulga, creating a small fog. It covered her face whenever the breeze came through. Despite the chill in the air, she found it comforting. She cradled her apples in her hands and placed two of them down. She went to clean off the first apple but realized her dress was dirty. *A little dirt won't hurt*, she thought.

She looked up at Mulga. He appeared captured by the scene in front of them.

"Have you ever been here before?" she asked curiously.

He nodded softly. She recalled the stories her father and Saga told her about his kind. They were gone according to history. He must have been by himself for so very long.

"Do you have any friends?" she asked as she took a large bite of her apple.

Mulga titled his head. "Friends?"

She nodded as she swallowed. "Yes, friends. Someone you talk to."

His eyes moved around in his head. After a long pause, he shook his head. "Mulga has no friends."

That's sad, she thought. "Everyone deserves a friend."

"You have friend?"

Frigg thought for a moment. "Not many," she confessed. "I'm the daughter of a lord. I'm usually in the castle all day and away from the other children. There was this girl, Astrid, who I used to be around all the time a few years ago, but she moved away when her father was called to Ravengale. At the time, she was my best friend."

"Best friend?"

"That's a friend that you like more than all others," Frigg explained.

"What does best friend do?"

Her eyebrows lowered and she looked up at him. She shrugged.

"Nothing important. My father's best friend is the king, and my father told me the king would die for him. So I suppose that your best friend would die for you."

Mulga kept her cupped in his hands as he nodded and managed a small smile. "You Mulga's friend?"

"Sure," Frigg said, feeling a little embarrassed. "We can be friends."

A cardinal swooped in and landed on Mulga's nose. The giant shook his head, but it didn't scare the bird away. He tried to focus on the bird, and his eyes went cross.

Frigg spit the apple from her mouth while laughing uncontrollably. The fierce look she always saw on his face was replaced with the goofiest expression. She laughed so hard she fell back while cradled in his palms.

Mulga watched her. "What does Frigg do?"

She still couldn't stop laughing. The imprint of him cross-eyed stayed in her mind. Her laughter finally died down. "You said my name," she realized.

"Frigg?" As he asked it, he seemed to realize it, as well, and a massive smile engraved on his face.

Frigg giggled. "Yes, Frigg."

"You, Frigg. Me, Mulga."

"Yes, I'm Frigg, and you're Mulga."

His lips parted, and he showed his teeth as he smiled. "Frigg, Mulga, friend."

The cardinal flew off, and Frigg watched it soar into the sky. Mulga's chin trembled a bit when it left.

"What's the matter?"

"Gone," Mulga said.

"Yes, he had to fly away. That's what birds do."

"Mulga like bird," he muttered.

"Well he's not completely gone," she said. "You have the memory of it, right?"

"Memory?"

She tried to think of a way to explain it. "Can you remember the bird? I mean, it was here, and you know what it looks like, right?"

He nodded.

"Well, close your eyes and remember it."

Mulga closed his eyes tightly and then opened them. "No bird."

"No, not here but in your mind. Imagine."

"Imagine?"

"Close your eyes," she said. He did as he was told. "Now think of the bird again, but keep your eyes closed. Remember he landed on your nose. Do you see him?"

After a short while, his snagged tooth rose, and his lips arched upward. "Imagine…"

Frigg smiled, too. "That's because you imagined him. You can always do it long after you've seen him. If you forget, just try to remember the moment."

"Remember…" the word lingered on his lips as he said it. Mulga opened his eyes, and his smile remained.

Frigg finished her first apple and went to take a bite from the other but stopped herself. "I don't mean to be picky, but do you know if there are green apples? They're a little more sour, but I prefer them."

"Green? Apple?"

She held the apple in her palm. "Do you know what this is?"

He frowned and shook his head. Frigg raised the fruit up to him. "This is an apple."

He gently tilted Frigg to his left palm, and then used the fingers of his right hand to take the apple. "Apple?"

"Yes!" she said. "That's an apple, and it's red."

"Red?" he asked.

"The color."

He handed her back the apple. "Red apple."

She smiled up at him. "Yes, that's a red apple."

His snaggletooth rose when his lower jaw embraced the smile that came across his face. Frigg admitted to herself that she found his smile cute. The hideous faces she had seen him create through his fits of anger made her think he could never be anything but ugly. His eyebrows were always lowered, his nostrils flared, and his lips arched downward when she met him. Today, she saw a different, more pleasing side to him.

Her curiosity got the best of her. How could a giant learn to speak some words but not know colors or objects? "Who taught you how to talk?"

His silly smile faded, and she thought she hurt his feelings.

Mulga placed her down on the ground and rose to his feet. He turned away from her and looked up to the cliffs. Beyond them, deep in the distance, was a cluster of mountains.

"Mulga," Frigg gently said.

The sky rumbled. In the distance, Frigg saw grey and black clouds with flashes of lightning. *A storm is coming.*

Mulga turned and picked her up with his hand. He ran toward the edge of the platform.

He leapt over the edge, and they dropped to the ground. Her hands grabbed his choker tighter, and she closed her eyes. Mulga landed hard on the ground below, and Frigg couldn't hold her grip. Her eyes shot open as she started to fall. Mulga managed to reach down and catch her just before she hit the ground. He placed her back up on his shoulder.

"Hold on," he said slowly.

The giant landed on another cliff and scaled it. This didn't look to be the same way they came, and she wondered if he was taking a shortcut back to the cave. She wanted to ask what alarmed him, but she concentrated on holding on, instead.

When they reached the surface, Mulga leaned down and placed his knuckles on the ground. Using his hands, as well as his feet, helped him pick up the pace, and Frigg's eyes filled with tears from the wind as it brushed her face.

He pushed through the forest effortlessly. The next thing Frigg knew, she was in the opening with the lake and his cave. He dropped her gently to the ground and pushed her into the mouth of the cave.

"What is it?" she finally asked.

By now, the grey clouds covered over them, and a loud crack hit the sky. Mulga nearly ran her over getting inside. Frigg stayed at the mouth just as the rain began to fall. She peaked her head into the cave. Mulga's shoulders hunched forward, and his chest heaved. His eyes lowered, and he growled. Another bolt of lightning flashed, and she watched the massive giant race to his corner of the cave.

"Mulga," she called to him. She couldn't see him. She walked around the bones until she saw him curled in his corner. "Mulga, are you afraid?"

The giant stared at her with wide eyes. When the sound of thunder echoed in the cave, he backed away again and sat against the wall.

"Mulga," she called gently.

"Fire, come now," he said.

"Fire?" she asked. "There's no fire that comes from a rain storm."

"Fire come," he repeated.

She sat down next to him. He snarled each time the thunder cracked in the distance.

"There's nothing to worry about," she assured him. She reached forward and gently stroked his hand. His eyes looked to her, and the fear faded. "I won't let anything happen to you."

"Frigg protect Mulga?"

She stifled her laughter at the very idea. "I'll protect you. I won't let the fire get you."

"How?"

She tried to think of something that could comfort him. She stroked the small ruby around her necklace. It gave her an idea. "Do you know what this is?"

"Shiny," he answered.

"Yes, but do you know what it means?"

He shook his head.

"It's a necklace of friendship and protection," she said to him. "It is filled with my friendship and care, so it will protect you."

He lowered his head to get a better look at it. "Small."

"It is small, but its purpose is bigger than you." She smiled up at him. She removed the necklace from around her neck and let the ruby slip off the lace. She then motioned for him to come closer. It took her a few moments, but she finally got the necklace to fit on the choker around his neck. "There, now the thunder can't harm you."

"Mulga safe?"

She nodded. "It'll protect you like it protected me. When I first got it, I didn't think it would work, but it brought me here to you."

Mulga sat back, and the charm touched his flesh. He kept rubbing it with his finger, and a small smile came across his face.

"Mulga stay," he said to her. "Frigg stay?"

"Of course," she replied. *At least for now*, she added to herself.

CHAPTER SIXTEEN

The storm shook through Direwood for hours. Each bolt of lightning startled Mulga, but he kept his finger on the small ruby Frigg gave him, believing in its power. He sat against the wall much like a frightened child would.

As promised, Frigg stayed next to him the whole time and kept him company. She would try to talk to him every now and again, but he only gave one word replies. It was quite clear to Frigg that, as large and strong as he was, he still feared small, insignificant things. She'd known long ago that storms couldn't harm her, and fire could be contained if managed properly. The mystery of his fear stayed in her mind, and she hated that she couldn't help him. She began to understand what he was; he was just as much a child as she was, perhaps even younger considering his inability to comprehend things.

The small hole in the cave's ceiling just above him shone a fleck of light. Frigg touched his foot and looked up. The storm had finally receded. He looked at her, and she gave him a smile.

She stood up, knowing his fear was long gone, but then something caught her eye. In front of Mulga was a wall, away from her view when she was first brought here, shrouded in the darkness because of the storm. It looked to have drawings on it. The pictures by no means were masterpieces that would have awed anyone who looked upon them, but, to Frigg, they were the most beautiful pictures she ever saw. Two large figures stood side by side. One of them wore what she guessed was a crown, while the other looked to be female, carrying a child in her arms.

"Who are they?" Frigg asked as she pointed at the pictures.

Mulga touched the picture with the crown. "Father."

"That's your father?" she asked.

He nodded. "Father...king."

"Your father was a king?"

"Father, king." Mulga's finger brushed across the female figure.

"Who is that?" Frigg asked.

He crossed his arms and rocked them back and forth. "Mulga's mother."

For some reason, Frigg never thought of giants like humans. Even in the stories, she just assumed they existed by some other means.

He touched the female picture again. "Mother."

"You have a mother?" she asked.

His sunken face looked at her, and he shook his head. "Mother gone..."

She wanted to ask how, but she caught herself. If his feelings reflected his expression, she worried it would bring back a horrible memory.

Mulga pointed at his mouth. "Mother help Mulga speak."

Her eyes opened wide. "She's the one who taught you how to speak?"

Mulga nodded. "Mother help speak."

Frigg frowned. "At least you can remember your mother. Mine died giving birth to mw."

"Frigg's mother die?"

Frigg lowered her head. "I don't even know what she looked like."

His hand brushed against his face. "No remember?"

Frigg shook her head.

Mulga rocked his arms back and forth. "Mother hold Mulga."

Frigg smiled. "What else?"

Mulga looked up and tried to say something. Finally, he pushed his lips out.

"She kissed you?" Frigg asked.

Mulga nodded excitingly.

"Well that means she loved you," Frigg said.

Mulga's face went blank, and he opened his mouth. "Mother love Mulga?"

"Of course! That's what mothers do," Frigg said.

"Frigg's mother love Frigg?"

"I think she would have," Frigg whispered. "She didn't get a chance to. Everyone tells me I look like her, but I don't know because I never saw her."

His eyes darted once more as he asked, "Frigg...imagine...mother?"

She couldn't help but smile because he remembered what she taught him. A single tear rolled down her cheek.

"What does Frigg do?" he asked.

"I'm crying," she admitted. "I do it a lot lately. I think this is the first time I did it when I was happy."

"Happy?"

"You remembered what I taught you about remembering," she said. "You're very smart, and what you just said is very sweet."

His hands ran down his face. "Why crying...happy?"

"Well you mostly do it when you're sad."

"Sad?"

"It's the feeling you get when you think about your mother being gone."

He slowly nodded. "Mulga sad when he thinks of mother."

"What do you think of when you remember her holding you?"

Mulga smiled.

"That's happy," she explained.

Mulga looked down at her. "Mulga happy with Frigg."

She couldn't help but chuckle softly as she wiped her eyes. "I'm happy with you, too. Especially since you don't want to eat me."

He grunted and then smiled.

She peered at him and asked, "Did you just laugh?"

Mulga shook his head furiously. She started to giggle again because he didn't want to admit to it. She looked back at the pictures. For the simple minded giant to have drawn them, based on just memories, amazed her. Even Mulga stared at them like the drawings were the true flesh and bone of his parents.

Frigg dusted off her dress. "Come on."

Mulga grumbled and remained still.

"The storm is gone," she said. "We're going to go outside and have fun."

"Fun?" he asked.

"I'll show you," she said.

They left the cave and walked out toward the lake. Frigg walked around and gathered some pebbles while Mulga watched her in wonder from where he sat near the embankment. Frigg picked up two rocks and placed them on top of two small boulders. She walked backward twenty paces and placed the pebbles she had gathered down near her feet.

"Mulga," she called to him with a wave.

He eagerly stood up and went to her. "What Frigg doing?"

She picked up one of the pebbles and showed it to him. "Astrid and I used to play this game in Southrend when we were little. You put a small rock on top of a surface. We used a tree stump, but we'll have to use the boulders." She showed him the pebble. "You take a pebble, toss it, and try to hit the small rock on top of the boulder."

"Why?" he asked.

"Because it's fun," Frigg said as she tossed her pebble but missed the rock. "Now you try."

"Frigg didn't hit," he replied.

"I know. I tried, and now it's your turn. If you hit the rock, that's good. Whoever hits their rock the most, wins."

Mulga lowered his eyebrows. Frigg picked up another pebble and threw it, this time hitting her rock on top of the boulder. Frigg joyfully laughed and looked at Mulga who still didn't seem to understand.

Maybe he's nervous, Frigg thought. She turned and faced the rocks while she spoke to him. "Just pick up one of the pebbles and toss it at your rock."

Mulga shuffled beside her, and Frigg assumed he finally felt comfortable enough to try her game. In a blur, an object hurled toward the boulders, but it wasn't a pebble; it was a boulder twice the size of the ones on which she put the rocks. It crashed into the boulders and reduced them to rubble.

Frigg backed up from the sudden noise and looked over at Mulga. He glanced at her, and exposed his teeth in an effort to smile at her. When the shock of the situation wore off, she couldn't help but laugh.

"I'm not sure you understand the concept," she giggled. "But you did win."

"Mulga win?"

Frigg gave an emphatic nod. "How strong are you?"

Mulga looked around and then finally shrugged.

"Could you crush that rock?" Frigg asked as she pointed at a boulder a few feet away from them.

"Crush?"

"Can you hit the rock and break it?"

Mulga galloped toward the boulder. He raised his fist as high as he could and pounded it into the rock, smashing it into hundreds of pieces. He did it with little effort, and Frigg stood with her mouth dropped.

He gave her that goofy smile again. "Mulga crush."

"You certainly did," she agreed.

Frigg stepped slowly toward the rubble. She picked up what she thought was a small rock, but it turned to dust in her hand. She slapped her hands together and watched the rest of the residue blow into the wind.

"Does it hurt?" she asked.

Mulga shook his head, turned away from her, and walked toward another small boulder. Once again, he raised his hand, and his fist crashed down onto the rock.

She giggled at how easy it was for him, and Mulga slowly made his way back to her. He sat down, legs crossed, and stared at her. "Frigg happy?"

"Very much," she replied. "I'm more impressed than anything else."

She got very serious for a moment and looked at her friend. He tilted his head. A deep knot started in her stomach and spread its way through her entire body. "They won't understand you," she whispered.

"Understand?" he asked.

"All anyone will see is a monster when they look at you," she said.

He raised his eyebrows.

"If anyone finds you, they'll try to hurt you," Frigg realized.

"Hurt Mulga?"

"Yes," she confirmed. "They won't see you the way I do. They won't be your friend. If they know you're here, they'll hunt you down and try to kill you."

"Kill?" he asked the question, but his face seemed to know the word.

"When my ankle feels better, and you show me the way out of here, you must stay here," she begged. "Do not come after me. Stay in the forest in your cave far away from men. You have to promise me."

"Promise?" he asked.

She knew he didn't understand certain words, but this meant life or death. She stood up with her fists clenched. "You can't leave here! Do you understand? All the men you encountered are nothing compared to an army. You may be big, and you may be strong, but you can't survive against thousands of them."

"Men won't hurt Mulga," he said.

She dropped her head. "Men will hurt you."

This time he smiled and motioned for her to come to him. She was hesitant, but he assured her with a second unfathomable wave of his hand. When she walked toward him, he placed her on his shoulder.

"Hold on," he said. "Frigg fall. Mulga catch."

Mulga rushed through the forest once again. Frigg held onto him for her life, yet she enjoyed traveling through the terrain at a rate the fastest warhorse would envy. The pounding of his feet shook her, but her grip tightened like an iron link on a chain.

Frigg smiled as Mulga leapt over rock walls and raced by trees with a single push of his hand. Frigg thought the trees would snap back and knock her from his shoulder, but his speed kept her from any harm. He headed back to the mountains, but, this time, they looked endless and too high for even Mulga to climb. The giant moved like a spider scaling up a wall. His fingers dug into the rock surface, and he propelled himself up while gripping the next portion of the rock ahead of him.

The air got thinner, and Frigg had to take deep breaths. The temperature dropped, and the sun bothered her eyes. She felt light-headed. She felt compelled to call out to Mulga, but she knew the wind was too hard for him to hear her. Besides, it might not have been a good idea to distract him while he scaled up a mountain.

Her grip loosened around him, but she kept hanging on. She closed her eyes and prayed, asking the gods to make the journey end soon so she didn't fall. He said he would catch her, but, at this height, that would be impossible.

When they finally stood on level ground, Frigg stared in admiration at what spread out before them. It was a city, much like Southrend, but this one was erected inside a valley nestled between two mountains high in the heavens of Direwood and far from the sight of men. There stood endless rows of damaged and crumbled pyramids. She could make out statues and pillars still holding up structures. Stone fountains spewed murky water with moss and algae spreading across what were once gardens and prayer altars.

"What is this place?" Frigg murmured.

She turned around and caught Mulga's eyes looking to the vacant city. He walked forward until he stood next to her. "Home."

He said the word with reverence. She gazed at him while he stared at the ruins below. With so much of it covered in plants, she knew it was vacant for quite some time. With cautious steps, she went forward. Each brick in the road leading to this ancient place was massive, and she feared she would fall into one of the small gaps. She carefully leapt over them, but her ankle still stung. After seeing her wince, Mulga picked her up and held her in his palm.

They stopped at a pool just inside of the city. It bubbled with a strange black substance that Frigg recognized as the liquid Mulga placed on her wounds. He went to the jar by his waist and opened it before dipping it into the pool and filling it to the top.

"So this is where you get it," Frigg said.

He placed the cork on top of it. "Help Frigg."

He quickly smiled and headed into the city. The structures grew even larger as Mulga and Frigg approached them. This was a city for giants, Frigg guessed. She was nothing more than the size of an insect compared to it. With the forests being so small for Mulga, she finally saw a place fit for him. The stone seats surrounding the fountains would have been the perfect size for him. The water from the fountains came out stained in a brown residue. Many of the monuments surrounding the fountains looked destroyed. Only the legs of a statue remained of what must have been the body. Even the statues still intact were aged by the nature of the mountains. Rainstorms must have come through and eventually dulled the sculptures from their once beautiful existence.

They walked through what she assumed to be housing areas for the citizens—each house a pyramid-style home. Only a few of them remained while hundreds of others looked destroyed down to their foundations.

"What happened here?" Frigg asked.

"Thunder," Mulga answered.

He seemed to be drawn to something, and, as she turned in his hand and looked out, he walked closer to the largest pyramid inside the city. The base had a squared-off entrance instead of a door. Frigg shrunk in Mulga's palm as they walked into the darkness. When the light of the sun vanished, she could still hear Mulga's footsteps. He suddenly stopped.

"Where are we?" Frigg whispered.

She heard a creaking sound on her left side and then saw a great explosion of light ahead. Mulga pulled down a kind of stone lever that opened up the top of the pyramid. A series of mirrors reflected the sun above them, and it bounced from one bronze shield to another until the entire inside of the pyramid filled with light.

Frigg gasped when she saw the inside—rows of pillars running all in front of them with staircases that led to different sections of the great structure. Dried torches hung near the pillars along with braziers. They were filled with dirt and growing plant life. Frigg felt stuffy, and her nose closed up with dust. Thick cobwebs hung in every corner like cloth covering over the stone.

Mulga walked toward the center of the pyramid. Used candles stood on an altar with dried up dripping wax. In the center of the table, a book sat open to the middle of the pages. A layer of dust covered over the words, but Frigg could still see through to some of the writing.

She looked at Mulga, and he placed her on the table in front of the book. She didn't step on the paper; she feared that even a small step could damage the parchment. Mulga gently pushed her aside, took in a deep breath, and exhaled, making a cloud of dust rise up in front of her. Frigg shielded herself with her hand, sneezed twice, and waited for the dust to dissipate.

She searched the top of the page for a place to start. *"Let this be written in the tongue of humans, so that in times to come they will understand what happened here. King Torvald of the humans has agreed to leave the North World, returning it to its rightful race of the giants. His terms are for us to travel to the Black Mountain and kill Valstrath the Vile, the last known dragon of the world. It is a risk to go after the great creature of the sky. The North World has always belonged to us. It would be much easier to just destroy the humans, but many of my kind believe this is a peaceful resolution. Even if the humans have the capability to only kill one of us, as King of the Giants, I must rely on saving all lives. Six of our greatest and most powerful warriors will go to the Black Mountain and rid the North World of a threat far more dangerous than the humans."*

There was a break in the page, and Frigg walked around the book to get a better look at it. *"It is now the fifth day of the attack on our city. Our six noble fighters did not return in victory. Instead, we have been attacked from the heavens by the children of Valstrath. Valstrath was not the last of the dragons, but his kind run into the hundreds. The storm that has come through Direwood has been raging for five days, and the dragons have been using the climate as a way to stay hidden within the clouds. Along with the rumbling thunder, comes the wrath of their fire from the heavens, destroying our homes and killing many of our kind…"* Frigg gasped as she turned and looked at Mulga. "That's why you're afraid of storms and fire! You think a dragon comes with them and will burn you."

Mulga looked at her. "Frigg know about giants?"

"Just from stories my father told me, but this may help me understand them better than anyone ever has," she said looking back at the book. *"It has been rumored that the dragons are under the control of one of the human kingdoms and have been unleashed only by a ruby that's said to control them…"* her mouth dropped. "Lord Gustav and the ruby he wears!" Frigg exclaimed. "That's why Halvar was able to go to him without being killed. Gustav's ruby controls dragons."

"Dragons," Mulga said with a growl in his voice.

"There's still one left," Frigg said to him. "Before I met you, I was brought to the Black Mountain, and one was there. That's why Gustav is so confident about killing my father and the king. He's going to use the dragon!"

"Dragon," Mulga said again, but the anger faded. "Dragon will hurt Frigg."

"I know," Frigg replied. She looked at her friend. "Gustav has an agreement with the dragon, but I'm not sure what it is."

"Frigg scared?"

She nodded. "I'm very scared. I need to get back to Southrend. There is no more time I can waste. If Halvar lets that dragon out, then my people are in danger."

"Mulga take Frigg home."

"You can't! They won't understand you."

"Frigg Mulga's friend," he said.

Frigg paused. Mulga taking her home would be the safest way. Nothing the world had to offer could harm her while she was with him. He could scare away any creatures and outrun armies if they encountered them. She lowered her head. "You can take me, but, once you do, you have to come back here and never return to Southrend. You come here and stay here forever. No matter what!"

His eyes looked sad, but he submitted with a nod and held out his hand to her. Frigg jumped to his palm, and Mulga turned to walk away. He pushed the stone lever, and darkness returned to the pyramid.

Frigg stared at the ruins of the city as Mulga carried her. If dragons could do this to a city built by giants, what could one do to Southrend? Hundreds of dragons may have wiped out the giants, but they were tall and mighty. A few hundred humans, even thousands with an army, were nothing compared to one mighty dragon—especially the one she encountered.

Mulga stopped at the edge of the mountain and placed Frigg back on his shoulder. He ascended down a little at a time just to be safe. Frigg felt the powerful wind again and kept her eyes on Mulga, so she didn't have to look down. The journey down took much longer. Mulga certainly seemed more confident in climbing up than he did in scaling down. After a short while, the mountain sloped a little, but Mulga remained cautious.

When he placed his foot on one of the rocks, Frigg heard a loud crack. Mulga looked at her in panic. She felt a rush of wind below her and realized they were falling. As she held tightly onto Mulga's choker, Frigg heard him grunt in pain while colliding with the rocks on the way down. With one strike of his body against stone, Frigg lifted in the air and lost grip of the rope. She let out a shriek, and Mulga shift his body in the air, reached out his arms, and cupped her in both hands.

Everything went dark as she spun around inside his hands. When she heard Mulga yell, she stopped caring about her own wellbeing. They finally came to a crashing halt. She rolled forward again with the light of the world returning to her. She was now out of his hands, but she kept going forward. The world was a blur as she tumbled forward. In a panic, she reached her hands out for anything and felt her fingers grasp a vine. Her sudden fall instantly stopped as she hung from the side of a small hill. They crashed close to ground level as she saw the forest ahead of them, and all of her concerns concentrated on the fate of her friend.

She spotted Mulga's motionless body at the bottom of the hill. She let go of her vine and carefully made her way to him. His entire body lay limp; his arms and legs sluggishly hung over the brush. She ran her hands against his body, but at no point did he move or breathe. She gently touched his face, but his eyes remained closed.

CHAPTER SEVENTEEN

Frigg sighed with relief when Mulga finally moved. His eyes opened, and he looked around. His shoulders heaved slowly as he exhaled, making the leaves on the ground shudder and shift.

"Mulga!" she cried to him.

"Frigg fall…"

"And you caught me," she finished for him. "Please just be quiet." Her hands rubbed across his face.

"Frigg hurt," he said to her.

Frigg touched the side of her head and felt a small cut. The blood trailed down her cheek, but the adrenaline from seeing Mulga on his back numbed any pain. "I'm fine. I'm worried about you."

"Mulga strong," he said weakly.

"I know but just stay down for a few moments until I know for sure," she said. He tried to smile but winced instead. "Stay down. Please."

He didn't look very happy about it, but he gave in to her request by relaxing his body. Frigg felt a little better when Mulga wiggled his toes and moved his arms. She prayed it was just a rough fall—that he was only bruised and needed a few moments to recover.

A few branches snapped in the forest next to them. Frigg didn't pay much attention at first, but then the snaps grew louder. Frigg slowly stood up next to her friend and watched three dark forms appear through the brush. With the sun in front of her and the brush very thick, she couldn't quite get a look at them. Several more shadows followed until the trail in front of Frigg was covered in dark shapes. Glowing, red eyes peered out at her as she heard a low growl.

"Black wolves," Frigg whispered. She remembered what Rangvald said to her. Her scent drove the first two insane, and their obsession must have somehow been passed on to the others in the pack they joined.

The largest wolf pushed through the forest and growled. Frigg couldn't move, but when Mulga stood up next to her, she snapped out of the trance. He scowled at the wolves, but she could see his lips trembling.

"Mulga, no. We need to run," Frigg said.

Frigg looked around and realized they were surrounded. With Mulga falling down the mountain, he may have lacked the strength to scale back up.

The black wolves stood a few feet in front of them as they snarled through the drool pouring from their mouths. Frigg worried these wolves combined could put Mulga down in his wounded condition.

Mulga let out a roar like he did the first night when the wolves covered themselves in the darkness of the forests, but these wolves didn't quiver in his presence. They looked fierce. Not even a giant could stop them from getting what they wanted. Frigg stopped counting when she reached twelve; there were just too many of them.

The first of the wolves lunged forward, but Mulga threw a fist and struck it midair. The wolf drifted back beyond all the others and crashed into the ground. Even the sight of one of them beaten didn't stop the wolves. Two of the creatures leapt at Mulga. He threw his fist down, striking the top of the first wolf's head and forcing it to the ground with a thud. The second wolf latched onto Mulga's forearm and bit down. Mulga tossed his arm to the side, and the wolf crashed into the rocks on the mountain. It let out a yelp and fell.

With Mulga distracted, a few of the black wolves headed for Frigg. She drifted back and tripped over her own feet. Three of them sprinted right for her, but Mulga charged in with his shoulder and tackled all three of them. He repeatedly threw his fists while punching the beasts and knocking them away. As each wolf came forward, Mulga released a backhand and a hellacious roar.

The wolves finally hesitated, but their numbers still looked to be countless. Mulga quickly turned around and grabbed Frigg. He lifted her up to the cliffs as high as he could reach and placed her on a platform. "Frigg, run."

Before she could scream at him, three wolves jumped on his back. One of them sank its teeth into Mulga's shoulder. Mulga reached his fist back and punched the wolf, but the other two quickly clamped their jaws into him.

Frigg's eyes filled with tears as more of the wolves attacked. She wanted to stay to make sure he was all right, but Mulga yelled out, "Run!"

Frigg scampered over the rocks behind her. She scaled the side of the mountain and saw the forest up ahead. The sounds of fighting echoed behind her and let her know Mulga still held his own.

When her feet touched the ground of the forest, she picked up the pace. The twist in her ankle still bothered her, but the thought of black wolves helped her ignore the sensation. Tears pressed the sides of her eyes as she ran. She kept going until her body couldn't go any further. She leaned her hand on a large oak to catch her breath and sucked in air to get it back. Her chest burned, and her legs ached.

Behind her, she heard a snap. She scurried around the tree and put her back into it. She heard something behind her sniff the air and then growl. She couldn't contain the shaking in her body, and she felt it rattle against the bark.

The steps seemed to get closer, and she no longer had Mulga to protect her. Suddenly, she felt herself running. The forest flew by her as she ran. The creature behind her kept getting closer until she heard the sounds of breathing next to her. With just a quick glance, Frigg confirmed her worst fear; a black wolf had found her. Out of the corner of her eye, she watched the beast dive in her direction. She found her bravery and ducked at the last moment. The wolf soared over her, and she ran down the slope of the forest. A second wolf came from nowhere, and she darted to the side once more. The wolf pounced on the ground where she once stood, lost its footing, and rolled down the slope.

She couldn't outrun them forever, and she could feel herself losing her breath again. The sweat poured down her face. She could hear the sounds of a river nearby and headed straight for it. Just as she thought she had almost reached the bank, she tripped over her own feet and hit the ground. She rolled over and saw one of the wolves headed straight for her. It bent down and went for her foot, but she pulled her leg away just in time. The beast grabbed the bottom portion of her dress and tugged at it. Her hand desperately searched the ground, and she felt a stick. Gripping it with both hands, she picked it up and swung. The stick struck the massive wolf across the face. Unfortunately, it did little to stop him and only enraged the creature more.

The wolf pounced on her, and she jammed the branch into its mouth before it could bite down. It growled with the stick in its mouth, and its spit oozed onto her face. She could hear the branch breaking from the pressure of the wolf's jaws, and she panicked. The wolf finally bit through the stick, and Frigg rolled to the side just as it tried to lunge on top of her. She kept rolling and let go of one half of the stick. She raised her body up and saw the wolf jump back toward her. Out of instinct, she placed the stick in front of her. The wolf's body covered over her as she heard a sickening yelp. The wolf trembled violently, and then it went still.

Frigg pushed with all her strength to get the creature off of her, but it was too heavy. She squirmed to the side until she was free. Blood soaked into her dress and made the fabric stick to her skin. She still remembered there was one more. At the moment, there was no sign of it, but she couldn't be too careful. She headed toward the river just up ahead, but a recognizable pain soon traveled through her body. The wound on her forearm must have torn open during her struggle with the wolf, and she felt the blood soaking into her wrapping.

A rustling in the woods behind her made her stop. She knew it was the other black wolf, and it was gaining ground on her. To the side of the trail sat a small ditch in the earth. Without so much as a thought, Frigg dove toward it and rolled until she felt her entire body drop into the hole. She immediately felt a crunch at the bottom. A familiar stench stung her nose.

Animal corpse! Her time in Mulga's cave helped her recognize the smell, and now half of her body dripped with blood and rotting flesh. She remembered the black wolves' obsession with her scent. She wondered if she coated herself in the blood, as horrid as the thought was, would it get the creature away from her? With her eyes closed, she rolled the rest of her body over the carcass and nearly threw up from the overwhelming stench.

Just above her, the creature came to a stop. It kicked up dirt as some of it dripped down the ditch. Frigg closed her eyes and could hear the creature sniffing. It softly growled, and she feared her plan had backfired. The sound of its feet picked up again, and she heard it run off. She finally breathed but instantly regretted it because of the smell. She crawled out of the ditch and checked around her to make sure it was safe.

She stumbled forward and headed for the sounds of the river. She couldn't wait to wash off the blood of the animal's remains coating her body. Just up ahead on the trail stood a man. When he turned, she noticed the golden hammer crest on his tabard. Relief came to her while tears swelled in her eyes. It was a warrior from Southrend!

Father? She wondered as she anxiously looked around. He had to be with them somewhere. No warrior of her city would travel this far alone unless her father was behind the journey. She walked slowly at first, but then her speed picked up and turned into a full sprint. She opened her mouth ready to scream out, but something hit her from the side and threw her to the ground.

All the wind inside of her escaped, and she rolled in agony. She thought it might be the other wolf, but she realized the beast would have held onto her with its jaws. She looked up and saw the figure of a man standing over her. The sun shone behind him and blocked her from getting a good look.

"I knew I shouldn't have let Halvar and those fools take you," a familiar voice said. "If it were up to me, you'd be dead already, but Gustav insisted."

He reached down and grabbed her by her dress. Frigg kicked and tried to scream, but he put his hand over her mouth and stopped her. He pulled her up, and Frigg looked straight into the eyes of Rangvald. They were bloodshot and full of rage. A voice called out not far away from them. Rangvald kept her in his arms and hid behind a tree. She could feel his breath on her skin.

"Make a sound, and I'll break your neck," he threatened.

The wolf no longer posed the greatest threat in the forest. Rangvald's deathly grip made her understand how easily he could kill her—a slight pull to the side and she would be gone from this world.

He sniffed the air in disgust. "You stink, girl."

She was still too scared to say anything. Of all the people to find here in Direwood, it had to be the one man who secretly plotted against her father. Rangvald must have joined the party to try to throw them off or personally deal with her when he found her. The brute pulled her away from the tree when Frigg heard someone yell her name deep in the forest, and she wished she could scream back for help.

Rangvald carried her forward, and the calls of her name faded in the distance. She didn't know where he was taking her, but she suspected his intentions weren't to keep her alive. His grip around her felt tight, but she could get an arm out if she really tried. She counted inside of her head, and, when she reached three, she pulled out her arm, threw it back, and connected with his jaw.

Rangvald cursed and dropped her to the ground. Frigg immediately ran forward as her torn shoes touched the rocks and gravel that covered the ground. The sound of Rangvald unsheathing his sword made her pick up her pace, and she jumped through the bushes of the forest. She didn't realize it, but there was a drop in the ground on the other side of the bushes. Because of her small size, she was able to catch herself just in time and continue forward. After several feet, she heard a crash, and she instinctively turned to see Rangvald fall forward and smash his face into the earth. He yelled angrily and tried to get up, but he immediately went to his knee in anguish.

This was her chance to get away from the traitor and find one of the other warriors of her city. She needed to head back toward whomever called her name but make sure she stayed away from any path Rangvald could use. She heard the river and headed for the crashing sounds of water.

Beyond the bank, she spotted a warrior, but he headed away from her.

She thought about yelling out to him, but she didn't want to give away her location. Somewhere within the forest, Rangvald and the wolf still stalked the grounds.

She reached the river and started to cross. With each step, she dropped further in the water, but the center of the river looked shallow enough. Besides, some of the corpse's blood and entrails washed off her body. Her dress gained weight, but she pressed forward while it dragged her down. When she reached the embankment, she ran forward again. Just when she hit a trail, Rangvald emerged behind one of the trees and grabbed her by the neck. With little effort, he raised her off her feet and pulled her toward him. Blood from the open wound on her forearm gushed onto Rangvald's chest armor.

Each breath felt harder to take as his grip got tighter. He pulled her face to his. "Where do you think you're going?"

Frigg stretched out and bit into his cheek. Rangvald roared in pain before she pulled her head back and ripped off a piece of his flesh. The warrior tossed her away, and Frigg hit the ground on her side and violently spat the piece of his cheek. She let out an anguished gasp as she cradled her forearm, but it was drowned out by Rangvald's scream. Frigg tried to stand, but she felt a familiar, sharp pain in her ankle, and she could no longer run. She crawled on the ground, but Rangvald didn't need to go far to reach her.

The warrior's chest heaved in rage. He looked down at her as the side of his face poured with blood. As Frigg desperately crawled away from him, she looked behind her and spotted a tree cave. She knew it would only delay the inevitable, but, if she was going to die, she would make it as hard for him as she could. He seemed to know she couldn't get away from him this time and took short steps. He was a scary site with his face and armor covered in a mix of his and Frigg's blood.

She stuffed herself in the small tree cave and gripped the roots with her hands. Rangvald lifted his sword and gave her a wicked smile. The forest fell deathly silent, but, as Rangvald took a step toward her, a branch snapped. Rangvald paused for a moment and looked to the side of him. His eyes grew wide with fear. Frigg heard a low growl.

The wolf, Frigg realized as she stared at her blood pouring down his chest armor. "Do you know what the good thing about black wolves is?"

Frigg asked.

Rangvald must have realized what Frigg meant as he looked down at his chest in horror. The massive form of the wolf jumped at Rangvald and tackled him to the ground. The vivid sounds of armor denting and the large warrior screaming pierced through the forest. Frigg pulled herself from the cave and limped away. Even as she thought about the horrible things Rangvald wanted to do to her, she couldn't help but feel sorrow over his fate. She could hear the wolf tear through the flesh. Rangvald's screams turned into gurgling, and then there was nothing but a chilling silence.

Frigg couldn't walk any further. She collapsed and sobbed on the ground. A growl echoed close to her right ear. Frigg slowly turned her head and saw the wolf staring right at her with fresh blood dripping from its mouth.

No emotion came to her as the wolf quickly closed the distance between the two of them. Her eyes went dark out of instinct to not see what was about to happen, but an explosion of sand and dead leaves erupted in front of her. She opened her eyes and saw a gigantic fist.

Mulga stood on her side covered in lacerations and soaked in blood. His eyes looked to her, and a smile covered his lips. "Mulga…crush."

She managed a small laugh, but it faded when she saw the anguish in his face. His whole body twisted to the side and collapsed to the ground. Frigg rushed to him and pushed at his head. "Mulga! Mulga, get up!"

She could tell he was breathing as his eyes darted back and forth. He finally managed to smile again.

"Are you all right?" she asked.

"Mulga…fine," he assured her.

She placed her hand on his face and gently stroked it. Mulga exhaled slowly. In the distance, Frigg heard a single voice calling her name once again.

"Frigg!" She recognized it immediately.

"Father…" she said hopefully.

"Frigg!" She knew the voice belonged to her father, and her heart warmed at its sound.

She rose from Mulga and limped out toward the trail. Several hundred feet away she saw her father. His back was turned away from her as he looked in the opposite direction. With everything inside of her, she screamed, "FATHER!"

Damari spun around. When his eyes met hers, he raced down the trail toward her. Frigg limped forward as much as she could, but her ankle wouldn't let her go very far. With thankful tears in her eyes, she dropped to the ground and opened her arms. Damari quickly reached his daughter, picked her up, and hugged her tightly.

"Thank the gods! I never thought I'd hold you again, little love," he said softly. He inspected her and patted her down. "Are you hurt?" She tried to speak through the sobs, but her body just heaved in his arms. Damari saw the gash in her forearm. "What happened?"

"Rangvald," she managed to say.

"Rangvald?" He gasped.

"He betrayed you in Southrend," Frigg told him. She tried to calm herself because she could see the confusion in her father's eyes. "He killed Olaf in the castle and handed me over to the Wild Men. Gustav said he was going to give him Southrend after he killed you."

Damari's eyes narrowed. "Rangvald?"

"Lord Damari!" a voice called in the forest.

"Over here!" Damari yelled. "I'm in the trail. I found her."

Southrend soldiers came through the forest and joined Damari. The heavyset Loke and Brynjar were among them. They all looked tired from running.

"Loke, Brynjar, find the others and have them meet us here," Damari commanded. "We need to get back to Southrend quickly. Gustav has patrols on the road, and we need to leave this place as soon as we can."

"Yes, my lord," they both said before running off.

Damari inspected Frigg again as he brushed the hair from her face. "How did you survive out here all by yourself?"

"Someone helped me," Frigg confessed.

Damari looked confused as Frigg pulled away from her father and then held out her hand to him. He took her hand as she slowly led him away from the trail. The sounds of Mulga's breaths got louder, and Frigg felt her father's hand tighten around her own. He stopped suddenly, but she kept dragging him forward.

"Frigg," he said quietly. "Frigg, slow down. There's something..."

Before Damari could finish his sentence, Frigg pulled him into the opening where Mulga laid on the ground. His intense breathing had formed a tiny hole in the ground near his nose. His shoulders heaved up and down. He tried to move his head when he heard Frigg and Damari come through the brush, but he grimaced when he attempted even the smallest movement.

Frigg's eyes swelled again when she noticed the blood coating his grey skin. The sound of her father unsheathing his sword made her jump and turn.

"Frigg, get away from it," he said sharply.

"No!" Frigg said as she raised her hands in protest. "Don't hurt him."

"Frigg...that's a...that's a..." Damari stammered in disbelief. "That's a giant."

"I know," she whispered. "And he's very hurt."

"I need to kill him then," Damari said taking a step forward.

"NO!" she screamed. Her father stepped back in surprise. "He's my friend."

"Your friend?" He asked as he pointed a finger at Mulga. "That is a monster."

"If he wanted to kill me, he would have done it when he first found me," Frigg said.

"Found you?" Damari asked. "What do you mean?"

Loke, Brynjar, and a group of ten warriors came through the brush and collectively stopped short in disbelief at the sight of Mulga. Frigg positioned herself in front of her friend. One of the warriors raised his bow with an arrow nocked and ready to let loose. Damari's eyes cut the warrior with rage.

"Lower your bow in my daughter's direction before I slice your head off," Damari said while biting down on his teeth.

The warrior lowered his bow. "But my lord...it's..."

"I know what it is!" Damari yelled. The Lord of Southrend turned back to Frigg and slowly approached her. "Frigg, please step away from it."

"He's not going to hurt me," she insisted. "He's my friend. He saved me from the black wolves. Why do you think he's hurt?"

Damari glanced to the dead black wolf not far away. "That was one of them?"

Frigg nodded. "There were twenty or more by the mountain. He fought them off, so I could run away."

"Why would a giant save a little girl?" Loke asked.

"Because he's my friend!" Frigg screamed. A sharp pain ran through her head.

"Frigg..." Damari began. Mulga rolled over on the ground.

Damari and his men backed up with weapons drawn. They gawked at how large the giant was when he slowly got to his feet and his head rose to the tops of the trees. Frigg looked up at her friend and saw his expression. It made her rethink whether or not Mulga would harm her father. His face reminded her of the time when he saved her from the bear. His bottom lip curled up, his eyebrows lowered, and he glared at the men.

Frigg placed her hands out in front of her and bounced them up and down slowly. "Mulga, calm down."

"Men," the giant said in a whisper. The sound of it chilled her to the bone.

"Do you see the one in front of all the others?" Frigg asked softly.

Mulga nodded, and his eyes turned in the direction of Damari.

"That's my father," Frigg replied. "If you hurt him, I will be very upset. I will cry."

Mulga's face lifted from its intensity. "Happy cry?"

Frigg shook her head. "No, sad cry. It will make me feel the way you do when you think about what happened to your mother."

Mulga's eyes widened and his mouth opened. "Mother...burn."

Frigg nodded slowly. "That's how I'll feel."

His eyes darted back and forth, and then he nodded slowly. Behind her, Frigg heard the warriors take a step forward. Mulga's anger returned, and he struck the ground with his fist. Sand exploded in the air, and the ground shook. Each warrior backed away in fear, but Frigg knew Mulga could have hit the ground a lot harder if he wanted.

"Don't startle him," Frigg begged.

She could feel the rising tension in the air. She knew the warriors were afraid. They seemed moments away from attacking her friend simply because he was a giant. Mulga looked ready to defend himself, and the last thing she wanted to see was more bloodshed. Mulga gave a low growl toward them before his eyes rolled into the back of his head, and he collapsed on the ground.

"Mulga!" Frigg yelled.

She ran to him, but her father grabbed her before she could get any closer.

"He's hurt!" Frigg yelled.

"That is not our concern," her father replied as he began to carry her away.

Frigg felt the tears falling from her eyes as Damari's men surrounded the fallen giant. One of them readied a spear as he walked around toward Mulga's head.

"Don't hurt him!" she begged.

"Fall back now!" Damari yelled while he effortlessly tucked Frigg under one arm.

"My lord," Loke began.

"Fall back now!" Damari said again. "We have to get back to the city at once."

The warriors slowly backed away from Mulga. Frigg couldn't tell if he was breathing or not. All she could see was that he lay on the ground with his eyes closed.

"I have to see if he's okay," Frigg cried.

"You're safe," Damari said to her. "And that's all that matters."

CHAPTER EIGHTEEN

Frigg's tears stained her face when she finally stopped shedding them. It had been hours since she last saw Mulga lying motionless in the forest. She had no way of knowing if he was alive or dead. She went numb just to stop the tears from flowing, and, just like with Tadeas, she replaced her sadness with anger to mask how she really felt inside.

The carriage bumped up and down along the road. Frigg's eyes felt like she could sleep for a year, but every few feet the wheels struck a stone. She opened her eyes with every jolt. Damari looked at her with concern while his fingers brushed through her knotted hair. "I think the first thing you need when we get home is a bath."

She still felt angry and sad, but she couldn't fight the smile on her face. She bit down on her lip to conceal it.

"I'm sorry, Frigg," her father whispered. "I have to get you home."

"I need to know if he is safe," she said as her voice cracked. She bit down again. She was tired of crying. She couldn't think about what may have happened to him; she wouldn't be able to contain the sadness.

Damari nodded. "This wouldn't have happened if I kept you better protected."

"You did all you could," she assured him.

"If I had, you wouldn't have been in the hands of that creature."

"He's not a creature. He's my friend."

"Your friend?" Damari asked with a small laugh.

"Yes, he saved me," she said.

"That doesn't matter," Damari insisted. "It may like you, but it also has a hatred for men. I saw it in its eyes."

"He's not an *it*! He's a *he*. He has a name. Mulga."

"Mulga," Damari repeated with a nod. "It's a strong name, a worthy one for what he is, but he is still part of a race that once wanted to destroy us."

"Not him," she insisted. "He would never do that."

Damari sat back and glanced out the slightly open window in the carriage. Frigg heard the men outside chattering indistinctively.

"He saved you from wolves?" Damari asked.

Frigg nodded. "There were so many of them. He fought them off to make sure I was safe. I ran away, but two of them chased me while he fought the others. Then Rangvald tried to capture me. He planned on killing me just before you found me."

"I can't believe I was fooled by him," Damari said with a sigh.

Something had been bothering her since the day she was captured. It ate away at her when she sat freezing in Mulga's cave. "Where were you when I was taken?"

Damari looked sadly at his daughter. "I was charging in with the men in the courtyard. I was nearly inside when they took you away." He leaned forward and exhaled. "I should have known it was Rangvald. We taught him how to get you out in the event of an invasion. If that wolf hadn't gotten to him..."

She could see the rage in his face; it painted his flesh crimson. She reached her hand out and grasped his. "It's okay. I was kept safe."

Damari laid his other hand over hers and squeezed her fingers gently. "I thought I lost you."

She could see the pain on his face. She could only assume his expression mirrored her own. "Do you think he's still alive?"

Damari looked confused for a moment. "Mulga?"

She nodded, afraid of the answer.

He combed his fingers over his face. "I'm not sure, little love. He was wounded pretty badly. He could have bled out..."

She choked back a sob when he spoke, and Damari could see the thought injured her. He simply stroked her face while she held back her emotions. She finally asked, "Why wouldn't you help him?"

"I don't know how to help giants, Frigg. Besides, Gustav and his men were all over the North World trying to reach you before we did," Damari explained. "He could have had over a hundred men out here somewhere, and, if we stopped to help a giant, they could have attacked and captured you again. I was not going to let that happen."

Frigg looked down in shame. Her friend may have been gone, but her father thought beyond her situation to that of the kingdom. She knew he looked out for her safety first.

The threat of Gustav reminded her of something else. "Gustav is a great threat."

Damari nodded. "I know. He is the greatest threat right now."

"No," she said. "There is an even greater threat than him."

"What are you talking about?" Damari asked.

"A dragon," Frigg said. "I saw it with my own eyes when I was brought to the Red Mountain. Halvar spoke with it and even sacrificed a little girl. I watched it burn her alive."

The horrible event flashed in her mind, and she shuddered from the vivid memory. Damari's lips twitched in an attempt to say something, but he seemed to choke on the words. He sat across from her making noises that never conjured a sentence. He finally swallowed. "A dragon?"

Frigg nodded. "It was terrible."

Damari leaned forward and grabbed her by the hands. "Listen to me and listen carefully. Watch your words. Giants are one thing, but dragons..."

"Father, it's true!"

Her father opened his mouth to say something, but a call from outside the carriage interrupted him. "My lord!"

Damari moved inside the carriage and kicked the side door open. "Stay here, Frigg."

She didn't even hesitate to ignore his command. She was right behind him as she dropped to the hard ground with a wince.

One of the warriors at the head of the party tried to contain his horse and stop it from bucking him. Ahead on the road stood a valley with a towering rock wall on each side. Damari made his way to the warrior. He glanced behind him at Frigg every few steps. His angered glare silently reprimanded her for following him.

"What is it?" Damari asked.

"The valley up ahead is the quickest route, but I fear it will also make us vulnerable to an attack if Gustav knows we're traveling back."

"We did spot a few of his scouts on our way to Direwood," Brynjar said. "We haven't seen any signs of them since we've headed back, but that doesn't mean they aren't out there."

Damari took a deep breath. "If we went around, how many days would we lose?"

Brynjar shrugged. "Maybe a half day—could be a full day depending on our pace. We should plan on camping for the night if we travel this way once we reach the forest. We don't have much daylight."

Damari looked dead ahead at the valley entrance. "There are only fourteen of us, and we're no army. We should be able to get through quickly. We can't lose any time if Gustav plans to attack Southrend within the week."

Brynjar bowed his head. "Of course, my lord."

Damari turned and headed back to the carriage. He grabbed Frigg's hand as he walked by her. "I told you to stay in the carriage."

Her head dropped as she walked with him. "I understand what's going on, Father. You can no longer shield me from this."

Damari grunted. "Is that right? To think, I thought I had a few more years of you being innocent and thinking this world was good."

"I've found that it isn't," she replied softly.

The carriage swayed far worse through the valley. It leaned to the right then immediately shifted to the left. Once again, Frigg lost all thoughts of getting any kind of sleep with the rocky ride and her thoughts still dominated by the safety of her friend. Her father sat across from her. His eyes never left hers. Every so often, he would give her a small smile. His face seemed blank and cold, yet his eyes looked gentle and soft. She realized he appreciated her being there. The days she was gone must have been just as harsh on him as they were for her, and she knew the pain he must have gone through.

"You're quiet," Frigg said.

"I'm just thinking," he replied.

"You haven't said anything about the dragon," she realized.

Damari took a deep breath. "Do you really think you saw a dragon? I mean, the dragons have been gone for many years."

"Same thing with giants," Frigg reminded him.

Damari laughed. "Do you know what the king is going to say when I tell him I saw a giant in Direwood? If it weren't for the other men who were there to witness it, he'd throw me in the dungeons for such madness. And now you also want me to tell him about a dragon that you may or may not have seen?"

"I've seen it," she said in frustration. "With both my eyes, I watched Halvar speak with it, and it spoke back."

"Are you sure you weren't dreaming?" Damari asked.

His tone was back to talking to her like a child, but all it did was fuel her anger. She was about to plead her argument to him, but a disturbing yell echoed outside that gained their attention. Damari's eyes grew twice their normal size. "Stay here! I mean it!"

Frigg worried as her father rushed out the side door of the carriage and took his sword from its scabbard. There was a fight in the air. Frigg felt the same odd feeling she had the night she was captured. A barrage of pounding sounds slammed against the carriage. An arrow broke through the wooden roof and missed her by a few inches. She dropped to the floor and continued to hear the arrows pelt against the carriage. She also heard voices yelling and swords clashing. Screams of agony and gurgling followed shouts of aggression and fury.

Frigg didn't move from her place on the carriage floor. She thought if she blinked it would give away where she was. The arrows hit the carriage less frequently, but she still caught the hint of arrows whistling through the air.

The door to her carriage opened, and a Wild Man peered his head in. His mouth dripped with spit as he hissed at her. She let out a yell just as a sword exploded through the chest of the Wild Man. One of her father's men stood covered in blood and dirt. He reached for Frigg, about to snatch her up, but he was pushed aside by three Wild Men. The carriage door slammed shut and she heard the guard who tried to save her grunt—and then nothing.

The door opened once more, and the first of the three Wild Men reached down to grab Frigg. She kicked and punched with everything she had. She connected a few times but not enough to get him away. Her hands reached up and she grabbed ahold of the one arrow that nearly struck her. With a twist of her wrist, she heard it snap. She jabbed the broken arrow into the side of the head of the Wild Man. When the arrowhead pierced his flesh, he went limp and dropped to the ground.

The second of the Wild Men leapt into the carriage. Frigg kicked him back with her feet, screaming from fear and the pain in her ankle, and crawled to the door on the other side of the carriage. With a desperate push, she felt the door collide with someone. Three more Wild Men waited on the other side, and the closest one reached for her.

She dropped to the ground and rolled under the carriage, barely avoiding the Wild Man's hand grasping for her. She rolled to the back of the carriage and crawled out. She tried to run away, but the stone rocks hurt her feet. She only needed to take one bad step on her damaged ankle before she lost her footing.

She turned to her back and saw the Wild Men coming toward her. Six of them advanced with their weapons covered in blood and ready to take her away once more. She crawled backward for a few feet but knew it was useless. The first of the Wild Men stopped in front of her. He lowered his blade and offered his hand out to her.

Frigg knew better than to trust a Wild Man. Beyond where she sat, she heard the grunting and yelling from the fight. The Wild Men were too many, and her father's guards were too few. Frigg knew the only reasonable thing to do was to give in quietly.

She reached up toward what she thought was her fate, but a thunderous quake in the earth behind her made her pull her hand back. A massive shadow covered over her and blanketed the Wild Men who stood before her. Frigg laughed softly. With a tilt of her head, she saw who she already knew was there. Mulga, still covered in his own blood, took one deep breath and carefully stepped over Frigg. With one quick strike, all six Wild Men crashed into the stone wall on the side of the valley. Their bodies twisted in unnatural directions, and splatters of blood painted the ground.

With her life now safe, Frigg looked and saw several more Wild Men attacking her father and his remaining men. Her heart sank. Before she could say something to Mulga, the giant rushed forward and slammed his fists into the ground with each step.

Mulga grunted loudly. Frigg watched while arrows made their way into his shoulders and arms. At the top of the rock wall, several archers picked off her father's men with their bows, and then turned their aim at Mulga. The giant looked up and gave a loud roar before he leapt to the rock wall. With one quick jump, he stood at the top. He swiped his arm in front of him, and Frigg saw the bodies of Wild Men scatter into the air and crash to the valley below. Mulga even grabbed one archer and tossed him from one side of the wall to the other. A faint sound of agony followed when the body of the archer struck another on the other side. The giant jumped across one side of the wall to the other while grunting and roaring. The limp bodies of Wild Man descended to the ground below.

Damari's small party was dwindling quickly. Another group of Wild Men fought past them and headed her way. She caught a quick glimpse of her father, still fighting amongst the battle. Loke broke from the main fight and hacked at the Wild Men trying to get at her.

A Wild Man struck Loke with a sword across his shoulder, but he ignored the pain and stepped in front of Frigg. He winced when he blocked the attack of another Wild Man. He countered and cut the warrior's throat. Loke, panting from all the fighting, took position in front of Frigg as his sword dripped with blood.

Two more Wild Men approached. The first fell quickly as Loke bested him with his sword. The second attacked just as Loke killed the first, and it amazed Frigg that Loke even blocked the blow. While their swords clashed, Loke reached for a dagger at his waist, removed it, and jabbed it into the neck of the Wild Man.

Loke backtracked his way to Frigg. When he reached her, he turned to prepare for another possible attack.

"You all right, my lady?" he quickly asked.

Frigg could only nod as she looked beyond the warrior to the main confrontation. The carriage blocked some of the fight, but she could still hear the clashing of swords and the grunts from the warriors who wielded them. In the middle of the fray, screams echoed and made Frigg jump. She went to stand, but then a body came hurdling through the air. It fell to the ground several feet beside her with an explosion of blood. She recognized the painting of a Wild Man, and, before the horrible image could burn into her memory, another body headed toward them from the sky.

Mulga slammed into the ground a few feet in front of Loke. The warrior's hands shook while he gripped his sword. He looked up at the giant as he backed away.

"I'm not going to hurt her," Loke gasped. "I'm her friend." Loke looked back at Frigg, and, with a high-pitched voice, said, "Please tell him I'm your friend."

"Mulga," Frigg yelled up to him. "Don't hurt him."

Mulga growled at the frightened warrior, but the sound of running feet forced the giant to turn around. Damari, Brynjar, and one of the remaining party members ran up to them. They all came to a sudden halt when Mulga turned and released a low growl.

"Mulga, no!" Frigg said sternly.

The giant turned his head back to her. His eyebrows lowered and a vein pulsated from his forehead.

"Mulga protect Frigg," Mulga snarled.

Damari walked around the giant to get to Frigg, but kept his eyes on Mulga the entire time. "Mulga doesn't need to protect Frigg."

Mulga grunted at him again. Brynjar and the other warrior readied their weapons. Damari finally took his eyes off of Mulga and looked at Frigg.

"I'm all right," she said.

"No wounds?" Damari asked.

Frigg shook her head. "Mulga and Loke protected me."

Damari gave her a once over anyway. Then he turned back to the giant. Mulga stood still as his chest rose up and down. Damari looked at Brynjar and the other warrior and motioned for them to lower their weapons.

"I don't think that's a good idea, my lord," Brynjar said.

"He could crush us in an instant," Damari admitted. "I don't think making him angry by showing him aggression is such a good idea."

"Mulga like to crush," the giant said.

Brynjar gulped. "I'm sure you're pretty good at that."

Despite the warriors lowering their weapons, Frigg could still feel the tension. It was as thick as when her father and his men first encountered him. Frigg rose from the ground and approached her friend.

"Frigg," her father called.

She held out her hand to him to assure him she would be okay. Mulga's eyes rested on her, and all his aggression and anger seemed to lift.

"They're not going to hurt you," Frigg said to him as gently as she could. Mulga's glance darted to each man. She could still see unrest in his eyes. "These men are trying to protect me."

"Mulga protect Frigg," Mulga repeated. "Bad men hurt Frigg."

"There are no more bad men," Damari interrupted. "I guess we can thank you for that."

"More men will come," Mulga said.

"My lord," Brynjar called. "I'd hate to agree with a giant, but there could still be more of them out there."

"Are you suggesting we listen to this thing?" the other warrior asked.

Now that the mayhem of the battle was over, Frigg took notice of the other warrior. He wasn't wearing the colors of Southrend but, instead, the symbol of Astongale. He looked to be about her father's age. He was a lean warrior with a few scars across his face.

Brynjar glanced at the warrior. "Our whole party was just wiped out by Wild Men, Asger. Do you really think there may not be more of them out there? Or worse, Gustav's forces?"

"So what do you suggest, Brynjar?" Damari asked.

"Take him with us," Brynjar replied.

Asger scoffed. "What would that help?"

Brynjar approached the warrior. "Would you attack a party that included a thirty foot giant?"

Asger couldn't find a reply and simply grunted before he turned around and walked back to the carriage.

"But is he willing to come with us?" Damari asked.

Mulga's expression changed. Frigg knew he understood. Mulga stared at Damari, and the Lord of Southrend looked back, unafraid of the massive giant.

"Frigg," Damari called while his eyes stayed on Mulga. "How well does he understand?"

"Mulga understand," Mulga answered for her.

"Is that right?" Damari took a few steps toward him. "Since you insist on protecting Frigg, will you cooperate with me?"

Mulga looked at Frigg. He seemed confused. Frigg took a step forward. "Do you promise not to hurt my father or his men?"

"Mulga not hurt Frigg's father," Mulga said.

"And his men?" Frigg asked.

Mulga looked at the men in disgust, but then he turned to Frigg with a gentle nod. "Mulga good for Frigg."

"I'm afraid that's not enough," Damari said. "Loke!"

"My lord," Loke answered from behind him.

"Leave the carriage here. It's useless now. You and Asger take the reins and make restraints," Damari commanded. "We'll use it to wrap around the giant's hands, so he can't hurt us."

"He won't hurt you," Frigg promised. "He doesn't need to be tied up."

"Frigg!" Damari snapped. When he realized his tone, he took a breath and gently grasped her shoulder. "What do you think the people of Southrend are going to do if we bring a giant into the city with no restraints?"

She suddenly realized her father's plan. The pit in which Alatrex died so many years ago would soon have a new prisoner.

"No," Frigg quickly said running to Mulga. "You have to go. Leave now!"

Mulga's eyes darted between her and her father. "Mulga protect Frigg."

"You don't need to!" she shouted.

"Frigg?" Mulga asked.

The truth sat ready on her tongue, but she worried about how he'd react if she told him. She knew he wouldn't hurt her, but she wasn't sure about her father and his men. She had an obligation to keep everyone safe.

"You should leave," Frigg said to him. "Please go."

Mulga shook his head. "Mulga stay with Frigg. Keep Frigg safe."

She sighed and looked at her father. Damari wouldn't glance in her direction. She could tell he was ashamed to do so. Surprisingly, Mulga allowed his hands to be tied when Asger and Loke brought over the reins, but Frigg caught a slight smirk on Mulga's face. She knew he could snap them with little effort, and she tried to return his smile. She turned her back to him knowing he wouldn't be smiling if he knew what was in store for him in Southrend.

CHAPTER NINETEEN

Asger and Loke were given the order to pull Mulga while on their horses. Frigg sat with her father on his stallion, and, every so often, she looked back at her friend. Mulga just glanced around the valley with innocent eyes. Frigg wondered if this was the first time he traveled outside of Direwood.

By nightfall, they had left the valley and reached the Red Forest. Home was only half a day away, but Brynjar feared traveling at night could get them ambushed once again. They took refuge near a small rock platform overlooking the river. This allowed Damari's men to see if anyone approached, and they couldn't be attacked from the rear.

When they reached the forest, Mulga needed to duck so he didn't hit the trees. When they stopped, he sat against a rock wall several feet away from their camp with his bound hands in front of him. Loke watched over him from a distance.

Damari walked into the forest and away from the camp. Even after a short while, Frigg began to worry for him. He didn't tell the men where he was going or what he was doing. He simply commanded them to get the camp ready and protect his daughter. Then he left.

Asger angrily tried to get a fire started. He gathered a few logs and dried up brush, so, when he made a spark, it would ignite quickly. Frigg glanced over at Mulga whose eyes stared at Asger. The giant knew what was about to happen, and his eyebrows flared.

Frigg turned back to Asger. "I wouldn't do that if I were you."

"Do what?" Asger asked.

"Mulga doesn't like fire," Frigg replied.

Asger looked at the giant in the short distance and chuckled. "Is that right? Well it's freezing out here and will only get colder as the night goes on. I don't know about you, little girl, but I don't plan on freezing."

"You will address Lady Frigg as, 'my lady,'" Brynjar instructed from behind Asger.

Asger rolled his eyes at Brynjar. He turned back to the logs and scoffed before he continued to try and get a spark. Within a few moments, smoke rose up from the sticks, and the spark ignited some of the dead brush. Then the ground rumbled. Asger quickly stood with his sword drawn and looked out into the darkness.

"Hey! Hey!" Loke's voice yelled from beyond the camp.

Mulga's dark shadow stood over them. He slammed his fists into the campfire and caused an explosion of dirt. Even in the darkness, his snarling teeth showed clearly. "No fire!" The giant said.

Asger fell back from the impact of the giant's hands, and his eyes grew as wide as the valley through which they just traveled. Despite the event, Brynjar didn't move from behind Asger as he smiled like he was impressed with the giant.

"Mulga," Frigg gently called. "Go back near the wall with Loke."

The giant kept his stare on Asger. Mulga's eyes were nearly bloodshot with rage.

"So, what's the plan? Freeze to death?" Asger yelled up to Mulga.

Mulga looked ready to take a step toward the human, but the moment Frigg rose from the ground he came to a halt. "Go back to the wall with Loke," Frigg demanded.

Mulga's aggression faded, and he hung his head. Mulga took the slow steps back to the rock wall, walking by a shocked Loke as he did.

Brynjar motioned with his head for Loke to follow the giant. After a slight hesitation, the chubby warrior did as he was ordered.

Behind them branches snapped with the sound of footsteps. Damari returned from the forest with a pile of logs in his hands. He curiously looked at what should have been the camp fire and saw a small cavity in the ground instead.

"What's the matter?" Damari asked.

"It seems our tall *friend* is afraid of fire," Asger answered in a raised tone as he rolled his eyes.

Frigg laughed nervously. "I did try to warn him."

Damari could see the incensed look in Asger's glare. Her father dropped the logs and dusted off his hands. "I guess that means no fire for the night."

Asger's whole body tightened, and he clenched his fists. "We are to be cold?"

"We'll only be here a few hours," Damari assured him. "By midday tomorrow, we'll be back in Southrend."

"That's not going to stop my fingers from freezing off by morning," Asger complained.

"You should have brought a heavier fur," Brynjar replied while he leaned up against a tree with a piece of bread in his hands.

Asger sneered and walked off into the darkness as he whispered curses to himself.

Brynjar chuckled softly and took a small bite of his bread. When Asger was out of range, Brynjar asked, "Are all the king's men this sensitive about the weather?"

"People from Astongale don't know our storms, our lands, or our weather," Damari reminded him. "I find this weather rather soothing."

"It is a bit chilly," Frigg admitted.

She heard Brynjar's steps behind her. He placed a heavy fur over her shoulders. She already had one of her own, but the chill pierced it.

"I'm fine," she assured him.

"Nonsense, my lady. I see you shaking even now. Give it a few moments, and you'll be warm. You'll also need it to help you sleep through the night," Brynjar told her.

"Brynjar," Damari called. "Make sure Asger doesn't go too far. When you find him, see if you can catch something for the morning."

"You think that giant will allow us to use fire in the morning?" Brynjar asked.

Damari slowly exhaled. "See if you can find anything to at least get us through until tomorrow."

"You have no food?" Brynjar asked.

"I ran out last night. How about you?"

"Just ate my last piece of bread," Brynjar replied.

"Then find something if you can."

Brynjar bowed his head. "Of course, my lord."

Damari built a small tent for Frigg while Brynjar searched for Asger and possibly something for them to eat. She sat across from her father but turned her body to watch Mulga as he sat against the rock wall in the distance. She still felt infuriated about what she assumed her father planned for the giant and hadn't said a word to him since they made camp.

"Frigg," Damari finally said. Her eyes left Mulga for a moment, and she turned back and faced her father. He motioned with his head for her to join him. She kept her gaze on him as she knelt before him. "What are you angry about?"

"You're going to throw him in that pit, aren't you?" Frigg asked.

Damari clicked his tongue. "Do you not know me at all, little love?"

"What do you mean?" Frigg asked.

"That giant of yours got rid of more Wild Men with a brush of his hand than a rank of my finest warriors," Damari reminded her. "All to make sure you were safe. Any man, or creature, who protects you like that will forever be in my debt."

"Then you know that he is good?"

Damari sat back. "It doesn't matter what I know. The people will not understand."

She nodded. "That's what I fear, too."

"Asger has to think I want him captured," Damari said. "He's going to run back to the king and tell him, but, with Gustav's forces coming, Graylyn will not care about a giant right now."

"Will you get in trouble with the king?" she asked.

"You let me worry about that," Damari replied. "Tell your friend, since he insists on waiting until you're safe, once he sees the city he must break his restraints and leave. Will he understand?"

Frigg nodded quickly. Damari leaned forward and motioned for her to go to Mulga. Frigg jumped up and headed in her friend's direction.

Loke stationed himself as far away from the giant as possible. He rose from a kneeling position when Frigg approached.

"My lady," he began.

"Loke!" Damari called from the camp. "Come here."

"But, my lord…"

"Now!" Damari insisted.

Loke took one last look at Frigg before he walked toward the camp. Mulga's head hung down, but he heard her gentle steps and raised his chin. His silver eyes glimmered in the moonlight.

"Frigg look worried," he said.

Frigg knelt in front of him and looked up at her friend. "You can break those ropes at any moment, can't you?"

He gave her that familiar smile as his snagged tooth rose with his lips. "Mulga strong."

She carefully looked at him. "Do you remember what I told you in Direwood? Do you remember me telling you to leave and never come back once I got home?"

Mulga nodded. "Man not understand Mulga."

"Good," she replied. "I don't care what anyone says about you. You're very smart, Mulga."

Mulga nodded emphatically. "Frigg help Mulga be smart."

Frigg smiled. "Then you know that once we get to Southrend, you have to break those ropes and go home."

Mulga shook his head. "Mulga keep Frigg safe."

"I'll be safe once I get to Southrend. I promise," she said.

Mulga lowered his head and grunted. "Mulga stay with Frigg."

She took a few steps closer to him. "Is there something you're not telling me?"

Mulga looked at the sky while she stared up at him. Finally, he shook his head. "Mulga stay with Frigg."

"Why?" Frigg asked. She stepped even closer to him. "Mulga, tell me the truth."

He didn't look at her. His lower lip quivered. It looked like he tried to find the words but couldn't. "Mulga don't understand."

"You don't understand?" Frigg asked, and then she looked into his eyes. The gaze of loneliness was all too familiar to her. She could see it in her own eyes when she looked at her reflection. Mulga was alone most of his life, and, now that he found companionship, he didn't want to let it go. "You don't want to be alone."

Mulga slowly nodded. "Mulga miss Frigg, like Mulga miss bird."

"You'll just have to imagine me," Frigg said. She could feel the tears starting. Even if all went well, she could never see him again. "You want me to be safe, and I will be once I get to Southrend. I want you to be safe, and the only way to do that is to go home."

"Home?"

"Yes, home. Go there and never come back," she begged. "Even if you miss me, you must stay away. You're strong, but you're not strong enough to stop hundreds of men. Do you understand?"

Mulga nodded sadly. "Mulga understand."

Frigg didn't know what other words she could say. She hoped her friend understood the gravity of the situation. She suspected armies and cities were images he couldn't even comprehend.

Frigg sat down on the grass and spun her thumbs around one another. Saga would always reprimand her for the action, but it helped her think. She didn't know what tomorrow would bring. She might make it home, but Gustav and his army planned on destroying her home and killing everyone inside just to gain the crown. The world was far from safe.

She was about to go back to the camp, but then her eyes caught something. In the darkness, Mulga replicated what she was doing with his own thumbs. She couldn't hide the smile. She didn't meet his eyes. She thought if he noticed her staring, he would stop.

Frigg pressed her thumbs together and moved them up and down. In her peripheral vision, she saw Mulga do the same. She held back her laughter and rubbed her thumbs on the sides of her nose. Sure enough, Mulga did it, too. She could no longer contain the laugher and allowed a silent giggle to escape her.

"Frigg," a call came from her rear. Frigg turned to see Asger standing behind her. "Step away from that creature."

"He's my friend," she insisted.

"He's your friend?" Asger asked.

Frigg bit down on her lower lip. "You wouldn't understand."

"The only thing that needs to be understood, little girl, is that creature will die once we reach Southrend," Asger said as he pointed an angry finger at Mulga.

Before Frigg could say anything, Brynjar came up behind Asger, grabbed him by the shoulder, and turned him around. "How many times must I tell you? You will refer to Lady Frigg as *my lady*."

Asger looked ready to reply, but Brynjar's fist struck him in the side of the face. Frigg quickly stood when she saw Brynjar standing over Asger with a clenched fist and hatred in his eyes.

"You little..." Asger began as he rose.

Damari marched over and got between them. "What is the meaning of this?"

Asger took a finger and wiped the blood from the side of his mouth. He chuckled lightly while his eyes burned into Brynjar's. "When we return to Southrend, I will see you whipped for touching a personal bodyguard of the king."

Asger walked away and left Damari alone with Brynjar. Damari didn't seem too angry about his action, but he certainly didn't look ready to condone it, either.

"We should get some rest," Damari suggested. He walked toward Frigg and held out his hand to her to follow him back to camp. Mulga's eyes must have caught his attention, because, when Frigg took her father's thumb, she saw him looking up at Mulga.

"What is it?" Frigg asked.

Damari motioned his head toward Mulga and even allowed a small smile to come to his face. "He doesn't trust me."

Frigg looked back to Mulga and could see an expressionless face on the giant. It was as if he was fixated with Damari.

"I don't think he likes you, my lord," Brynjar said with a laugh.

"It's not that," Damari noted. "It's the same look I would give someone who tried to take Frigg away from me."

CHAPTER TWENTY

Frigg awoke to someone calling her father's name. When her eyes opened, she saw Brynjar standing over her.

"Sorry, my lady," he whispered to Frigg.

"What is it?" Damari asked as he rolled to his back and rubbed his eyes.

Brynjar took a deep breath before speaking. "Asger is missing, along with the horses."

Damari's eyes narrowed. "What do you mean missing?"

"I mean he's not here and neither are the horses," Brynjar said. "Before he left, he told me he was going to look for some food."

"But how are the horses missing?" Damari asked.

"I wanted to check the trails to see if anyone may have followed behind us," Brynjar explained. "When Asger went to look for food, I backtracked from the trail. When I came back, they were gone, and now I woke you to tell you."

Damari lifted his upper body from the ground. "Do you think the Wild Men or Gustav's men killed him?"

Brynjar shook his head. "Hard to say, my lord. If they took him, he must have wandered pretty far."

Damari rose and looked in all directions, as if somehow his glance would find Asger. "Should we look for him?"

"Without the horses?" Brynjar asked.

Damari looked at the tree to which the horses were tied, and Frigg followed his gaze. Sure enough, they were gone.

"You don't think the giant…" Brynjar began.

"My lord!" The familiar panicked cry of Loke came as he ran toward them from the rock wall. "The giant—he's missing!"

Frigg turned quickly and looked to the rock wall where Mulga once sat. All that remained was the outline of his body in the dirt.

"How does a thirty foot giant leave the camp unnoticed?" Damari asked in outrage.

"I was looking for Asger," Brynjar reminded him as he motioned toward Loke. "It was his job to look after the giant."

"I-I-I feel asleep in the night," Loke stammered. "I thought I would hear him get up."

"Do you think the giant took Asger and ate the horses?" Brynjar asked, looking sickened by his own question.

A gentle rumble shook the ground. Frigg stood up and looked in back of her at the trees parting in the distance. She heard Loke, Brynjar, and her father unsheathed their swords, but Frigg already knew it was Mulga. When the closest tree parted, she watched the giant emerge with his hands still tied but cupped together. When he closed the distance between Frigg and himself, Mulga stood over her and opened his hands. Large quantities of fruit spilled out in front of him and fell to the ground.

"Red apple," Mulga said.

Frigg couldn't help but laugh. She turned around and looked at the confused group of men behind her. "You said you were hungry," she told them.

"He brought enough fruit to feed a village," Brynjar said.

"Mulga," Damari called to the giant as he approached him. "Do you know where our horses are?"

Mulga looked at Frigg. It was clear from his expression he didn't understand what Damari asked.

"The creatures that were tied to that tree," Frigg clarified. "Did you see what happened to them?"

Mulga shook his head. "Mulga not hurt creatures."

Damari tightened his body as he turned away from the giant and looked into the forest ahead. "Well, with the horses it wouldn't have been so long, but now we have to walk the rest of the way."

"I'll keep us on a safe path, my lord," Brynjar assured him.

"I know you will, Brynjar." Damari placed his sword back in its scabbard. "Grab what you can for the journey."

Brynjar picked through the fruit and looked for ones that weren't bruised. Frigg shuffled through the pile. Mulga lowered himself and watched her carefully until she grabbed two apples. She looked up to her friend and noticed a glimmer in his eyes while he studied her.

"Thank you, Mulga," she said with a smile.

Loke grabbed the ropes of Mulga's restraints as if he truly held power over the giant. Frigg knew with just a small pull Loke would be launched without a chance to stop it. The chubby warrior's brow dripped with sweat from having the duty of looking over the giant. Before Loke walked forward, Frigg held out her hand to him and motioned for him to stop.

"Mulga," Frigg called to the giant. She held out her hand to him, raising it as high as she could get it. Mulga's eyes darted. Frigg softly nodded to him. Mulga was about to hold out his own hand to her but realized it was much too large. Instead, he used just his pointer finger. He reached out until it touched Frigg's hand. Frigg looked to Loke afterward and said, "Now you try."

Loke's eyes went wide. "Are you crazy?"

"Do it," Frigg insisted.

Loke took the ropes with one hand and raised the other toward Mulga. Mulga slowly reached his pointer finger out and touched Loke's hand.

"Loke's a friend," Frigg said to him. "Loke, friend."

"Yoke, friend," Mulga said.

"It's not Yoke..." Loke began.

"Trust me," Frigg interrupted with a small smile up to Mulga, "Don't try to argue."

"Yoke, fat," Mulga said.

Frigg had to hold in her laughter.

"You're one to talk," Loke replied.

The party set out through the forest and walked through difficult, slim paths filled with hedge plants and ornamental bushes. Even with Frigg being as small as she was, she found it challenging to get through without a thorn sticking her every so often. She glanced back and saw Mulga gingerly taking steps through the path. His head nearly struck the trees, and he had to duck down most of the journey just to get through.

Brynjar traveled ahead of the camp, and, as they emerged into the plains, they saw him standing on top of a hill looking toward them. It wasn't until Frigg and the rest of the party reached him that she realized he wasn't looking at them at all. His sight was beyond them in the horizon to the north.

With a blank expression, Brynjar pointed outward. "They're coming."

Frigg turned to look. Because of her small size, she couldn't see beyond the trees of the forest from which they emerged. Mulga picked her up, and she found herself being raised in the air.

"Frigg!" Damari called in alarm.

Frigg settled on Mulga's shoulder. When she looked down to her father, she noticed his concern for her safety. "I'm fine."

Mulga reached his tied hands out to the distance. "Man coming."

On the horizon, Frigg saw a dark mass starting to fill the landscape. She looked down at her father and asked, "Gustav's men?"

Damari nodded and reached up toward her as if commanding Mulga to put his daughter down. The giant held out his hands in front of his shoulder, and Frigg jumped into his palms. Very slowly, Mulga placed her back down.

"I suspect we have an hour or more ahead of them," Brynjar surmised. "They're in no hurry to reach Southrend."

"We should get moving then," Damari replied as he brushed by Brynjar and started to walk through the plains.

Without any forest or nasty trails to get through, the rest of the journey was only harsh because of the wind. Instead of getting back to the garrison by midday, the high sun started to set in the west, and they would only have light for a few more hours.

A small cluster of trees in the distance gave Frigg hope because she knew just beyond the hills in front of them would be her home. She picked up her pace. At some point, her father would have to release her friend. Though she didn't look forward to the goodbye, it meant she would finally be safe from the world outside her home.

The thoughts of hope nearly slipped away as fast as they came when she remembered the army on the horizon in back of them. She couldn't help but feel concerned about how Mulga would get back to Direwood once her father released him.

When they reached the small cluster of trees, Damari stopped and looked to Loke. "Cut the restraints."

"My lord?" Loke asked.

"You heard your lord," Brynjar said.

Damari looked to Brynjar and nodded his head in thanks. That's when Frigg assumed Brynjar suspected the release of Mulga from the start.

"I only question the command because, if the king finds out, he will not be happy," Loke explained.

"The only ones who know about Mulga are us," Damari reminded Loke. "We tell the king we found Frigg in Direwood and were attacked in the valley just as it happened, but, instead of him coming to our aid, we fought off the ambush and escaped."

Loke took in the story, and, after a few moments, nodded to himself. He removed the sword from his sheath and cut Mulga's restraints.

The ropes hit the ground, and Frigg took two small steps toward her friend. Mulga looked down at her with the same saddened expression that she knew mirrored hers.

Frigg was about to say her goodbyes, but a rumbling sound took over the earth. She looked to the hill that stood before them and Southrend. A cavalry of warriors rode over the hill by the dozens. Each of them was heavily armored, and their faces masked by war-helms. It couldn't have been Gustav; this army arrived from the other direction. The ranks of horsemen rode around the cluster of trees and blocked off the small party from retreating or getting away. Mulga stepped in front of Frigg. He clenched his fists and stood ready to attack the army if they got anywhere near her.

When Damari's small party was completely surrounded, the army of horsemen lowered their lances and slowly rode forward. The leader raised a hand to the others to stop them from coming forward as his horse trotted out toward the party. A second warrior rode closely behind. When the warrior raised the visor in front of his face, Frigg saw it was none other than King Graylyn. The second warrior did the same, revealing the missing Asger.

Graylyn stared speechlessly at the giant. "So, it is true."

"I told you, my king," Asger replied.

Graylyn gave the warrior a sharp look, and Asger's shoulders dropped. The king glanced in Damari's direction as he dismounted his horse.

"What is the meaning of this?" Damari asked.

Graylyn met up with his friend and patted him on the shoulder. "I'm glad you're all right." He then saw Frigg and slowly approached her. Mulga immediately stepped forward. Frigg heard armor clanking together as the king's army advanced. "Do not startle the creature!"

At the king's command, the army stopped, and Graylyn stood bravely in front of the giant. Mulga lowered himself just enough and let out a low-pitched growl.

"Mulga, no," Frigg quickly said.

Graylyn chuckled at the sight. "He seems to be very protective of you."

Frigg's heart sank. Mulga stood surrounded by the very thing that tried to kill him every time it came in contact with him. If the army came after him, death was inevitable, and the fate of her friend unknown. His strength could stop many of them, but there were too many lances aimed in his direction.

Bravely, Graylyn got down on his knees a few feet in front of Frigg. "You look dirty, young lady. No worry. We'll get you cleaned up and in clothes that suit the Lady of Southrend."

Mulga growled once more.

"Mulga," Frigg warned. She looked up at the giant and shook her head.

Damari looked back at the king with his arms stiff and his fists balled. "What is the meaning of this?" The second time Damari addressed the king, Frigg heard hostility in his voice. Graylyn gave Frigg a small smile and turned back around to Damari.

"Asger returned and told me about your discovery," Graylyn replied as he walked back to Damari. The king cautiously glanced back at Mulga. "I have to admit, at first I did not believe him. I thought he was mad, but he assured me of the tale of a giant found in Direwood who fiercely protected your daughter. The scribes will write stories about this for many years, my friend. I can assure you of that."

"I'm not interested in stories," Damari spat. "I want to know why one of your men would run off in the middle of the night. He took our horses and stranded us in the wilderness with Gustav's army on us."

Graylyn turned to the north. The army could not yet be seen from the hills in the distance. "It seems Asger was afraid that at some point you'd let the creature go without informing me. That is another thing he told me which I did not believe." Graylyn stood right in front of Damari and stared at him. "That wasn't going to happen, was it?"

Damari did not make eye contact with the king. Graylyn walked back toward his horse and motioned with his head toward his men. A few of the cavalry shifted, and six men came forward with a long iron chain they struggled to carry.

Frigg's eyes went wide, and she looked up at Mulga. The giant rocked back and forth. His fists came up, and his eyebrows dropped. Frigg watched while his entire body went stiff, and he lowered his shoulders.

"Mulga, no!" Frigg shouted as she backed away from him.

The giant glanced at her and then softened his aggressive stance at her shout toward him. "Man hurt Mulga."

Archers emerged from beyond the cavalry and walked forward with arrows nocked and bows raised in the direction of Mulga. Frigg didn't know how many arrows her friend could handle, but she didn't think he could survive the countless number the king planned to use.

Frigg got as close to Mulga as she could and whispered, "They will kill you. You can't fight them all."

Mulga rocked from one foot to the other. His eyes looked at every archer and warrior who approached. Swords were unsheathed, and the tension of bow strings echoed. Whispers were exchanged between warriors in preparation. Confrontation hung in the air. Frigg feared she would throw up. The tingling of anxiety and fear made her shake. In one last attempt to stop her friend from being harmed, she reached her hand up to him.

"Please." The word came like a soft squeak.

Mulga stood up straight. He snorted and lowered himself to the ground in a kneeling position. He held out both of his hands and put them together. The warriors kept their aim at him with their bows, and those with hand weapons kept their stances like statues ready to attack at the slightest sign of aggression. The cuffs of the chain were crafted from iron, much like a sword. After they went around Mulga's wrists, a spike went through two links in each cuff, clasping them together. Mulga softly growled while one of the warriors chained him, and Frigg could see the man gulping and shaking from having to do the task. He quickly backed away and kept his eyes locked on the giant.

"Bring forth the carriage," commanded Graylyn.

Frigg turned around and looked up at her friend. "If you resist them, you will kill many of my people, and they will eventually kill you. Please, do as they say, and I will do all I can to release you."

"Man not listen to Frigg," Mulga said.

"You have to let me try," Frigg begged.

Mulga grinned. "Frigg protect Mulga?"

She tried to hide her smile. "I'm trying. Please let me try."

His stern expression returned as he nodded. "Mulga trust Frigg."

A carriage with twelve horses came over the hill with a long, empty platform attached to the rear. When the horses were turned back around, the middle of Mulga's chains were attached to a link on the carriage, so the horses could drag the giant forward.

Frigg's stomach was still in knots, but she found comfort seeing Mulga relaxed and not showing any signs of struggle.

Her father grasped her shoulder. "He'll be all right."

With a faint look up at him, she replied, "You don't seem so sure."

Damari looked at her briefly before turning back to the king. "My lord, I request a few horses for my companions and myself. I wish to get my daughter back to the safety of the city as soon as possible."

Graylyn mounted his own steed and looked at Damari for some time before he nodded. He turned to a few of his men and commanded them off their horses with a simple gesture of his head. Three of the king's warriors dismounted and walked the reins of their horses toward Damari, Brynjar, and Loke.

"Frigg!" Damari called.

Frigg stayed in front of Mulga and planned to walk with him the whole time. Mulga jolted forward just as the carriage started toward the city. "Frigg!" Damari called again, this time with a little anger in his voice.

With her head down, she walked to her father and held up her hand. With one quick tug, her father pulled her onto his horse and placed her in front of him. Even as they rode, her eyes stayed fixed on Mulga. She could feel her father picking up the pace, and, if he kept going, they would be ahead of the king's men and out of view of her friend.

"Please slow down," Frigg begged.

Without a word, her father reined in the stallion and kept it at a slow trot.

Brynjar's horse galloped beside them. "What do you think they'll do with him?"

"They'll throw him in the pit, much like the last one," Damari guessed. "That's if he doesn't go wild and try to get free once we reach the city."

"He won't," Frigg assured him. "I asked him not to."

Damari exhaled loudly. "Frigg, your giant has never seen a city before or the amount of people Southrend has. He may get there and feel overwhelmed."

"Should preparations be made?" Brynjar asked.

"Just ride ahead and make sure the warning bell is sounded," Damari said. "I want all our people inside and safe before Gustav arrives. Command our men to take their posts and prepare for war."

Without a word, Brynjar put his heels into his horse and raced forward. Frigg could hear him snapping the reins as his image faded into the distance.

Loke rode his horse beside Damari and kept his eyes on the giant. Even though Mulga walked slowly, his steps still moved faster than the horses dragging him. He looked in all directions at the men surrounding him. For as large and as strong as he was, Frigg still saw fear and anxiousness in his eyes. He looked much like a child—innocent and fearful of the unknown. The thought of him being hurt or hurting her people crept back into her mind.

Frigg looked away from her friend just as they crossed a hill, and she finally saw Southrend in the distance. The chime of the warning bell faintly echoed, but it grew stronger with each stride of the horse. Frigg saw lines of people rushing inside as the guards on the wall assembled. Distant yells were unclear, but she knew the warriors of the city were preparing for battle. Frigg did not know if Brynjar told them about the giant, and the thought of the people seeing him for the first time caused a lump in her throat. She found herself holding her breath.

Hunters returned from the nearby forests, and many stopped in awe to gape at the thirty-foot giant being pulled toward their home. Some ran in panic, yelling a warning the whole way home with just a single word. "Giant!"

"Loke," Damari called.

"Of course, my lord," Loke said as if he already knew the command.

The heavy warrior pushed his horse forward and gained a lead on the party as he approached the front gates.

"Father, what's going to happen?" Frigg asked.

"It'll be all right, Frigg," he father assured her with a distant voice.

He stared at the king, but Graylyn didn't return his look. The front gates of the city stood wide open, and hundreds of warriors, along with commoners, emerged from the city. The soldiers readied their weapons, and the archers on the wall nocked their arrows. Even the commoners held pitchforks and shovels.

The whispers from the approaching crowd grew louder. Their eyes fixated on the creature they never thought existed. Frigg looked back at her friend. Mulga swayed back and forth, and his eyes darted in different directions with each new sound. He first looked to the wall with the archers and then to the front gates with the warriors. His eyes went to Frigg for comfort, but new sounds from the commotion of people took his attention away from her.

Graylyn held out his hand to the rank. He rode forward alone and met the hundreds of soldiers at the front gates. Many of them wore the colors of Southrend, but a mixture of them wore the colors of Astongale.

"Silence!" The king yelled to hush the crowd. "Silence at once!"

Frigg kicked her leg over her father's horse and awkwardly dropped to the ground on her bad ankle. He shouted to her, but she ignored him and went straight to Mulga. The king's guards stood in front of her and blocked her from getting to him.

She stopped in shock and stared into the eyes of the angry and determined soldiers. Mulga grunted behind them, and it made the warriors turn their heads in alarm. They still didn't move, so Frigg thought of the only thing she could do to calm him.

"Be strong, Mulga!" she shouted. "It'll be all right. I promise."

Not even she believed her words, but the giant gave a slight nod.

"The giant will be placed in the pit," Graylyn announced over the noise of the people.

Even the king's command did little to comfort the people. The shouts started once more, and Graylyn looked to the carriage and nodded for the giant to be brought forward. When Mulga moved, hundreds of the occupants of the small garrison suddenly grew silent. The giant stood with his arms chained and a sunken expression on his face. His snagged tooth rose with every soft breath. He had to duck his head to get inside the gate as the crowd muttered insults of disgust and harsh judgment about how hideous he looked. Each new whisper felt like a dagger in Frigg's heart. Not only were they insulting her friend, but it confirmed what she feared most: no one saw him the way she did.

Mulga hesitated. The carriage tugged at the chains, but it was like trying to drag a mountain. Frigg immediately locked eyes with Mulga. She softly nodded to him, hoping he would understand and continue to cooperate, but her expression didn't seem to help him. He looked ready to snap at any moment. His shoulders came forward, and his face tightened. The crowd grew louder. Each new voice added to the chaos and tension in the air.

"You disgusting creature!" Came one shout, followed by an object tossed in Mulga's direction.

The eerie sound of a splat echoed as dirt suddenly covered Mulga's eye. The giant pulled at one of his hands so he could wipe away the mud, and it pulled the carriage backward making the horses neigh in fright. A hushed panic fell over the crowd while Mulga dug his knuckle into his eye to clean the dirt. A moment later, more objects were tossed at him. Rotting food, clumps of mud, soaked rags, and even small rocks made the giant grunt and moan. They had little effect on him physically, but Frigg saw the anger in his face.

A group of guards whipped the horses until they forced Mulga further into the garrison. The crowd was deafening. They shouted every obscenity they could and continued to pelt him with rocks and sticks from the ground.

Frigg tried desperately to rush to her friend, but Brynjar grasped her in his arms and picked her up. She kicked and tried to pull herself from his arms, but he was too strong. She shouted Mulga's name over and over, trying to get his attention, but she was drowned out by the mob of her own people.

As she was carried off, she saw Mulga's head dart in every direction, as if looking for her to see what to do. She could only pray that he would still cooperate, but the crowd kept jeering and mocking him. She remembered what if felt like walking through Gustav's camp when his guards treated her similarly. Frigg's heart broke with each shout, and she could do nothing to help him.

CHAPTER TWENTY-ONE

She wiped away the tears as Brynjar gently placed her on a chair inside the front of the castle, and then stood in front of her breathing heavily. He put his hands on his knees and bent over to catch his breath.

"I know you may be angry with me, my lady, but I needed to get you out of there," Brynjar said.

Frigg quickly rose from the chair. "I need to know if he's all right! I need to know he didn't go crazy!"

Brynjar grasped her by the shoulders as he kneeled down. "Trust me, my lady. If he got angry, we would have heard it by now."

"Please, let me see him," she begged. "I need to see him…"

The front doors of the castle burst open as Damari and Loke entered. Damari looked his daughter over and then glared at Brynjar. "I swear by the gods I am going to kill Asger for what he's done."

Brynjar tilted his head and smirked. "You need only to ask, my lord."

"Not now," Damari replied. "We have other things to worry about. I knew if that giant came into the city that's the reaction the people would have. It's by some miracle that they got him into the pit."

"So he's safe?" Frigg asked.

Damari looked at her and nodded. "For now."

"What does that mean?" she asked.

"Frigg, go take a bath and get dressed," Damari commanded, ignoring her question. He walked by his daughter and headed into the castle.

"What does that mean, *for now?*" She shouted after him as he disappeared into the hall.

"Frigg," Brynjar said to her as he kneeled in front of her once more. "Do as your father says and take a bath. When you're done and dressed, I'll take you to see him."

"I'm not sure Damari…" Loke began.

"I'll handle Damari," Brynjar cut in as he rolled his eyes at Loke. He looked Frigg in the eyes. "Go, my lady. I promise I'll get you to see him."

Frigg took comfort in Brynjar's words and found her way to the bath chamber. A few of the maidens in the house prepared the water. The steam rose high into the ceiling, near scorching, but she knew it would be the only way she could scrub off all the grime. They attempted a conversation with her while she cleansed herself, but she ignored them or gave them one-word answers to their questions.

The once clear and soapy water turned black. The maidens scrubbed every portion of her face and combed through all the knots in her hair. It felt quite painful considering the filth nearly dreadlocked most of her hair. The worst to come off was the blood. A few dry portions clung to her skin. Each time she looked over her body at the blood, another horrible memory surfaced of her time in Direwood. She vividly remembered running through the forest knowing her father was out there somewhere while a traitor and a beast pursued her. She could still hear Rangvald's screams as the wolf devoured him. Her mind brought her back to when the wolf charged her, and she had accepted death until Mulga saved her. The thought of Mulga lingered in her mind until the door to the bath chamber burst open.

Damari stood at the entrance of the door and looked to the maidens. "Is she ready?"

"We got most of it off her, milord," one of them answered.

With his firm expression locked on her, a small smile slowly emerged. "She almost looks like my daughter again." The smile faded, and he looked to the maidens once more. "Finish up in a hurry. I need her."

"Yes, milord," they all said at once.

Three maidens tugged at her hair as they all braided it from different parts of her head. Her forearm was freshly treated and wrapped. A young girl brought in a heavy white dress for Frigg to wear for the evening. The feel of clean clothes against her skin made her shiver. Another maiden quickly wrapped a long white fur with a hood around her. When Frigg stood up, she glanced toward the mirror so she could see herself. Two portions on the top of her head were braided to her scalp and all the way to the back of her head where they connected into a tail. The rest of her hair on the sides and back were combed straight and flowed down to her shoulders. She finally recognized herself again, even if her hair wasn't curly anymore.

She gave all the maidens a quick thank you, knowing they deserved praise for their effort, but her thoughts stayed with Mulga. She hastily headed for the door and opened it to see Brynjar and Loke already waiting for her.

"You look beautiful, my lady," Loke said with a slight bow.

She ignored his admiration. "Take me to see Mulga."

Silence hung over the castle as she walked between the two of them. They passed hundreds of guards stationed all around the castle. Since her return, it seemed her father would not allow an outsider inside without a proper fight.

When she reached the courtyard outside, she heard the shouts in the distance. Her stomach twisted again, fearing the worse. *Did they harm him?* She knew the answer to her question would be found once she reached the pit.

The commoners gathered as close to the entrance of the pit as they could. Soldiers forced the people back with their swords drawn and shouted for the crowd to control itself. Brynjar and Loke pushed people aside so Frigg could get through. Once at the entrance, she could hear the rumble from the pit. Ferocious thuds vibrated the ground as soldiers engulfed the entrance and stood several feet away from the slope to the pit below. She could hear Mulga yelling and roaring. At the edge of the pit, stood Graylyn, Asger, and her father.

"He will stay in the pit until we figure out what to do with him," Graylyn was saying.

"The people are restless," Asger said. "They fear the giant will escape and destroy the entire city. I think we should kill him and be done with it."

"If Alatrex didn't escape that pit, then he won't either," Damari shouted over the noise of Mulga. "He is smaller and nowhere near as powerful."

"You mean to tell me that thing has yet to grow to its full size?" Asger asked.

"He is not a thing!" Frigg said with all the power of her voice.

She gained their attention, and all three men turned in her direction.

"Lady Frigg," Graylyn greeted. "Nice to see you in better condition."

Mulga continued to pound inside the pit. As Frigg got closer, she looked down and immediately saw why he was going wild. All along the path leading to the bottom of the pit were dozens of lit torches.

"Put the torches out," Frigg demanded.

"Excuse me?" Asger asked. "For what purpose?"

"He's afraid of fire and lightning," Frigg reminded him.

Asger scoffed and nearly started laughing. "I forgot. A massive monster afraid of a tiny flame."

"Put the torches out now!" Frigg commanded.

"If it calms the creature..." Graylyn began.

Damari cleared his throat loudly.

"Sorry," Graylyn replied as he looked to Frigg then back to Asger. "If it calms *him* down, do it."

"But if I go down there..." Asger whined.

"For the love of the gods," Brynjar cursed as he headed into the pit and started putting out the torches. Loke eventually joined him. When the two warriors reached the bottom of the pit, the giant roared with such force it vibrated the ground.

In a panic, Loke sprinted up the pit to the top, but Brynjar scaled slowly with no fear of the giant. He waved his hand in front of his face. "His breath is more frightening than his anger."

Ignoring the words of the king and her father, Frigg headed toward the bottom of the pit. Now that the torches were extinguished, she could hardly see Mulga. She recalled the last time she visited the pit and the massive skull of Alatrex hidden in the shadows against the wall.

"Mulga," Frigg called softly.

Mulga's silver eyes glimmered for a moment when he looked in her direction. He was nothing but a black mass, but she could see the comfort in his eyes.

"Frigg?" he asked.

"Yes," she said. "I'm right here. Are you all right?"

He snorted, but his eyes looked above him at the cage covering over the pit. "Man fear Mulga. Man lock Mulga away."

"You're scaring them," Frigg said gently. "And, based on your actions, I do not blame them for fearing you. You have to calm down."

She could sense his rage. His shadowed chest heaved, but she saw him relax a little.

"Frigg protect Mulga?" he asked.

"I will protect you," she promised him.

Mulga looked beyond Frigg as an orange hue crept in Mulga's direction and gave a bit of light to his enraged face. Before Frigg could turn to investigate, a burst of flames ignited on the side of her, and she jumped back. The brazier next to her lit and caused the flames to spread in a circular pattern around the skull of Alatrex.

Immediately she looked to her friend. His eyes grew wide, and he backed away as best he could. The fire was nowhere close to touching him, but he still kept his distance. He raised his bound hands and hid his face from the light.

Graylyn stood near the skull of Alatrex. His eyes locked on Mulga, and he grinned when he saw the giant's fear.

"I told you he was afraid of fire!" Frigg yelled.

"I know, my lady," Graylyn replied. "Finding this creature's weakness is very fortunate for us. Perhaps now he will behave and listen."

"He would have listened to me," Frigg said.

"I'm sorry, Lady Frigg, but I do not have the time to wait," the king told her. Graylyn inched as close to the giant as he could without being in range of getting hit. "Do you understand what I'm saying to you?"

"He understands…"

"Silence!" the king demanded.

Frigg flinched. She was about to say something back to him, but she felt her father's hand on her shoulder.

"I will ask you again, giant. Do you understand me?" Graylyn repeated.

Mulga rose with his lower lip still quivering, but he summoned some courage as he said, "Mulga understand man."

Graylyn nodded. "Good. Now, I will put the flames out, but only if you stop trying to escape. If the flames are put out, and you continue this behavior, then I will ignite them again, and you will see what happened to the last giant we had in this pit. Understood?"

Mulga continued to fight his fear. He lowered his eyebrows, and his top lip curled upward. Despite the aggressive expression, he nodded. "Mulga obey man."

"Asger," Graylyn called.

The king's soldier came down the pit carrying a bucket of water and tossed some of it at the flames. The first splash didn't extinguish it completely, but the second and third attempts returned the pit to darkness.

Even in the shadows, Frigg could see the king's grin as he embraced his psychological victory over the giant.

Graylyn turned and headed back up the pit. Damari gently guided Frigg and made her do the same. Frigg kept looking back at Mulga. She watched him slowly sit down against the back wall and look up into the clear sky.

"Have we heard any word of Hackett and Egil?" Damari asked Graylyn when they reached the top.

"Nothing." The king grimaced. "Gustav is holding most of the North World, so even if I sent word for forces from anyone, he could keep them blocked off and delay them from helping us."

"So, we're on our own?" Damari asked.

Graylyn turned and looked back down the pit at Mulga. "It seems so. Come the morning, Gustav will attack."

"Then we should prepare," Damari stated.

Graylyn softly nodded as he faced the Lord of Southrend. "Give your commands. We'll discuss strategy in your meeting hall."

"Of course, my king," Damari replied with a bow of his head.

Graylyn took one look at Frigg before walking off with his men. Damari exhaled and looked to the bottom of the pit at Mulga.

"What will happen to him?" Frigg asked, fighting the tears in her eyes.

"I'm not sure, little love," Damari told her honestly.

"He will die, won't he?"

Damari looked at her and gently stroked the side of her face. "If I must be honest, I don't know. Your giant is the least of our worries at the moment. Gustav and his army—they are the threat." Her father paused. "I'm sorry, Frigg. I know how much he means to you."

"If you do, then please help him," she begged.

Damari scoffed, but Frigg could tell he wasn't mocking her request. "That will be rather hard to do, but I will try."

Frigg could hear the cage slowly lowering over the pit. "No! Please, let me see him before you close it."

Damari looked at the guards lowering the cage and held out his hand for them to stop. He then looked to Frigg and nodded, permitting her to see her friend before the bars were lowered.

Without a moment's hesitation, she headed back down toward Mulga. Even in the shadows, she saw the defeat in his eyes as he sat against the wall, chains shackled to his hands while he stared up at the stars. Her steps echoed as she scaled down the pit, but he didn't even look in her direction. She could hear his faint breaths. He finally glanced at her but then looked back to the sky. His lips twitched, and his face pulsed. She wanted to explain to him that she didn't know what to do, but she didn't think he would understand. *How will he believe I'm trying to save him when he is in chains?*

"Mulga," she gently called as she reached the bottom. "Are you all right?"

He kept his eyes upward and didn't move.

"I know you're mad at me," she said. "But please talk to me. Talk to me like when we were in your cave in Direwood."

"Mulga not in chains then," he whispered.

"Don't you understand that it needs to be like this until they know what to do with you?" Frigg asked.

He snorted as he leaned off the wall and stood up. "Frigg warned Mulga about men. Said men would kill Mulga."

"I'm trying to make sure that doesn't happen."

"Men fear Mulga," he said. "Men always kill what they fear."

"I won't let them kill you," she insisted.

"Frigg small and weak. Men many and strong," he said. "Men ignore Frigg."

"My father is one of those men. He will listen to me."

"Frigg's father no king." He lifted up his shackled hands and showed Frigg how both chains connected to two boulders on the floor. "Mulga strong but not as strong as chains."

"Even if you escape, they will try to kill you," she tried to explain. "You may kill many of them, but they will eventually defeat you."

Mulga's face dropped. His eyes drifted toward the wall where the skull of Alatrex lay hidden in the darkness. Small flickers of starlight gave a hint of it.

Mulga's restricted hand pointed at the skull. "Mulga's father?"

She could no longer contain the tears. She answered Mulga's question with a shameful nod. "They starved him. He promised to kill every one of my people if he ever got out. They had no choice."

The giant's silver eyes looked to her and then darted back and forth as if he was trying to make sense of what she said. "Mulga to die?"

She feared the answer was yes, but she still wanted to assure him that he was safe. Even for a brute such as Mulga, he seemed to understand. Frigg stared at the ground. "I don't know." Mulga rose slowly and pulled at his chains. Frigg stepped toward him and exclaimed, "Mulga, no! They will kill you!"

"Mulga already dead. Mulga kill men."

"No," she yelled with the tears still coming from her eyes. "One of those men is my father. I won't let you hurt him. The others are my people."

He shook his arms in anger and rattled the massive chains. "They throw things at Mulga! They yell at Mulga! They chain Mulga!"

Frigg did not fear him because she knew his true heart; he would never hurt her. "I told you not to come with me many times. I warned you…" her voice nearly broke. "I will get you out. I will find a way. You have to trust me."

"Mulga get out alone. Frigg can't help."

His angry replies worried her. This wasn't the giant she had grown to love. This was the giant Saga told her about in the stories who destroyed everything in its path. If he kept showing aggression, the king would see him as a threat. Mulga needed to be calm, or they would not see the same kind soul she did.

She finally broke from her sadness and replaced it with anger. "You'll never get out! They held your father in here, and he was bigger than you! He never broke out! How do you expect to?"

"Mulga trusted Frigg." He took a step toward her. The ground rumbled, but the chain restricted him from getting too close. "Frigg said not to harm man, but man chain Mulga. Now, Mulga will die!"

She could no longer mask her sadness with anger as the tears streamed from her face, and she sobbed once more. "You are my friend. I won't let them kill you."

Mulga breathed in and out. He backed away and sat against the wall. He dropped his hands to the ground as the chains fell on the stone. "Mulga has no friends."

The words twisted at her heart. She wiped away the tears that poured from her eyes, turned away, and headed back up the slope. She knew there was only one person to talk to about saving him, and, for once in her life, it wasn't her father.

CHAPTER TWENTY-TWO

Frigg walked quickly through the halls of the castle. She passed dozens of guards bearing the mark of both her father's house and the king's. She caught a few of their glances as she passed by and wondered if they could feel the anger coming off her.

She spotted the meeting hall straight ahead. A rank of twelve guards stood post outside the doors and blocked her from getting inside. She paused and glared at the guard directly in front of her. Then she made sure her eyes looked to every guard, so each soldier could see her conviction.

"I wish to speak to the king," she stated.

The first guard chuckled. Several more joined him in their mockery of her. "Why would a little girl think she could command us?"

Her eyes fixed on the guard who taunted her. He wore the colors of Astongale, of course; her father's men wouldn't dare speak to her that way. "Considering the fact that I will one day rule this kingdom because of my bloodline, I would figure a warrior such as yourself would know that you will one day take commands from me. You may as well learn to respect me now even though I am still a child."

The smiles and glances changed rather quickly. The guard gave a bow of his head. "You're right, milady. I apologize. The king is currently meeting with his advisors. Perhaps it would be best if you came back."

"I want to go inside. Now!" She said it quietly but firmly.

The guard looked taken aback but bowed and said, "I think you'll find the conversation boring, milady. But if you insist…"

He looked to the others and nodded his head. All at once, they moved away from the entrance. The guard reached for the handle and opened the door for Frigg. He gestured with his hand for her to go inside.

Frigg suddenly felt hesitant. She walked forward, but, this time, she didn't have to force her head up as she walked; it came naturally.

Loud voices bombarded her ears almost instantly. The king once again sat in her father's chair while her father and Brynjar stood before him alongside warriors who wore the colors of the king's personal army. They all shouted different strategies toward the king. Each one would talk, finish half a sentence, and then get interrupted by someone else. The fighting against Gustav hadn't even begun, and yet they were verbally going to war with one another.

Frigg stayed against the back wall and paced slowly around the room while she looked at the crowd of shouting men. They reminded her of wild dogs the way they aimlessly barked at one another. Her father remained silent. He seemed to take in all he heard from each man but never gave an opinion.

"If we meet them in the field, we will be slaughtered by their numbers," Brynjar chimed in. "The best we can do is get the war machines ready and pelt them with rock throwers while we stay behind the walls."

"The king's men do not cower behind walls!" Asger shouted. "We meet them in the field, we show them our strength, and we send them to the afterlife."

A roar came from the king's men, but those wearing the golden hammer of Southrend didn't join in the enthusiasm. Frigg saw her father subtly shake his head. His hand came to his chin, and he gently rubbed the recent stubble of facial hair.

"Trying to show them we are stronger will only get us slaughtered," Brynjar argued.

"If you're afraid of war, then perhaps you should stay inside with the women," Asger replied. "As for me and my men, we will face them head on."

"Then you will be the first ones the gods mock once you reach the afterlife," Damari said. The entire room fell silent. Asger lowered his eyebrows in anger, but the Lord of Southrend did not look worried. Damari paced around the men as he continued. "Gustav will laugh at us all if we take him head on. That's what he wants. He wanted me to get angry when he captured my daughter. He figured I would become emotional about the situation and foolishly take him straight on." Damari finally saw Frigg. Instead of getting angry with her for being in a room filled with warriors, he just nodded to her. Damari then turned and faced the warriors again. "I'm ashamed to say it would have worked if she were still in his hands. I would have gathered every warrior in the garrison and marched out to get her back. But what would that have done? It would have left Southrend defenseless. I would have been crushed by his numbers. My daughter would probably be dead, and our king would have lost another ally in the battle against Gustav. If I could finish this war in some kind of fair fight, then I would. I would fight him myself, or have my best one hundred against his best one hundred. That clearly isn't going to happen. He has the numbers. Therefore, we must fight smarter than him."

"So we cower?" Asger asked.

"You may call it cowardice. When the battle ends, and we have won, I shall call it victory," Damari told him.

The room went silent once more. Every warrior seemed in his own thoughts. Even the king sat silently with his head leaning into one of his hands.

"Wait," Asger said. The spoken word almost echoed in the silence. "We're standing here trying to find an advantage against his numbers, and we already have the solution."

"And what would that be?" Graylyn asked.

"We use the giant," Asger recommended. "Tell him we'll give him his freedom if he helps us fight the invaders."

Frigg finally stepped forward from the shadows and announced, "He will not fight for you."

Everyone within the council turned and looked at her. She kept her head up high and looked each of them in the eye as she searched through the room.

"This is a place for men," Asger said when he noticed her. "We are speaking of war. What does a child know of war?"

Her father looked ready to go after the king's loyal warrior, but Frigg stepped forward and said, "I know he will not fight for anyone who placed him in chains."

"Then we kill him," Asger suggested. "Now, leave at once, child!"

"She will one day rule this kingdom," the king spat as he rose. "Or have you forgotten?"

The entire room hushed. The Lord of Southrend glared at Asger. His eyes burned into the side of the warrior's face.

"My king," Asger began, "I didn't mean..."

"Leave me alone with the future queen of the North World," Graylyn said and motioned toward the door.

Each member bowed his head softly to the king and exited the room. Damari stopped just as he turned and looked at Frigg. He softly dropped his head in a nod to her and walked out. She knew it was his way of telling her to be strong.

When the door closed, Frigg felt a slight chill in her body. *Stay strong*, kept going through her head, and the concern of keeping her head up clouded her thoughts. She kept her face stone and showed no emotion in the king's direction.

"It is true that you have no place at this meeting," the king stated as he settled back into her father's chair. "A part of me almost agrees with Asger. You're nothing but a little girl—too young to understand what is going on here."

"I am the last remaining member to have your blood in their veins," she reminded him.

Graylyn nodded. "I'm aware, and you have my sister's spirit."

"I wouldn't know," Frigg admitted. "All I hear are stories. I don't even have an image of her in my mind though nothing would compare."

"Your father loved her dearly," the king told her. "I admit that even as one of my greatest friends, I still didn't think he was worthy of her. In my eyes, no one could be. You'll never understand how it feels to be protective of something so pure and beautiful that it tears at your soul to think about harm coming to them—not even trusting your greatest friend with caring for her because you are the only one who can truly protect her." The king leaned forward. "I couldn't protect her from her fate. What enemy was there to blame when she died? You? You were just an infant—pure and beautiful as she was. However, I admit that I hated you for some time."

"I'm sorry," Frigg whispered.

"There's nothing for which to be sorry," he replied. "Over the years, I learned to accept her fate. That is what a king must do. He makes choices, and he accepts them. I could train with a sword my whole life, but death will eventually find me. There is no magic potion to cure it, no warrior strong enough to fight it, and no army that can hold it back. The only thing we must do is head straight for it, look it in the eyes, and say, 'I do not fear you.'"

"You think I'm brave enough to do that?"

The king grinned. "As I said, you have my sister's spirit. So I know you are."

Frigg couldn't help but look down as she blushed, but she raised her head in strength once more. "There is one death that you can avoid, Uncle."

The king's face sank when she called him that, and his eyes softened when he looked at her. "That's right, I am your uncle. Sometimes you forget your true relationship with someone when they always call you *lord* or *king*. Perhaps that's why so many kings find it easy to make difficult choices."

"Well, you are my uncle."

"I am your king first," he reminded her. His fingers dug into the arms of her father's chair. "I have a feeling I know the death of which you speak. Your giant, is it not?"

Frigg nodded. "I need to know what your plans are for him."

He seemed to force a grin. "And what do you feel would be the right choice?"

"I feel I am unworthy to make that choice."

"Nonsense," he said as he rose. "One day you will rule. That is your birthright. Many times in history children were forced to rule even younger than you."

He stood before her as his shadow covered over her. She gulped. "I would let him go."

"Let him go," he said slowly while he walked toward a table on the side of his chair. A chalice sat on the surface with an empty goblet. He filled the cup to the top with mead and took small sips from it. "Mercy is a good quality. Many of us are born with it in our hearts, but, unfortunately, it can be a terrible flaw when it comes to the safety of so many we rule." The king returned to her father's chair and took a long, slow swig. The drink dripped from his beard when he finished, and he wiped it away with the back of his hand. "Did you ever wonder if perhaps we have been wrong about the giants—that perhaps your giant isn't the last one? Maybe there are other giants out there who are older and remember what humans did to their kind. Perhaps they teach your friend about what happened. Its mind about our kind could change, and it could come back—this time not as your friend."

"He saved my life," she whispered.

The king leaned forward. "Did you ever ask yourself why? You see, you believe it's because it has a good heart, and it's your friend. The gods know I cannot imagine what you went through while in the hands of Gustav. I *can* imagine the terror of almost dying, escaping, and then being in the care of that creature. It must have been a relief to feel you were safe, and that you were not alone. I have another theory—one that will perhaps open your eyes to the truth."

"And what do you think is the truth?"

"It didn't kill you because it didn't understand what you were. It was taught to hate men, but, in its eyes, you were just some weak creature. Let's be clear; the moment it discovers you are a creator of men, it won't hesitate to kill you."

Frigg summoned strength in her voice. "I don't believe that."

"You don't believe because you do not wish to, and you are foolish," Graylyn said, sounding almost gentle. "You're young, my niece, and you still hope the world is not as it is described in legend. You pray the violence and the actions of wicked men are gone, but they are not. You saw with your own eyes what men are capable of when you were outside the protection of those you love. You were spoiled in your upbringing—

an expected way of life considering who your father is. Tell me, after being captured by that traitor, Gustav, do you now realize the world in not a nice place?"

Frigg stepped toward him. "It may not be, but I know there is good in Mulga's heart. If you let him go, you will never see him again."

The king scoffed. "I wish I could believe that. With him out there, there is always a chance he'll come back."

"How can you be so cold-hearted?"

"You think me cold?" he asked. "It's not coldness, Lady Frigg; it's what is best. You want to hear the harsh truth? If Gustav rode to the gates of Southrend with a white flag and asked if I would honor our previous arrangement to marry you, I would be forced to say yes."

"Even after all he's done?"

"There would be severe punishment. That I assure you. The sad truth, the one no one else will tell you, is that it would still be what was best for the kingdom. Being a ruler doesn't mean making the decision that you want to. It means making the choices that are best for the kingdom. If he surrenders now, and gives in to those demands, then thousands of lives would be spared." The king paused. "There will be thousands who die tomorrow, my lady. Fathers who will never hold their wives again or play with their children and young men who have only become warriors will litter the battlefield and never take another breath in this world. These are the harsh realities. If I could stop that by marrying my sister's only daughter to Gustav, as a king, I would be forced to do so."

"But he's a monster."

"A monster who has the largest army in the North World," he reminded her. "Men like him can be useful. They can be controlled if you bribe them properly. A giant on the other hand, well, he will learn one day, whether you want to believe this or not, that our kind is the enemy. He will always see us as a threat because we see him as such."

"Then see him as I do," she begged.

"I do not have that luxury," Graylyn told her. "Your giant will die, Lady Frigg—not because I want it, but because the people will feel safer in a world where they know giants do not exist. Even if I believed as you do that it should live, my choice would remain the same because so many of our people fear its existence. If there's even a chance that it will come back and cause us harm, death is the only choice."

Without another word, Frigg bowed her head to the king and turned around.

"My lady," the king called after her.

Frigg stopped a few feet from the door and turned. "Yes, my king?"

"A true ruler finds something worth fighting for. I congratulate you on finding that."

His words brought her no comfort, and she forced herself to turn from him before he could see the tears about to fall from her eyes. She paused before she reached the door and faced him once more. The king looked at her with curious eyes. She fought for Mulga and it did little to change his mind. *The dragon*, she reminded herself. *Father said not to tell him, but he must be told.*

The door burst open before she could say anything, and Asger and Damari rushed in. Their sudden entrance, and her father's worried look, made her forget anything she was about to tell the king.

"It's Gustav," Asger announced. "He rode here with four of his men and raised a white flag."

Frigg turned back toward the king. It had to be a coincidence. Gustav would never ask for those terms, but the sudden appearance of the Dragon Lord worried her.

Graylyn rose from her father's chair and rushed toward the door. Asger and the king disappeared as Frigg went to follow them. Damari stepped in front of her and stopped her from going forward.

"Where are you going?" Damari asked.

"I'm going out there with you," Frigg replied.

"You most certainly are not," Damari said with a raised tone. "I will not risk your safety around that man."

"I want to look him in the eye and show him I do not fear him," Frigg said.

"I don't care," Damari replied. "You're staying inside."

"I am not!" she shouted.

His eyes narrowed, and he grabbed her by the shoulder. "I am your father. You will do as you are told, and I'm telling you to stay inside."

"And I will not," she said bravely, but her voice nearly cracked from emotion.

"Why are you defying me?" he asked through gritted teeth.

Frigg looked at him carefully. Fighting back the tears, she threw his own words back at him. "The proudest day in a father's life, when it comes to their children, is when they stand up to him."

His infuriated face faded, and he let out a light laugh. "You certainly do have your mother's spirit...as well as her memory."

Her father reached out his hand to her, and Frigg grasped his pinky finger. When they left the castle, Brynjar already had horses prepared for himself and Damari. When he saw Frigg walk out with her father, he looked to the closest stable hand and gestured with his head for the boy to retrieve another horse.

The king sat mounted next to Asger and two of his other soldiers. He stared at Frigg as the stable hand brought out a white mare. Damari went to pick her up, but she held out her hand to stop him. With one swift movement, she was atop her horse and sitting proudly.

"You are joining us?" Graylyn asked her.

Frigg just nodded and kept her head high to show how she wouldn't allow anyone to command her otherwise.

Brynjar winked at her as he mounted his own horse. "After you, my lady."

Graylyn led the way with Asger beside him while Frigg, her father, and Brynjar rode behind them. The gates of Southrend opened slowly. Beyond the darkness outside, Frigg saw two mounted warriors; one held a torch, and the other held up the white flag. Between them could only be one man. As Frigg got closer, Gustav's arrogant grin confirmed her assumption. She found it odd that he lacked his trademark ruby and looked strangely naked without it.

"Well, if it isn't the King of the North World with the Lord of Southrend and my betrothed," Gustav mocked.

"You're no longer betrothed to my daughter," Damari said.

"If it brings you comfort, she will die quickly and by my own hand," Gustav said.

Damari reached for his sword as Graylyn shouted, "That is enough!"

Gustav chuckled at Graylyn and replied, "I haven't even begun."

"I have to admit, Gustav, it was rather clever having your soldiers dress as Wild Men when you abducted my daughter," Damari said.

Gustav laughed once again. "I thought the ruse was rather brilliant myself."

Damari looked to the two mounted warriors and then beyond Gustav. "Is Halvar with you? I wish to meet him in the field once the time comes."

"He couldn't make the battle," Gustav replied. "He has other things that require his attention."

"Such as?" Graylyn asked.

"And spoil the surprise?" Gustav asked as he raised his hands.

"Did you come here for terms or not?" Graylyn asked.

Gustav's face went cold. "There are no terms. I simply wanted to tell you that I grant you one last night of living before I burn this place to the ground. I offer none of your lords, soldiers, or commoners safe passage anywhere. Come the morning, I will attack with my full force and make sure that even the rats infesting this pathetic city are dead." Gustav looked directly at Damari. "And mark my words, Lord of Southrend, you will watch me kill your precious daughter."

Gustav tugged at the reins of his horse and rode away into the darkness. His two men followed behind him. Graylyn gripped his sword and kept his eyes on the horizon.

"I look forward to meeting that man in the field," Graylyn finally spoke.

"That would be a foolish strategy," Damari said.

"And what would you suggest?" Graylyn asked with a whip of his head toward Damari.

"Father," Frigg called gently.

"We stick to the plan," Damari replied, not hearing Frigg.

"Stand back and allow him to crush us?" Graylyn seethed. "By nightfall tomorrow, your city will be dust."

"Father," Frigg called again.

"Not if we anticipate and wait for him to make a mistake," Damari said.

"What mistake?" Gralyn asked. "He has the numbers, and he has the war machines. Nothing will stop him."

"FATHER!" Frigg yelled this time.

"What?" he yelled back. Damari took a breath and looked back at

Frigg. "I'm sorry, what is it?"

"A warrior will throw an ax at an enemy, while a smart warrior will make sure it is sharp and accurate before he throws it," Frigg reminded him.

Everyone looked at her in befuddlement, but it was Damari who eventually smiled. "That's right."

"What does that mean?" Graylyn asked.

"But, Frigg," her father began. "That would mean..."

"I know," Frigg cut in. "But it may be our only chance."

"What are you two talking about?" Graylyn asked.

Damari looked directly at the king. "I think my daughter may have found a way for us to win."

"How?" Graylyn asked.

Frigg smiled. "With the help of Erland and my wits."

CHAPTER TWENTY-THREE

Of all the mornings Frigg awoke in her bed, the day of the battle felt different. A deep tension hung in the air. A chilling silence gave her chest an unsettling feeling, and that all too familiar knot in her stomach had returned. A battle would be fought, and thousands would die to claim the title of King of the North World. It didn't make much sense to her. She thought of it as madness. She may have been a child in the eyes of everyone who looked at her, but even she could see the ignorance of war.

Frigg noticed the white dress hanging in the corner of her room. Her white fur hung behind it. The air had a chilling sting as she rose from her bed, and she knew it would be a cold day.

She would have to take a great risk, but how could she not, knowing the sacrifice that so many others would make? As she dressed, she reflected on her role as the future ruler of this world, and how she needed to make a stand.

When she walked out of her room, a row of guards joined her as she traveled through the halls to leave the castle. Once outside, the cruel chill of the day crept up her entire body. Not even the heavy fur she wore stopped her from shivering—though Frigg was unsure if she shook from the cold or from nerves. Her arms tingled with anxiety, and her throat felt dry. The very thought of the risk she was about to take unsettled her.

The walk to the front gate was long. Frigg passed by hundreds of commoners who whispered to one another—no doubt questioning why an eight year old headed toward the front of the city where the soldiers gathered. She raised her head, stayed brave, and ignored their gossip. Even someone small like herself could make a big difference; she just needed to show them.

As she reached the front gates, she watched as the soldiers prepared the war machines. The rock throwers were loaded, and the ranks of warriors readied their weapons and armor for when Gustav's forces broke through the wall. It was not a matter of "if" but "when." Thousands of men from both Southrend and Astongale stood between Gustav's men and innocent lives.

While scaling up the stairway to stand on the wall, Frigg's knees tingled, and she felt a sharp drop in her chest. There was no railing, and a simple push could have plummeted her to the ground below. She finally took a breath when she reached the top and didn't look down. Her father, Brynjar, Loke, Asger, and the king stood at the edge of the wall and looked out at Gustav's army.

In the distance, Frigg could still see the torches. The sun hadn't completely risen, yet she could feel the glow of its light. Gustav's forces gathered around their own war machines, positioned as close to the city as they could bring them. The rock throwers and bolt throwers stood in the front line while incoherent shouting by the warriors surrounded them. The first rank of Gustav's soldiers gathered behind the war machines carrying wooden ladders. Frigg glanced toward the forest in the distance and saw hundreds of trees had been reduced to stumps. Gustav's men worked into the night preparing ladders to scale the wall, and, by the looks of the force, they were ready to begin their assault.

"We will stand behind these walls, and have them bombard us like insects?!" Asger asked.

"We have war machines, as well," Damari reminded him.

"We have the walls and places we can take cover from his rock throwers," Graylyn added. "They have nothing to protect them."

Asger looked to Frigg and said, "You better be right about this plan of yours, my lady."

"You must know a man's weakness before you attack him," she replied with her eyes still focused on the army.

"Brynjar, take my daughter back to the castle and watch over her," Damari commanded.

"My lord," Brynjar began. "I'm one of your best swords. I think perhaps I should stay here and be with you and the others."

"He's a far better swordsman than me, my lord," Loke cut in. "I can look after her."

"The fact that he's a better swordsman is exactly why I want him to look over Frigg," Damari said.

Brynjar's face dropped, but he nodded. "As you command, my lord."

Brynjar stood beside Frigg and directed her with his head to go forward. Frigg looked at Gustav's army one last time. The realization that all those men in the field, so very close to her home, were all out to kill her father and his men scared her.

"Father!" She said.

Damari turned to her, and his face of intensity gave way to a smile. "I'll see you soon, little love."

He seemed so sure, and, although she didn't quite believe it because of her fear, she felt a little at ease because she heard the words in the voice she trusted the most. She wanted to reply, but she knew any word that found its way from her mouth would be followed with tears.

She turned and headed down the stone steps back to the ground level. The streets felt lonely, even with Brynjar's angry steps next to her. She looked up at his clenched face. It was clear he wasn't happy with his command. She took no offense, knowing he only wished to fight and defend his home.

When they entered the courtyard of the castle, ten men stood at the front entrance. Brynjar approached them and looked them over. "The escape route to the south?"

"Protected by a hundred men," one warrior replied.

"Remove them from the post, and have them head to the front of the city," Brynjar commanded.

The guards stared for a moment before another one said, "But then it will be left unguarded."

"I know," Brynjar replied. "These are the commands of Lord Damari.

His daughter stands beside me as a witness."

Frigg tightened her face and looked at each of them. "Do as he says."

"Then there will only be us to defend the castle and Lady Frigg," the first warrior said.

"We want them to come in," Brynjar assured him. "The only thing I need to know is whether you are willing to die for this. If not, you may leave now, but know you will not be welcomed back in this city. I will make sure every outpost, garrison, and village knows of your cowardice."

The first warrior took a step forward and kneeled before Frigg. "We will all die for you, Lady Frigg."

The remaining men unsheathed their swords, struck them on the ground, and went to one knee. In unison, they said, "Lady Frigg."

"Remember, no matter what happens, stay out here in the courtyard," Brynjar told them.

Frigg and Brynjar walked inside the castle and through the empty halls. When they reached Frigg's bedroom, she sat on the bed while Brynjar closed the door and took a seat in a chair just in front of the door. He pulled his sword out of its sheath and pointed the blade into the ground while he griped it tightly with both hands. He focused on the door but remained silent. Frigg felt her hands tremble.

"Scared?" Brynjar asked without looking in her direction.

"Very much," she admitted.

"If you're right, you're very brave for doing this," he said.

"If I'm brave, then why am I so scared?"

He chuckled. "Bravery begins because of fear, my lady."

"Not sure if I believe that."

"Perhaps talking will help ease it."

"I'm not sure what to say."

"Say anything," Brynjar replied. "Silence will only swell your fear."

Frigg thought for many moments. "I worry about my friend."

"The giant?" Brynjar asked. "I wouldn't. I feel sorry for any man who thinks he'll march into that pit and take on a giant."

"It's not that," she said. "The king told me he was going to kill him regardless of the outcome of this battle. So, even if we somehow manage to survive, Mulga will die. If Gustav wins, he'll fear him, too, and have him killed."

Brynjar sat in silence. "If this plan of yours works, maybe he'll reconsider."

"The king won't," she said. "Now talk to me."

"About?"

"Say anything."

"I hope this works," Brynjar whispered.

"Are you scared?" Frigg asked him.

He nearly looked at her but stopped himself. "Only a fool wouldn't be."

She knew he wanted to be among the warriors outside, fighting with her father. She recalled rumors of how he was one of the greatest swordsmen in the south. How useless he must feel protecting her.

"Are you willing to die?" Frigg asked.

"Pardon me?"

"You asked the men outside if they were willing to die," Frigg reminded him. "But what about you?"

Brynjar grinned. "I'm here, aren't I?"

"But you'd rather be in the front."

"It is true that I wish to be there, but there is no greater honor than defending you." She watched his head drop. "Before I left with your brother, I told your father I would protect him. I failed." Brynjar sighed. "I will not fail now."

Before she could reply, Frigg felt the ground quake. A horrible rumbling vibrated the entire castle and shook the floor.

"That's the front of the city." Brynjar said without moving. "It has begun."

Frigg wiped her sweaty hands on her dress. She walked to the window and slowly opened it. A strong, cold air touched her and made her teeth chatter. Her eyes looked to the south, but she couldn't see much. A fog had settled on the land and restricted her vision.

"I can't see anything," she said with a sigh.

"Doesn't matter," Brynjar said. "Light a few candles."

Frigg did as she was told just as another quake shook the castle. Frigg heard Gustav's war machines fire relentlessly upon Southrend. Frigg feared that each strike pelted the front gates and weakened the stone wall. At first, the quakes were separated by a few moments, but soon they came right on top of the other. Each one felt more powerful and closer than before, and Frigg knew death followed with each impact. Even when the ceiling above them shook, Brynjar stayed in place and glared at the door.

Frigg passed the time with meaningless questions for her protector. Brynjar sat like a stone without even the slightest shake. Hours went by, one strike after the other, as Frigg felt her body jolt with each hit. The darkness settled in, and a clear sight of Brynjar turned into a shadow.

Frigg heard another sound, but she knew it wasn't the war machines. Incoherent voices from outside her window gained her attention. Brynjar's head snapped toward the voices. He rose to his feet and stomped his way toward the window.

"What is it?" Frigg asked.

"They're here," Brynjar said softly.

He turned, snatched Frigg by the hand, and swiftly pulled her toward the door. With a kick of his foot, they were in the hall. Frigg nearly jogged to keep up with him. "I told you."

"Yes, you were right, but now comes the hard part," Brynjar replied.

There came a sudden eruption above Frigg, followed by a rumble so intense she couldn't even hear herself scream. Brynjar shifted to the right and then was violently thrown to the left. The ceiling above them started to collapse on top of them. Frigg went to move, but she felt a jerk on her arm as Brynjar pulled her forward. The rubble from the ceiling wasn't completely displaced, but a few more strikes and the stones would collapse on top of them.

Brynjar gained his feet and pulled Frigg once more. A second strike rumbled throughout the castle, but it sounded farther away. The entire palace creaked around them, and the ground felt unsteady.

Brynjar pulled Frigg down the spiral stairs and rushed through the long halls of the first floor. The entrance to the castle was in sight just as a third and fourth explosion knocked them both to the ground. Behind Frigg, the ceiling finally crumbled leaving nothing but large stones and dust. She coughed violently as she breathed in the filth and, eventually, had to hold her hand over her mouth. A large stone sat in front of her and stopped her from getting down the hallway. She saw a dusty hand grasp the other side of the stone as Brynjar appeared and saw her slouched forward on the ground.

"Are you hurt?" He asked while the entire castle quaked from another strike.

She shook her head. She still heard other rocks and stones falling in the distance from the impact of the war machines.

"You have to grab my hand, Frigg!" Brynjar yelled over the noise. "I don't know how much longer this part of the ceiling will hold. We're almost out of the castle."

The ceiling creaked above her. The wooden braces barely kept the stone from falling on top of her.

"Frigg!" Brynjar called. "Come now! I've got you."

She felt a small comfort in his confidence. She rose to her feet and reached up. The stone was much too large, and, even when she got on the tips of her toes, she was still inches from reaching him.

"Jump, Frigg," Brynjar commanded.

Her first attempt grazed his fingertips. The second one slapped his hand. The third time she jumped Brynjar just needed to touch her fingers as his entire hand grabbed hers and pulled her up. Frigg heard the ceiling behind her fall in, and Brynjar dragged her away as more rocks collapsed.

After Brynjar pulled her near the door to leave the castle, he paused. The castle was still unsteady, and Frigg felt her feet eager to run. The strikes to the castle ended, but the sounds of the falling ceiling still echoed.

"We have to run," Frigg said.

"Not yet. We do not want to spoil it," Brynjar replied.

Within a few moments, faint yells came from down the hall. At the first sight of a warrior wearing black and red, Brynjar tugged at Frigg's arm and pulled her out the castle doors.

When the ten warriors outside saw Brynjar and Frigg, they quickly stood back from the castle and watched some of it collapse. Six of them removed their swords while the other four backed away from the entrance with bows and nocked arrows.

Brynjar jogged by them holding tightly to Frigg's arm. Just before they reached the gates, Frigg heard the whistling of arrows. With a quick turn of her head, she watched Gustav's men pouring out of the castle.

The sight gave her a jolt of energy and made her run faster to keep pace with Brynjar.

Her protector kept his eyes forward. Frigg could hear the yells of devastating blows as swords struck one another. When they traveled through the empty streets of Southrend, whistling arrows screeched toward them, missing them by inches. Brynjar nearly got struck, but he ducked down an alleyway and picked up his feet once more.

"Don't look behind you!" he shouted. He kept turning down different pathways to make sure that if Gustav's men came around another bend they didn't have time to stop and aim weapons. "We're almost there."

They entered the Common Quarter, which sat empty and silent. Brynjar removed his sword from its sheath just as he pulled Frigg behind him and stood in the empty streets of the city. Gustav's men poured into the square by the hundreds, but they drastically slowed down when they noticed Brynjar and Frigg standing alone.

Brynjar stood between Frigg and the warriors, positioning his body to catch anything aimed their way. All Frigg could see was his back, but she heard the tremble of footsteps.

"Now!" Brynjar screamed.

An explosion of snaps echoed through the square followed by arrows pouring into the crowd of Gustav's men. Warriors of Southrend stood up from crouched positions on the wall and let loose their projectiles. It was close to impossible to miss in a crowd so large. Some of the arrows merely struck armor, but the surprise stunned the army. Gustav's men looked for ways to reach the archers, but no staircases went up toward the wall.

Galloping erupted from the alley around the Common Quarter as a cavalry of horsemen rode into the square. Frigg caught a glimpse of her father before he and a hundred mounted warriors crashed into the crowd. The height of being on horseback gave them a great advantage as each of them only needed to swing downward in order to create a devastating blow.

The archers on the wall used large sling-shots to fire buckets of tar toward Gustav's army. They screamed from the heat of the substance. Flaming arrows followed the tar, and fire immediately spread throughout the mob of men. Their shrieks chilled Frigg's body—each one as horrid as the first.

The final part of the plan came together while Frigg and Brynjar retreated backward. Erland's stand against the Wild Men and remembering the Common Quarter didn't have stairs helped inspire her plan. Brynjar and her started to retreat from the battle, it was up to the warriors of Southrend now. They scaled up a slight hill in the streets, and Frigg could see warriors of Southrend coming in from the rear. Gustav's men continued to pour into the square, but every warrior who attempted to chase her down was ambushed by a force in hiding. Gustav's army was still stronger than the tiny ranks Damari gathered for the attack, but the element of surprise began to even the numbers.

"Now get to the front of the city," Brynjar commanded her with a gentle push. "Find the king and stay there!"

"But what about you and my father?" Frigg asked.

Brynjar didn't get a chance to answer the question. Six of Gustav's men pushed their way through and started to come for them. Brynjar readied himself and stood between them and Frigg. The first reached him only to swing a sloppy attack while Brynjar ducked and cut him down with a single blow. Brynjar stepped forward and struck the second warrior's sword from his grasp and stabbed him through the heart. Brynjar quickly removed his blade from the warrior and immediately struck down the next two. When the final two warriors came at him, Brynjar needed only to block a few strikes before they, too, fell before him.

"Go now!" Brynjar shouted as more of Gustav's men broke through the battle and headed toward them.

Without hesitation, Frigg turned and ran as quickly as she could. The sounds of clashing steel faded into the night when she put distance between her and the battle. After a few hundred feet, she stopped and caught her breath. She saw Gustav's men running down the pathway toward her. She didn't know Brynjar's fate, nor did she have time to feel anything about it. With each moment that passed, she saw more men coming her way.

Brynjar may have commanded her to go to the front of the city, but she knew she would never make it with so many of Gustav's men trailing her. It would only be a few short moments before they closed the distance and captured her. She thought of the only safe place left and sprinted down the closest alley.

She never wanted to look behind her because she thought even the slightest delay would slow her down. She ducked through alleyways and slim paths just to try to gain some distance. For a moment, she feared she was lost and would be unable to find her destination. Perhaps it was fate or the will of the gods that made her see the gateway into the pit. The footsteps behind her echoed loudly, and she could tell they were gaining ground.

She nearly collapsed into the gate and pushed it forward. After three quick steps, she lost her footing and fell to the ground. She felt the familiar pain in her ankle from the previous days. She crawled her way to the pit, hoping she could somehow get inside and release Mulga from his chains. Then she realized the cage was over the pit, and she didn't have the slightest idea how to open it. She turned to face Gustav's men. The warrior in front of them held his massive sword and headed straight for her. There were at least ten of them, but Frigg knew many others followed behind.

Fear covered her eyes when she saw the evil expression of the warriors who surrounded her. She summoned all the energy that remained in her tired body and screamed, "Mulga!"

Her voice echoed throughout the city. It may have even pierced the ears of the gods themselves, if they were listening, but it did nothing to the warriors who stood over her.

Suddenly, a reply to her scream shook the very foundation below her feet and vibrated throughout the pit. "AAAARRRRGGGHHHH!"

Mulga had answered her call, and, this time, Gustav's men froze in their steps and looked around for the source of the mighty voice. Inside the pit, Frigg heard Mulga thrashing around while the chains shook and clattered. The men in front of her still didn't know what was going on. Frigg watched as the cage launched into the sky above her. The massive steel structure rotated in the air until it crashed over the gate that surrounded the pit. One of the massive stones to which the shackles were connected sat on the side of the pit with an empty chain hanging from it. Frigg watched in awe as she remembered the stones were forged into the earth at the bottom of the pit. She saw another stone soar over her head. The shadow of the boulder covered over two of Gustav's men who tried to yell but were silenced when the large stone landed on top of them.

The cold and menacing looks on the faces of Gustav's men vanished and were replaced with utter fear. Frigg felt a push against the earth below her, and Mulga's form rose from the pit and landed directly in front of her. Her friend heaved from his chest as he grunted. The grunt turned into a slow and rolling growl as he stared down the men standing inside the gates.

"Men hurt Frigg," he said. "Mulga kill men!"

Even with one hand still chained, he swung forward with such power the boulder whipped in front of him. Mulga knocked the closest of Gustav's men away while the massive rock collided with even more. Mulga pulled his arms together and smashed the ground in front of him. Gustav's men who tried to flee lost their balance. While they fell to the ground, Mulga struck each of them over and over again. The first strike proved fatal, but he took his aggression out on their corpses with a second and third.

More of Gustav's men charged in ready to fight back. Frigg looked on in horror as arrows struck him. The warriors took advantage of the distraction and cut at the giant's legs. Mulga grunted, but his thunderous strikes came with even more power while he ignored the petty injuries of their attacks.

Mulga tossed the stone connected to his shackle, but it imbedded itself in the wall. For a brief moment, his hand was restricted. With a roar of rage, he ripped the shackle from the chain and snapped it like a twig. The broken pieces of iron rattled to the ground. With each swipe in front of him, three or more men were flung to the side. The gates to the pit seemed cluttered and overwhelmed. More of Gustav's men charged inside to take on the giant.

Just as Frigg feared the worst, arrows suddenly struck Gustav's men. They fell at an alarming rate. From behind the mob, she watched her father ride in with the remaining forces who battled at the Common Quarter. Mulga stepped back from the fight and stood next to Frigg. With arrows sticking out of his arms and chest, she watched his eyes dart back and forth. She realized he didn't know the difference between the men.

"Mulga!" Frigg called. Her friend looked down at her. "The men wearing red like the apple—they're the bad ones."

Mulga grinned and rushed forward. Once again, Frigg watched the bodies of Gustav's men get thrown through the air.

Gustav's men were still too many, and the last of Damari's men was killed by three warriors surrounding him. Only her father remained, and Frigg saw him surrounded and get thrown to the ground. Her heart jumped in her chest when she saw a warrior raise his blade, but Mulga picked up Damari with a swipe of his hand and tossed him behind the battle. Damari rolled on the ground until he reached Frigg and looked back to the fight. A series of pounding strikes into the ground shook throughout the pit, and Frigg witnessed the remaining warriors of Gustav's forces retreat.

Mulga took a few steps forward and roared. The last of the soldiers fled as he pounded his chest. Mulga raised a fist when a single form ran toward them, but restrained himself when he recognized Brynjar.

Frigg's protector looked battered and bruised with dented armor and several cuts across his face. "My lord, it's Gustav."

Damari rose to his feet and gingerly limped toward Brynjar. "What do you mean?"

"He's coming right now," Brynjar said. "After we killed all of his men in the square, and you came here, more ranks came through."

"How many?" Damari asked.

"Too many," Brynjar replied.

Mulga turned toward Damari and said, "Go. Mulga fight men."

"You could die," Frigg said.

"Bad men killed Mulga's father. Mulga will save Frigg's father from bad men," Mulga said.

Before she could say another word to him, Mulga put his fists into the ground and galloped toward the sound of charging warriors. He vanished into the darkness, and all that could be heard was his roar and the screams of fearful warriors.

"Brynjar," Damari called. "Go to the front of the city at once. Find out what's going on and if you can bring men back here."

"Of course, my lord," Brynjar replied.

Like Mulga, Brynjar rushed away into the darkness until the sound of his boots faded. Damari grabbed Frigg by her hand and walked around the bodies scattered on the ground. Once they left the pit, Damari started to limp toward the front of the city. Frigg kept turning around and looking in the distance. She did not want to go forward without knowing her friend was safe. She felt her father pull at her.

"Frigg, he's going to be..." Damari grunted in pain.

Frigg saw an arrow pierce through her father's armor just above his shoulder blade. A second struck him in his back, and he collapsed forward. Frigg let out a scream.

Behind them, four of Gustav's warriors emerged from the shadows, along with Gustav himself. The Dragon Lord held his blade out and walked directly toward Frigg. Damari rose from his feet and met with the first of Gustav's men. A quick exchange of strikes ended with Damari stabbing the warrior in the chest. He quickly readied himself for another. Gustav walked around the fight as Damari started to lunge toward him, but the Lord of Southrend quickly realized he needed to keep his attention on the men who surrounded him.

"RUN!" Damari screamed at his daughter.

Frigg sprinted down the empty streets of Southrend with Gustav trailing her. The Lord of Westerland gained with every stride, and Frigg felt the pain in her ankle once more. She turned down the next street, but the wall surrounding the city towered before her. When she tried to turn back, Gustav stood with his sword out and stared directly at her.

He lunged at her, grasped her by the back of her hair, and pulled her into him with a twist of his arm. Her back was pressed against his chest as he raised her into the air. Frigg's arms flailed about until her hand touched the hilt of a dagger at his waist. She removed it and clumsily stabbed it into Gustav's side. The Dragon Lord yelled as he tossed her against the wall.

He clenched his teeth as he removed the dagger from his flesh. Gustav pressed on the wound and winced. His face quivered with rage while he stood before her, but he laughed softly when he noticed her expression of horror.

"Very clever. Very clever, indeed, knowing I would rush a major amount of men through the rear of the city," Gustav said. "Who figured it out? Your father or the king?"

"I did," Frigg managed to say. "I used my wits. You showed me your weakness."

He winced again as he leaned forward. "And what is that?"

"You didn't want to give us a day to stay alive," she told him. "You needed a day to redirect your men around the city without detection, so you could kidnap me and kill me in front of my father as you promised."

He chuckled lightly and stood up straight. He placed his bloody hand back on the hilt of his sword and looked ready to raise it. "As I said, very clever, little girl. Looks like I won't be able to kill you in front of him after all. I'll just have to hand him your head instead."

Gustav dramatically raised his sword over his head. Behind Frigg, in the darkness of the shadows, she saw two glimmering silver eyes. She relaxed against the wall and started to stand up.

Gustav stared at her curiously until the vibration of a footstep behind him made him slightly turn his head. His eyes went wide at the sight of the giant. Mulga snorted, and Frigg watched him bring up his hand and slam it down toward Gustav. She turned away just as she felt the thud in the earth and heard the splash of blood and flesh against the stone. Gustav didn't even get a chance to scream.

"Mulga crush," the giant said.

Frigg kept her eyes closed tightly as Mulga picked her up and cupped her in his hands. He placed her down far away from the horrid sight of what remained of Gustav's body. When she touched the ground, she turned and looked up at him.

"Frigg safe now," Mulga said.

"Father!" Frigg remembered with a turn of her head.

"Frigg's father safe," Mulga told her. "Mulga save him from bad men."

"Gustav's men?"

Mulga smiled. "No more bad men."

Frigg heard the voices through the thick smoke behind her. She could vaguely see movement in the distance.

Mulga looked up and said, "Frigg's men."

With a glance at Mulga, she quickly said, "You have to leave. You're free now. Go back to Direwood and stay away from here."

"Mulga help man," he reminded her.

"It doesn't matter," she said. "They'll try to put you back in chains. Do you understand? It doesn't matter that you helped. They fear you because of what you can do, and they fear you'll turn on them. Most of them aren't like me. They'll kill you."

"Mulga stay with Frigg and keep Frigg safe," he said.

"I'm safe," she assured him. "Most of the bad men are gone."

"Mulga stay," he insisted.

The voices sounded closer, and Frigg knew they would put Mulga back in the pit. If he resisted, there would be more violence and unnecessary deaths. She realized she would have to resort to something she would regret for the rest of her life in order to get him to leave. She pretended to be angry and looked directly at him. "I don't like you! I never did!" Her false expression didn't hold. Even as she lied, the tears found a way beyond her eyes and ran down her cheeks. "You're ugly, and you're stupid. I don't ever want to see again! Now go away!"

As if her words weren't wounding enough, she picked up a small rock by her feet and hurled it in his direction.

Mulga shifted his body so the small stone would bounce off his shoulder. He stood before her like so many times before, but, this time, a glimmer of light fell from one of his eyes and ran down his face. The very look he gave her shattered her heart as intensely as hearing about her brother's death. She forced herself to look him in the eye. Mulga sniffled slowly and turned away from her.

"Frigg still Mulga's friend," he muttered.

Without giving her another glance, he leapt up to the wall surrounding the city. She heard him jump forward, and a small quake was felt from the other side. His steps slowly faded into the night until Frigg could only hear the fires crackling around her from the aftermath of the battle.

Her knees hit the stone ground as she put her hands to her face and sobbed into her palms. The words she said to her friend wounded her far worse than it did him. At least, that's what she told herself. The very friend who saved her many times heard her last words of malice and hatred toward him. She felt disgusted with herself, but she knew it needed to be done in order for Mulga to be safe.

CHAPTER TWENTY-FOUR

"Frigg," a gentle voice called.

She turned to see her father through her tears. She hadn't heard his footsteps, but she suspected he stood there for many moments. He gripped his wounded shoulder and struggled to stay up.

"Father!" She called as she rose and went to him.

He stopped her from jumping into his arms and motioned with his hand for her to calm down. "I'm all right. Your giant came just in time."

He bent down and inspected her for wounds. Damari wiped her tears and looked at her warmly. "It's all right, little love."

"Did you hear?" She asked as her voice cracked.

He nodded with an equally wounded expression. "It's what you had to do."

Her face swelled with emotion as she tightly wrapped herself around him and hoped her embrace would release the hurt she felt. He softly hushed her. No words would make her forget the pain of having to harm her friend.

"Lord Damari!" The call came from the fog behind them. Loke appeared and sounded out of breath. "My lord, you're needed outside the gates of the city."

"What is it?" Damari asked as he gently broke his grip on Frigg.

Loke calmed his breathing and said, "Ravengale and Morendorn, my lord. They joined the fight. Our scouts got through. The battle has been won."

"Get Frigg," Damari commanded as he stormed off.

Loke reached out to Frigg to carry her, but she shook her head, still ashamed of her words. She wiped the tears from her face and walked after her father. Loke stayed next to her, but she still had to pick up her speed to keep pace with him. Frigg saw the carnage she only heard and felt while in the castle as she walked through the streets of the city. The fog that set in wasn't fog at all but smoke caused by fires. Some of the buildings were reduced to rubble with flames spreading to the quarters around them. Bodies of villagers and soldiers alike littered the streets—evidence of Gustav's rock throwers and war machines. As horrible as the sights were, Frigg couldn't get the final image of Mulga's face when he walked away from her for the last time out of her mind. The heat of the fires made her forget about the cold as she and Loke tried to keep pace with her father.

Warriors from the battle outside trudged in from the fields, carrying the dead and wounded warriors who fought bravely against Gustav's invasion. She could hear screams both close and in the distance. The battle may have been over, but the pain of warfare had yet to cease. Her nose smelled the stench of waste and death. Children her own age ran in all directions and cried for their parents as they ducked away from the horrors.

An immense explosion went off above Frigg. She looked up to see the stones of a building falling toward her. She felt picked up from behind, and she imagined being elevated in the air and placed gently on Mulga's shoulder. Instead, she opened her eyes to see Loke, who grabbed her before the stones of the building could crush her.

"Walk carefully, my lady! Some of the buildings are still unstable!" He shouted through the noises of the city.

The smoke in the front of Southrend thickened, and the fires blazed with a deadly intensity. This was where Gustav's army focused their attack. Damari vanished into the smoke at the front gates. It wasn't until they were twenty feet or so in front of the main wall when the smoke finally faded and Frigg took in the sights of the main battlefield. Bodies were piled on top of one another like hillsides. Helmets, swords, and limbs scattered across the landscape. Frigg looked down to see her white shoes stained crimson from pools of blood.

Damari's pace finally slowed when he looked around the battlefield in bewilderment. "Did Graylyn attack?"

Loke nodded. "Asger baited him into doing it when he saw Ravengale and Morendorn. With Gustav attacking from the rear of the city, he thought he could take out this force."

Before Damari could say another word, two warriors approached him. One wore a tabard with two crossing swords, colored yellow and orange, while the second wore a tabard with wings, colored purple and black. From Frigg's studies, she knew the crossing swords of Egil, Lord of Morendorn and the purple wings of Hackett, the Lord of Ravengale. Hackett was a brute of a man, scarred and dirty, with a bald head and a knotted chin beard, while Egil was fair-skinned, lanky, and blonde.

Both lords stood with sunken faces. Behind them, Frigg caught a glimpse of warriors rounding up the remaining men in Gustav's army. The defeated men walked with their hands on their heads in a line away from the city.

Damari stood before Egil and Hackett and bowed his head. "You'll never know the debt I owe the two of you."

"None required," Hackett said. "We only wish we could have arrived sooner, so that many lives could have been saved."

"I thank the gods that you came at all," Damari said. "Have you seen the king?"

The two lords exchanged a troubled glance, and Hackett asked, "Have you?"

"Is he..." Damari began.

"Not yet," Egil cut in.

"He was asking for you earlier," Hackett added.

Egil motioned for Damari to follow him, and they made their way through ranks of warriors who stood in gloom. The crowd parted, and Frigg saw King Graylyn lying in the dirt. A trail of blood darkened the drag marks on the ground where he was obviously pulled away from a pile.

Brynjar knelt at the side of the king and tried to hold his head up. Damari bent down on the other side and grasped the hand of his brother-in-law and king.

"They were everywhere," Graylyn said as his eyes focused on Damari. "It was like the war with the Wild Men all those years ago. They surrounded me, but my sword must have sent a hundred or more of them to the afterlife."

Damari hushed him. "Be still, my friend."

"Friend?" Graylyn asked. "What kind of friend doesn't believe the word of his most honorable ally? You have never lied to me. I should have believed you about Gustav. I should have known his intentions. To think, he nearly killed the last remaining thing I have of my sister." Graylyn's eyes rested on Frigg. He closed them for a moment and winced, but he quickly forged a smile upon his face. "Frigg, there you are."

Frigg dropped to her knees at the side of his body and brushed his face with her fingers. "Uncle."

He lifted his other arm as best he could. "You know I used to hold you with just this one hand?"

"Yes," she whispered.

He grinned as his lower jaw quivered. "Not for much longer." He coughed violently, and blood spat from his mouth. His glazed eyes looked upon her again. "Brynjar was telling me that your giant saved him and many others."

Frigg nodded. "He saved my father and me, too."

"I was wrong about him," he admitted. "I should have also listened to you."

"It's all right," she replied quietly.

Graylyn raised a shaky hand and extended his finger to wipe away a tear from her eye. "You hush now. One day, you will be a queen. I made a promise to your father, and I will uphold it. Let all here bear witness to that vow. When the final breath in me leaves, the new king will be Damari of Southrend until you come of age."

The remaining warriors around Graylyn stayed still, as if already mourning the death of their king. They all heard his command in the silence that surrounded the aftermath of a bloody battle.

Graylyn looked at Damari. "You must rule better than I did."

Frigg watched her father try to keep his composure. "I will rule in your name, as you command, my king."

Graylyn tightened his grip on Damari as his body stiffened and briefly convulsed. His head struck the ground and tilted until his wide eyes looked right at Frigg, and the life within them faded.

Frigg watched death take her uncle. She thought it would be dishonorable to look away from him in his final moments. A few days earlier she would have run from the scene, but how much those few days had changed her.

Damari rose from the ground and kept his eyes on his friend. He slowly looked to two of his own warriors. "Take his body inside."

Frigg had to control her tears. She followed her father as he searched the battlefield. The bodies were piled up over pools of blood drenching the ground. Frigg saw too many dead eyes looking into the nothingness that surrounded the sodden field.

"Damari!" Her father looked up to see Egil walking toward him with a warrior in chains. Egil tossed the warrior to the ground, making the prisoner fall to his knees. Long hair covered his face and dirt and blood covered over the tabard he wore, but the colors of Astongale were still visible. Egil grabbed the back of the warrior's head, pulled it back, and revealed the dirty face of Asger. "I found this one deserting the battle."

Damari slowly approached. He kneeled down to look into the defeated eyes of Asger. "What was he doing?"

"Running like a coward," Egil said. "I thought he was the enemy until I saw the colors of Astongale."

Damari stared at Asger while he rose to his feet. He looked to Egil and replied, "I will not kill him. Let him live forever with his cowardice."

Within that quiet field, came a faint swooping sound. Frigg stopped to listen to make sure it wasn't her imagination. As Egil and Damari discussed what to do about Asger, the faint sound in the distance gained her attention, and the hair on the back of her neck rose. It got even louder the second time she heard it. Finally, it brought with it a gust of energy she felt go right by her. *Swoosh...swoosh...swoosh.*

From the heavens, an object fell to the earth. Damari pulled Frigg back just as a body struck the ground with a crashing sound of armor and a burst of blood.

No one seemed to want to go forward and inspect it. Finally, Damari cautiously walked forward. No living being could have survived the fall, but he still removed his sword and held it ready.

Damari kicked the body and rolled it over, but it was covered in so much blood the face couldn't be recognized. A dented and damaged helmet lay discarded next to the body.

Damari reached down and picked it up. He faced away from Frigg, but she tried to walk to him. Brynjar gently grabbed her by the shoulder and stopped her. Damari finally turned and showed his men the helmet. The ghoulish mask of Halvar stared back at them. Frigg wiggled free of Brynjar's grasp and got close enough to see the body, but something else gained her attention. The necklace Gustav had worn with the large ruby on it was around Halvar's broken neck, but the charm was missing.

"Why did he fall from the sky?" Brynjar asked.

Frigg's heart sank at the exact same time the swooping sound returned.

"My lord!" screamed a guard on the wall. "It's a..."

In a blur, a goliath of a shadow flew down and grabbed the warrior but vanished back through the smoke as quickly as it came. Frigg's whole body jolted.

"Brynjar, get Frigg back inside!" Damari screamed. Brynjar immediately picked her up and ran with her in his arms.

The form of the creature returned to the sky and blocked out the light of the moon. Frigg watched from Brynjar's arms as it descended toward the warriors on the ground. A sudden discharge of fire lit up the darkness and covered over the field. The line of fire exploded and made its way toward the kneeling Asger. The coward who had deserted the battle looked behind him at the carnage and screamed until the fire found him, and he exploded into ash. Other warriors fell to the ground engulfed in flames as they rolled their bodies to try and put out the fire. Their screams quickly faded as they became motionless, and the fire consumed them.

"Dragon!" screamed one of the warriors watching from the wall as another streaming flame came from the sky and covered the landscape. Nothing remained in its path but an explosion of cinders.

Chaos consumed the city once more. Commoners and warriors alike ran in panic. Brynjar crashed into groups of people and knocked them to the ground with his shoulder so he could get by. Frigg looked into the sky and saw the dragon soaring above her with its wings ripping through the air.

The creature turned and headed downward once again. A single breath of fire engulfed the entire Common Quarter of the city with explosions of debris from shops and wagons. Frigg feared her and Brynjar had no place to run. Her protector crashed through the door of one of the buildings just as the flames took over the ground outside and broke through the stone wall of the small store they entered.

Frigg screamed as she felt the heat of the fire all around her. Then the fire receded and an eerie silence followed. Brynjar rose to his feet and looked out the open door and gasped. "By the gods."

He helped Frigg up from the ground and pulled her outside. Charred bodies littered the ground with their mouths open—killed just as they let out their screams of suffering from the inferno. The conflagration covered the shops, wagons, and small carts as the wood cracked and popped. Beads of sweat formed on Frigg's forehead from the heat.

The bodies came in all forms: men, women, and children. Frigg thought of the warriors on the battlefield who knew their fate could possibly end in a battle much like the one fought. They expected that sort of death, but the people burned by the flames of a dragon died without warning. Everywhere Frigg looked innocent lives lay scattered all across the ground.

She closed her eyes and tried in vain to block the images from her thoughts. She felt Brynjar pick her up again, and she buried her head in his shoulder. When he carried her through the courtyard, she caught a glimpse of two guards; both had been burned black and their armor melted.

Frigg could hear more explosions and the cries of her people in the distance.

Brynjar placed her down and held her by the hand. "It's Valstrath the Vile."

"Valstrath the Vile?" Frigg asked. "But Alatrex killed him."

"That's why you never believe stories," Brynjar said.

They ducked through the empty allies of the city. The warrior was much older and stronger than Frigg, and she started to lose her breath.

"We have to slow down," Frigg said through heavy gasping.

"We can't," Brynjar replied. "We'll take cover in the castle."

"The castle is nearly destroyed," Frigg reminded him.

"Not all of it," he said.

Just as they turned a corner to head to the castle, a great gust of wind came over them. Frigg watched the dragon's body clip the side of the buildings above them. Hundreds of bricks fell to the ground ahead of them and smashed the gate leading to the castle. A mound of stones and wreckage now blocked their way to safety. Based on how Valstrath flew right into the building, Frigg realized no place was safe.

Brynjar headed for the entrance despite the blockage. Frigg leaned into the wall as her knees shook. Looking up, she felt relieved thinking the buildings were too close together for the dragon to dive down and reach her—but there was still the fire. Brynjar tried to move the boulders, but it looked impossible. They couldn't climb over the rubble either. There was no place to step, and each of the boulders was packed into where the gate once stood. The wall surrounding the castle was too high; the spikes at the top prevented anyone from climbing up and over.

"Frigg!" Brynjar yelled. "There is a small gap in these ruins."

"The dragon can fly," Frigg said in a quivering voice. "Even if I get through, he can get to me."

"Not if you run fast enough." He turned and held out his hand to her. "Run to the castle, and find your way to the escape route through the tunnels. Stay there until your father or I come for you!"

She hesitated, but he stiffened his hand as he held it out. She found her courage and ran to him. The hole Brynjar found seemed rather slim. Instantly, Frigg imagined the boulders collapsing in further when she tried to crawl through. The swooping above her head quickly erased that fear from her thoughts. Perhaps it was better to be crushed by rocks than get burned alive.

Inside the courtyard, the dragon dove, and its front claws grabbed onto one of the statues. It pulled the statue effortlessly from the earth and tossed it into the side of the castle. Stone collided with stone, and the noise echoed as the side wall to the castle crumbled. The crashing continued after the sound of Valstrath disappeared.

"He flew away," Brynjar said. "Here's your chance."

"He just went into the courtyard," Frigg told him.

He dropped to one knee and looked directly at her. "Frigg, you must go. It's the only way. If we try to run someplace else, there's a chance he could get us. He can't get to the tunnels."

There was no time to argue. Brynjar picked her up and tried to stuff her through the small hole. She slimmed her body like she did many days earlier while trapped in the cage just outside of Direwood and willed her way through the hole. She got a bit stuck toward the end but managed to free herself and get inside the courtyard.

When she hit the ground, she quickly got up and looked back through the gap at Brynjar. He briefly smiled when he saw she made it. "Now run, Frigg. Run as fast..."

In one violent motion, Brynjar disappeared from her sight. Frigg looked to the air and saw Valstrath flying into the heavens with Brynjar in his jaws. Brynjar screamed, but his voice faded into the night sky with the dragon's figure. Frigg's legs shook again. The knowledge hit her that she was alone, and she wondered how far away help could be.

She pressed her back up against the rubble that blocked the gate. She felt far too scared to try and run to the castle; it felt like a world away. The pillars surrounding the garden still stood, so she figured she could use them as a way to hide when Valstrath flew over. The first pillar wasn't far from her, so she sprinted in its direction and quickly put her back into it.

Her whole body quivered when crashing and chaos suddenly took over the courtyard. She heard stone rolling around and then silence. She peeked out from her hiding place and saw that Valstrath knocked over several of the pillars in the courtyard. She suspected the dragon knew where she was hiding. She darted to the next pillar and hugged it tightly.

On the far wall, she heard Valstrath land, followed by a whimper. With a quick look, she realized with horror that Valstrath held Brynjar upside down in his mouth. The dragon sank his teeth into Brynjar's waist and blood poured down the warrior's armor and soaked his face and hair. His groans became a painful scream, and he let out one last cry as Valstrath ended Brynjar's life with his mighty jaw. Valstrath's wings expanded, and he lifted from the wall, landing on the ground with a thud and spitting Brynjar to the ground in disgust. Frigg didn't move from behind the remains of a destroyed pillar. She heard a rattling sound and saw the end of Valstrath's tail with its back spikes shaking rapidly.

Frigg stole another glance and stared at the black scales and the red underbelly of the legendary dragon. His wings spread out to the side, ready to fly off again, until they retracted and tucked to his back. With a quick snort, his nose exhaled two gusts of smoke. A strange kind of rumbling came from his throat as his massive head swayed from side to side, and his orange eyes gazed around the courtyard. Miniature horns covered his head and grew in all directions, running either upward or downward. On the crown of his head, two large, black horns extended in a spiral toward the heavens.

"I can sense your royal blood, little one," the dragon hissed. "It lingers with your stench of fear. I haven't forgotten your essence since I smelled you in the cave when you were brought to me. Halvar and his pathetic lord told me you would be my gift when I fulfilled my duty. You wretched humans think you can tell me what to do?" The dragon laughed from deep in his throat. "We haven't been properly introduced, however. You are Lady Frigg from what I remember. Do you know me? My name is legendary in this world."

"Valstrath," Frigg mouthed. A brush of powerful wind hit her, and Frigg looked out to see Valstrath's tail crash into the entrance of the castle. Much like the gate to the courtyard, the stone fell to the ground and blocked her entry to safety.

"There is no use running," said the chilling voice she remembered from the cave. Valstrath's whole body ran across the stone ground, and Frigg shifted her own body around the pillar as the dragon passed her. He headed toward the courtyard gate. With a swipe of his claw, he destroyed another pillar, picked up a massive rock, and jabbed it into the top of the rubble. The rocks compressed into the entrance, and there was no longer a hole through which Frigg could crawl. The dragon turned, and Frigg crept around the pillar to get out of sight again. "Every path to get away from this courtyard has been blocked off. All there is now is to face your fate."

The dragon crawled back into the center of the courtyard. He stood so close to her she could reach out and touch his scales. She peeked her head out slightly to look at the crumbled wall of the castle. There seemed to be a tiny section her small frame could squeeze through to get into the castle. If she ran and climbed to it, she could attempt an escape. Just as she ducked back around, she heard the dragon turn its head in her direction.

She saw a small piece of the pillar in front of her, and an idea came to her. She slid to the ground and grabbed the rubble. While she tried to contain her trembling, she tossed a stone to the side of her and heard it strike the ground. Valstrath exhaled loudly. With an explosion of fire, the warmth hit the side of her face and told her the dragon fell for the trap.

She summoned her bravery and sprinted away from the pillar toward the broken side of the castle. When she hit the stones, she quickly scaled them. One of the stones dragged downward, and she lost her grip. She heard another explosion and thought she was finished. She tried to run into the castle, but the floor gave way and collapsed. When she struck the ground, she saw the fire go over her head. The relief of not being burned alive delayed the effects of the fall, but they immediately kicked in when she exhaled. Her elbows felt broken, and her knees throbbed. When she tried to get up, she realized she was still outside. If only the floor hadn't collapsed; she would be inside and out of danger.

"You cannot run from me," Valstrath said in a booming voice. "I will destroy every piece of this castle if it means getting to you. Your ancestors are the reason I was put in chains by Alatrex and those pathetic giants. Your kind was too weak to fight me on your own. Now, the giants are nevermore—relics of the past your kind doomed when they were sent after me."

Frigg crawled forward, hidden by the rubble of the castle, but she knew Valstrath would eventually find her if she stayed in one place. She found another pillar, this one fully intact, and she hid behind it, hoping her body would recover from the fall.

"Your blood calls to me," he roared. "It won't matter where you go. I will find you. You...will...be...mine!"

Frigg felt a crash in back of the pillar and let out a scream. She ignored the pain in her legs and ran away. Just ahead of her stood the stables. She said every prayer she had ever known as she ran and made it inside just as another burst of flames hit the entrance. She jumped to the side, but not before some of the fire singed her feet. She let out a loud cry of pain and crawled further inside the stables. In a panic she removed her shoes and tossed them away. She could hear the cackling laugh of Valstrath just outside.

"Do you think this stone structure will keep me away?" he asked while his feet stomped the ground. "I would be angry with you, but what fun is the reward without the splendor of the chase?"

She watched his black-scaled body pass by the small open windows and even caught his orange eye peering in one of them. She managed to get to the wall and get out of his sight.

A loud crack hit the sky. For a moment, Frigg thought it was the dragon breathing his fire. Then she heard the sounds of the rain pouring down from the heavens along with the rolling thunder following it. Frigg doubted there would be enough water to put out the flames of Valstrath the Vile.

Her feet throbbed, and she felt scared to look at them. She glanced up to the second floor of the barn with its piles of straw and saw the small open window to get out the back. She hoped Valstrath would try to come through the entrance—that his obsession for her would cloud his judgment. The stone walls would delay him for a moment, but, eventually, his powerful strength would get him through.

With tears of pain, Frigg got to her feet and hobbled from brace to brace to keep herself from falling. She made it to the stairs just as she heard an eruption outside. From the window at the top of the barn, she could see flashes of light. Valstrath's fire seemed directed away, and she could only thank the gods that it wasn't aimed at her.

She got halfway up the stairs of the stables before she heard a crash behind her. She turned to see the front wall of the barn crash inward. The wall completely collapsed as Valstrath's tail broke through. The stones fell, and she looked up and saw the ceiling coming down on her. She rolled off the stairs and fell on the straw just as the wreckage brought down the staircase. The rain poured into the barn, and she caught the flashes of lightning in the sky. Frigg couldn't tell if each rumble was the thunder or a growl from the dragon.

She dug herself in the hay and hugged her entire body, trying not to shake, while the rain came down. She heard his growling pants as he searched inside the broken stables. She could feel his hot exhales of smoke above her. She wrapped her hand around her mouth, convinced that a slight breath would help him find her.

"You're close." The power of his voice vibrated her body. She risked a slow glance and saw him staring at the barn window that had yet to collapse. His head was right above her. "Did you escape?"

He crashed into the back of the barn. Frigg rolled in the straw and sprinted under his body and out of his sight. She ran back out in the main courtyard, running forward as the hard rain soaked her. She stopped cold in her tracks as a horrible sight stood before her—nothing but a circle of fire all around. The flames leapt so high she wouldn't be able to get by them without mortally burning herself. She knew the hard rain would eventually put them out, but it would take more time than what she had.

She heard his approach behind her. She stood out in the open with nowhere to run. He had scorched everything around her, and now his orange glowing eyes set on her. She was trapped.

A smile covered the dragon's evil face as his neck turned behind him and exhaled another blaze of fire, so, even if she got beyond him, she couldn't get away. His massive body slowly stepped forward. His wings expanded in the air and flapped once before they folded to his back. The gust created by the mighty wings brushed against her, and she nearly fell backward.

"I'll give you tribute for bravery, little girl," he said. "Most of your kind stand frozen in fear before the inevitable."

She could hardly keep her eyes open with the rain, and the sky lit up once more as the lighting flashed across the heavens. She backed away as much as she could before she felt the heat of the fire behind her. Another few steps, and it would scorch her tiny frame. Valstrath stopped several feet in front of her.

"Now, little one, stand still," he requested.

Her eyes closed, and she stopped trembling. *After a few moments of pain, I will see my mother and my brothers,* she told herself. It was the only thought that brought her comfort.

CHAPTER TWENTY-FIVE

Frigg heard a deep howl come from beyond the fire. When she opened her eyes, she saw Valstrath looking around in confusion. A massive form quickly pushed its way through the blazing wall and ran with such force the ground reverberated. Mulga suddenly appeared through the flames and took two massive steps before his fist came back, and he threw it forward, colliding with Valstrath's face.

The dragon was surprised by the hit as his entire body flew to the side and crashed into the wall that surrounded the city. A burst of rubble and bricks fell to the ground as Valstrath's body nearly broke through the wall. The dragon roared in anger and rolled away from the wall before he regained his feet.

Mulga stood right in front of Frigg as his breaths came out in grunts.

Valstrath's nose ran with blood. He lowered his body and crawled to the side. "What is this? A giant who comes to the aid of a human girl? Your ancestors would call you a disgrace."

"FRIGG MULGA'S FRIEND!" Mulga screamed as he grabbed the remains of a broken pillar and hurled it at Valstrath. The ruin hit Valstrath in the face just as Mulga rushed toward the dragon and took advantage of the distraction.

Mulga struck the dragon with his shoulder, pushed him backward, and slammed him into the rubble of the castle. Mulga unleashed a fury of punches to Valstrath's face, but it seemed Mulga's strength had finally met its match. Valstrath's front legs grasped Mulga's body and slammed the giant on his back. Mulga could no longer reach the dragon's head, so he punched him in his underbelly.

Valstrath's claw grabbed Mulga's head and repeatedly slammed it into the stone ground. Frigg collapsed to the ground with worry. The dragon stared directly at her and crept over Mulga's body. The panic came back to her, and she started to crawl backward. With three quick steps, the dragon was right on top of her, but, before he could touch her, Mulga picked him up and flung him to the side. Valstrath's body collapsed most of the pillars until he struck the city wall once again.

Mulga grabbed the dragon's tail and flung him away from Frigg before he could cause her any harm. The giant let go of Valstrath, but it turned out to be a mistake as Valstrath's tail whipped back and hit Mulga in the chest. Mulga lifted in the air and flew across the courtyard before he struck the ground and rolled.

A terrible groan escaped Mulga's lips, and Frigg quickly rushed to his side. "Mulga!"

The giant slowly got to his feet and gently pushed her to the side. "Stay away."

Frigg grabbed at his hand, but he pushed her behind him again. Valstrath headed toward the giant. Despite his obvious pain, Mulga ran at the dragon and leapt in the air with a fist prepared to strike. Valstrath caught the giant in the air like a fly and slammed him back to the ground. With one claw holding Mulga down, Valstrath pounded into his head with the other claw until the ground cracked.

Tears filled Frigg's eyes. *I have to do something.* The wall Valstrath crashed into earlier held the bolt thrower with the dragon spear, but the collision destroyed most of the walkway to the top. The platform where the bolt thrower stood was still without any damage. A narrow staircase led up to the platform, but she would have to somehow get by the broken walkway in order to get to it.

She already knew she wasn't strong enough to fire the enormous device, but if she could somehow cut the tension of the rope it would fire the dragon spear. Her eyes drifted to Brynjar's corpse still lying on the ground and a sheathed dagger around his waist. Her throbbing feet ran to him, ignoring every affliction that consumed her.

With a quick pull, she removed the dagger from its sheath and headed for the stairs. Though the pain in her feet felt worse with each step, Frigg knew she needed to save her friend. When she reached the top of the wall, the walkway was nearly destroyed. All that remained was a slim, brick path that would hardly fit her small feet on it. She looked down and realized just how high in the air she stood. Her head felt dazed, and a strange tingle trembled down her legs.

Mulga remained stuck under Valstrath, but the dragon wasn't pummeling him as badly as before. Her friend grasped the dragon by his jaws and directed his head to keep the stream of fire away. Small bursts of flames escaped Valstrath's mouth, but they were nowhere close to Mulga. Valstrath's claws dug into the giant's sides, and Mulga let out a scream of pain.

Frigg swallowed her fear and kept her mind on Mulga. She started her walk across the slim, brick pathway. She leaned on the exterior wall with her one hand and tightly gripped the dagger in the other. She feared her foot would slip off the slim path at any moment. *Don't look down*, she thought as she kept her glance on the bolt thrower that seemed miles away. With every groan Mulga made, she picked up her pace.

She slipped on the wet stone and nearly fell below. Her legs dangled over the side as she held on with one hand and the other kept the dagger in her grasp. She couldn't help but look down. This time Mulga wasn't there to catch her. She forced herself to check on her friend below. Mulga had somehow rolled himself on top of the dragon repeatedly punching Valstrath, but, within a moment, he was slammed to his back again. Cuts and slashes covered his flesh, and blood seeped from the wounds.

She found the strength to pull herself back up and continue down the walkway. The bolt thrower was only a few feet away and the platform still intact.

With a lunge, she made it, nearly falling once more, but her perseverance was stronger than her small frame. She stood up and grabbed the bolt thrower, but it wouldn't budge. Even the strongest of men needed to use every ounce of power they possessed to lift it and aim. Despite knowing she didn't have the strength, she tried to aim it toward the dragon, but she was too weak.

When Valstrath collided with the wall, the bolt thrower lowered toward the ground. If she cut the tension now, it would miss by five feet or more. The struggle between Valstrath and Mulga moved away from where the bolt thrower was marked. The two titans still struggled, and her friend still fought the good fight. She may have heard Mulga yelling in pain, but the dragon also roared in excruciating agony every so often.

Through the thundering rain storm and the roars of both the monsters, she called out to Mulga from the depths of her soul. "MULGA!"

The giant's head turned toward her even as he was pinned to the ground. With a mighty roar, Mulga released his arms from Valstrath's claws and grabbed the dragon by the throat. Mulga pulled the dragon backward while he crawled and lifted Valstrath high in the air.

Mulga held Valstrath within the target of the bolt thrower, and Frigg knew this was her chance. She took the dagger in both hands and raised it above her head. With a mighty push downward, she cut the rope's tension, and an exploding sound echoed throughout the courtyard. Frigg fell back from the force and then heard a roar that sent a chill down her spine.

She saw the dragon spear sticking out of the back of Valstrath near one of his wings. The dragon released Mulga from his grasp and tried to flap his wings to get away. The dragon spear took its effect as Valstrath roared and moved away from Mulga. His lurid screams pierced Frigg's ears.

Mulga rose from the ground and charged the dragon. He leapt on the back of Valstrath and wrapped one arm around the dragon's neck. With the other arm, he pounded his fist into the back of Valstrath's head. The dragon flapped his wings with a painful roar and tried again to fly into the air. Mulga weighed him down, and the dragon spear stopped him from getting away.

Valstrath finally managed to get in the air with Mulga still on his back. The two behemoths headed in Frigg's direction. With another punch to the back of Valstrath's head, the dragon's whole body fell downward, and Frigg knew its tail would strike the platform.

Frigg tried to quickly walk down the slim path, but she lost her footing. Just as she began to fall, Valstrath's tail hit the bolt thrower and an explosion of stone and bricks fell with Frigg. She closed her eyes, waited to strike the stone ground below her, and prayed for minimal damage.

She finally stopped falling, but the stone didn't feel as bad as she thought. She opened her eyes, and there stood Mulga with her safely cradled in his palm.

"Frigg fall. Mulga catch," the giant said.

Even with his lacerated face, he managed a smile toward her. With an exhale of relief, she returned one. She looked over his entire body. His grey and green skin hid behind all the blood he shed from his many lacerations. Valstrath did his damage, but thankfully there didn't look to be anything mortal.

The rain subsided then, and the roaring thunder and lightning seemed to pass. The ring of fire Valstrath created finally died down. A small amount of fire still burned, but the size of the flames was nothing as it once was.

Before she could properly thank Mulga for saving her life, Valstrath's massive form flew right over top of them. He turned in the air, and headed right toward the two of them. As quickly as he could, Mulga placed Frigg on the ground and ran toward the dragon. With a thundering leap, he soared into the air, and his fist collided with Valstrath, knocking the dragon to the ground. Mulga kept his relentless attack, throwing punch after punch. Each hit made a sickening crack as the dragon backtracked in the courtyard.

Frigg heard a crash and watched ranks of warriors finally break through the rubble that blocked the gates. The charging men flooded the courtyard but came to a quick halt when they saw the giant and dragon battling.

Damari pushed his way to the front. He watched the battle between the two beasts before his eyes found Frigg near the wall.

"Father!" she screamed.

Damari put his blade away and ran to her as several of his guards followed closely behind him. Frigg limped toward him, but Damari closed the distance in seconds. He picked her up in his arms and hugged her tightly.

With the battle in back of them still going on, Damari grasped Frigg's face with his hand and brushed away her hair. He shifted his body, and the two of them looked at Mulga and Valstrath. Mulga battered the dragon with punches until Valstrath used his elongated neck to knock Mulga away. He flapped his wings and flew into the air.

Mulga recovered quickly and ran in Valstrath's direction. Using the wall to boost himself, Mulga jumped in the air and landed on Valstrath's back. They rose together in the air. Because of the smoke from the fire, Frigg could no longer see them.

She broke from her father's grip and headed out of the courtyard, ducking between guards. She sprinted through the city with her eyes looking up to the sky. She couldn't get a good look at what was going on between them. She thought she saw Valstrath spinning in the air, but the image was nothing more than a blur.

Her heart sank, and she could feel it pounding against her flesh. Her father called from behind her, but she barely heard him. Her only concern was for Mulga.

The stone hurt her feet. She could feel herself losing breath. With her eyes trapped on the sky, she nearly collided with warriors in the city. A few of them jumped at her, and she realized they were trying to capture her for Damari. Her desire to reach Mulga was far more important. Because of her size, she could duck under their grasp and run around wagons and carts, so she didn't get caught.

The whistling sound of Valstrath spiraling through the air was nearly drowned out by the grunts of the two creatures as they tangled with one another. Frigg finally managed to see Mulga hitting the dragon over and over again with all his strength. His other hand grabbed Valstrath by the neck and directed his head, so he wasn't hit with the dragon's fiery breath. Each time there was a burst of flame, Frigg thought the worst, but the flame extinguished itself into the cold, dark sky with no sounds of pain coming from the giant.

Something on the ground caught her eye. A small glowing light instantly made her curious. She recognized Mulga's thick choker with the ruby of friendship she gave him still attached. She picked it up and carefully inspected it. Though Frigg didn't quite believe the myth of the charm, she still felt worried for her friend.

Valstrath roared as they continued to soar. Frigg stepped away from the broken front gate of the city and looked up into the night sky. Their silhouettes danced in the stars. Mulga continued to throw thunderous blows and received a painful screech from the dragon each time they landed.

"Frigg!" Damari's voice yelled from behind her.

Any other time she would have turned the moment he called, but her eyes wouldn't allow her to look away. She felt her father stop next to her, and she knew his own eyes looked to the fight between the two creatures.

In the echo of the sky, she heard a horrid sound—a deep roar of agony that made her heart jump. Frigg realized the two of them were falling from the sky. She saw Mulga go limp and fall under Valstrath. He was no longer tied up with the dragon.

Valstrath looked like he was about to ascend in the air just as Mulga seemed to regain consciousness. His massive hand reached for Valstrath's back leg and pulled the dragon back down to him. They spun again—so quickly that Frigg couldn't get a good look at them, and they slammed into the earth creating a debris of sand, dust, and rocks. The ground beneath Frigg's feet shuddered.

There was nothing but a cloud where the two landed. Frigg failed to get a glimpse of her friend. When she tried to run, she felt her father grab her by the arm and pull her back.

"Let me go!" Frigg screamed. Tears replaced her fear. They streamed from her eyes as Damari wrapped his arms around her. "MULGA! MULGA!" Frigg cried.

She could barely make out a black shadow coming from the dust. The shape of Valstrath's head peaked through the smoke, and his narrow, orange eyes locked on Frigg.

Damari wrapped Frigg up and ducked just as the dragon inhaled.

"Hello, my..."

Mulga's arm went around Valstrath's neck, and he pulled the dragon against his own body. His other hand knocked Valstrath in the side of the face twice. The dragon turned his head and nearly tossed Mulga away. The giant landed on the top of Valstrath's neck, gripped one of the dragon's horns, and held on. Valstrath whipped his head in every direction, but Mulga's grip wouldn't loosen.

Mulga's other arm stretched for the wing of the dragon and removed the spear still imbedded in his back. Mulga reached up and then threw his hand down. A nasty chomp echoed when the spear pierced the top of Valstrath's head, went through his mouth, and out the bottom of his jaw. Mulga pounded the top of the spear as it burrowed further into Valstrath's skull. Bursts of blood spewed from the wound as the dragon tried to pull his head up and fly away. Mulga wrapped both his arms around the dragon's neck and squeezed, holding Valstrath in place. With a final strike to the spear, it spiked the dragon's head firmly into the ground. Even that didn't stop the dragon from trying to fight.

Mulga kept his grip as he straddled the dragon. With a furious roar, he turned the dragon's head in his hands. A sickening snap created an explosion of blood as Mulga pulled Valstrath's head away from the spear. Mulga screamed in rage until he completely removed Valstrath's head from the spear and slammed the lifeless head of the dragon into the ground. Valstrath's body went limp and fell over with a thunderous thud and one last groan of despair.

Damari's grip on Frigg loosened up, and she exhaled the breath she didn't know she had been holding inside. Mulga stood over the body of the dragon as his chest heaved. He grunted several times and roared once more at Valstrath's carcass, but his emotions changed the moment his eyes met Frigg's. The rage left him, and she saw a glow in his silver eyes—the same one she remembered back in Direwood when he said her name properly for the first time. His breathing returned to normal, and he stood tall and proud. His mouth curled up into his familiar half smile with his snagged tooth rising high above his lips, but then it faded into trembling.

Frigg smiled back, thinking his rage still consumed him, but, because of the darkness and how fast he moved while fighting Valstrath, she had somehow missed the wound on his upper-shoulder. A row of teeth marks pierced his flesh, and blood dripped down the whole left side of his body.

Mulga followed Frigg's gaze and looked at his wound as if he never knew it was there. Agony covered his face. He looked back at her with glazed and watery eyes. He took two steps toward Frigg, reached out with his right hand for her, and collapsed forward. He hit the ground with a crash.

Frigg broke her father's grip and rushed to him. Her face welled up, and her sight blurred from the tears. She dropped and grasped the side of Mulga's face with her arms. She looked at him in horror.

"No, no, no, no, no," she kept repeating. "Get up! Get up!"

Mulga shifted his head and looked at her. He smiled at her with his snaggletooth rising as best he could to try to cover the pain in his face. "Frigg."

"Get up!" she cried. "Get up, Mulga, get up!"

His eyes darted, and he looked confused. His glassy eyes finally looked back to her as his lower lip quivered.

His body bled from the smaller wounds Valstrath gave him, but they seemed like nothing compared to the shoulder wound from the dragon's bite. She watched the blood ooze to the ground at an alarming rate.

Frigg pounded his chest with her little fist. "I told you to leave," she cried. "You were okay. You were going to live. Why did you come back?"

She buried her face in his cheek and sobbed. She felt a push on her shoulder and thought it was her father. When she backed away from Mulga's head, she saw it was the giant's finger, gently touching her cheek and getting rid of the tears. It did little to help since more flowed through her eyes every second. When they subsided for just a moment, she saw his smile once more.

"You should have stayed away," she said grasping his face as best as she could. "Why did you come back?"

He gave a shaky smile. "Frigg...Mulga's...best...friend."

She felt her face swell. "What am I going to do without you?"

"Imagine...Mulga," he muttered.

His silver eyes looked at her lovingly before they turned empty. He looked beyond her as she saw his head lower just slightly into the ground. One last gasp came from his mouth. Then a chilling silence.

She leaned her head into his nose, crying loudly and squeezing his head as if her grip would breathe the life back into him. She screamed into the silence of the night, but Mulga never moved. She leaned her body into him and stroked his face.

She gave out one last scream before the sobbing consumed her, the word no repeatedly falling from her lips.

CHAPTER TWENTY-SIX

She could still feel the fire on her face, drying the residue of tears left on her cheeks. Her father built the largest pyre he could for the giant who saved them. The flames rose high into the heavens. Frigg clutched Mulga's choker tightly and wrapped it around her hand with the ruby cupped in her palm.

An orange glow lit up the grim faces of each warrior and commoner who gathered outside the city to pay homage to Mulga. No one spoke or made a sound as everyone's head hung down—but not Frigg's. She kept her eyes on her friend, still expecting him to rise from the flames. She looked to the shadow of his face as the fire burned around him. She was numb—much like when Tadeas died. It wasn't until she knew her father's eyes looked at her from the side that she felt some emotion again. He had watched her cry far too much, and she knew if she started again it would break his heart. It would only take eye contact with him for her to fall apart, so she fought the urge to turn in his direction.

Her father reached his hand out to her, and Frigg grasped his pinky finger. He turned his hand and stroked hers with a few of his fingers. It was a small comfort. Even as the flames engulfed Mulga's body, she waited. It wasn't over—not yet. He would rise from the pyre, roar into the heavens, pound his chest with his hand, and walk away.

She watched Mulga's head turn to ash. She knew then it was real, and she allowed her head to drop. He wouldn't get up and run into the darkness, disappear into the forests of Direwood, and stay hidden. The last of the legendary creatures was gone—nothing more than ashes being blown away by a northern wind.

The tears she thought were cried out came back. They sat in the back of her eyes and waited for her to give in and let them out. As Mulga's ashes spread through the air, the only comfort she took was knowing he would always be there in some form. The last piece of him brushed into the wind, and her eyes blurred.

Frigg wondered if her father wanted to say something to her but could not gather the words. She still refused to look at him, knowing her daughterly instincts would take over, and she would sob to him like she did so many times in the past. A part of her wanted to do so; she wanted nothing more than for Damari to hold her tightly in his arms and find the right words to say. She even tried to imagine what those words were, so she could feel better.

Her father had just lost his best friend, the king. He had lost so many warriors fighting against Gustav and Valstrath. The last thing she thought he wanted to do was try to figure out how to solve her sadness over the death of a giant.

She didn't remember much after that. A few guards escorted her and her father away. She could vaguely remember her people as they called her by her title, wishing to honor her, yet she couldn't return a gesture of gratitude. Her father would have been angry with her in times past, but he seemed to understand her callous grief and did not reprimand her.

For days, she never said a word, not even to Loke as he watched over her as he promised. She walked through courtyards and sections of the garrison without a word. As Saga told her, the people began to base their attitude on hers. After a while, she stopped going out in hopes her absence would build the morale of Southrend.

With the castle nearly destroyed, she and her father stayed in the guest quarters. The silence finally began to bother her. She hoped someone would be brave enough to say something, but they all remained silent. While her father was off handling affairs in the city, she sat with her head leaning on the palm of her hand, stabbing at the food on her plate she didn't intend to eat. She half hoped it would eat itself, so she didn't have to force it down to appease the servants and her father. She heard him checking on her, asking the servants if she said anything that day or managed to smile. It shattered her even more when they revealed the truth. Even then she waited for him to talk to her, but he would enter the room, look at her, and walk off without saying a word. She would stare in his direction when he was gone, hating that she wished for his words but couldn't ask for them.

One afternoon, she sank her fork into the sliced apple on her plate. To her surprise, a smile emerged on her lips as she looked at the skin of the apple. "Red apple," she whispered.

"Apple?" she conjured Mulga's voice in her mind.

"Yes, this is an apple, and it's red," she said under her breath.

"Red?"

"The color." She picked up the sliced apple with her fingers.

"Red apple," she remembered him saying.

"Princess Frigg," Loke said her name from across the room, interrupting her thoughts. Frigg looked up at her bodyguard. "Did you say something?"

The smile she managed to find with the memory of her fallen friend disappeared. She could only shake her head toward him and look back at her plate.

"You should eat something, princess. Your father will worry if you don't," he said.

Frigg nodded. She looked down at her cold food and watched her fork graze the meat in repetition, but she could still feel his eyes. His footsteps came toward her, and he stood by the seat next to her.

Her glassy eyes looked up at him, still fighting the tears that wanted to come out. She kept her chin up, so she didn't reveal her sadness.

"May I sit, princess?" he asked.

She hesitated, wondering what would make him want to sit with her. She finally nodded.

"Are you all right?" he asked gently. He shook his head and added, "Never mind, of course you're not. It's a stupid question."

Her fork went into the sliced apple, and she went to put it in her mouth but stopped herself. Her mouth trembled too much to even eat.

"I was glad to be given the duty of being your bodyguard," Loke said. "Your brother meant a great deal to me. I want you to know that I will protect you with my life."

When he didn't get a response from her, he stood up. Frigg quickly put her hand over his and stopped him, but she wouldn't look at him.

"Stay," she said with a crack in her voice.

"What do you want to talk about?" he asked.

"Nothing...just stay," she managed to get out.

"As you command, princess." His other hand went over hers and rubbed it for a moment. He pulled his hands away and sat with her. Several moments went by before he asked, "Can I say one thing?"

She nodded.

"Your brother was always harsh with me. One day, I asked him why, and he said it was because he thought I could be better than I was. He also promised me something. Can I tell you what that was?"

With a lump in her throat, she nodded in permission.

"He said, 'If you ever fall, I will be there to catch you.'"

The statement struck her, and she let out a whimper. She felt her body tremble. The tears she tried to fight off found their way to her eyes.

"I'm so sorry, princess," Loke gasped. "I didn't mean..."

"No," she cut in, looking at him and finally smiling. It was the first one she showed anyone in many days. "I know you will."

She went back to her food, but still didn't eat a thing. After the servants took away her untouched plate, she headed to her room for the night.

During the day, the pounding of hammers echoed throughout the city because of the builders trying to restore what the battle and Valstrath destroyed. Hackett and Egil offered to stay and help with the rebuilding, which her father readily accepted. The sound of hammers kept her mind occupied, but at night, with the outside world hushed, she had no choice but to deal with her own thoughts.

She reached her room while Loke shadowed her the entire time. When she walked inside, he stopped outside the door and took his post. She closed the door and prepared herself for bed.

Just when she was ready, she heard her father outside the door talking with Loke. They spoke of the damage to the city, the many fallen men, and what the future held for their people. She felt selfish that those things didn't dominate her thoughts, as well. So many others had died. All across the city, her people lost loved ones.

With thoughts of Mulga still stirring in her head, she crawled into bed and pulled up her bearskin. She looked to the ceiling and tried to block everything out. Her father entered the room and stood in silence—still not a word said to her since her best friend turned to ash.

He walked over to the brazier near the window and shuffled the embers with a poker. After he finished, he strolled over to her and stood on the side of her bed. He stared at her while his hand rested on the hilt of his sword. He looked her over and even adjusted the bearskin with one hand.

"Good night, Frigg," he whispered. He gave her a quick smile and turned for the door.

Every other night he did this, she let him walk out. Tonight, though, she couldn't fight it anymore. "Father," she called.

Damari turned and looked back at her, his saddened face mirroring hers. "Yes, little love."

She clutched the bearskin and pulled it up to her neck. "Can you tell me a story?"

His head dropped in thought as he walked to her slowly. He sat on the edge of the bed and looked over her. "What kind of story?"

"Any story," she said. The tears welled in her eyes, and she tried to fight it. Her father's stories were always about giants. She couldn't handle a story about giants. Not now. Not ever again. "But please, don't tell me one about giants."

Two tears fell from her eyes and trailed down to her chin. She almost started sobbing again. Her father hushed her gently, and she gained control of herself. He kissed her ever so softly on the forehead, looked upon her, and gave her a gentle smile.

"I'm not going to tell you a story about giants," he said. He swallowed, and his own eyes got misty. "I'm going to tell you a story about *a* giant—the story of Frigg's giant."

Her mouth quivered, and she closed her eyes as tightly as she could. When they opened, the tears fell down her face again, but she felt a smile emerge as Damari returned one of his own.

She did fall asleep eventually, although she didn't know exactly when. She wanted to stay awake to hear her father describe Mulga, to tell her what he had remembered about him, and to imagine him in the world again. He may have been gone, but, as Damari told the tale, for just a little while, even if she knew his irreversible fate, Mulga was still alive.

Made in the USA
Middletown, DE
23 January 2021